METAERIE™

Winding the Strands

By

Jonathan Davenport

Every project ends, but perhaps each ending is also a new beginning... All I know is that just as I will go on the same rides over and over again at a theme park if I like them, favorite stories stay alive as long as they continue to be told. Thanks for letting me tell mine!

JD

Here we are at last, at the beginning of the end. I started with rules, and ended with premises... Yes, I broke my own rules once in a while, shush. First, I apologize that this took me so long to finish. Second, I regret nothing. Third, I know it's too long and could have been 2-4 books...but that's not how I envision a story line.

Here is my vision: Every scene must be a scene and need to be seen. If it is in one of these volumes, it is important. Maybe you don't see exactly why right now, but at some point in these revelations the point will reveal itself. Or not. There is no beginning and no end. You just get to walk into the story, already playing out long before you arrived, and then walk out again, as it continues to play on without you...

For those who are waiting for the gaming – these novels are hereby declared to be the canon and history of my world that will be the foundation of the system to come next!

For those who want this world to grow, expand, and mature beyond what you have seen here – there are plenty of tangential stories already percolating!

For those who enjoyed the stories but want shorter installments – you're in luck too! The tangents will be storyline introductions of a much briefer nature to lead

3

into playable modules and frameworks for future Metaerie gamers.

To my wife, who has endured the most 'shushing' of anyone this last year, thank you Sweetheart for tolerating me! To the rest of my family and friends who have found me off by myself mumbling, scribbling, perhaps drooling from hunger, thirst or just miniature comas, thanks for the food, drink, and periodic reality checks.

To those who have played, swapped stories, and in some cases been included in the tale, thank you so much for entertaining me.

And to those loyal fans who have waited (not-so) patiently for this installment, I appreciate you all!

JD

Chapter 1

The Old One Lives

The bracken hanging from the stone wall left semi-circular shapes in the rock where the wind blew them back and forth constantly. They were actually dangling roots from plants above exposed by the excavation of the prison.

Above the chamber's only occupant was a ceiling made of layers of peeled logs, each laid perpendicular to the next. There were at least a half dozen layers, each log as big around as a small barrel. Above them were head-sized rocks a barrel high, then hand-sized, then eyeball-sized, then an earthen layer deep enough to bury an average man standing upright.

Wind and water both entered the chamber through small shafts perhaps two handspans across near the ceiling and exited the same way via even smaller holes in the floor. The latter lower tubes had been bored into the native rock by a stone mason who was also a fairly accomplished mage. As he had been present when they were created, the prisoner knew they were magically protected from any exploitation on his part.

He was desperately tired. So tired his bones ached, his hearing was going in and out, his eyes were rarely open, and his neck had the strength of a windless sail. He was only awake because he had heard the voices that meant food was coming...

He did not see the chunks of meat fall out of the upper tube, but he heard the slap when they hit the floor. He leaned toward the spot, sniffing – and heard the clinking of the gems underneath him as he repositioned his bulk. Over time he had adjusted to relieving himself in the corner where there was a drain box of sorts with a mortared border a few handspans high, filled with white quartz stones the size of chicken eggs. There was a hole above this as well; it let in sunlight and water (and let him know he had active keepers present at all times because when he torched it once water came down right away when it was not raining).

He sniffed at the meat. It was a new smell. He had eaten many things in his extensive lifetime, men not the least, but his favorites had been hooved. Cattle of many shapes and sizes, stags of every color and even sheep and goats – he enjoyed them all. This smelled to be of the latter ilk. He smelled no spoil or rot, only fresh blood, and he was literally starving so he ate it, every

10

piece, and licked the floor where they had lain.

He sent his thoughts up the tube, questing for an open mind...and found nothing. Nothing. Not a sound, not a response, nothing.

The chamber was big enough to turn around, but not wide enough to fully extend his wings. It was tall enough that when standing on his back legs his head could not touch the ceiling without jumping as high as he could, and it made his ancient hips ache when he landed. He was certain that if he burned the logs, once they collapsed he would just be buried alive, so for now starving to death seemed a slower option that allowed continued hope for a change of the status quo into his favor... He remembered that he was the oldest living creature in his world and could afford some patience. He settled down and went to sleep.

***

Chapter 2

Dragon Meet

The hills around the high glacier bowl had been scoured by roving patrols for a week in preparation for the coming gathering. The elevation favored dragon life in almost every way. The thinner air let them take flight quicker, stay aloft easier, and kept them cooler. The hills were too steep for non-flying creatures to approach with speed, and there were no approaches where even a rabbit could hide for long, so stealth was also impossible. There was still snow on the ridge lines, but the sparsely treed talus slopes supported very little animal life. Most of the arrivals brought food with them. Only treachery and/or hidden magic could put them at risk here. The former seemed unlikely; the latter was almost expected.

Ariene had just finished ruminating those points to her daughter Sylvia from a large hollow high up the cliff wall on the highest ridge when a flight of large red dragons arrived. The outsiders here in the high mountains, the reds were heat-seeking cave dwellers, notoriously unpredictable, and usually mean. The two silver females watched Aurelius greet the new arrivals from the solid gold dais he lay on at the inner/upper end of their protective glacier bowl.

The platform had originally just been an enormous gold vein exposed by erosion. It had since been shaped to hold the regent's large and robust gold dragon form. Most recently additional stones had been added all around just below the top edges, made from the bags of gold pebbles Auron had when he was killed.

Fortunately, as much as the reputation of dragons dealing enigmatically and capriciously with other races was usually well-founded, it was not that way between them.

When the flight of reds landed, the leader, an enormous female, came to rest mere inches from Aurelius, who did not budge. She touched her snout to his briefly and said clearly for all present to hear, "I do not challenge. I mourn with you, and I will support you." Neither looked away. A lone tear rolled down the High Priest's cheek scales and made a metallic 'clink' when it hit the stones at her feet. She leaned in further and touched her snout to his horns, igniting them with a magical crimson flame.

When she pulled back, he said, "Thank you, Rowena. We need your help."

***

Chapter 3

Counting Dragons

After millennia of interbreeding (and inbreeding) there were almost no colors of dragon that could not occur in the natural course of their genetic mixing, but some were quite exotic. The Counter was likely the best known, even ahead of Aurelius. Born from a black father to a white mother, instead of some shade of gray his whole body was a patchwork of white and black, in a repeating pattern that appeared differently depending on the angle from which he was viewed. His friends and family just called him Chaos, but to dragon kind he was the keeper of all numbers; how many there were and of which types, their disparate abilities, how far away were their lairs, how old they all were, how many young had resulted from each union – in fact no one else even wanted to count the number of things he counted...

Of course, the way Chaos kept up his accuracy was to constantly update his data. The new arrivals all had to be interviewed after presenting themselves to the Regent. None dared refuse. Not because they would be threatened with any violence or shunning, rather the opposite – the Counter would follow them everywhere and listen to every little thing they said and ask questions not only of them but of all around them until his relentlessness was either answered or simply became too much to stand. Only a few had tested him on it, and none had failed to succumb to his utterly polite and genuine interest in the knowledge he sought. One gruff old green was overheard saying, "After a thousand trips around the sun you would think he would lose a little interest... but, no, he's still like a pup with a bone..."

Today Chaos the Counter sat at a stone table, a pale elf with jet black eyes, hair, fingernails, robe and boots. The books he wrote in had pages of the brightest white, like puffy summer clouds, and covers of the darkest obsidian polished to a shiny black glass mirror-like finish. His styluses were just as shiny, his ink just as dark, and both were enchanted.

The stylus' he used transcribed his interviews exactly as they occurred, and only in the appropriate book. The ink was his own stomach acid mixed with shavings from his claws and melted together and magicked to etch the words into the pages. No water damage would destroy these works.

The books were all filed in his table/cabinet,

itself a powerfully magical storage device that collapsed down to the size of a gaming cube. Currently three of his five styluses were scribbling furiously, pages turning like autumn leaves moving ahead of an evening breeze.

When he finished with the last of the arrivals, he turned to Aurelius. "Sir," he said with polite candor, "we are not all present."

"We know the Old One is missing," replied Aurelius, "who else?"

"Young Audhan, the Elvish Arch Mage's adopted charge, has not been seen in nearly a full turning, not even by Rrahmus. Roary of the direct red line has not been found though searches were made. And Bianca, cousin to silvers and whites, went hunting months ago and did not return, though she knew of this gathering." Chaos' statements reverberated across the glacier and met with initial silence.

When Aurelius did not respond, a low buzz of side conversations began. Ariene and Sylvia listened to Argenta comment from behind them, "Two reds, two golds, one white/silver – and all well-known. Auron was perhaps just bad luck. The others remain to be seen. We need to investigate…"

Aurelius stood on all four legs, stretched, shook his head and tail so hard the spikes and horns whistled

17

like the tip of a fencing sword in the hands of a master.

"You all know what my family has lost, what, ergo, our race has lost. Auron was a fine young dragon, kind to all who deserved it and likewise firm. An adept fighter, if a bit impetuous, I will never forget his ready smile and mischievous eyes and his ability to poke even me into humility with his with wit and sincerity. His perspectives made me a better father, and, I hope, a better Regent. Though my male line is ended, I will continue if you will have me. I need no challenge; I will step down to pursue this threat that indirectly brought about Auron's demise if another choice is preferred."

Though not without precedent, his pronouncement took even his family by surprise. He had hidden his feelings well. Ariene launched from her perch above and headed straight for his back, changing to elven form as she landed squarely in between his shoulders and wings as gently as a wingless dragon-in-elf-form can, her naked body still slightly silvery iridescent as she hugged him tightly around his neck, her tears falling freely.

Aurelius did not budge, but he dipped his head to see molten silver drops splash into the rocks at his feet, the droplets harden immediately in the cold air of the glacial bowl and tinkle to the ground like a series of tiny bells ringing.

From across the slopes around him, dragons of all colors but of similar size and age, mostly between two and five hundred years, came forward from their groupings. Dozens of them, each representing hundreds more, began to bow, dropping one front and back leg to a knee and curling that wing in front of their chest in deference.

Only Rowena and a large black male called Dubhan looked around to assess their followers first. His look took longer as one eye was missing from a previous tussle with Aurelius' grandfather Orondack centuries earlier. Both saw a majority of nodding or bowed heads, turned and bowed as well.

"All right then," said Aurelius. "Rowena, I leave it to you to discover Roary's fate. I will sort out Audhan myself. Ariene will work with her white cousins to track Bianca. I am confident that other servants of Mortalya are tracking down the Old One. We need to discuss this other-worldly mage who is trying to destroy our magic."

Dubhan uncharacteristically spoke first: "We were approached by the renegade witches to support their rebellion. After a thorough interview as to their logic and goals, we declined, as in our estimation it could only lead to our own eventual demise. Many of the men and witches in that region did not share our longer term view, however. Sadly, some are just misguided and in need of leadership. Some are actually horrible excuses for humans. The rest are largely beyond selfish or evil but are rather voracious seekers of wanton violence with no sense of order at all. I believe you and your family and friends killed most of them. Their then-leader never came to any of us directly that I know of..." He paused to look around for confirmation – all heads shook side-to-side indicating a negative response and therefore the truth of his statement. "... so, if you have actually seen him you are ahead of us..."

Ariene sat up on her husband's back, swiping at her elvish eyes with the backs of her hands. "His name is Baru Dall. He is a powerful mage, yet wants to destroy magic here, in Metaerie. He seems to think that when magic dies here it returns to the old world, his world, specifically when magical creatures like dragons and pixies pass on, because our life forces are here due to a spell, the original spell. Though it may be just a false assumption, it would explain Baru Dall's apparent hypocrisy of being a user of magic and trying to destroy it. If he is really from our old world, and it does gain magic when it dies here, he may simply want to increase the magical ability available to him in his own world, and if no one in the short term in his world is paying attention, he may be able to harness it all for himself…"

She slipped around Aurelius' neck to the ground, moved to his left and in a second was a large silver dragon rather than a naked elf. She continued, "We also believe the Human Arch Mage, Craddagh, was tortured into becoming a lich and supporting Baru Dall. Ironically, our best partners in this have been pixies, Original Men, adventurers for hire, and … vampires."

The collective response was one of derision, indicated by hundreds of forced snorting, exaggerated exhales. "I have seen both gold and blue-eyed vampires now in addition to red. The blues we missed as they just appeared to be human. The gold is a new development… Rrahmus' brother-in-law, dead for a decade, was bitten but not killed, then killed but not buried, then raised but not anchored to an evil master as his infector died before he was buried. Upon waking he wandered and found his original self to be largely intact. He re-entered the lives of those he cared about and <u>chose</u> his new path. I believe that we, as he did, must make a choice, as our race did in millennia past, to come together to preserve our existence, to commit to each other one more time, to set aside our wants and squabbles and fix our world."

Rowena stepped closer and said, "We are already prepared to be supportive, definitely <u>not</u> to undermine or hinder, but what help can we provide? These magicks and spells are well beyond most of us to even understand, much less counter or overcome..."

From far down in the lower part of the bowl, a deep voice was accompanied by the thuds of a lumbering step coming forward. An enormous white male named Blanchet, so bright he looked like a walking snowbank with eyes and wings, rumbled, "We have to find where the magic goes."

Chaos, from his table, said, "We need a tracker then."

An old blue named Azular said in a surprisingly high-pitched voice, "Only a tribrid can track dragonkind life force, or magic in general. Are there any left?"

Chaos, of course, knowing all about his kind, said, "Yes, there is one, called Sugarplum by his mother before she succumbed to insanity and flew toward the sun. He is here."

There was a squeak from above the hollow that Sylvia and Argenta were still in far above the conversation. They both looked out and up. They saw nothing.

Aurelius, however, took a deep breath and closed his eyes. When he spoke, all could hear it as if he were speaking inside their heads. "Sugarplum, come to me now."

Thousands of dragons, their interest piqued, their already amazing senses heightened, and their focus sharpened, heard and saw nothing. Until a figure appeared just in front of Aurelius' nose.

At first there was just a shimmering outline of a smallish dragon, head bowed in deference. Aurelius, ever imperturbable, said, "Plumley, we need you. Will you help? There may be some risk..."

The shimmering stopped, revealing a purple dragon's body with shiny gold wings. The horns on both sides of its head were lop-sided, longer in the back, forks of blood red. The talons were dark, deep ocean blue, and they matched the spikes on the tops of the wings while the spike on the tail matched the horns.

Sugarplum (Plumley to everyone but his mother) was quite the collection of bold coloring, but his size was only remarkable due to its lack. He was the size of an extra-large war horse, quite small by dragon standards, but also quick, quiet, and strong. His invisibility and inaudibility were innate, and it was rumored that he could teleport himself freely to anywhere he had previously been without fail. He dipped his head lower briefly, and said, "Of course I will help, sir, in any way I can."

***

Chapter 4

Pixie Meet

The ancient pixie woke to the sound of childish laughter. NOT the sound of children laughing, which usually gave him joy, and NOT the sound of child*like* laughter, that innocent, happy peal of joy when adults revel in the pure and innocent pleasures of their youth, which usually made him chuckle. No, this was that laughter that accompanied mature people reacting to one or more of their number doing something terribly juvenile – and it filled him with dread...

Grimly he began his 'check for stupid' mental checklist. Smell of smoke? No. Screaming? No. Unexplained pain and/or bleeding? No. Boots tied together? No. Weapons where they should be? Yes. 'Okay,' he thought, 'what are they up to?!'

The bench that he laid on was just a flat slab of rock that had split from the adjacent cliff face when struck by lightning and the top of it landed squarely on an ancient stump. It inclined slightly upward at the cliff end, a perfectly not-quite-flat place for repose, especially now that thick moss covered the top and the space underneath was hidden by the surrounding ferns just enough to hide a pixie if need be. As he sat up, he brushed some of the moss from his hair, though no one else would have noticed. There was more laughter, and then he remembered. Turning, he flew up to the top of the cliff and looked into a great rocky bowl on the other side.

The gathering was almost complete, only a few tokens had not been returned. Each had gone out with one of their partners, scores of magically trained falcons. All were accomplished hunters that were also homestead defenders and early warning as well as messengers. In this case they were sent out with as many as half-a-dozen wooden, coin-shaped tokens with Slawhit's likeness on them.

The tokens went out two moon cycles past. They had begun to come back in half that time, each with another tied to it, belonging to the respondent. As his glance took in the dozens of buckets full of tokens, he also saw some of his more nefarious cousins taking turns trying to scare Flaw into invisibility. He knew they would argue that they were helping to get the young one over his fear response as soon as he told them to stop. He did it anyway.

As the protestations came, so did an ancient bellow of, "Bite your tongues!"

Thousands of noisy little men, women and children went dead quiet. The eyebrows that looked like unruly spider webs the morning after a mosquito feast went up, somewhat surprised that they all listened. "Well," he added, "not <u>too</u> hard – don't hurt yourselves…"

When no chatter started back up, he settled onto a large round rock that looked over them all. He surveyed them, with both pride and nostalgia. He would love to claim to be unaware as to how he had become the eldest of his race, but the truth was he had simply outlived his forebears, his peers, and even many of his own children, his siblings' children, cousins – it made him feel sad and alone even in the throng of thousands that revered him, mostly because he had outlived his own wife.

'Enough of that maudlin bat guano,' he thought. "My children!" he thundered. "Long ago we came to a point where we understood that our existence was at risk if we failed to act! I know, I was there… I am the last of our 'originals'. I saw firsthand the terror and horror wrought upon our friends by this new evil." He paused, drawing them in, getting quieter.

"I do not know if it will happen again, but I <u>do</u> know that it <u>can</u>, and that alone should drive us to investigate the origin of <u>how</u> it happened. I need some of you to help me – I need to know exactly where this 'Dark One', the one called Baru Dall, entered our world. A daunting task, I know. But if we can make a world of our own, searching a relatively small part of it should be easy. The only difficulty may be that some that need asking might rather kill you than talk to you, so we will need some partners in this I think. The High Priest and Priestess were there, at the spot where the psychotic mage was seen to depart our world as his forces were being vanquished. We can start there, and backtrack as far as possible, take the first step on our own. Who is with me?!"

The response was as cacophonous as the colors that assaulted his eyes.

***

Chapter 5

Supportive Dwarves

From her time as a shield maiden and later mistress of her father's house, she had learned the hard but necessary lessons of logistical planning by balancing funds, materials and labor to make any event possible. From farming ventures to garden parties, from trading goods to combat, the commonalities of supplies, work and timing were constant.

Now as the matron to the leader of their clan and village the differences were only that of scale and seriousness. Their decisions impacted more people, involved more moving parts and required more lead time to plan (and more funds). She said as much. Leif looked at her lovingly and said, "Wife, I leave it to you to plan. Grim asked for a tithe from us all, and I'll get him at least that, but I need you to ensure that it makes sense..."

He regarded her analyzing his expression for a moment with a double squint then turned back to his brother. "Yar, ten percent only makes sense if it is balanced. I'll get the funds, the missus here will determine the supplies, you figure out the manning.

Let's try to have it all in motion in under one moon cycle, okay?"

Receiving nods all around, they put their thoughts into actions.

***

Chapter 6

The Protégé

"Are you sure you want to do this?" came the whisper one more time.

"You sayin' I can't?" was the return swipe.

"No...just not sure this was the best choice to 'learn' from as a beginner..." This sounded genuine and not at all condescending.

The figure wedged into the corner of the back wall of the cave and its ceiling was small but thick. The clothes were all black, like those of his mentor, who was wedged there as well, having free-climbed up there next to him. They had used the slight imperfections in the rough-hewn wall to leverage themselves into place high above (four or five barrels) their intended target.

They had timed the patrolling guard's rounds, waited until he passed from view, then scrambled up above either side of the chamber walls next to the passageway where he went, the corners of the entry giving two directions for grip. They did not have to wait long.

The clumping of the heavy footsteps warned them of the guard's return. So did the smell. Brine was fairly certain he was smelling the decaying flesh trapped in the ogre's teeth from its last meal. The enormous walking figure resembled a cross between a hill giant and a hideous legendary she-devil. At least two barrels high, this one's skin was a mottled mess that resembled a full body bruise in varying stages of healing, deep dark purple to bile yellow. The ogre's huge bare feet hit the rock floor like steel boots, its talon-like toenails scraping visible lines into the stone. Fortunately for the two extra-large flies on the wall, it did not wear a helmet. As the black stringy hair passing under them gave way to nauseatingly colored neck and shoulders, they dropped.

Both elf and dwarf pulled out daggers from their belts with both hands. The ogre heard nothing over its own disastrously noisy feet. The impact, from twice the guard's excessive height, wrenched the blades from Brine Drake's thick-fingered hands. Pill Von Ferret, however, master thief and experienced adventurer (truth be told many had called him an assassin...), planted both of his elven daggers into the ogre's exposed neck and began to hand walk down its back using the daggers like ice axes on a crevasse, securing one at a time by poking a new hole every handspan.

Looking up, Pill saw Brine's daggers sticking out of the ogre's left shoulder, dark blood dripping down its back. Looking down he saw Brine, both hands swinging small hand-axes at the ogre's legs. Inexperience was briefly given the advantage in the form of lucky coincidence.

Brine's right-handed swing to the left at the ogre's right leg missed – and severed its left heel tendon. The matching left-hand swing to the right ended up striking forward, straight into the front of his target's left shin bone.

The ogre fell to its left, attempting to inhale so it could bellow for help. The resulting crack was it breaking its own left kneecap on the rock floor, and the disgusting squishy sucking/popping noises were from air and blood entering its lungs where Pill's daggers had left extra holes in them. The ogre's collapse brought Pill's feet down far enough to stand, remove both daggers and then slam them into both of his victim's ear holes.

Seeing the ogre's delayed response finally coming – a club made from four pieces of barrel staves banded tightly with iron, capped with a polished black stone ball – being whipped over its back like a cow's tail switching at a fly, Pill simply released his daggers and dropped flat to the ground. The make-shift mace struck its wielders own spine so hard that he fell face down, unable to move his mottled purple and yellow colored legs.

Paralyzed and weaponless, having lost his grip on his club, the ogre once again tried to bellow, this time in anger and fear rather than pain and surprise, equally unsuccessfully. He only felt the short sword pressing through the base of his neck for a moment, then deflated through the holes in his back as the blade blocked his airway. The resulting blood bubbles looked like a boiling red mud puddle. Brine decided that this was the time to show Pill his breakfast a second time before retrieving his axes from the ogre's left leg bone and daggers from its left shoulder. He avoided eye contact with Pill.

"Well," he said finally, pausing to inhale, exhale, and inhale again, "that was <u>way</u> different than just defending myself and my friends…"

"And…?" asked Pill, leading the young dwarf's thoughts.

"Did we <u>have</u> to do that?!"

Pill knew what Brine needed – justification – and said as much. "Brine, I can't tell you that this was the action of 'good' people. I <u>can</u> tell you if the situation was reversed, <u>he</u> would not have hesitated to kill <u>us</u>, and while that makes him in this case just doing the task he was assigned, killing him from ambush was definitely 'bad'... The real question is 'was it necessary'?" The elven thief paused.

"Well?!" said the young dwarf impatiently, "Was it?!"

Pill regarded Brine with his multi-colored hazel eyes for a long moment, the dwarf feeling like his mentor was staring right through him. When he spoke, his voice was hollow, echoing in the darkness. "No. Necessary is breath, water and food. All else is choice. We chose to support the King. He chose us to complete this reconnaissance and raid. The keepers of this place chose to put this guard here to stop us and those like us. Could we have completed our task without killing the guard? Perhaps. If our skills or equipment or number of personnel in our little group were different. But they were not. Could we have bested this ... thing ... in a straightforward fight? Again, perhaps ... but it did seem unlikely. So, to complete the task assigned to us within the capabilities possessed by us, I say our method was optimal, our results undeniable, though perhaps to the chivalric our morals might seem questionable." Here the elf paused and joined his young friend on one knee then continued.

"In the argument of Just versus Unjust, the

dead never argue. Only the living can feel guilt, and only friends can betray you or be betrayed by you. If it comes down to my life or that of one I know would kill me without remorse, I choose to live, and without any guilt."

After a long pause Brine looked up and said only, "That has to be the most words I have ever heard you say." Pill just laughed.

"All right," he said, "let's get what we came for and get out of here."

***

Chapter 7

The New King is NOT Loved by All...

The King observed his errand boys entering the rear of his audience chamber. The site of his return, his validation by Carnis, Craggen and the former King's personal guards. It was where he proclaimed simultaneously his intent to rule, to resume trading with their newly re-established partners, and that he wanted all who might disagree or challenge to come forward to discuss their reasons with a guarantee of non-violence and to not fear reprisals. The invitation was declared to be 'open forever' he had said, but he expected attendance at a formal coronation in no more than one full tide cycle. It was time they dealt with their world as a force all their own. He wanted them to use their skills to become a permanent part of their regional economy. They were unparalleled fishermen, divers and swimmers – if they combined that with Fallon's coastal trading routes they would not have to fight their neighbors alone and would need fewer of their numbers dedicated to their warrior caste.

The first few days had seen two tries at (literal) backstabbing, one attempt at poisoning, and at least a handful of vicious rumors. The most popular of these, that Runebane had murdered the old King in his sleep, was dealt with by the old King's guards immediately and violently, but not lethally. The rumor mongers were made to publicly denounce their own statements, standing on platforms in their own village centers, with the guards they essentially called liars standing next to them, their tridents conspicuously present between accuser and defender...

The would-be backstabbers both underestimated and (literally and figuratively) overlooked the new King's closest personal bodyguard while attempting to assassinate Runebane. The first of these had dashed by Hak down some stairs as he followed the new King. The bloody-tipped trident that the would-be assassin carried pointed forward and low like a jouster's lance definitely gave away his intentions. The gnome was far faster and much stronger than the trog expected. Hak's sword clanging into the stone wall of the stair well after passing through the assassin's neck was the first indication to Runebane that anything was amiss. The second was the sodden thumping of the even-more-bulbous-eyed-than-normal head rolling unevenly down the stairs past him. Hak just nodded once, wiped off his sword and assigned one of the younger trogs to find out this one's story – his name, family, friends, job – and then called for the King's Guards. He was only answered from below. Three of them swarmed around Runebane, taking in the grisly scene with grim resolve. Hak moved back up the stairs and found the fourth King's Guard, dead, face down in a pool of his own blood, three gaping wounds in his back.

The second backstabber tried a few days later in the audience chamber. A group of southern coast fishmongers came to offer their support for the new national plan. A handful shared how their dealings with Fallon's people had been very positive in the past, that their biggest problems lay in dealing with the ogre threat at the border.

After a good discussion and sharing of information and intentions, they turned to leave. A southern guard that had accompanied them was behind one of the fishmongers that was in turn behind the King. He pulled out a dagger and drove the fishmonger closer to Runebane to stab him with it. His flippered hand came up short when it fell to the floor spurting blood out of its severed-at-the-wrist stump, the dagger clattering on the stone floor.

As all eyes dropped to the detached hand, seeing it lose its grip on the dagger, they missed the now-screaming assassin's fate become complete. The sword that took the hand off was reversed, now blade up, and was brought up from the side straight through the guard's neck at the underside of his jaw and continued straight up following the back line of his jaw through the top of his head, cleaving his face completely off.

One of the fishmongers, seeing the gnome wiping the blood and brains off of the sword that was taller than its wielder, blurted out, "You're <u>real</u>?! I thought you were a statue!"

Runebane responded, "It seems to be my good fortune that he is not…"

With all further audiences canceled that day (the room needed a serious cleaning, especially after a few sympathetic retchings at Hak's face removal handiwork), the King set Hak to training his guards to better anticipate and react to these things. It did not help what came next.

***

One day about a week later the King was out walking through a market in his capitol city. The palace sat just below the top of a rocky point above a horseshoe-shaped deep-water harbor. The arms of the arc were well-developed pier facilities, the sizes of the vessels getting smaller the nearer they came to the apex. Under the shadow of the cliff below the palace were shops carved out of the rock face with storm covers that spanned their entire length. What were essentially enormous shutters hinging on iron rings above the shops hung down in front of the entrances. When opened and propped up they became full length sunshades (troglodytes being generally unconcerned with rain). It was the only location that the King could not see from his balconies above and had been a favorite haunt of his as a youngster. It was so familiar that it blunted his natural caution.

Eager to share a childhood nostalgic experience with his savior and protector, Runebane took an offered local delicacy from a vendor he did not know.

The dish needed some explanation, so Runebane showed Hak how to eat it. A whipped jellyfish spread on thin toasted hard bread covered with a thin, also roasted, filet of a local whitefish was placed on a plank with the back of the cracker laid on the leading edge of a wedge block. By holding the plank in one hand and pulling the wedge (and therefore the food) toward you, once could munch the leading edge and even if the cracker broke awkwardly instead of losing it all over the ground it was still on the plank.

Hak was noisily crunching his third pull of the wedge as Runebane looked on with approving laughter when his eyes rolled back in his head and he fell to the ground unconscious, bubbles of orange foam on his lips.

In his distress of getting his guards to help, the King did not see the vendor slip away into the crowd.

* * *

After getting the news that Hak had not had a negative reaction to the food but had in fact been poisoned, Runebane finally awoke to his new reality. Fortunately, his bodyguard's gnomish constitution kept him alive long enough for the royal healers to decide what to do to help him. It was his discussion with his priests about the differences in how to treat a poisoned gnome versus a poisoned troglodyte that sparked a strange realization. He had always thought he and his people healed well because of their partial troll lineage. His top priest said otherwise.

"Your Highness," he began hesitantly, "over the centuries we have learned that this poison which your protector has survived would have killed you, or any of us, in minutes. We do not regenerate like our reputed ancestors the trolls...nor have any counter measures tailored to snakes or lizards helped either, giving the lie to the alternate theory that we have that ancestry either." He put his hands together in front of him and bowed deferentially.

"What are you saying?! What <u>are</u> we then?!" cried Runebane.

The priest looked at the King conspiratorially and said, "There is one of our order, very aged, who many know where to find your answer..."

***

That conversation with his priests weeks ago had spawned this moment. Receiving a nod from Pill, accompanied by a haphazard salute by touching the end of a sealed tube made of a large bone briefly to the side of his forehead let Runebane know that his question had an answer. Now to find out what it was...

The King called for his royal mage. The troglodyte that approached, slowly with age, wore robes that covered all but his face and flippers. The latter were mottled with spots, some dark, some almost clear enough to see the bones underneath. The former had tithed to gravity. So much so that that his lower eyelids would not rise far enough to meet the uppers, the net effect being that his eyes no longer truly closed. The sighing exhale that signaled his arrival lasted for longer than his companions' comfort level. When he spoke it was as if he had just awoken from a nap where he stood.

"Yes, sire……….. What would you wish of me?"

The King paused as well, unsure why. He shook his head slightly and said, "My elvish friend here has an item I would like you to examine and give me your expert opinion about."

Pill stepped toward the mage, offering the bone case to him, holding it in the middle. The mage gave his staff, a piscine spine covered in solidified clear pitch, to the thief in order to hold the case in both flippered hands.

"Engraved on the outside of this rather light whale bone are the words, 'The History of Trogar and Lodyma'."

Grasping the end that had a cap on it, he remarked, "This tube is sealed. It is capped with stitches through the bone and the holes filled with melted wax. I presume something required to remain dry must be inside." The ancient hands moved so quickly that the dagger they produced seemed almost magical. The old mage spun the whale bone while holding the dagger under the stitched leather laces, severing them all in a flash. He extended the tube toward Pill, saying, "Young elf, the cap if you please?"

After Pill pulled the cap off with a 'pop' that

echoed throughout the hall, revealing a hollowed-out bone and the edge of a scroll of paper inside, the aged mage deftly plucked it out. Continuing to use Pill as his table of convenience he handed off the whale bone tube as well. The thief rolled his eyes but took it.

Showing further dexterity and familiarity with old rolls of paper, the mage unfurled it top to bottom and held both ends gently but securely and read, "Trogar was a handsome specimen of his amphibian race. His bulging eyes, nimble tongue and flippered feet were quite well suited for swimming and hunting insects in the coastal swamps. His favorite place, the darkest, foulest, mud bog was dry that summer, so he hunted further inland, in a cleaner pond with surface pads covered in colorful flowers. It was there that the pixie girl Lodyma found him. She was smitten. She watched him for days before she finally approached him in frog form. No one really knows what happened next, but their union did not result in a single offspring but rather the hatching of thousands of eggs. Lodyma left after laying the eggs, but Trogar remained, protecting them. Lodyma returned to see Trogar only to find him trying to wrangle thousands of tadpoles. Her love grew even greater and this time she caught him and kissed him in her pixie form. Her unspoken wish was magically granted, and Trogar became a larger, walking, talking frog/man. Their young, however, were soon beyond the size of their parents, but had neither wings nor magic. As the spawning required no air, only water, they did not truly appreciate how many hatchlings there were as they were submerged. Most frogs have so many eggs because due to predation very few survive to adulthood. These hatchlings were larger than their normal predators in days. By a few weeks they were coming out of the water and the pond was overrun. Soon their food supply was almost gone. Trogar had a magically developed voice, but no language yet, so Lodyma led them out to the river that fed the pond. They followed it from bend to bend, eating the fish, from backwater to backwater, closer and closer to the river mouth, following the ever-larger fish. The final pool before they reached salt water was large and shallow, teeming with small aquatic life. They stopped there and Lodyma began teaching her children to weave and lash grass and wood into doors on cave entrances in the cliff walls to protect themselves. The area where they chose to live was named for them by Trogar himself as he learned speech from Lodyma alongside their young. He called it Civit Rana. Their offspring were called 'troglodytes' by her family, a simple combining of their two names.

Later generations, able to speak and learning to read and write, decided after being attacked by ogres in the north that a more violent and hardy ancestry would serve them better. Stories of trolls had come to their knowledge, so a troglodyte shaman invented the new origin story that they were descended from trolls and ogres. The new leader when Trogar finally died began raising and training the first troglodyte army, instilling a new martial mentality. And it worked, so this story, and all who would tell it, were silenced. All but me. I have eluded them and will hide the account where they will never look – in an ogre temple. I have paid them to keep it with their own holy relics, some of which I have seen. Many are terrifying, magical, and not of this world. It is certain I will be dead soon; my tale is too well known. Someday I hope this is found by those who value truth and history.

- Godfrey GillSnatcher

- Great-great-grandson of Trogar and Lodyma

***

"Well, your opinion Arken?" Runebane's inquiry was imperious but genuine.

The ancient mage took a moment to respond. He turned the old scroll around, examined the edges and back, sprinkled some dust from a pouch at his belt in the air and then dragged the ancient document through it as it sprinkled slowly to the ground. Arken Rune-Reader opened his droopy eyes as far as he could, cleared his phlegm-filled throat long enough for all present to once again feel both individually and collectively awkward, then spoke.

"Majesty," he began, "this document is of the proper age, language and materials, sealed and preserved, to be genuine. However, old writing does not have to be truthful... Where was this obtained?" This last was directed at the elf holding the tube it had arrived in.

Pill looked to Runebane, who nodded. "One of the eldest of your holy order told us a story handed down in his family of an ancient ancestor being part of a force sent to kill a rogue priest centuries ago. They found him in a coastal cave north of here, deep into what is still the domain of the ogres. My pupil here," he said, indicating Brine Drake, still clad all in black, "may be new to the skills I am teaching him, but he is well-versed in underground structures and activities. We went to the caves, searched for a nearby village, then stayed out of sight. Brine here noticed after a few days a location where ogres were arriving fresh and dressed and equipped as warriors. They disappeared and reappeared at the opening of a small tent next to a rockface and did not come out all day until another showed up." He paused. "The two things it told me was that it was an entrance to a larger space, where they could eat and relieve themselves, and that it was important enough to guard all day and all night."

Runebane interjected, "The old priest told us his forebear had been instructed to kill the 'rogue', do not talk to him, and bring back all he possessed, especially any writings. Specific mention was made that none of his companions could read..." With that he waved his flippered hand for Pill to continue, which the elf did.

"We found some old, valuable and strange items in the temple. Some that probably don't belong in our world and may need to be dealt with someday... but the ogres, and whoever drives them as they seem vacuous at the individual level and incapable of internal leadership, will know the location is compromised. Perhaps their mages keep written records, but in this location the relics were unholy objects – the scroll you hold was the only document present."

"King Runebane, if I may..." said an as yet silent priest.

"Indeed," replied the King, "what is it Haulis?"

The speaker's skin was the light green of the underside of a new spring leaf. His eyes were especially bulbous and extra far apart compared to his companions'. His brown robe covered everything but his head and his flippered hands which were currently held slightly to either side, palms up, fingers as splayed apart as they could achieve.

"Your Highness," he began, "this would absolutely explain why our attempts through the generations to heal and minister to our people as we would to trolls or ogres or even reptiles has failed so miserably. Also, our lack of physical tolerance to dry climates, our webbed hands and feet, our large eyes – it just makes sense."

The room enjoyed a brief collective murmur of agreement before Runebane raised one flippered hand for silence.

"Very well," he said, his voice resonating. "As of this day forward our people will refer to themselves and each other as 'Froglodytes'. Arken, Haulis, communicate this to the people via your mage and priestly brethren throughout your networks in every village and town, every farm and freehold." In a quieter voice he said to the thieves, "And to our allies and partners as well, please. We need to emphasize our differences from my predecessors…"

Brine was wide-eyed but remained silent as his mentor merely nodded.

Runebane's voice rose again, "This history shall have duplicates made and sent out as well, to be taught to all Froglodytes, to restore our true lineage!"

Arken Rune-Reader and Haulis Heart-Mender exchanged a brief look then responded in unison, "As you command Your Highness."

When the chamber cleared out, Runebane kept only Arken, Haulis, Pill and Hak behind. The three former troglodytes leaned in close together. Runebane said in an only half-joking conspiratory manner, "In addition to copying and distributing this history both orally and in writing, I want you both to pursue medical and magical testing to see if we can categorically support this with present-day facts and evidence. I am quite certain this will lead to more attempts on my life, perhaps even an outright challenge, though I believe Carnis has the only legitimate chance, and we support each other. Any other concerns?"

Arken's droopy eyes almost closed completely he was smiling so widely at his king. "Highness, I am rather excited about potential testing and helping our people live longer and healthier lives!"

Haulis was circumspect, as always, "My King, I trust you will support my experimentation efforts within a willing test group?"

Runebane only blinked his bulbous eyes once before he said, "Of course. Start with the sick, old and infirm. Move on to the criminal and deranged if it does not go well…"

Haulis smiled. Smartest-of-All indeed.

Arken lightly touched the younger froglodyte's voluminous sleeve, saying, "We will, of course, synchronize our efforts and compare results my King."

Haulis nodded in agreement, echoing, "Of course."

The two trundled off together. When they were well and gone, Pill said, "I really hope this all turns out how you want it to…"

"Well," said the King, "the real question now is, will my people support us?"

The remaining trio faced inward, each watching the backs of the other two through the gap between. The elf and gnome both shrugged.

"So…what next?" asked Hak.

Pill rolled his eyes, and replied, "I have no idea. Associating it with a martial success may help…"

"And yet," said the King of the Froglodytes,

"why would they?"

The other two met his eyes and each other's and said, "Why indeed?"

***

Chapter 8

The Ogres are Hungry

It was time to attack. It would be a total surprise. They planned to leave no one alive. The sun had been down for hours, the fires had burned low and were banked for the night. The village was asleep. The vision had been clear this time. He knew the artifact was going to be here. It would be in the possession of a female. As shamans go, devoutness was not his forte, but as a simple being he knew what he saw and could remember it, even in visions.

Dagrog Torax was a direct descendant of the Ogre-Father and the Witch-Mother. He viewed the dwellings before him through the trees, knowing which ones held living beings and which were empty. He also knew that no help would come for those he was about to kill; he had foreseen it.

In a mere half an hour the dozen dwellings of the village were empty of life, its inhabitants well on their way to becoming breakfast. Some were being roasted on spits over fires, both made from their own fences. The very ground turned grayish-white and the fire died at the approach of an almost shadow. That was new. The voice that filled his ears was not new.

"No survivors, no one missing?" came the cold direct query.

"We watched for three sleeps. No one else," was the rumbled response.

"Did you find it?" The eyes glowed briefly in expectation.

"Not yet. The vision is incomplete," said Dag.

"What does that mean?" This was deceptively soft-spoken, and the ogre knew it.

"The visions are always right. The scene is right. The time may not be." His response was matter-of-fact.

"I trust both your ability and your assessment. Don't burn the houses. Stay here. Wait for it to arrive, get it for me, and bring it to me. I will be moving toward the final portal. It has to be right... May the Hags will it for us..."

Dagrog squinted as he began to feel even his not-entirely warm flesh turn cooler. "May the Hags will it..." he responded.

***

Chapter 9

Lost Froglodytes

The two Froglodyte soldiers that accompanied the King's magical and religious emissaries along the coast in the direction of the ogre borderlands were just along to make sure the mages and priests sharing the King's decree and their race's new name and recently found history remained safe in the endeavors.

They were used to being met by their fellows stationed in outlying areas with desires for news of home, family, friends and fellows. In one village, however, one asked after the guard that had tried to stab the King.

The senior soldier responded before anyone else present could, saying, "He sounds familiar, was he with a group of fishermen or traders...?" The affirmative response let him continue while the others held their breath, "Was he a friend? Did you serve together here?" Another positive answer. "Perhaps we should visit your garrison for a meal, some fellowship and see what we all remember?"

That evening found the traveling soldiers in a shack atop the central low bluff near the middle of the village; high enough to avoid coastal storms and provide an excellent view for responding to threats.

With bunks lining two walls and tables and benches down the middle it was perfect for the expected austerity of the (now) froglodyte barracks life. They normally didn't cook much of their food anyway and the local climate never got cold enough warrant a fire. It did have a fireplace so they must not have built it themselves. It was partially filled with fish bones, some with tiny bits of flesh still rotting on them, the stench permeating the entire volume of the structure. To the visiting froglodyte soldiers it smelled lovely from the moment the door opened to let them in.

Unfortunately, it also masked the smell of the dozen ogres hiding behind the bunks. When the host soldiers were exchanging introductions from the center tables, placing the four newcomers all facing inward, their backs to the bunks, the ogres stepped out in pairs and eight of the twelve skewered or hacked or smashed their unwitting victims with spears, axes and clubs. The next day the local troops talked in the village about 'seeing off' their counterparts. No one went looking for them.

When the 'wordspreaders' began to return to the palace to report their efforts to King Runebane about their visits communicating his proclamations, it was weeks before anyone asked after the missing group.

***

The delegation that did not return on time was awaited. The wait was not rewarded. Runebane's advisors had given their minions specific locations and numbers of days to visit and to return. They knew that delays happen, but also that unlike social or trade movements, when there was a King waiting most would at least send a messenger if they could regarding any possible delay.

The particular party in this case was senior and experienced. The royal support group was concerned, then nervous after a few days, and at a week downright worried. They told the King as much.

"Sire," said Arken, with an obsequious bow, "we have had no word from the northeastern coastal contingent. They are a quarter moon cycle overdue."

Runebane knew very well where they had gone. It was the route that ended at the outpost along their borderlands with the ogres that he himself had both defended and fled many years before. He exchanged a look with Hak. They had discussed his various assassination attempts at length, and both knew one had started in that region.

"Let us handle this one carefully. While I do not want open war with the ogres, neither do I intend to ignore the possibility that it may already exist... Send a column, slowly, that way. Send another via ship to the adjacent port. Instruct them to arrive simultaneously if possible, to suspect everyone, believe no one, secure the town and port, and send back any suspicious actors to me for interrogation."

"Yes, sire, it shall be as you say."

The two columns left the next morning, the ground troops traveling light, the ships laden with supplies.

Neither was heard from for over a month. That was when a dock worker came to them with a piece of flotsam from the harbor that was identified as belonging to the missing ship.

Another meeting of the leaders, another worry session – this time a different decision.

"First," said the King, "begin raising troops to replace the columns sent, but at triple strength. Hak," he turned to the gnome, "you train them – violence first, logic later. Size and endurance, and hopefully a few who can lead on their own. Craggen," he said, turning again, "reassign some of your most likely subordinates, make an advancement plan – this could be a large-scale, long term effort. Pull in our reserves from the south and west, I want them <u>here</u>."

The scrambling began as soon as he turned and left the chamber. Over his shoulder, he called back, "Send me the most senior naval, merchant and trading ships' captains in port, today."

***

The ogre chieftain gestured toward his troglodyte table companions with a leg bone still dripping a little black blood, the flipper still attached. "Well, at least we have enough to eat for quite a while… keeping most of them alive so they won't spoil, brilliant I tell you!" The motley-skinned speaker grinned slyly as he asked, "Not that I wouldn't bash the skull of my own cousin for a good meal, but why are you fellows so taken with killing your own king?"

"Oh," said Dramin, exchanging a look with Tarlek, "you could say we're just paying him back…"

***

Chapter 10

The Frogs of War

Craggen was of course the obvious choice to lead. He fully supported Runebane, his troops were loyal to the death, and he was both ruthless and cunning. He and the King met with all of the ground and naval leaders, culminating in a simple, layered plan of simultaneous intelligence gathering and asymmetric action.

The two froglodytes having served together were aware of where each other's strengths lay. Runebane knew which questions needed answering, and Craggen knew how to get the answers.

They first tasked one ship to approach from well out to sea, not traveling near the coast where they could be warned by lookouts. That ship would have three more in hailing distance behind them, but invisible from the shore. They would send a boat to shore, under the pretense of never having been there before and being unsure of the depth, when in fact it was to scout the port and risk as few of their number as possible. They were to discover if any other ships were there, who they belonged to, and how they were manned.

The froglodyte warship, captained by the old King's first mate, Roglok, would switch crews with part of all of the trading ships of Fallon's, everyone around the inland ocean knowing of their partnership by now. It seemed reasonable, but no one really knew what to do with the information once they had it.

Craggen asked their small group, "If the ogres are moving against us in force, we need to know that. If they are not moving/advancing but have just taken over the port village, that is different... Losing an envoy and two entire columns is really bad and must be answered. The real question is why? What is their goal? Is it related to our recent desecration of their temple?" This last was directed at Pill.

The elf thought a moment. "I don't know. Maybe? No one now living saw us, I know that. If they had, an elf and a dwarf raiding a temple together is barely believable on its face, and it definitely would not implicate *you*..."

Runebane agreed. "I reckon this is something else. An advance party, preparing for an invasion? But why us? And no movement in a moon cycle? I propose it is the location that is at issue, not the occupants. The ogres, or whomever they are working for, need that port. But again, why? That is what we need to find out."

Hak growled and said, "Too bad none of our dragon or pixie friends are here. They are so very useful for quick movements, reconnaissance, and decisive action."

"Very well," said Runebane, "Pill, I need your help. Your foreign eyes may notice what we 'Froglodytes' have become blind to…" Hak looked worried. Runebane continued. "Master Upgood, I will be just fine for a week or two while you oversee training, and I promise to be extra careful."

***

The ships departed, and the recruiting was quick, easy, and netted unusually competent candidates. Hak was impressed. Craggen brought in his three main combat commanders to discuss a training plan. They all liked Hak for his humor, skill and appetite (the last was fast becoming legend). They respected him for his brutality and lethality. They had seen him fight against their own comrades at Fallon's, seen his strength and ferocity overcome any lack of size. They paid rapt attention to what the shorter, younger gnome wanted them to do with the new volunteers… Weeks passed; the new troops were mostly ready…

Carnis was worried. He said so. "I am uncertain

that without help we can withstand any level of an ogre attack, much less an actual invasion. Occasional border incursions notwithstanding, we have never gone toe-to-toe with ogres and won."

Runebane, sitting at his council table covered with maps, charts and ledgers surrounding a lunch of day-old fish salted with dead flies and brown, brackish wine, agreed, but with a positive view. "We've also not done it and lost either!"

Gjork, Craggen's most senior captain, said, "Sire, I think it will be simple math unless we fully incorporate an asymmetrical strategy. It takes three of us in single combat on average to bring down an ogre. In a fixed defense we could likely get those odds to work. If we go on the offensive, though, the math is reversed, and we likely need nine to their one... and as we have no information at all we don't even know how large of a force they have put into the field to begin to compare and estimate any chances of success!"

"Sire!" announced a royal herald, "Pill Von Ferret!"

The weeks he had been absent had not been friendly to him – the elf looked a bit peaked.

"Pill!" shouted Hak and the gnome ran to tackle his friend. Luckily for Pill, he collapsed before it could happen. Hak stopped in his tracks, dejected and worried.

The looks of concern exchanged by all present spoke volumes, but their only source of information to answer their questions was unconscious.

***

When he awoke, Pill was immediately aware of his stomach telling his brain about its concern that his throat may have been cut. With a sigh he opened his eyes, revealing his occupation of a room he had no memory of, but on a low stool next to his head was a cup and a pitcher. Turning to sit up and put his feet down brought a groan. Overall soreness, a few recent wounds and bruises, but none matched his hunger headache.

Pouring what smelled like beer and honey into the cup, the exhausted thief gulped down the mead in one quaff. It was a start. He felt it trickle down through his entire system. He poured another cupful, which lasted just as long. He stood up to go find food and almost lost consciousness. Catching himself with one hand the elf eased himself back down onto the bed he had just vacated. As he was downing a third cup of mead, the door opened, and he was soon eye to eye (though he was seated) with a familiar ruddy face.

"H'lo Pill – how ya feelin'?" The gnome's tone was hesitant.

"Starving and weak. You?" came the honest but sarcastic response.

"Ah! Gotcha," the last trailing off as the enormous booted feet at the end of the short, stumpy legs bolted away making a close copy of the sound of rolling thunder on the stone floor of the hallway outside the chamber Pill occupied.

In moments the thunder returned, but with a tray of wonderful smells attached to even more wonderful tastes – fresh bread, smoked fish and some spiced boiled potatoes. Washed down with a few more cups of mead...

When the food was gone, Hak asked, "Pill, where's Brine?"

"As far as I know, still on the ship... have they not returned?" The thief's eyes narrowed a little.

"No, but I don't know if that's good or bad," said Hak.

"Well, my father always said, 'If you haven't seen a body, anything is possible.' Of course, he turned into a vampire, so there are many layers between 'good' and 'bad'..."

The gnome spent a moment wrestling with the

68

layers of logic, lost, and said, "I'll be right back!"

***

When Hak returned, followed by Runebane and Carnis, Pill's headache was subsiding. Hak had more food and Carnis another bottle of mead and three more cups. The rack of steaming bird meat Hak extended was devoured before Carnis could pour four cups from his bottle. Runebane chuckled.

The King of the Froglodytes said, "So, Royal Thief, regale us with your exploits..."

***

Roglok had altered the plan. They had sailed with a half dozen ships. Two merchant traders with large holds were loaded with newly mustered Froglodyte warriors from across their lands. They stayed the farthest from shore, only able to see the middle two ships. Those had full crews of experienced sailors and soldiers and more sails, though they had shorter overall profiles, making them quicker and more maneuverable. These ships kept pace with two fishing boats, the crews fishing with a massive net strung between them. These last two were in sight of and closest to shore, and the extra cargo stayed below the side rails out of sight. Part of that extra cargo included Pill on one ship and Brine on the other. Their plan was to wait for the fishermen to go ashore to sell or trade their catch and sneak into the port town and see what was going on, hopefully to find the missing frogmen, get back on board, then meet the rest of the group at sea and make a better informed plan.

***

Runebane, who had not eaten, briefly interrupted, "How was the fishing?"

The elf laughed, "It was the only thing that went well..."

"Sorry," said the King of the Froglodytes, "please continue..."

***

Per their norm, the fishermen cleaned most of the day's catch each day, salted the meat and sealed it into barrels. The rest they ate. Pill did not have to imagine Brine's horror at the lack of cooked food – he got to see his protégé's greenish face staring at him in between retches while the crews ate in shifts – but froglodytes at sea would not normally have fire on board at all, so to avoid any outward appearance of anything out of the ordinary, Brine just had to endure.

It was dusk on the second day that he saw the scouts watching them from the land. They were hiding, back in the undergrowth of some coastal copses of overhanging trees along a cliff. He couldn't make them out, but from their size they could only be ogres. Well over two barrels high, these were all huge, and once they moved they were clearly fast, agile and athletic – in other words, these were soldiers. And they were well south of the normal froglodyte border. Finally, once they sighted the ships, they (well, at least some of 'they') moved along the shore, staying even with the ships. Their eventual arrival was to be no surprise.

When they did get close to the port, late in the evening on the fifth day, there were no beacon fires on the pier to guide their approach. The fishing captain said, "We must wait for daylight, I'll not risk sinking us." It seemed reasonable, so they anchored out in deep water offshore and waited for morning.

***

"I don't know what happened after that," Pill said, "We woke up in jail cells, listening to the discussion of which of us were to be eaten first... Ogres. Yech."

He paused. "My favorite was to be slow roasted, as the cells we were in were so damp and cold and my jacket was not with me. At least I'd die warm... but, upon wiggling my feet I remembered that while ogres are large, cunning and somewhat mystical fanatics, individually they aren't too bright..."

Sitting up a little straighter the elf recounted what he remembered after that point with clarity and detail. "I got above the cell door after picking the lock and opening it – when the roving guard looked in I garroted him with my belt. He banged me up pretty good before he passed out, but he didn't succeed in raising an alarm. I unlocked the rest of the cells, but only found part of the crew and none of the fighters. I saw a large double door barred at the end of the passage, more of a cavern really, it got taller as it went deeper. I found hundreds of mostly starving froglodyte soldiers and sailors. They said the ogres didn't care; they would eat them anyway."

Runebane sighed, Carnis fumed, his amphibian nostrils flaring. Hak looked ready to vomit. Pill went on. "I didn't see Brine or any other ships' crews, so I figured it was just our ship that was captured. The fishermen were okay but the other prisoners had no chance to escape on foot, so I decided to try to clear a path to the docks for them to steal a ship, then come back and create a distraction to give them time. Of course, I didn't know how to get to the docks, so I took a few sailors with me. It was surprisingly easy. There was a back door, likely for bringing in supplies, that led down to a few switch-backing stone staircases and right to the docks. The nearest pier had two empty ships, neither of ogre design, both unguarded. We made quick work of getting them filled and underway – and no one noticed."

After a bit more mead for everyone, Carnis asked, "Did you expect them to come back here?"

Pill shook his head, "No. Time was critical, I just told them they should find the other ships."

Hak said, "How'dja get away? And how long ta get here?"

Pill exhaled slowly, then said, "As the two ships slipped their moorings and a handful of oarsmen each set them on the way out of the harbor, I made my way toward the only light I could see – a bonfire near the middle of the settlement. Turns out it was actually a dinner celebration, and some of the main courses were still kicking and screaming. I figured to get what information I could, but couldn't let them see me... I found a hooded robe and snuck around behind what seemed to be a table for honored guests. Oddly, a few froglodytes sat there with the ogre chieftains, unbound, drinking and eating with them. That's when I saw my father's jacket. It lay on a smaller table behind them, my belongings spread out almost like a display next to it."

He drifted off a little, then snapped back to the present. "I listened for a while. The ogres frequently made fun of their dinner's antics while it was cooking, and poking fun at the two dining with them as well. They did not seem amused, but they tolerated it. They both wore robes, one with your religious symbols and several pendants on chains and leather strings around his neck. When they all went to the bonfire, I scooped the table's contents onto the jacket, gathered it like a sack and walked off into the darkness. After a few minutes I put it on, filled my pockets, lit a torch with my tinderbox and began setting fire to houses as I ran out and down the road to head here. That last bit took me three days, only stopping to eat and drink a little whenever I could." As if to emphasize this the thief took a long drink from his cup.

Carnis turned to stare into Runebane's curious eyes. "We are betrayed," he said.

"Yes..." said the King, "but by whom?"

Hak, ever the pragmatist, said to Pill, "You need some new weapons then I guess?"

Pill smiled, saying, "Please and thank you."

Just then a herald announced himself, which made them all look at him like a bird with gills. He said, "Sire, there is a rather insistent dwarf to see you. With the attacks of late I deemed it best to not allow it without your protectors knowing about it in advance, and … well, they are here with you…" The smiling spearman was rather proud of himself, but his expression changed to confusion as he was instantly the only being left in the room.

***

They found Brine being restrained by two more spearmen, who, when Runebane said, "Let him go!" obeyed their king immediately, and the poor young dwarf fell to the ground abruptly.

When he looked up, it was to see two hands offered, Pill's and Hak's. He accepted their help to rise, then squeezed them both in a dwarven bear hug.

"Oh! Thank the gods you're alive! I was SO worried! They all told me how you saved them but that you went back to create a distraction, and then the flames were so high we could see them in the dark over the horizon! I …"

"Ssshhh…" Pill said softly, ruffling his shorter companion's hair. "I'm okay. Thank you for your concern." The elf smiled. "Now, tell us your news…"

"Oh! So, we saw a small boat come out to meet yours, but it was just a couple of, um, froglodytes, so we weren't worried. Then your ship sailed into the harbor, following them. A few hours later the boat came back, but our captain declined the escort, said it was fine to wait until daylight. They didn't want him to wait, but he would not budge, and said, 'No, thank you and good night!' and didn't even let them come aboard to discuss it." Long inhale…

"As they rowed away I whispered to him to ask why he did that, and he said, 'Dwarf boy, I was at Fallon's keep several times when the Arch Mage was imprisoned there, bringing supplies and eventually the King ~ those two are Dramin and Tarlek, the very mage and priest that betrayed him and got your dad killed! I'll wager they've done some magic to the other ship to capture it. Just lucky they didn't recognize me… I wasn't a captain then. As soon as they are out of sight, we sail to meet the other ships and tell them of this treachery!' So, we did, and he did, and the King needed to know, so he sent the fishing boat we gained from you sending two back here with me in it, and here I am!" the dwarf, finally out of breath, smiled at everyone.

Runebane exchanged a look with Pill. He said, "You just missed meeting my old advisors when you came to rescue your uncle. We dropped them into Fallon's ancient fountain, getting rid of them for good, or so we thought at the time… The old king jumped into it on his own to avoid personal combat with me…also avoiding answering my challenge, but instead abdicating in front of his own guards, many of whom are still with me today. If they survived, odds are he did too. I may still have to kill him… They are likely the two you saw eating with the ogres. It explains the ease of my troops' betrayal – only a friend can betray you after all. Brine? Did Roglok stay? If so, did he tell you his plans?"

The dwarf nodded frantically, "Yessir! Yessir, King, sir! He said he was going to help some big, ogre rowboats to find the bottom of the ocean!"

Runebane smiled. "Yes, that sounds like him…" He turned. "Carnis, with the sailors we have out, what odds do you give any ogre force to outdo them without the surprise and deception they had until now?"

The old froglodyte fighter had been quietly observing and only advising the King in private for months. Asked for a public opinion, he regarded his comrade (now King!) for a moment, then said succinctly, "None, sire."

"And an invasion?" the King went on.

"None. Ogres are clansmen. No one but the Hags themselves can keep them from fighting each other for more than a few days at most. We can reinforce the three main villages just short of the coastal border region now with our newly raised volunteers. Giving each a triple strength column will secure them well, then we have each push out a reconnaissance and some raids in conjunction with the ships until the ogres run out of food and just quit the field, which they will inevitably do anyway even if we do nothing at all. We'll need to get word to Roglok how to signal the shore troops, but I believe it will be easily handled, now that we have the information we needed, and the resources properly allocated." The old commander looked around. "To challenge, they need *you*. Even if they should sneak around *me*, only the old king, Craggen and myself can pass the trial; he quit and Craggen and I don't want to…so if he is <u>not</u> with them, either he is coming here or is perhaps actually dead? Either way, our allies need to know that their betrayers are back and enlisting the aid of the ogres… I say you go, take the thieves and their 'spoils' with you and return Fallon's ships. I'll direct the actions at the border then return here when I can."

After several seconds of silence, Runebane said to all present, "Well, that presents a few issues, but they are manageable I believe." He turned to meet the gaze of the one person everyone else was already staring at – except him. He, Hak, was glaring at Runebane. "Oh, no-no-no-no-no! No ya don't! Ya can't get rid o' me that easily! <u>You need me!!!</u>"

"Hak...I am about to be a father. Mistress Toss is about to be a <u>very</u> busy governess, and if you want to see her at all you need to be near where <u>she</u> is...which will be here. I am sure I will be back very soon, and well-guarded the <u>whole</u> time. Besides, with Carnis gone, I'm leaving <u>you</u> in charge!"

"Wh-wh-what?!" sputtered the gnome. "I'm no King! I can't even spell King!" He looked around at them all, eyes pleading along with his words, "Tell 'im you guys! No one even likes me, I'm too mean, I always order people around..." He noticed they were all smiling and stopped, clamping his mouth shut.

"Sounds pretty 'kingly' to me!" laughed Runebane. "Throw in an assassin or two, and we could be twins!"

The rest of the group drowned any potential gnomish response in raucous laughter.

***

Carnis had just finished coordinating his detailed instructions to Craggen, who left leading the first ground column to secure their border. Pill approached him and asked, "Carnis, who are 'The

Hags'?"

The veteran froglodyte fighter leaned against the stone training yard wall watching the newly trained troops marching out for a few seconds, then said, "I really only know part of the story, and you're the one with the direct link to the Goddess of Death, but apparently they were a group of evil women with divine powers not of this world or even of the last one, but from something even before that. They were imprisoned in the earth below the bottom of the ocean in our old world, and the spell that created Metaerie cracked it open. Still trapped from going back to their origins, they simply came out of the water. They apparently cannot drown, and they seem to inhabit this dimension only partially... If you see one you will know it! They are mostly shades of purple, hair, skin, eyes and fingernails. They can fly, but it is slow, almost like they are still under water. They have no men, and they are hideous to look at, I don't care what race you are... they have bumps of extra flesh and gouges where flesh should be, like they never fully matched their presence in this dimension." Carnis paused, shaking his head, eyes closed, as if to rid himself of the visual memory.

"Anyway," he continued, "not only are they singularly ugly, they are also enormous, the smallest runs two barrels tall! To the north there is a mountain riddled with caves, right next to the ocean. At least that is how it appears to us. In reality it just goes down under the water, with caves above <u>and</u> below. The Hags live in those below the water. They roamed around our inland sea here and at some point found the giants in the coastal hills, otherwise described as large, ugly, evil men with yellowish skin, eyes and fingernails. Truly it was a match made in hell, if there is such a place. The results were easy to predict – two uglies, two larges and two evils – put them together and you get large, ugly, evil offspring. The coloring and abilities are the only variables in the mix. Most are physically strong and of mostly yellowish pigment. Some are purple, with innate magical abilities. Those are apparently from their goddess, though they never say her name. Usually the coloring is consistent; the yellower they are the stronger they are, the purplier the more innate magic they possess." Carnis paused, considering. "Haulis is the expert, but apparently these 'Hags' are of a fixed number, and they can't die, but once they breed they take their hill giant mate down to an underwater cave and live off of the corpse until the young ogre is born... They are ravenous, but reclusive, both about mating and eating, so a sighting would be rare indeed, but their young breed with each other, and much faster, months not years, so their population has grown. Stupid they may be, but they fear <u>nothing</u>."

***

Chapter 11

The Dark One's Trog Helpers

The mage stared at his troglodyte minions. He realized now that they had failed him utterly. They had turned a minor task he had given them into a grand scheme of their own. Not only had they failed to complete the task and obtain the objects he needed, but in the process they had turned their entire race against themselves, and ultimately against him, drawing in powerful and numerous additional opponents along the way. Their independent scheming had resulted in his total defeat, his efforts being completely thwarted. His anger was palpable in the air.

It was only while checking on his recruits from the ogres that were guarding the old red dragon that he had discovered them, attempting to escape the Red Desert to the sea. Not doubting their loyalty or competence he had set them to task to lead the less intellectually inclined ogres in obtaining the relics they claimed they had been forcibly removed from before. Now he knew better.

"I have a few questions. And if the answers are sufficient, I will give you some guidance and direction to help you understand what it is I need from you and why. And then I will perhaps clearly explain how slowly and painfully I will torture and kill you if you go off on your own again and ruin my plans. Do you understand?" said Baru Dall.

The nodding responses were emphatic. It was all they could do as they were currently trussed up, bound and gagged, hanging, heads downward over a fire that had been allowed to burn down to just embers for cooking. Their upside-down view of Baru Dall hurt their eyes and brains – he was a little hazy, blurring in and out at times.

"First question: If you fail to do exactly as I say, will you survive?" the out-of-focus mage said softly.

The two trogs went completely limp, motionless and silent, then shook their heads from side to side in the negative, slowly and full of trepidation.

"Second question: How many pieces of you can I cut off and feed to the ogres before you die?" This was said in a genuinely curious tone, contemplative and speculative.

The upside-down duo's only response was for their already bulbous eyes to get far larger in fear.

"Follow up question: How many pairs of waterproof boots can I make with your hides?" Without waiting for a response that could not be made, he voiced one more query, "Last question: If I send you out with another chance to obtain what I need, instead of subverting my allegiances to your whims of revenge, do you think you can finally do what I want?!" this last rose and rose in volume until by the end it was a booming echo that made even the ogres present tense up a little.

The nodding from the flippered captives was less emphatic than earlier, but much more sincere.

"Then let me make this abundantly clear. You had special knowledge and placement and skills that led me to you initially. You wasted them. I don't give third chances, yet you still have knowledge that keeps you at the top of the list of qualifications. These ogres are currently staring at their future meals if you fail. They will be with you the entire way. I have protected them against your magicks so that you have no possible sway over them. Now, here are your tasks: One – Go with the ogres and find and retrieve the items you already told me you had; bring them to the port near the river fort fountain. Two – wait for me there until I come to retrieve the items. Three – Once I recover the relics I need, take your king to reclaim his throne and advise him to assist me in all ways possible. The ogres tending the Old One will bring him to me when the time is right.

85

HAVE YOU GOT THAT?!"

The nodding this time was absolutely crazed in its frantic enthusiasm.

The dark form before them was by now somewhat incomplete. His form was clear enough, but when he moved his edges were … poorly defined. Wispy. Cloud like.

"Tell me again," he said, with a terminally laced undertone, and one of the ogres sliced their gags away.

The priest sputtered a little, spitting the filthy cloth out of his mouth, and said, "It seems I can only raise my own kind for further service in death…" The flailing amorphous arm in front of his face cut him off.

After a moment's silence, the quasi-humanoid cloud said, "I _need_ you to be able to raise _ogres_. They, at least, are a fighting force worth preserving… _your_ kind will only be helpful if I can keep the ogres from eating them!" The mage laughed long, maniacally, and loud at that. When he finally stopped, Dramin and Tarlek both felt the menace in his words, "And I'll wager they could carry you around more easily if you were legless… They get a nice meal, you can still cast spells, and your usefulness in a fight doesn't change at all, at least not when the ogres are on your side…" This time the laughter lasted even longer.

"Now," he said suddenly calmly, "I need those relics. They were magical before this world was created, and are magically linked to both. I just need one of them to physically get my body here. One!! The early histories I found here said, 'The Elves had magical items.' Nothing in them said anything about dragons being able to look like elves. My histories only talk about dragons, witches and faeries. There are no elves or dwarves, troglodytes or ogres in the old world, my world. Those early men that arrived here may not have known either, they may have actually not realized they were dealing with dragons."

Dramin raised the courage to interject, "O Dark One," he began, "I am sure that the elves have magical items now, but perhaps it was not so in antiquity... early magicks were simple, usually personal items. We tracked some in the possession of some of the escaped dragons. I am confident that Rrahmus had some as well, we just never got to see in his chambers. And now I think that perhaps the Human Arch Mage that you enslaved may have had some as well! We should return to his holdings and search them!"

Baru Dall, unused to being interrupted, first wanted to backhand Dramin's froggy-fishy face, but was quickly drawn by the allure of an easier potential path to getting what he needed...

"Very well," he said. "Take two boat loads of ogres with you. Return to Rrahmus' and Craddagh's chambers and find me one of the relics I need. I will instruct the ogres not to eat you...yet. Remember without this my time here is finite; I am already beginning to feel the pangs of hunger."

The Dark One's voice went to a whisper. "I need all of this to make my plan work." His figure began to fade out completely. "If any of it fails, the last thing you shall contribute to this world will be fertilizer donated by an ogre."

The scythe-like scimitar blade cut audibly through the air prior to severing the ropes holding the trogs' feet to the beam of the supply shed above – their combined sodden impact as they slammed to the ground was very similar to a net full of fish dropping to the deck of a ship. The ogres laughed, making lip-smacking sounds as they cut their other bonds. The trogs laid there for a long while silent with their thoughts.

**

Chapter 12

Roglok's Return

"What happened after I lit the town ablaze and left?" Pill asked.

Roglok had just returned. He had left two triple strength columns in charge of cleaning up and re-establishing the border defense as well as two fully manned ships, only one to be in port at a time, with the other patrolling the coast constantly to watch for invaders. "After your fire was mostly out, the ogres discovered their food supply was gone. We sat offshore with the fishing boats, our other ships out of their view. They decided to challenge us in their long rowboats, several dozen warriors in each. As soon as they were closer to us than the shore, we signaled the attack. Our ships approached and each went after a boat with our large, deck-mounted cross-laid bows. We used grapnel heads with ropes attached first – they have folding barbs that lock out when pulled on. Once they were being towed, our mages flung bolts of lightning at the crews and balls of fire into the boats." Roglok paused, remembering.

He continued, "Ogres are generally quite stoic.

They yelled, but only in anger at their predicament. As their boats burned, broke apart and sank, some tried to swim toward us, others clung to the flotsam. Our spears and tridents took care of the former, and soon the sharks came for the latter."

Roglok's demeanor was quite serious and sad. "These ogres were mostly warriors who could row the boats and board us, but a few were actual sailors. A sailor's two biggest fears at sea are fire and sharks, and we inflicted both on them. I doubt that any survived."

Pill waited.

"On land," said the froglodyte captain, "the other columns arrived and began clearing out the last holdouts. They captured a few and sent them back with me – you may want to talk to them..."

Carnis, listening quietly this whole time, finally asked a question, "What about supplies?"

Roglok said, "They are good for a while, we gave them all of the fish from the two ships' catches while on the way there, plus all non-essentials from our stores as well. We returned quickly, but the fishing crews are coming back slower, fishing their way toward us now."

The senior froglodyte commander nodded curtly, said, "Well done," turned and left the room.

Roglok told Pill, "This behavior is out of character for the ogres. I have <u>never</u> seen or heard of ogres attacking <u>anything</u> in boats. Their strength lies in, well, their strength..." He paused. "They are ground fighters who smash things. Their mage class only follow the will of the Hags and the appetites of their warriors — they don't need much beyond food, which is likely the only reason historically that they have attacked us — to eat us. This was different. They didn't want Runebane to know they were coming. Some had already left — one of the crew you rescued confirmed that the two of our people among the ogres were the same ones that tried to board my vessel, Dramin and Tarlek. That can't be good." The old sailor looked down at his aging gnarled flippered hands. "I served the old King. He was horrible. He is <u>not</u> missed. The changes in our society as a whole since his departure are all positive. I am sure it is treasonous to say, but I would rather kill him myself than let him undo it all by returning. Unfortunately, that is not how 'froglodyte' culture works." The heavy-lidded bulbous eyes bored into Pill's now. "I can't do it...but anyone not of our people could..." He too left the room.

Left alone with his thoughts the elven thief realized that beyond Roglok's implicit request might lay a mercenary benefit as well — he might approach King

Runebane with a proposal of this own...

***

Chapter 13

The Last of the Traitors

The Froglodyte helmsman stared at the group on the dock below him in abject disbelief. Waiting near the gangplank was his King, a gnome, an elf, a dwarf, and two dozen of the largest, meanest-looking and muscular trog – er, frog – fighters he'd ever seen.

Out to starboard, already raising sail, was another ship. Not a froglodyte ship, though the crew were mostly his old shipmates; sailing it back to Rose Castle was half of the point of their voyage, or so he'd been told. It seemed silly, really. The ship's original leadership had arrived in the capital port looking for Dramin and Tarlek, so they were taken to King Runebane. He put them in leg irons in the feeding hall and chained them to the floor while the rest of the crew was sent for with an invitation to a royal feast. In short order the humans had become prisoners and the ship outfitted to return to Fallon, the former crew now condemned cargo. If HE were in charge, he'd have given the ship to, well, himself. He wasn't, though, so he just steered this one and watched the group before him get aboard, leaving his King and the sour-faced gnome behind.

***

"Well," said the helmsman to the thief, "we should arrive tomorrow about midday I think."

Pill, accustomed to maritime travel as much as any other conveyance, agreed. "Perhaps sooner – the winds are quite odd." He had been checking the helm's azimuth himself at least hourly, noting that rather than the typical correction for side winds there had been none made – correctly, apparently as that was what made him notice that there <u>were</u> no side winds, a phenomenon he had never encountered on this side of the inland sea before.

He asked the helmsman if it was common, as the froglodyte sailor had much more maritime experience than the elven thief and adventurer. Surprisingly, he also had never seen it happen before. He relayed his conversation to his companions. Brine Drake had no real maritime experience other than their first voyage to Civit Rana, but a few of their froglodyte bodyguards had, and one said, "I hadn't noticed, but when I went out fishing as a young pollywog the winds were a well-known constant, always in a right-hand circle. The smaller the boat or raft you had the more you had to pay attention not to stray too far out, especially in the colder months for then it was often stronger."

It was Brine who reminded Pill, "Tara and the crazy dark mage controlled the weather some, remember Pill? I think the Dark One used her abilities mostly to enhance his magic, to have a greater effect on storms."

The older thief looked at his apprentice thoughtfully, and said, "You're right, Brine, he did. But he had some skill of his own... I'm not sure how much effort or ability it would take to do this magically... Or for that matter, to what purpose one would do it. For now, I just hope it means we get to Fallon's quicker and we can ask my uncle."

They left the subject and conversation at that, unease shared by all.

***

Chapter 14

Uneasy Magic

The smell assaulted him like a physical wave of lethal chemicals.

Laying on his stomach, face down in a small pool of his own drool, the Arch Mage pushed himself up with both arms onto his knees then rocked back until he was sitting on his heels. Comically, his conical hat had folded down in front of his face, but he heard no laughter. Wondering how long he had slept, he swept it up and back with one hand and snugged it down a little tighter on his head with the other.

His task had been to create a potion. It had seemed simple enough. Potions were his specialty after all, how hard could it be? Locating, divining, tracking – the more specific the requirement and the reference materials, the easier the magic. And this was so specific it should have been the easiest of all he had ever done...

So, why did his mouth feel like that of a fish dying on the shore and his head like he'd had a moon cycle's worth of ale in one sitting?

The fire under his cauldron was cold dead; not

an ember or a wisp of smoke was present. At least a day then. A look inside it told a different story. He almost recoiled, but hesitated, the glowing red contents bubbling slightly, and each burst added to the foul odor surrounding him.

He touched the liquid with a finger, expecting a boiling hot mass as he got close, but the anticipated heat was not present – the potion was cold.

As he contemplated the ramifications of that, and while searching for some empty bottles, there was a tap at the door.

Yar Drake looked at him excitedly when he opened the door, asking, "Well?! Did you try it?!"

Rrahmus shook his head violently, certain he was dehydrated and delusional.

"Here now, give way crazy dwarf, he's weak!" Fallon's voice preceded the man himself, holding a familiar goblet and bottle in one hand, and a basket with bread and honey pots peeping out above its sides. Rrahmus smiled, drank the proffered drink in a gulping, dying fish rush, grabbed a bread loaf and held the goblet out to be refilled while rending the end of the loaf off in his teeth.

After two glasses and one full loaf he stuck a finger into a pot of honey and put it straight into his mouth. Then he finally acknowledged Yar.

"Glad to see you my friend. I am still so sorry about the circumstance of our last parting," the mage said softly.

"Much has happened since then, and while I miss my brother every day, the tasks I have did not diminish when I went home – if anything they increased. I am taking care of both of our families now." The normally dour dwarf looked positively ill. "I came to fetch Brine for a family meeting. We have much to discuss."

Fallon and Rrahmus exchanged a glance, the mage with raised eyebrows, the fighter briefly crossing his eyes then rolling them.

"Ah!" said Rrahmus. "What my large-hearted friend here has elected me to relay to you is that Brine sailed with Pill to go on a mission for Runebane a few seasons past. Did he visit after returning from the Red Desert?"

"He did, but he didn't stay long. He was obviously uncomfortable. It was like he thought we blamed him for Wonder's death or for not wanting to work the mines. He was most awkward around his Ma… When he left he gave her every bit of coin he had left, took what gear he could carry, and followed the elf into the night, both all in black and armed top to bottom with more weapons than I could count. Don't get me wrong, I trust Pill to take him under his wing and do his best to teach him and train him. It is just that Wonder was the first of my kin and my generation to die. The suddenness and gruesomeness aside," both man and elf winced at this, "he reminded us all of our mortality. Dwarves as a rule are long-lived, stoic and durable. We are also often accused of being 'grudgy', but there is no one left alive to kill, no group to harass, just absence and loss. And so, we, myself included, must move forward." He paused. "But where I used to feel fairly invulnerable, now I fear losing more loved ones, even more than losing my own life. If the past year has taught me anything it is that it is easier to be missed than to miss those that cannot return..."

Rrahmus ate more bread and honey and drank more mead before he responded. The bottle empty, he set the goblet down on his stone-topped potion-making worktable with a clink. Fallon put the mostly empty basket next to it.

"Yar," Rrahmus began, "based on how the events that precipitated your brother's death came to pass, I would say we're not done yet with our rooting out of this evil. I don't know how that will play out, but I am mostly certain now that the dark mage Baru Dall set the trogs on their path toward capturing me, specifically, and maybe the dragons as well, though I am uncertain if he knew they could take elven forms...and therefore did not know who or what they were other than the spiritual leaders of good creatures. All of which has to mean he is not of *this* world."

Fallon picked up the logic trail as Rrahmus tapered off in thought. "We need to know where he came from, and how he got <u>here</u>. To do that we need two data points – arrival and departure points. The latter is easy enough, we were there – I'm sure Myron, Aurelius and Ariene can spot it down to the footprint. The former leaves some investigation requirements... We may need a fairly robust search party to go through what is likely still 'enemy territory', filled with the survivors and kin of those we killed that sided with the Dark One originally, and I'll bet many of <u>them</u> are still pretty 'grudgy' after just a year. I know those lands. Most of the men there are hearty folk, but not the brightest. They are easily convinced by a charismatic presence to do damned near anything, but once decided they are not easily swayed to <u>change</u> their minds. The trick will be, instead of trying to counter their current positions, to give them a new cause to rally behind that supports <u>us</u>..."

***

Chapter 15

Talking Takes Too Long

"We need a more reliable method of communication," came the muted mumble from under the flopped-over top of the ridiculously pointy hat.

"Why? Are we under attack?!" was the response from the aging fighter who was startled into full awareness from his previous 'dozing off' status.

"No," said Rrahmus, "I just hate all of the 'message sending', waiting, response writing, more waiting, multiple meetings where everyone has to introduce themselves over and over again, establish relationships, trust-building, then when they've all come together it's not what was expected, not everyone shows up, the plan has to be altered, then finally you set off... only to get a key player killed and have to adjust before the actual task is even begun..."

As the Elvish Arch Mage finally ran out of breath, Fallon held up a hand to stop him before his rant could continue. Rrahmus paused.

"Is there something new you want to tell me, or are you just rehashing the last few moon cycles?"

The hat spun and inflated against the air

pressure created with the force of being thrown at him, and fell short, coming to rest upright on the ground at Fallon's feet.

They had rehashed their plight several times a day for a few days now, with no advancing thoughts to be found.

"The dragons, pixies, dwarves, witches and even the 'Froglodytes' are fully on board with supporting us, but no one seems to be truly convinced that it's a pressing issue since the crazy mage is gone, his army is defeated, and his remaining followers are scattered. I want to tell them all about Dramin and Tarlek's possible return, the likelihood of Baru Dall being back as well, at least in some sort of projected form, but still think writing it down and sending messengers is a risky proposition. This needs to be communicated securely, face-to-face. Add to all that, no one has heard from Mortalya, not even Pill accidentally, and we have no new source of information, no imminent threat, just leftover speculation and rumor. What is missing you ask? My own people. The elves are completely disinterested..."

"Really?!" asked Fallon. "I thought you told them everything?!"

The Arch Mage rubbed his forehead slowly,

tired and frustrated. "I did. It did not get them excited." He waved a letter at his old friend with a deep blue wax seal, freshly broken. "Just being forced to acknowledge that they have an Arch Mage is painful enough. That I have chosen not to live among them is worse. Pill and I and my apprentices were the only elves involved or impacted... I need to go back anyway – after meeting with the families of my two apprentices who were killed at Icelle's I said I would. I need to recruit some replacements, and some fairly well-connected families' second sons couldn't hurt our cause..."

"You're talking about going to your grandfathers'..." Fallon started –

"I know! I know. It could take a while to get back, assuming I collect some followers," interrupted the Arch Mage.

"Because that will be your biggest problem..." muttered Fallon. "You don't intend to go alone, of course..."

"No. I think three apprentices of varying experience, a stout-hearted healer and one competent swordsman would be fine. You have to stay here. Aren't you about to launch another new ship?" Rrahmus ended with the question to lead his friend away from arguing to accompany him.

Fallon knew what his oldest friend was doing and rolled his eyes before he answered to make sure Rrahmus <u>knew</u> that he knew. "I am. And still recruiting the crew. Maybe you can find me a few more of those elves with natural magic knot tying abilities – young Krygon has grown quite adept at it! He still can't come close to the Yeomring boys, but, then, no one can... You should take them too! They keep beating up my students in the training yard."

They both laughed.

***

Chapter 16

Heading Home

The Yeomring brothers sat back against the stone wall in the passage outside Rrahmus' chambers on a newly installed bench, relaxing, talking quietly, periodically poking and punching each other.

From the matching bench opposite them a handful of mages who looked, dressed and (usually) talked like sailors or dock workers with pointy ears sat quietly and stared at the only other person present.

Seated on the other side of Rrahmus' door was a human girl whose beauty was such that even the elvish men could not fail to notice. Unlike the brothers, they also knew who she was and therefore rather than risk offending her they simply refrained from speaking entirely.

Her boots were reddish-brown soft brushed leather that laced up the back and came up above her knees. She wore lighter brown woolen breeches tucked into her boots. They were cinched at her waist with a broad belt that matched her boots around her midsection that had three staggered buckles at her right hip. The blouse she wore looked like it might have fit her properly a year or two in the past...it was stretched to the point that all of the elvish apprentices fully expected one deep breath to rip it in several places...

When she had descended the stairs to approach the door, she had been wearing a hooded robe wrapped around her, avoiding getting her hair wet in the light misty rain that was falling. When she got to the door and looked at the five of them quizzically, Graham had offered, "He told us to wait ... quietly," with a sarcastic smile.

The subsequent removal of the hood with one hand and fluffing out of long, curly tresses of shiny dark auburn hair with the other made the previous 'quiet' in the passageway sound like a rockslide. All five males were literally holding their breath. The following drop of her hands to the inner edges of the front of her robe and flinging it up and around her shoulders by throwing both elbows simultaneously outward had tested the strength not only of her blouse's fastenings but its very fabric. Sean, having recently spent a lot of time with witch girls only thought that if it had fastened in the front the stays would have been ruined... He looked at Graham, who was looking back at him wide-eyed and open-mouthed.

Spreading the bottom of her robe slightly and

108

lifting it, she sat carefully on it rather than the bench directly. That had been at least a quarter of an hour earlier.

When Rrahmus finally opened his door, Fallon came out first. Taking them all in at a glance, he went straight to her. "Bronnie, I just want to say one more time that I think this is a really bad idea."

As Sean and Graham exchanged another look, she replied, "I know, but I have to start somewhere, sometime, or else what have I been training for? Mom would have demanded that you take me along by now..."

"And..." said a crazy elf in a pointy hat from inside the doorway Fallon had just exited, "she needs to get some real world experience away from Daddy's shadow, in a permissive environment, surrounded by confident and competent scary people that are on her side!"

"Um, Arch Mage, sir?" began Sean, "How long of a trip are you planning?"

"Days to months, young captain," said the mage, "what is your concern? Wait. Please, all of you come in and sit down and we can discuss it together."

Nobody moved.

Seeing their hesitation, Fallon murmured,

"They're waiting for <u>you</u> young lady…"

***

Chapter 17

Off to See the Elves

The instructions had been brief and to the point. It will hurt a little. It will be over quickly. You have to move out of the arrival spot or those following you can get hurt. Go with a weapon in your hand – just in case.

Graham went first. The Arch Mage read from a scroll then closed his eyes while facing a blank stone wall, then held a small hammer in one hand and a tiny chisel in the other in front of his eyes, wrists toward his face. He flipped his hands around abruptly, extending his arms (and the tools) toward the wall. Immediately an arched doorway appeared, the hole black as a moonless night, the edges smoking.

Graham held his longsword pointed downward in his right hand, his shield in front of his face and torso, and stepped in.

It was pitch black, and his boots struck a wooden floor, echoing with hollow thuds as he stepped forward. He whispered, "Really? No light? Great." He stepped further forward, more quietly, until he bumped into something solid, then froze, waiting.

The most experienced apprentice, Angus, came next. At the first step he snapped his fingers and his whole hand became a torch. As he folded his fingers down it shrunk and got dimmer, then brightened when he extended them upward and outward. Graham could now see that he was standing in what looked like an enormous wine barrel, half again as tall as he was.

Rrahmus was next, hands in front, vertically. He moved to the right side and sat down immediately on a bench that was mounted along the inside of the barrel wall.

The second apprentice to arrive, Fergus, was the youngest, and he quickly sat next to Rrahmus.

Bronwyn arrived holding her hammer in front of her face with both hands, head slightly turned in fear, squinting. After being greeted by Graham's lopsided sardonic smile, she quickly regained her composure and stepped to her left.

The last apprentice to arrive came through the portal like he was falling out of a tree, swearing as he fell to his knees and vomited on Angus' shoes. The latter shook his head and was in the middle of saying, "Really?!" when Sean came through with his left foot falling to the floor as if after a kick, or, in this case, a 'polite shove with a foot' as he would later describe it.

He looked around, then at the spewing fountain he had created, then at Rrahmus, to whom he said, "Well, he was in the way…"

They all regarded the elf on the floor with some curiosity. Graham, ever the brutal interrogator, said, "Weak stomach for magic travel? Or just scared?"

The elf mage apprentice looked up, haunted, and to everyone's surprise, answered rather quickly. "My uncle died doing this, right in front of me. He was just showing off, at a family gathering, and didn't know they had brought in an extra table for the meal. It cut him in half. Well, actually, part of his midsection just … didn't arrive. So, a bit of both I think." With that the mage leaned left and collapsed fully prone and closed his eyes while letting out a deep sigh.

"Well," said Rrahmus, "that would have been good to know a bit sooner!"

Without opening his eyes, the elf on the floor said, "I figured you wouldn't take me on as an apprentice if I told you. Every story about you is one of fearlessness and ferocity almost unheard of in a mage. I couldn't admit to fear…"

Crouching down, avoiding the vomit puddle, the Elvish Arch Mage said softly to his apprentice, "Geoffrey, you should have told me sooner…" *"I'm sorry sir."* "...that people tell stories about me. That is fascinating!"

Geoffrey opened his eyes and raised up to rest on his elbows. "What?!"

Rrahmus laughed. "Did you think I was going to hold your hand and tell you it will all be okay, I'll help you through it, you'll get over it in time?"

When the befuddled apprentice's eyes widened and he sort of half-shrugged in agreement, Rrahmus continued, "Oh. My. You did. Well, that may make this even more awkward – you see, I brought you home to stay, not to help me recruit. You've had decades to reconcile yourself with your fears and spent half of that time being less than honest with me by your own admission. Geoff, your services as my apprentice are no longer required."

The no-longer-an-apprentice-to-the-Elvish Arch Mage laid back down, and after a pause for a few deep breaths, said, "Thank you."

"My pleasure," said Rrahmus. "No one will ever know outside of this barrel unless you tell them – my story is that you wanted to be closer to home. Okay?"

"Yes, okay."

"Great. Now – let's get out of this empty vat and go find some actual glasses of wine..."

Chapter 18

Home at Last

Bronwyn could not stop staring at the lineup of Rrahmus' cousins seated against the far wall of the audience chamber they waited in to see his grandfather. The venerable and regal elf sitting at the end of the long, narrow rectangular chamber was pale, almost to the point of matching his snowy white flowing hair that trailed loosely over his shoulders.

Seated between Sean and Graham she felt tiny, though she was approximately the same size as the warriors seated across from her. Their armor gleamed, highly polished, no dents or scratches like on that worn by the Yeomring brothers. That gave her a feeling of comfort and safety, knowing they were battle-tested. She was still a bit annoyed, however, that even with her body separating them, Graham put his long leg out in front of hers and kicked Sean's foot to wake him up when King Kedrick began to speak, as Sean's reaction was to smack her arm without even opening his eyes. Brothers. Good grief. She kicked Graham, who laughed in a not-quite-muffled snort.

"Family! Friends! Guests! Welcome!" boomed

the King. "And especially our First Men descendants, and last but not least among them, my own daughter's son, the Elvish Arch Mage – welcome home Rrahmus!"

This last brought a cacophony of sound as the armored warriors recognized their cousin by grasping the hilts of the daggers they all wore in embedded metal sheaths on their leg greaves and, raising them slightly, slammed them home repeatedly, the hilts striking their armor with many differently pitched clangs that all ran together.

Rrahmus doffed his goofy pointed hat and bowed until the clanging stopped. "Thank you sire!" he said, putting his hat back on, "And thank you cousins all!" Then he turned and continued, "I have several tasks that I must perform here, and I need your help."

Before he could enumerate what those tasks were, his mother's father interjected (which as King was his lifelong privilege), saying, "Rrahmus my boy, please sit down and let me tell you where we stand – to better enable you to argue any points later..."

Rrahmus turned to face the King, smiled with aplomb, and said, "Thank you Grandfather!" and sat.

King Kedrick rose, inhaling as he did so, and generated a musical cascade of metallic tones as his silver robe revealed itself to be a full body chainmail made of tiny links so bright and shiny they reflected the light of the torches around the chamber differently and constantly. As he moved it looked like a rainbow of light. He gripped a staff taller than himself, the top shaped like an ornate cross, seemingly made out of the same material as his robe, but thick and solid.

Leaving the base in place, he moved the top of the staff toward the elven warriors in the gallery. "First and foremost, Elvish Arch Mage, you need to be reassured that with regard to issues that concern all beings of our world, you are not alone. You never will be, and, if you wish it, all of our available support the world over will come to your aid." He paused, turn and faced Rrahmus' guests, re-directed his staff, and continued. "Though you do not live among us, your good works are known to us as are the great deeds of your friends and companions." Turning again he faced Rrahmus directly. He dropped to one knee and placed his empty hand on the Arch Mage's shoulder. "Grandson, your power is only eclipsed by your curiosity, your love only by duty, yet it is in your fearlessness that you are weak."

Confused expressions filled the chamber.

"You see, when we work together, we are always stronger than we are alone. Perhaps without training, practice and experience we are less efficient, but that changes <u>quickly</u>! You are an amazing problem-solver, a ferocious fighter and an excellent practical teacher. You <u>need</u> to be a <u>leader</u>. Leaders recruit, assign, direct, train, mentor, assess and evaluate. Good leaders also fight – when they have to – but the best prepare their forces so well that they rarely have to engage personally, and then only decisively. I urge you to stay awhile among us and see how these tasks apply and are performed among us, your own people. I am sure that you have learned from others. Your lifelong friend, Fallon Rose, the Yeomring lads here's father Icelle, Morgain, and even the dwarves, Lorknowis love them, though I tend to see them as a bit <u>too</u> direct, there can be no doubt of their loyalty and support to the First Men; all of these you have learned from, but outside of your dabbling with a few dragons, and now I'm told some rather interesting pixies, you have left wanting your social education, your history even, of your own ancestors."

At this point King Kedrick stood and turned to return to his own seat, but his voice remained clear to all present. "I will not presume to ask you to leave your friends, your lodgings, your comfort zone. I will only suggest that as you <u>do</u> venture out the occasional journey home can be as much of an adventure and learning opportunity as somewhere new and hostile…"

Rrahmus should not have been surprised that his grandfather knew of his feelings, intentions and deeds and had already analyzed them and formed a response in decree form, likely already announced to his subjects before Rrahmus and his companions arrived.

He smiled and said, "Thank you Sire. I never doubted your support, only my ability to adequately communicate its need. I feel that perhaps my time away as it has lengthened has made me increasingly hesitant to return, my social shortcomings only increasing as well and adding to my embarrassment at being an ever poorer excuse of a diligent subject of your kingdom. I apologize and can only pledge to alter that negative spiral here and now. It appears I need to increase my recruiting so that I may avoid the excessive personal involvement that has plagued my last few decades since taking on this mantle. I admit that I didn't fully appreciate what it would entail!"

The polite laughter from everyone wearing armor around the room showed a full measure of respect for both Rrahmus' magic and his adept application of it in some well-known past exploits in brutal combat. He bowed his head briefly in response, then stood. Turning toward the King he continued, "My needs are simple to describe, but difficult to fulfil... I need to know how this 'Dark One' got here, where he came from, and if he can do it again. I need to know if our natural magic actually returns to the old world when we die and whether that threatens our existence. I need to find out why those who aided him were so willing to do so. I need to discover the fate of the Human Arch Mage. My suspicion is that Craddagh was somehow the lich we encountered both at Thea's tomb and at Icelle's. Was he destroyed? Perhaps. What about a successor? Did we destroy all of his apprentices too? Hard to say... but in our travels afterward in the regions his supporters were from, none came forward...and no one has had contact with Mortalya for several months."

As the Arch Mage paused to breathe, a strong baritone voice broke in from directly across from Bronwyn. "Perhaps you need a dedicated information gathering capability..."

The chamber became so quiet that the rustle of Rrahmus' robe as he turned to seek out the speaker was heard by all.

Seeing a face very like his own smiling at him, the Arch Mage smiled back reflexively, and shook his head. "Indeed, but of what use without a reliable method of communication?"

"What about Fallon's famous faeries?" asked Rrahmus' oldest cousin.

"Perfect to the task, but neither expandable nor repeatable, sadly."

"Surely you of all people has experimented..."

"Yes, I have. Sound, vision, even movement, but always it only works in one direction." Rrahmus clamped his mouth shut and let out a frustrated exhalation via his nostrils.

"Well," came the response, "if it were easy, it would already be done!"

The speaker stood at this and revealed an elvish warrior in his hundreds. As he stepped down to the central floor his armor did not clang, his boots did not clunk. His whole being seemed to gleam, but while it shone brightly, his armor was not decorative.

His appearance alone was the embodiment of a history lesson in Elvish ancestry. His shoulder-length golden hair hung in waves from under his helm. The full-face covering side-hinged visor was open, the latch chain looped to the right side, revealing creamy skin, high cheek bones and a long, straight nose under eyes like the sea at three different times of day all at once.

121

Though he had no mustache, his short-cropped beard was full and hung below his lower lip like two upside down arches pinned from end to end of his growing smile.

To anyone who did not know them, he and Rrahmus could have been brothers. Bronwyn, seeing the resemblance, asked quietly, "Are they...?"

"Brothers?" interrupted Graham. "No. They're..."

"Cousin!" Rrahmus nearly shouted as he hugged the elf warrior as best he could, robes and pouches catching and hooking on armor and weapons, making it quite the spectacle. The hall filled with laughter without malice, seeing unabashed love from two of the most serious characters in their race, the pair grinning like children at play with the grandfather, also grinning, looking on fondly.

"Tahmus," said Rrahmus, "I am sorry, I did not see you when we arrived, thank you _so_ much for being here!"

"I wouldn't have missed it for a world, not even ours," was the reply.

"I really _am_ sorry I stayed away..." said Rrahmus remorsefully.

"From here?!" the other scoffed, "I've been

gone as much as you… We have much to talk about – I don't think this was your crazy strange mage's first foray into our world…"

***

Chapter 19

Who's Your Daddy?

"What do you mean, 'That's it.'?" The voice was sarcastic and hollow and echoed up the dark, round tunnel.

The deep-toned words were followed by a higher pitched, frustrated, and equally sarcastic measured and monotone response, "No more. The end. Finished. All done…"

"Okay! I get it. Why is it the end?"

"Ah, different question. Because, my enormous colleague, it's a dead end. I can go no further."

"What now?! Back up the way we came?! I can't even turn around in here!!" This last began to have a slight tinge of mania, and it did not go unnoticed.

"Just start backing up. A little bit at a time, and we will be out in no time at all," was the calm and mature-sounding confident response.

"This is not okay," came through clenched, possibly grinding, teeth, but along with it came a scratching/shuffling sound as enormous booted feet searched their way backward up the narrow, low and round passage.

"Just warn me if you drop anything, you know … sharp…"

"Do shut up. I know you can see just fine in this ridiculous blackness that you convinced me to follow you into. I'm going." The tone of this was much calmer, more focused, if slightly resigned and bitter.

He was right of course. They were both half-breeds. In fact, they were brothers. Half-brothers. They shared the same human father, who turned out to be both a famous (or perhaps notorious?) ladies' man, and a horrible dad. They were pretty sure they had at least a handful of other siblings, and all were remarkably similarly aged.

For the moment, the half-elf named Farsight stared at the half-orc in the darkness. His ability to see into the inky tunnel and see his half-brother Hailee's face by its warmth had come from his elvish mother. Hailee, on the other hand, was larger, stronger and fearless in direct combat, but he could not see in the dark, was terrified of tight spaces, had a difficult time forming human and elvish words without concentrating, and was only in his current predicament because of his absolute and unwavering faith in his brother.

Hailee's faith in Farsight was well-founded. The thief was slight of build, fair-haired and pale, where the fighter was thickly-muscled and dark – hair, eyes and skin. Farsight's self-trimmed mop of fine, straight hair generally fell in a tousled mop over his forehead so far that it barely exposed his light blue mischievous eyes that twinkled when he smiled.

He smiled a lot. Including right now. He would never knowingly allow harm to come to his 'big-little' brother.

The sounds of iron-tipped boots scraping as their extra-large owner slid backward was occasionally accompanied by sparks as Hai-Lee's sword blade caught on the flinty rock floor of the tunnel. It was only a few minutes until Farsight could stand, though crouching. In a few more moments they came to an opening and both stood in the round chamber they had descended into less than a turn of an hourglass ago.

They were in the bottom of an old dry well, and the sky above was still the inky blackness of a midnight filled with clouds.

The half-orc waved at the face looking down at them as he and his brother stepped onto the small wooden platform in the center of the opening. The ropes coming down looped around a center log that spanned the top of the triangular cage/frame they were in. It had been hollowed and then placed around a narrower iron rod so it spun freely, the ropes from above went down to it from one side, up again to a similar spinning reel, down again, then up to the other side and through an iron ring set into a great boulder and tied to a post, one of a great many set in a circle around the stone walled parapet above ground that surrounded the well.

In a moment their makeshift basket lurched upward. One arm-length, two arm-lengths, pause. One, two, pause. The pattern continued until they were standing at ground level and able to step off onto the inner ledge of the stone wall and climb the stairs up, and then over, and then down a matching stair on the outside of the well.

The figure awaiting their arrival in the dark was (to Farsight), short, thick-muscled, and though well into his forties, beardless. Just now his features were blank and gray in the dark. The wavy red hair must have been from his mother, along with the lack of height and squared jaw of the dwarves under a tightly closed, thin-lipped mouth and slightly oversized round red nose. (He had matching ears, but they were usually hidden under a knitted wool cap even when he was not wearing a helmet.)

Even though he knew his brother had just

hauled them out of the well, Hailee jumped when Grunnach touched his arm and said, "Follow me. Quietly, we are not alone…"

They followed, slowly and (almost) silently toward an empty barn just off of the old village square that was centered around the well.

Once inside, Grunnach asked his brothers, "So? Did you find out where the water is going?"

The half-orc answered first. "Sort of," he said. "There is a tunnel at the bottom leading off on a tangent and down."

Farsight interrupted, "But it doesn't make sense – it ends, and there is no water in it."

"What?!" exclaimed the half-dwarf. "Then where does it go?!"

"Nowhere," the other two said in unison.

"That's not possible," the third said emphatically.

"Well," said Farsight, "It looks bored out, like a pipe maker's first pass through a stem – long, narrow, getting gradually smaller, but from half-again as tall as Hailee at the opening to so small I couldn't move forward crawling, and it ends in solid blank stone."

Their group consternation became instant silence and watchfulness. Any onlooker would have been left with no doubt about their familial tie as they all struck the exact same listening pose in the blackness.

***

The torchlight grew brighter. Farsight and Grunnach lowered their eyes while Hailee peered more intently.

"There's quite a few of them…" he said softly.

Grunnach looked up, his eyes adjusting, and squinting, said, "What <u>are</u> they?!"

Hailee answered, "Kobolds. Kobolds with prisoners."

Farsight added, "Not just kobolds – they are being followed by our psychotic sister…" Again, in brotherly fashion, all three shook their heads slowly from side to side.

As they watched, a dozen of the smallish creatures piled onto the recently vacated platform. Four more unwound the half-hitches Grunnach had used to cinch the line as he brought it up (matching how he had found it). When the rope went slack, they looped the remainder around a single post, moved to the edge and peered over.

When they seemed to lose interest in the contents of the old dry village well and began to talk amongst themselves, Farsight moved toward them without a sound.

The torches they had all carried had been placed into iron rings that were set into the perimeter of the stonework around the well. This bunch had brought enough for about one quarter of the circumference to be used. Their positioning put the light in their faces, the shadows behind them. They never saw the pair of dagger blades flash and kill two of them from behind with downward thrusts through the hollow between shoulder blade and spine, angled to pierce the lungs and penetrate the heart. The popping sounds as the blades were removed was only slightly louder than the thuds created when they entered, but as they were followed by the two kobolds on the left of the group falling to their knees and wheezing blood bubbles out of their mouths and nostrils, the two on the right turned to look in alarm.

The one farthest from the two stabbing victims now had his back squarely to Farsight as he approached. The half-elven thief did <u>not</u> waste his advantage. He plunged his shortsword up under the right side of his target's ribcage, also into a lung, but the larger blade had an even more devastating effect, coming out of the kobold's right pectoral far enough for it to see the blade, to know how it was killed before the blade holding it up was removed and collapsing to the ground.

The last of the four now saw what looked like a giant gnome girl with two bloody daggers biting off one of his dying companions' pointy ears. He shrieked and ran up the steps to the top of the well wall. A few steps later he was launched into space over the well as a pitchfork thrown by Hailee skewered him with enough force to send him several body-lengths through the air.

The four siblings all made the exact same quizzical expression when the shriek ended with a splash.

***

Chapter 20

The Newest Keep Story

Farsight had been through this area before, years ago. The stone structure on the river's edge was new. It was also well-constructed and oddly placed. There had to be a story behind the money, and he liked both. He wandered into the small village and found a tavern with some outside tables, bought a pitcher of ale with two cups and sat down to wait for some local conversation. He did not wait long.

The blacksmith was more than willing to join him for an ale and share the village's tale. It culminated with a murder that they had all approved of…

***

Theirs was a small village with occupants of many different races, who all shared their love of food, frolic, fishing, farming and freedom from people asking them about their pasts.

The murdered man had been a new arrival, and, with a dozen well-armed men in his employ and with a few large bags of gold, he had taken over the village. At first they all went out of their way to please him as he was very free with his gold. In short order he owned the tavern, the supply store, and controlled the trade in an out. That was when his men began harassing, then beating and torturing the locals.

Until one night a pale female elf came into the village and stopped at the tavern. At some point things went wrong, the entire population heard the screams. But none went looking. Later, another argument was heard, this one ended with sounds of a fight, many shouting voices, and breaking of buildings.

The next day, with the dust settled, and no one serving at the tavern, a few intrepid souls ventured into his house. They found him, though none of men-at-arms were ever seen again. When they shooed the flies away from his body, they discovered that several parts of him were missing and/or rearranged...

At first glance, he was stripped naked, tied to an armchair, and his eyes, ears, lower jaw and 'man parts' were all missing. But when his hands were cut loose from the chair and opened reflexively, his ears fell out of one and from the other there dangled a fleshy pouch that seemed to hold four rather than the expected two objects, explaining the missing eyes...

When he was cut loose the rest of the way he was found to be sitting on his lower jaw, tied down so tightly the teeth had cut into his flesh. They stopped looking for the rest. The number of pools of blood made it clear that his minions did not survive either, but the attackers were gone. The searchers looked around a bit more, seeing every drawer, cupboard and floorboard in the disarray of a hasty search. Finding no bags of gold, only a note, left in blood, saying, 'I'll be back,' they left, trooped back to the tavern and served themselves.

***

He had come back, their savior. His name was Roary, and he arrived with a dozen men-at-arms of his own, much larger and better armed than even those that they had removed had been. The village seemed almost uninhabited that day, but he had known it was an illusion of abandonment. Until recently the occupants had lived in fear of the brute brigand who had arrived a few years ago with bags of gold and a dozen well-armed minions. He intended to change that. He began walking down the main thoroughfare, a man-at-arms dropping off behind him to lean against a corner of a building at each such intersection of byways and alleyways. He reached the other end of the village before he ran out of men. He started his return walk, back to where he began, talking loudly.

"Good people! When your hated nemesis arrived, you catered to him, wanting just a part of his gold. Not until it was too late did you discover his cruel nature and that of his followers. I tell you now that I want nothing from you. Not only have I removed the brute, but each of my men here are committed to your protection and prosperity as well." At that, each man-at-arms laid down an obviously over-laden bag that clinked metallically as it was set down. He continued. "We are prepared to leave you alone, but if you'll have us, we are prepared to become a permanent part of your little community. If you agree, we will live here. I will build a keep for myself and my followers at the edge of the river, on the rocky bank where nothing grows, no one moors a boat or even casts a line to fish. I seek no tribute or recompense for eliminating your tyrant – I only wish to be part of your community! I will buy or barter for whatever I need, and if you accept us here, we will support you when you need it as well."

He had reached the end of his walk and turned around again. None of his men were signaling that anything was amiss. He continued.

"Do we have an agreement? Can I stay here, build a home, put down roots and be a part of your community, help to make it the safe haven it should be?"

One by one, doors on houses began to open.

From treehouses to mud huts with long leafy roofs to fired brick walls with wavy tiles to large stone boulder half walls and oil-soaked log upper tiers with second stories and split shakes, the building styles indicated the cultural mix of the population. Indeed, he now looked into the faces of human, dwarf, orc, elf and gnome alike, all wary of a trick. An older female dwarf, holding a pendant in her hand, approached him, held out her hand. He took a knee and took it in his. She asked, "Do you intend to be a good and supportive neighbor and take care of us all as you say?"

He replied slowly but unhesitatingly, "Yes, madam, I do indeed."

She smiled, let go of the pendant, reached out and patted his hair like a grandmother and said, "I believe you." Turning around, she announced, "Well, I believe we have a new neighbor!" Turning back, she said, "How would you like some food you didn't have to prepare for yourselves?"

***

They had started in hastily set up lean-to tents made of a few poles and some hastily stitched furs. It had been summer, and the tents were completely unnecessary to protect against the weather. The other residents were sure the new neighbors had some things that they didn't want seen, but after their kindness (*free kindness...*) they were going to be afforded a LOT of social latitude...

His quarters had grown repeatedly. From a log house of a few rooms to several wings, his followers upgrading from their tents to bunkhouses. Eventually all were connected by covered walkways allowing them to keep clear paths in snow, stay dry in the rain, and remain shaded in the summer sun. They patrolled the area every day and night, at least a pair or trio of them, checking on all of the villagers, hunting and sharing the meat, which in turn earned them some of the farmers' vegetables and the barman's drinks.

Then they began to build with stone.

Built on a promontory of stone that jutted into the river, they began to cut the edges of the native rocks square and straight down, leaving sheer sides in the water that were cut farther down than an average man was tall. Using the rock they had cut first as raw material, they first built two right-angled walls, the corners laid out at sixty paces from the river and thirty paces apart. The long sides of the rectangle they began creating were built up to five barrels high and stair-stepped down as they went along, the base set with a ground-up mortar in actual barrel rings placed around holes chiseled into the rock every two paces.

The narrow sides of the two walls left an intentional gap wide enough and tall enough for a wagon to drive through the middle before the archway connecting them above started. When the outer wall was completed, only one other gap remained, one man wide, high up in the middle of the upriver side. From that point a gate was installed, and no one but the newcomers could see what was being built.

Eventually the side walls that extended out into the river ended in large round turret towers with narrow horizontal windows extending three-quarters around. Every few days they went hunting, but every moon cycle they went out to obtain logs for lumber and firewood. From the smell the villagers believed one of them must be a master baker.

The gap in the upriver wall was given an odd downward left-hand spiraling staircase that ended underneath the same spot with a hallway/wall that went to the water's edge. The landward side was walled off, as was the river's edge for a few rods, but that wall ended in cut steps for a boat to easily moor and offload in several different heights of water.

The final touch was the carving out of the stone in front of the main gate parallel to the walls from the upriver river's edge to the gate, and from the other corner of the gate to the downriver river's edge, the end result was a canal on either side of the main gate. Then they built a massive drawbridge in front of the gate and an inner portcullis. The flat of the bridge was laid on the remaining stone, made of peeled and soaked logs and banded in iron.

Raised initially with ropes and pulleys like those used to raise sails on a ship, eventually they were replaced with a massive turnstile and iron anchor chain and a capstan, again like on a ship. The last step was to cut out the remaining stone between the two previous cuts, making a channel of river water that doubled as a moat. The keep was now in fact an island. Once they moved in they began dismantling the old wooden quarters, using some for internal building materials, and some for firewood.

***

The half-elf thief's pointy ears were at full attention to the entire description of the keep's building after the phrase 'bags of gold'.

The weather was warm and pleasant, and he bought the blacksmith sitting across from him another ale. The large florid-faced man was bald with an over-sized bristly and unkempt black and white beard. A few dozen rods over the smith's left shoulder he had a clear view of the recently mentioned drawbridge.

"So, they commissioned parts from you, but you never worked inside?" he led his new drinking partner to continue.

The smith, called, characteristically, 'Blackie' by the barman earlier, brushed his beard down with both hands then held it with one while he took a deep draught from his new cup with the other before he answered.

"No. There were two times they brought me in to fashion items in place. Some heavy forged-in-place floor rings and a special spring-closing gate," said the smith.

"Well, that sounds interesting! How do you build something like that...?"

***

A few hours later the thief had related to his siblings what he had learned. The fort was always guarded, the inhabitants seemed to have never-ending wealth, they periodically sent out up to a handful of the men but were never gone more than a few days. The blacksmith believed they had a hoard stashed nearby, and had even followed them once, but had awoken at home with a knot on his head... and never followed them again. Farsight had a plan...

They left in the direction that the blacksmith said they always went, positioned themselves along the road at every junction they came to, and waited. They did not wait long. Two days later three of the fort guards came through. They followed them to an abandoned village with a central courtyard with a well and a decent sized keep. The men went straight into the well.

The siblings waited, but the men never came out. Finally, the siblings grew impatient and they decided to go in after them, only to find the well dry and empty.

***

Two days had gone by since Hailee had fished out his skewered kobold from the well that had somehow filled with water silently and in mere seconds. Half of the kobold was now missing – cooked and eaten. Hailee enjoyed it, Yelsa tolerated it, Grunnach held his nose and chewed as little as possible. Farsight absolutely refused. They planned their ambush, arranged blocking items and made long wooden spears for standoff weapons – all to no avail. The water remained, the kobolds were still gone, and the half-elf was starving.

On the third morning they changed tactics.

"Well, we know gold came out," said Grunnach.

"Yes, and a dozen little devils went in, after at least three full-sized men," said Farsight.

Yelsa had tried to think of any way to penetrate the well without drowning but had concluded that a parallel well would take too long and that this was a magical problem. Two nights of prayer had not seemed to help, but she said, "I have to go."

Hailee, who they always assumed was the dumb one, even himself, said, "If we cannot rob from the source, what about the destination?"

"Huh," said Farsight, "backtracking a score of kobolds couldn't be too hard..."

So they did. It took longer than they thought. The kobold subterranean lair was only a day's travel, but when they arrived it was deserted. Not empty – there were dozens of bodies, exhibiting a variety of causes of death, but the most prevalent were spears and blades and the occasional crushed skull...

They had approached quietly and eventually wandered through the entire kobold town without speaking. As generally morally ambivalent as they were with regard to property, especially if it was shiny and valuable, the several family groups found together

143

struck a chord with the trio of partially-related males who had not grown up with their father as their primary role model.

While there were a few scenes that made Farsight glad he had not eaten much other than nuts, berries and an unfortunate rabbit in the past few days, he still made them search everywhere and take everything of value they could carry. They netted a few bags of coins, several edged weapons, and a large bag of apples, which the half-elf tried to consume all by himself. When they emerged from the lair's entrance cave, they easily found another trail, this one revealing the tracks of larger, booted feet, and it was fresh. It led them down a stream-paralleling path. Where the stream fed into a larger river lay a quiet hamlet, much like they envisioned the one they had been in for the past several days would look if it had been inhabited.

It was here that they discovered both some information about current events and a discouraging truth about their world. The tavern they entered solved the kobold massacre mystery in seconds. They saw a bunting on the wall behind the bar made of at least several dozen kobolds' ears of various sizes. Mere minutes later the local beer softened that backdrop as they listened to the story from the barmaid about how her entire village, several days travel upstream, was murdered in their sleep by kobolds a few months back, including her parents and her little brother. She had luckily been here, visiting her aunt, when it happened.

After a few more rounds she offered up how a group of adventurers for-hire had just returned the favor to the kobold town upstream three days earlier. She herself had paid for a round of drinks for them all in thanks, and the locals had taken a collection and donated items as well as money to the group before they took a boat and headed downriver.

"So, they were sent for? Or did they just 'show up'?" asked Farsight.

"We had decided to be proactive about our safety... My parents were killed in their beds in a midnight ambush. We started a night watch, collected and saved some gold and silver for a reward and sent word with our local traders to ask for help. We were enough in number to defend ourselves, but lacking the tactical skill and experience to risk a raid or attack of our own..."

Grunnach drained his mug and said, "So they answered the call then? These men who just left?"

"Actually," the barmaid said with the first non-smiling expression they had seen her make, "I'm not sure...it hasn't been that long, and I don't recall if they specifically mentioned being told. We had not even settled on a payment amount, and when they arrived, we just assumed it was the only reason such a group would come here. When we asked, they told us they would do it, and when we brought up payment, they said they would only take donations that we could afford. Very honorable, but very dangerous men this lot!"

As she spoke the barmaid's face regained a smile and she bit the left corner of her lower lip and tugged on the braid of her dark blonde hair that came down by her right ear, her brown eyes twinkling a little.

Yelsa caught Farsight's eyes twinkling along with the barmaid's and she kicked his shin under the table.

"Ah!" he said, then recovered quickly with, "They must have been! To take such a risk for so little reward. Were, uh, were any of them injured?"

Her face was fairly plain, not unattractive, just average, but when she frowned in thought she was decidedly cute. "Well. Now that you ask, it does seem odd that I did not see any bandages or even minor wounds... I can barely get away with that just serving dinner!"

"Just one more question," said Yelsa sweetly, her pronounced gnomish features almost comical on a frame so large (comparatively) and just looking at her made the barmaid smile in return.

"Yes?" she asked Yelsa expectantly.

"Did they wear their armor all of the time? And carry extra weapons?" asked the half-gnomish girl.

The barmaid paused, staring at Yelsa a bit quizzically, then said, "Your accent is fascinating!" Another pause. The three males exchanged glances. "They were wearing all of their armor when they arrived here and were all carrying spears and axes in addition to the swords and shields. When they left, though, they had a small hand cart they were pushing, square, you know? Like a peddler's. Wheels in front, handles in the back... It had plate armor, shields, spears and bows and stuff in it. There was one, I think he was their priest, who never took off his armor. He also never set down his hammer, only drank from his own waterskin, ate his own food, and I never saw him sleep. Oh! Excuse me!" she said and darted away.

The answer had rushed at them like a stream going over a fall, unstoppable. Their eyes all followed her, seeing a large human young man with soot on his face taking off a large leather apron and gloves as she stood by, arms folded in a scolding pose.

Their drinks quaffed, they rose as one, each placing an extra coin on the table and left without a word, unnoticed by the barmaid who was once again talking like her thoughts were a flock of birds fighting in a fir tree for seeds in springtime.

Once outside, Grunnach asked, "Downriver then?"

Farsight said, "Maybe we missed something?"

Yelsa said, "Perhaps the well was not the only way in or out. The well is obviously magically protected, that water didn't come from nowhere..."

Hailee summed it up, "We saw them go in. We could not get in. The kobolds went in but did not come out. The kobold village was destroyed in the time we waited. What if the men who did it were not here for the gold, but rather for the kobolds? What if they hit them from two sides, knowing how to get in? What if they knew each other? Oh! And that could mean the kobolds were the watchers of the hoard! I mean, what do we know about underground lairs other than they always have some type of treasure? Where do they get it? Or what if they stole it from this priest in the first place?"

The other three gawked at him. Experienced as

they were with orcs, Hailee's intellect was far keener than his full-blood brethren. His language skills had to fight around his teeth and tusks, but in this moment he was clearly understood.

"Well," said Farsight, "we also didn't fully explore the kobolds' cave – what if they were connected? An alternate exit maybe? What if someone else was watching?"

Yelsa's eyes gleamed. "The men were prepared for battle when they arrived. They left with no expectation of combat, but with a cart they didn't have before. Putting their armor and shields on it was a convenience, but bags of gold are heavy and easier to cart or float than carry..."

"Alright then," began Grunnach, "we have a choice – follow or move on...and if we DO follow, is it worth the risk? A dozen heavily armed and experienced fighters with a priest leading them? Sounds like a bit more to chew than perhaps we have teeth...when it was just go find their offsite hoard and steal from it without their knowing, that was one thing – head on? Or in their fort? Quite another for the four of us..."

Yelsa's smile grew more scheming. "I say follow. Make sure it went to that fort. I need some time with a mentor. Northeast of here is a temple I can go to. You three head back downriver and make sure where they took the cart. Since I know you'll frequent every inn along the path anyway, just make sure if you change direction away from the river to leave me word with the barkeeps. I will find YOU."

"Are you sure?!" asked Farsight. "We could just go with you...there's safety in numbers!"

"I'm sure there is," she said, "this is for me to do. Thank you, brother, but I'll be fine."

Hailee removed one of the no less than two dozen religious pendants he wore and put it around her neck. "I will find you if I have to!" He was also more emotional and familial than any other orc any of them had ever met. He received even more sibling gawking.

***

Chapter 21

Mynorca is Coming

"We need a better plan," said Hailee.

"You're just saying that because the last one ended poorly and it was <u>my</u> idea!" snapped Farsight.

"Ha!" interjected Grunnach, "The real bottom line is we are dangerously low on funds, and some of us will starve faster than others…"

Yelsa's eyes were wide and excited, her smile barely contained as her gaze flitted between them all. As their eyes all eventually met hers, they froze, all wanting to ask what she thought, but all equally afraid of the answer. When she knew she had all of their full attention, the smile spread in a wide, upturned, evil curl and she said, "Mynorca is coming. We wait."

Farsight spoke first, "How could you know that?"

The teeth disappeared, but the smug smile remained. Yelsa said, "It's what I do."

"So that's your new thing, huh?" asked Grunnach. "Anything else we should know?"

"Yes!" she said. "I can make food!"

"Well," said Hailee, "I guess your time away was

well spent! Let's eat..."

***

Chapter 22

Mynorca is Here

When she arrived, no one knew she was their sister. Her speech was perfect. Smooth like warm honey, clear like a cloudless day and pleasant like a doting grandmother. As they lounged separately on benches along the narrow track in front of the village's various establishments (Yelsa the church, Grunnach the smithy, Farsight the tavern and Hailee the stable) they all heard her before they saw her.

As the wagon rolled to a gentle stop in front of the inn, a perfect mid-range alto voice opined, "Aww, that is so sweet of you! Just let me get my things and I'll relieve you of the burden that is me!"

The two men on the driving bench did no such thing. The driver wrapped the oxen's reins around the hand brake, hopped down, placed a box on the ground and held up his hand for support to his dismounting guest. The stock boy also jumped down, ran to the back of the wagon and gathered up a rucksack and an instrument case equipped with a shoulder strap for traveling, then sprinted to be next to his partner.

The half-dozen other passers-by and all of the

shopkeepers froze in place.

When she stood up from her concealed position between bales of food and boxes of goods just behind the driver's seat her long curly hair in the morning light was like the sun itself, coppery and glowing over currently exposed pale shoulders that were being shrugged into a dark green leather waist length jacket covered in sewn-in copper rings that matched her hair.

She seemed to run to the ground, one booted foot hitting the box, the cloak trailing over her shoulder dropped on the driver's proffered hand. She flung her hair back and spun around, noting her entire audience, especially her siblings, before saying, "It IS a bit brisk! Help me with my cloak?" to the driver who was happy to oblige as his inability to speak continued as it had for hours prior to their arrival.

His assistant, who was NOT shy, just desperate to please the pretty girl, talked TOO much. "I'll help ya miss! Here's your stuff! D'ya need me to carry it for ya?" all came out as if his life depended on saying it as quickly as possible.

Her response, as the scowling driver placed her cloak about her shoulders, was charming and sincere, "Oh, no, I'll manage, thank you ever so much! I'm sure you have work to do..." Relieving him adeptly of her rucksack with her left hand, spinning it by the strap and punching her arm forward making it slam securely onto her back, her right hand draped the long shoulder strap of her instrument bag over her head and right shoulder, letting it trail from above her pack to her right, narrow side down.

The moves were those of someone who was both strong and well-practiced, quick and decisive. As she walked away, each hand lightly touched a corresponding helper's cheek as she said softly, "Thanks again," and went straight to the inn. Moments later, after the wagon had moved to the loading dock of the village store and began to be unloaded, she re-emerged, without her cloak and rucksack, and with only a cursory glance at the street and its occupants, turned and went straight into the tavern. The sound of her thigh high boots striking the wooden steps left no doubt that though they matched her jacket they were solidly made. The tops were not visible as her skirt of overlapping thick russet leather strips covered in black iron studs hung down past them. If one looked closely, though, a few of the studs showed shiny glints – scratches from being struck... Similarly, a few copper rings on her jacket hung slightly askew, some were smashed or dented. Most looked recent, and likely had matching bruises underneath...

The stock boy received a smack on the back of his head to get him moving again after she entered the tavern. He was still smiling. Across the road, unobserved, Yelsa rolled her eyes.

***

The plan was perfect. Mynorca's first night of singing in the tavern had elicited the desired response. The village men loved her, the village women hated her, and the pair of off-duty guards from the keep told their friends about her. And then told them again. And again.

The next day the half-breeds made ready in the morning and departed before midday. While getting some food from the inn's kitchen for the road both the innkeeper and cook asked the males why they were leaving, knowing the charming beauty was singing for them again that night.

Grunnach said, "Not really into singing or human girls." Farsight and Hailee echoed the sentiment and Yelsa found herself rolling her eyes again. The two villagers looked at all of them like they were square chickens or three-legged eggs.

After settling their packs and weapons, the four siblings marched away along the road upriver and out of sight.

Chapter 23

Growing Up Sucks

The 'little dinner party' was <u>not</u> going to plan. With Bronwyn gone Fallon had been forced to turn to his non-socially oriented or inclined staff for more help than either he or they were used to providing. Even Rrahmus would have been helpful by the main course, if only as a distraction. He was thinking he should have made it a luncheon in the training yard where he could have had a periodic excuse to hit something or someone and be motivated to smile sincerely as the forced ones were making his face hurt when the conversation finally took a welcome turn to violence.

"So, Fallon," began King Jankin, "do you see your trainers, sailors and traders as a military force?" His initially thoughtful gaze met the King's, but his hesitation led to a more formal follow-up of, "Master Rose?"

Unused to his title, rarely hearing it since it was used to refer to his late father, Fallon began his response slowly. "I think of them as friends and family," he said. "Some are with us for a short time, others a lifetime, and some of them both…"

He stood up, turned from the long head table in his great hall currently set with a score of place settings. Grabbing an iron poker, he used it to its namesake purpose in each of the three fireplaces that paralleled the table. As he did so he used it for occasional emphasis while he spoke.

"Do you remember when we were kids Lee? Before we owned anything or led anyone? Just trying to find the next fight, win the next battle, get the next reward, meet the next girl, tell the best tale of our exploits? Anyone who was not us was suspect, and whoever our parents or our priests said was bad became our mortal enemy with no value except as an obstacle to be removed, clinically, objectively, terminally. Growing up complicated *everything*."

He turned from the last hearth, tossed the iron clawed shaft to the stone floor in front of the largest, center fire with a jarring clatter and said, "No. Not a military force. An ecosystem of partners with various skills who have agreed to pay and be paid, duty and wages and profits. The net monetary gain of our ventures is split, shared, and a portion reinvested into more trade goods, more ships, more wagons, more horses, more people. As a rule, we do not take sides, we bring food and supplies to those who want them. That's it."

"But…" began the King of the Coast Men.

"I'm sorry. It isn't that I am unwilling to help a cause, it is that we are a large cooperative group of essentially profit-sharing volunteers. Make no mistake, as I have recently demonstrated, internal treachery is dealt with immediately and permanently, and the rest of the band is wholly onboard, but I can't 'command' them the way you do with your subjects…"

Sensing the overall disappointment, and in a few eyes outright disgruntlement, King Jankin had a moment of clarity. "Fallon, you are one of my oldest friends. Your situation, to us old campaigners, is almost ideal. Your men serve your greater plan – oh, sorry, and women – as willing partners in your risk, knowing you always have their interests as your own. You are genuine, so their respect for you is genuine as well. I, on the other hand, was *placed* as King, my cousins all dying in short order. I was not trained or prepared for all of this," he spread his hands out to his sides indicating his companions, to their growing discomfort at his admissions, "Rather, I was meant to lead soldiers in combat! I know tactics, weapons, motivations and survival methods and how to be an absolute terror in a fight. What I don't know how to do is to make farmers and shepherds be good neighbors, how to always have enough force ready to keep from looking like either a threat OR a target, how to keep my Lords and Knights from attacking each other, how to resolve disputes of 'honor' that start with some stupid perceived slight and keep them from ending in at least one less subject in my kingdom! Let's face it, I am <u>horrible</u> at this!"

Fallon turned at this, looked his friend in the eyes, and said, "What are you saying?"

Jankin the man sat back in the padded leather chair, his pale face stark against the dark wood and iron brads, haggard and tired. He took his crown, and iron circlet with hammer marks all around the base and wings of white gold sweeping upward on both sides and set it on the table. "Fallon," he said simply, "I need help. Your help."

The silence in the room now had a gravity of its own, sucking in extraneous sound so no one heard anything at all.

"Don't you see," he continued, "no one wants to be inspirationally led to pay taxes and tend cows and gardens. The bards do not sing of boring comfortable nights around the hearth with an average fire taking the chill from an average winter evening. They sing epics about sacrifice, loss, privation and despair, ballads about grand pursuits, impossible loves and fallen friends, and triumphant marches of grand victories and promises of fidelity and future loyalty. I know how to lead in battle. I do NOT know how to govern in peace."

The room filled with an interminable pause, the truth of the King's words weighing them all down like a leaden fog.

Finally a different voice broke in, saying, "Put your crown back on King, your people need you, whether you want them to or not, and whether or not you are good at it, even when they cannot see or hear you. It is, in every kingdom, the central point of its existence, that they do, in fact, have a king!"

King Jankin smiled broadly as four of his attendants almost broke their chairs in their haste to stand up from their chairs and prepare to defend him.

Icelle Yeomring stood in the entry of the great hall, and when King Jankin stood, turned and replaced the circlet around his head before facing him, Icelle bowed, and continued, "Lee, you've looked better…"

Fallon, Icelle and the King all began laughing infectiously, the whole room soon roaring together.

***

Chapter 24

How Dwarves Make Friends

The elf sitting across from Brine and Pill while they ate was the smallest the newly minted dwarven thief had ever seen. He reminded him of Flaw, the Furry, Large and Wingless pixie Pill had met before setting out to rescue his uncle, Rrahmus the Elvish Arch Mage, over a year ago. The rescue that ended with Brine's own father being killed.

But it wasn't just their relative size, it was the garish appearance; the elf wore a bright purple long coat over what looked like gold chain mail. His boots and gauntlets were steel but were bluish in color, like they had been heated too much or too often. And his hair was red. Not the copperish orange so prevalent in the tribes of men to the southeast or the burnt sunset orange of Brine's own people, this was the bright scarlet of fresh arterial spray, the color of poisonous berries, even evil vampire eyes, but it definitely did not belong on an elf's head...

The young dwarf was about to lose his battle with Pill's internal lesson voice in his head saying, "Sshh. Listen for the unbidden answers to the unasked questions – they are much more likely to be true!" He desperately wanted a name, a story, a background, anything!

When Fallon sat down next to the elf and said, "Hello Plumley! I'm afraid your message from Aurelius for Rrahmus will have to wait, you just missed him. I guess you can either follow him, wait for his return, or just tell _me_..."

The answer, to Brine's ears, was hesitant, more youthful than he appeared, yet intelligent. "Well, sir, there is more to it than just words, and I believe the Arch Mage may have need of his personal supplies, which likely reside here...?" Getting an affirmative nod from Fallon he pressed on. "And here I believe I am among friends, whereas I am unsure of it elsewhere... I think I'll wait here if that is amenable to you, sir."

"Absolutely!" boomed the old fighter. "Let me introduce you to some good friends right here. Pill here," he said pointing with a half-eaten chicken leg, "is in fact Rrahmus' nephew, and an old friend and adventuring companion. Brine Drake, there next to him (and dressed WAY too much like him if you ask me), is a wonderful lad whose father and I shared many an adventure, rest his soul. Ask them anything you need whilst I track down a little lady who can help you!"

As the owner of the keep they sat in stood up, the enormous table creaking slightly as he forced his bulk upward with his arms, Plumley shot a glance at both of their faces, seeing in return two eyebrows-raised-in-question gazes that were patently the same. Their patience was rewarded quickly with a response from an obviously shy, nervous and self-conscious being unused to such scrutiny.

"I was sent by Aurelius to help Rrahmus. That's all I know!" The words tumbled out like a basket of potatoes being spilled down a stairwell. Brine's eyes got wider, Pill's relaxed as he smiled patiently at their new acquaintance, sympathy and understanding inhabiting his expression.

The older thief said, "So, Plumley... you're kind of small. Can you fly fast?"

"Oh yeah! I mean ... wait, what?!" The smallish elf's expression was a montage of pride, memory, hesitation, realization, and resignation. "I take it I'm not your first encounter."

Pill's expression grew sad around his eyes though his mouth was smiling. "I traveled and fought alongside Sylvia and Auron to rescue my uncle, then later with their parents and aunt. Handy in a fight that bunch; too bad about Auron – I really liked him..."

"I didn't know him," Plumley said lamely.

Brine said quietly and with a slight squeak, "He was great! In his elf form with a bow or a sword he was pretty amazing, but as a dragon?! HOO-boy could he fight and fly! He ..." Pill's kick to Brine's shin went unnoticed by the dragon-in-small-purple-elf-form – a fact that did <u>not</u> go unnoticed by Pill.

"I don't really do that kind of thing," said Plumley, "not in either form."

After another long pause, Pill asked quietly, "Then what kind of things <u>do</u> you do...?"

The elf-dragon hesitated, then said, "I have some unique abilities and ... sensitivities. I don't really talk about it, even with my own family, and I am uncomfortable discussing it with you. Sorry." The cacophony of color stood abruptly, turned and walked purposefully away from the pair of thieves, hesitated at the exit, then left without looking back.

Brine and Pill exchanged a look, said nothing, and resumed eating.

Moments later Fallon re-appeared, with a tiny woman perched on his shoulder. Finding the two black-clad lunching partners but no purple clad new arrival with them, she tapped the big man's ear and said, "I know <u>them</u>..."

His look when Pill finally met his eyes, mouth full of a slightly-too-large bite of delicious fresh bread said several things at once though rather than speak he indicated the spot formerly occupied by Plumley with a spread-fingered open hand and a demanding, questioning and exasperated expression. The elf swallowed his bread and waited. Brine caved.

"He just left! He went out that way!" he said, pointing with his knife, a slice of butter on the blade. The tiny woman winked out of existence and Brine breathed a quick sigh of relief. Fallon and Pill both swiveled their heads to stare at him.

Looking from one to the other, the adolescent dwarf and fledgling thief said indignantly, "What?! I don't care how small she is, she still scares me!"

Pill said slowly, "All women should scare you, and rightly so, as most of them are fearless in the face of actual danger. If, by race, they had the size and strength we do, we would be largely useless in a logical world. As it happens, emotion and morality, good and bad, rule the world. Fear is a perfect example. You walked into an ogre temple without hesitation but are a quivering mass when confronted with a tiny female wingless fairy."

Fallon continued the thought, "Your real fear of

her is because you don't understand her, and you don't know what she'll do or say next – fear of the unknown is the greatest fear of all. Courage, however, is acting despite and even in the face of fear. Unknowns gradually lessen with age and experience, but mark my words, you will <u>never</u> truly understand women. Individuals, perhaps, with long-term exposure, can become almost known quantities, or at least give you an expectation of motive and behavior. Marriage can be like that…" The old fighter stopped talking and abruptly turned and walked away.

Pill waited until Fallon passed from view, then said, "We try to govern our actions with logic, but our motives are largely emotional, either in the moment, or when choosing the principle we follow that <u>drives</u> our actions. I chose to rescue Uncle Rrahmus because of our family bond, because of love. I took you on as a debt owed to your family for helping me, for your father dying, a sense of owing, of survivor guilt. I chose to kill that ogre with you being loyal to our agreement with Runebane, loyal to Fallon and Rrahmus. They all <u>sound</u> logical, but only if you accept the emotional premise of each first…now, what are we going to do about your propensity to give away everything even when unsolicited. I hate to use punishments, though sometimes they have their place…" The elf regarded the dwarf critically for a long moment. Brine wanted to speak so badly his whole body was starting to shake before Pill spoke.

"Go find Plumley. Make sure he is safe and keep him so. He may be a dragon but I'm not certain he even knows how to defend himself… Get him back here so Lily can take care of him, and you can thereby help her. I'm going to find my father."

Brine had brightened at the thought of helping Lily, completely unconcerned about tracking down a dragon. Pill just shook his head and sighed softly.

"Ok! I'll be back here as soon as I can!" said Brine, almost falling backward off of the bench in his haste. More elven headshaking.

***

Chapter 25

Finding Sugar Plum

The market was busy – the sounds, smells and sights overwhelmed the dwarf. Having until recently been a lonely tweenage miner who saw his own family only every few days, anyone else only weekly or even monthly, and then they were still all dwarves, Brine's brain was spinning.

The logic that brought him here was simple – hiding in a crowd made sense. When he had spent a few minutes looking for a purple robe and scarlet hair it occurred to him that his quarry would not <u>blend</u> with the crowd, so this location was <u>not</u> logical at all. Had anyone seen his expression go from eager to crestfallen they might not have realized the weightiness of the moment to him as his stoicism had greatly increased under Pill's tutelage. That same mentor had told him that frequently the easiest way to go back mentally and make a different decision was to physically go back to where you made the decision – so Brine turned around and did just that. As he climbed the hill back up to the gates of Fallon's keep he tried to distract himself from his failure by observing his surroundings in detail, working on other lessons he knew needed improvement.

Rose Castle was covered in historic art and symbols. He had seen them all enough times that he felt he should be able to describe them in detail, but if he looked away and said the words to himself then looked back, he found he had been inaccurate every single time.

The gate should have been the easiest. The central design of the enormous work of iron was a giant rose, woven of ribbons of iron as thick (and sharp) as sword blades, but each petal was a skull. Brine had seen the faces of the gate; when the sun was high the shadow made a beautiful rose, but when lit by outside torches at night, the castle wall beyond showed dozens of horrifying faces.

As he walked through the gate and the sound of his soft-sided boots was low enough to let him walk right up to an inattentive guard, Brine was busy remembering. So much so that he failed to see the guard (though he held a spear) start to draw his sword until he was a step beyond the man and heard the squeal of steel being dragged amateurishly loudly out of a scabbard. The dwarven thief spun to his right, his right hand slamming the guard's right hand downward, forcing his sword back into the scabbard. Continuing his spin on his right foot he swept his left behind the guard's right leg and with a quickly thrust left palm put the man down on the ground, hard, as a stout dwarf can do, the man's shoulder blades striking first.

Before Brine could decide whether or not to drive down onto the guard's armored chest or pull back to watch for responders to his actions, his target sprouted a tiny woman with a not-so-tiny voice. If he had been afraid of her before, when she was simply sneaky, smart and sarcastic, Lily now officially terrified Brine. Even the three other gate guards that had been springing to help froze in place when her shouting began.

"WHAT ARE YOU DOING?! Do you not recognize Brine Drake, one of the saviors of our Keep just a year ago?! Brine Drake, the young dwarf who drove the wagon that lured in an entire column of troglodyte warriors to their ultimate defeat just outside this very gate?! Whose father fell to his death just outside that wall rescuing the Arch Mage himself the very same day?! He who is now the protégé of Pill Von Ferret, the Arch Mage's own nephew, and an honored guest of US?! Did you not see him walk OUT of this very gate just one quarter of an hour ago?! Don't you EVER let

173

something like this happen again, do you understand?!"
She paused, and Brine noticed that the guard was
grimacing and had his eyes closed, his face turned to
one side.

The silence around them was complete, not
even any of the pack animals nearby were making a
sound. One of the fallen guard's eyes opened. Though
he spoke quietly everyone in a hundred paces heard his
words, "I am SO sorry."

The tiny wingless fairy turned around, still
standing on the guard's breastplate, and asked, "Brine,
do you accept his apology?"

The young dwarf took a deep breath, then said,
"Of course I do." He reached and offered his arm to the
fallen guard and said, "Here, let me help you up."

The guard made eye contact with the fairy,
who, looking at him over her shoulder, nodded. He
grasped Brine's forearm and pulled himself upright.

As he rose Lily leapt to Brine's shoulder and
whispered, "Spend a few minutes and get to know this
young man, he just helped us both quite a bit. Your
quarry is in the corner of the wall behind him, invisible
to you, but not me... come find me in the main hall in a
few minutes." And then she was gone.

Brine spent some time meeting all four of the

guards, finding out where they were from, their family names, some of their training specialties, and parted with four new friends.

As he entered Fallon's great hall, Brine saw Lily right away, pacing between two goblets that sat in front of Fallon and Pill. She waited impatiently until Brine sat down opposite them then said abruptly, "Here he comes," and she vanished.

"I'm already here..." began the dwarf.
"I think she meant me..." said a voice over his shoulder. Only the blue steel gauntlet pressing down on his shoulder kept the young thief from jumping up.

The smallish elf that sat down next to him said, "I apologize for any distress I caused. Let's start over. My name is Sugarplum and I have some special talents that the Arch Mage has need of to further his quest for the one called Baru Dall. I just hope that I can help."

Pill said, "Until my uncle gets back, there is someone else I think you should meet."

***

Chapter 26

Hunter Has a Rough Patch

He had wandered through the winter. From the reddening of the leaves that reminded him of the blood in his hospital tent falling like drops from tables to the bluish white ice of the frozen creek tops reminiscent of the faces he had found in the morning that had been pink with life and warmth the night before, his escape was an utter failure. Then he found the valley.

Now, a season later, Hunter was gaunt, pale, his eyes slightly sunken into hollows of haunted solitude. His hair was to his shoulders, shaggy and dark auburn from not having seen much sun. His beard, the same color, hid his neck under disordered curls like waves at a gradually sloped shoreline. His diet of snared rabbits and wild onions and potatoes had let him live in the cold and snow, but the rabbits weren't breeding fast enough, and the vegetables were gone. He had to leave.

Not knowing what lay ahead, he simply kept heading generally southward, and generally downward. Eventually the creek he followed became too wide, fast and deep to keep crossing and he stayed on the eastern edge. Occasionally cliffs forced him to travel quite a long way around, but he stuck with it until he left the snow and ice behind. When the river flattened out there were enormous trees spread out before him for so far that he could not see their end. That was where he found the first trail not made by wild game that he had seen in half a year. The only identifiable tracks on it looked like those of barefoot children. He decided that at least it had to mean there were food sources nearby; he followed the path.

***

When he awoke he was puzzled by his view. These were not children staring down at him, but they were the right size. Make that toddlers. They were studying him rather critically it seemed. The moment of self-consciousness made him want to smooth his beard, but instead forced his discovery of being restrained. Looking toward his feet he could see he was lying next to a downed tree and his arms were bound at his sides, tied to his own belt, and indeed his whole body was lashed to the log.

The voice that invaded his consciousness was not too high-pitched, but definitely female and definitely in charge. "Oh, for goodness' sake, cut him loose! He needs to eat, not miss even more meals because we chose to treat him poorly!"

Even as he took in his surroundings he began to salivate at the mention of food. It got worse as he began to smell fresh bread, crisped meat, and a bit of cheese. He drooled a little, and, unable to wipe it away due to his bonds, was slightly embarrassed.

The sounds of a hundred crab pincers clicking at once made him sit bolt upright in fear of being eaten…until he realized that he <u>had</u> sat up, his bonds were cut, and the sound was dozens of little sets of shears cutting the dozens of strings that had been holding him down. "There now. Isn't that better?" said the voice. Only this time it arrived in concert with a small female face's mouth moving in time with the words. At first it was just a disembodied head peering at him from between his feet, which was far more disturbing than just the disembodied voice.

As a dozen thoughts and questions swirled in his head, he shook his hand loose and rubbed (gently) a sizable knot on the back of his head.

"You fell," said the voice/head/thing.

"Into one of our traps…" said another, lower-pitched and as yet unattached voice off to his left.

"<u>After</u> being hit in the back of the head by a deer snare! He's too tall!" This was from his right, and, by the sound, an even younger female.

At a mere barrel and a half high, Hunter had never, that he could remember, been called "too tall" for anything in his life.

Hunter closed his eyes and shook his head like a dog trying to get water out of its ears. When he re-opened them the head was smaller, and it had a body. In truth it had simply jumped backward and into view, and likely would have only reached his knees had they stood side-by-side.

The diminutive female was studying him critically and made him self-conscious again. He swiped unconsciously at the strings draped loosely over his shoulders. Rolling his eyes at the futility, he said to her, softly, "Hello. My name is Hunter, what's yours?" in an upbeat, optimistic tone.

Her little brown face lit up when she smiled, her sparkly white tiny teeth were like jewels in the sun. And then she jumped. Easily a full two of his paces away, with no tensing, flexing or warning whatsoever, she jumped right onto his lap, one little foot on each thigh, and he barely noticed the impact. She still had to look up at him, and when she seemed about to fall, didn't flinch when his arms shot up to steady her. She just smiled bigger.

"I'm Chestnut! We didn't mean to hurt you –

sorry about that!" Her brown eyes twinkled with just enough mischief for him to be uncertain of the truth of that last part...

"We don't see very many big people around here..." she said leadingly, looking for him to supply some more information about himself. He could not oblige.

"Well," he said, "I don't even know where 'here' is, so to orient me, perhaps you could tell me what is nearby?"

By way of answer she pointed toward an odd-looking tree.

At least three barrels high and two wide at the base, it looked like a dead fir tree at first glance, but as Hunter's eyes focused he saw that the ends of many of the thick boughs had been shaved flat leaving vertical surfaces that had been written on. The inscriptions revealed the tree to be a navigational device. The listings showed a name and a sigil – Hunter guessed it was a number, as they were all similar, but what it was or what it represented he had no idea.

Looking closer, he saw 'Elves', 'Dwarves', 'Witches' and 'Goblins'. Based on the relative directions, he thought he knew where he had traveled to – or at least how to get back if chose to. As hungry as he was, with the food smells making him continue to salivate, he decided to just get his question answered. "What are the symbols? Are they distances?"

Chestnut giggled. The sound was like the childish joy of a naïve toddler. "No! Silly. It is how many nights of flying by owl."

"Just nights?" he asked.

"The owls do better at night, plus we can sleep if we want to!" Said brightly and most enthusiastically, it exceeded Hunter's patience for further interrogation. "So, is any of the food I smell available...?"

Over food so much better than he'd had in months it almost made him cry, Hunter learned all about his new friends, the little people of the high forests. Well, all that they would tell him, and the few pieces of that information that made sense...

First Chestnut quizzed him about his own background and upbringing while he ate. The meat was juicy and tender and hot, the bread was fresh and buttered, the drink was warm milk. He had not seen any cows nor could he imagine his new friends slaughtering or milking one if there had been any to be seen. Then he heard a goat in the distance, and it became clear that smaller herd animals were present, and likely adequate to the task of supporting the local miniature population.

He was about to ask a politely inane question about the goats when one approached with a tiny figure on its back, like a horse…

Hunter smiled in spite of himself.

The tiny male sat astride the smallish billy goat with the practiced ease and relaxed demeanor of an experienced equestrian. The goat was equipped with a bridle that connected from a bar in its mouth to leather straps around its head and under its horns. The reins attached to the bar and horns on each side. The rider pulled on them both equally at the moment, and the goat stood quietly.

A heavily nasal voice, deep, defeated and yet defiant spoke from behind him, saying, "Get that smelly thing out of here before it steps on somebody! Especially me…"

Hunter was now hard pressed not to laugh.

The goat rider's clothing was fur – likely from a relative of the creature he rode as the black and white splotches of color were extremely similar. The speaker that walked out from behind him wore tanned leather of almost every shade of brown imaginable, with many obvious patches where repairs had been made. His expression was simultaneously sullen and resigned, accepting of his fate yet certain that it would be bad...

Chestnut piped up, "Regor, what's wrong with you <u>now</u>?! No one is stepping on anyone. You always think everything will go wrong, but it always works out. So, stop it already! You're such a Patchy..."

"Yeah, Regor," said the rider, "Relax, will ya?!" and pulled high on his goat's reins, making it rear up, turn toward the taciturn 'Patchy' and slam its front hooves down so close to the pessimist's feet that he felt the earth shake under his toes. Regor flailed his arms and fell over backward. Hunter caught him with one hand behind his shoulders, set him upright, then turned his head away and forced a yawn to keep from laughing out loud.

The miniature male, having regained his footing with the slight forward and upward push of Hunter's hand, a fairly easy accomplishment as that hand was more than half of little Regor's size, turned, not in thanks, but to Hunter's surprise, in anger. "Hey! Watch where you're grabbin'! You could crush something you big oaf!" and then to the goat rider, "You Splotchies have no sense of danger, no sense of caution!" and finally, "Aw, Chestnut, c'mon, <u>someone</u> has to do the worrying around here..."

The little lady's laughter made all of the males

relax. "Oh, how my worrier and my protector are so alike and yet so different...and you, Master Hunter? Which are you?"

The human's eyes narrowed a bit and one measured breath expired before he spoke, "Neither, I suppose. I don't worry much, largely because I plan out most of my life and actions. And of late my charges did not really have to live to fight another day, so my protector skills were superfluous."

His response seemed to catch both Patchies and Splotchies off guard, uncertain how to interpret his meaning. Their concern registered with the young healer, so he elaborated. "Don't worry, I won't harm you. In fact, I generally do the opposite when I can..." As he spoke, he reached back to the knot on his head with one hand while briefly touching a pendant he pulled from inside his shirt. The pendant, his hands and the bump glowed like they were lit by torches for a few seconds. Unseen by his audience, the bump was gone.

None of his new little friends shied away at the sight, but Chestnut raised her eyebrows in understanding. "Come with me," she said, and she turned away sharply without waiting for a response. Her pace left no doubt that she was not waiting. He followed.

Chapter 27

Off to See the Witches

King Jankin rode loosely gripping his heavy warhorse's saddle with his knees, reins looped in front of him over its neck, using both hands to light his pipe – one to hold it, the tip of the index finger of that same hand ablaze, the other hand stuffing dried leaves into it.

Fallon, riding on his left, laughed and said, "What is that, lilac?"

Icelle, on his right, asked, "How much magic can you do, Warlock King?"

"Oh!" said Jankin, "No, no, no! 'King who is a warlock, fine, but not that! Hazelmoon would turn me into something unpleasant, like a shopkeeper, if she heard that! I can do a little, basic household practical magic – light fires, move things, see who is at the door, nothing too grand. Besides, I'm a horrible King…"

They rode in silence; the sounds and sights and smells were comforting to the old campaigners. Horse sweat, hot leather, flies buzzing, hooves clopping and the occasional waft of human or equine flatulence were all familiar.

"I did not choose this," he continued. "I was

happy. Going on quests, killing monsters and rescuing people, especially the daughters of wealthy old men... Now, I'm married to one of them and I send people like me on quests...!"

This time both of his companions laughed.

Fallon said, "Welcome to the last decade of my life... Responsibility, leadership, finance, logistics and every possible sob story along with it. Bad weather, bad choices and bad people – all worse to have to plan for than just bad enemies. And the worst can be the best and vice-versa! My longest known and most competent associate betrayed me, my worst was the most loyal and honest. Ability is only a portion of quality in a man..."

Icelle asked, "Do you think it makes you choose your allies and supporters faster and with greater accuracy in your assessments as to who will remain true? Or are you just less surprised when they fail you..."

King Jankin thought for a moment, puffed on his pipe, and said, "Yes."

***

That evening they camped at the base of a cliff. In the middle of its expanse, a several league long front, there was a channel where a river from high above had cut its way through the rock. The original waterfall had roared over the edge and pounded the ground below with enough force to create a deep pool far out from the hundred-barrel-high face.

Eventually the top of the falls had found softer rock well back from the cliff and bored completely through. Now the water came out like a spout a quarter of the way down the cliff and shot off to the left. It had made a newer, smaller, shallower pool, and a narrow stretch that joined the original pool. A bridge, made of stone fitted carefully with no mortar evident and said to be older than Metaerie itself rose gradually toward this narrow stretch, wide enough for two wagons to pass, smooth enough that their loads would not jostle. So smooth that there were posts and columns along the sides to anchor heavy loads to as needed to ensure that their teams would not slip and be dragged backward, and also so they could be used to keep the load slow going down and not let it roll onto the team in front.

Pill had described to Plumley (and Brine) how he had seen an occasion where a load was so heavy that the teamsters had wound lines around several columns, attaching the ends to the wagon and team harnesses making the bridge support the bulk of the weight and the team walked downward and pulled it right up. Then they'd tied it off like anchoring a ship, rewound the lines on the other side, hitched up again and let the team walk upward behind the wagon, letting the load down slowly.

The traders had been some of Fallon's father's sailors, and they'd told Pill it was no different than the pulley systems they used to manipulate cargo and sails and steering on a ship.

At dusk, cooking fires were being lit even as the last of their caravan was arriving, and Plumley disappeared. Only Pill and Brine seemed to notice, both immediately searching with just their eyes, finding footprints being created. Suddenly they stopped, the last two got really deep, and then there were no more. 'Wings are definitely useful,' the two thieves thought at the same time.

Not long after full dark a set of wings landed next to Pill – but these were visible and dark brown and seemed to fold down and become a cape on the back of their owner, Pill's father, Corvin, the vampire.

The gold eyes were still unsettling, despite being a positive indicator about Corvin's behavior and motivation. His speech still was not what the elven thief remembered of his huntsman father. As an adventurer Corvin had been a decent fighter and a deadly archer.

As a known vampire, his lack of creepy behavior almost made him creepier... Everyone that met him waited for him to pounce and kill them, the trepidation of impending death (and perhaps undeath?) sat in the pit of their stomachs like they'd eaten a live eel that wouldn't die...

Plumley in elf form was no exception.

Shy to begin with, Sugarplum's appearance was not easily overlooked; he stood out like the only flowering bush in a field of dead grass. As he also had the innate ability to make himself invisible, he did so freely and frequently.

When Corvin arrived and sat next to his son, he turned and stared directly into Plumley's invisible eyes. The little dragon was unnerved. Pill, easily deducing from his father-vampire's posture what he was doing, turned to stare at the same spot. Sugarplum appeared, shaking his scarlet hair violently, saying, "You two disturb me."

Father and son smiled together, quite alike except for one set of fangs...

"So, young dragon, why is it you are able to track the magical transit of an otherworldly being?" asked Corvin with no preamble.

"I'm not sure, but the story that suggests it is

probably only familiar in magical flying reptile circles..." replied the purply elf. "Some things we just don't talk about outside the dragon community."

Corvin just stared. Pill thought a moment, then told Brine to fetch Fallon.

When the young dwarven thief had scurried off, the elf turned back and said, "It is already evident by your very existence that dragon interbreeding is somewhat common. If you were all purple, it would seem easy enough to figure out – red and blue – but where does the gold come from? I thought metallics and chromatics were incapable of mixing bloodlines - ?"

"Well!" said Plumley, surprised, "You even know what we call ourselves – that's rare all by itself I think."

"My uncle has had dragon friends for a long time. What has only fairly recently become clear to me is that you can take other forms naturally – I thought dragons were just, well, dragons!" Pill sounded exasperated.

"My 'bloodline' is, as you may imagine, unusual. While it is not without precedent, as far as any of us knows, no 'tribrid' has ever repeated, though we cannot rule it out in the future. What I can say is that we have all been accidental...the mating of two dragons that did not know the other was a dragon, while in elf form. So, 'incapable' is incorrect. 'Largely undesirable' is probably more accurate." Plumley's response left them all quiet, considering.

Brine returned with Fallon in time to see Pill staring at Plumley-the-elf intently, then saying, "Can 'tribrids' reproduce?"

Just for a moment the four non-dragons – man, elf, dwarf and vampire – saw a pair of eyes flicker between humanoid and reptilian pupils. Unsettled would be an understatement it seemed.

"No," said Plumley glumly.

"Ah!" said Corvin. "No future bloodline, so you can project yourself. That's how you can track our target, the psychotic mage."

Plumley disappeared. Again.

Corvin did not notice. Neither did Pill. Brine and Fallon shared matching shrugs.

The vampire said, "You know, if that is instinctive, you should learn to control it better. It will help more when you actually need it if fewer of those you intend to elude know you can do it…"

The elf's clothing as Plumley reappeared was now a deep violet, and the hand holding his shaking head had blue-like-overheated-steel fingernails clenched in his scarlet shock of hair.

"At least try to do it out of view," suggested Pill, "behind an object, or inside, like in a room or cave or wagon... Oh, and to be clear, some of us can still see you, others can track you, and <u>no one</u> is threatening you... You need to also learn to differentiate between fear and danger – right, Brine?"

Pill turned to see his dwarf apprentice nodding in both agreement and chagrin, and then...disappear.

***

'What the heck?!' Pill thought, 'Brine can't ... Oh, you have GOT to be joking ... Now?!'

'Ah," said a familiar but long unheard voice. 'I am sorry, this is my fault.' It was the sincerest it had ever sounded.

Everything he saw was familiar...and yet different than he remembered. The dead dwarf in front of him was young, laying in repose in only a white robe, eyes closed, hands clasped at his mid-section. The wrong-ness of it took a moment to become clear – he was face-to-face with Brine Drake, but the deadly pale youngster was lying flat, so Pill was... hovering over him? And then it all happened in a rush. Brine's eyes opened, but they were dark. His mouth opened,

194

showing sharp canines. His nose elongated and was also dark. Even as his entire face grew furry, the dwarf's short arms became even shorter, now ending in paws with sharp, curved claws that were reaching up to slash at Pill! Brine was a badger.

'I am SO losing my mind!' Pill thought.

The snarling Brine-badger began to curl forward to be able to reach Pill, who fought to fling himself backward to avoid contact, but found he could not, saw a bone-handled dagger appear just below the badger's ribcage, angled inward and upward, penetrating its heart. As the blade disappeared, the blood that followed it out of the newly made opening stopped flowing quickly.

'Yep. Lost it,' he thought.

***

"No," answered the long absent voice in his head. "Your mind is as keen as ever, clever thief. You are correct, you should not have seen that. I do apologize…"

'I've said Brine's name dozens, maybe hundreds of times before now! What does that mean?!'

The scene before him was a wooded glen, filled with bright green grass and pine trees whose needles were also a deeper but still vibrant green. The trees had branches widely spaced with bark that was a brightly hued brown. The trees themselves were <u>not</u> widely spread out, and while sunlight seemed to filter through, none directly struck the ground. Between two larger tree boles in front of him was a large old stump. What looked like a young tree growing out of its center moved suddenly, the bark 'fluffing', turning out to be the feathers of a great owl. As the tree knots came into focus Pill saw they were eyes – <u>her</u> eyes.

'It happened before,' he said, 'but I didn't understand it. I had called out several names and nothing happened at all, but later, I named Myeer and saw his death. But this is far worse than Myeer dying an old man, this is <u>me</u>, killing a young friend! What changed?!' he cried desperately.

"Everything, I'm afraid," the owl-goddess replied, spinning her owl head completely around twice, almost making Pill nauseous as a result. The owl chuckled.

"Yours was not the only fight you see. I was lost – trapped – by those who hate me, what I represent. What changed...? Who knows exactly? More than likely, without our connection, you were to be unable to perform a task that would have prevented the eventuality of him dying before you, regardless of how...

196

but once that changed, the ancient bond with my medallion freed me. So, while I mourn with you at the loss of your friend that is to come, I remain pleased by its side effect."

'You – you are death – aren't you?' asked Pill with a bit of trepidation.

"No," she answered, "I am the idea that all creatures can die, that we each fill up the world for a time, each serve a purpose, both in life and in death. It is the how and when that matter. Some of our cultures accept the deaths of the aged as inevitable and are incensed by the deaths of the young as having left life unlived or incomplete. Others embrace all death fatalistically as the meal that they have been served. In other worlds and times there are elves like you that revere all life; they will not kill any living thing if they can avoid it and will only fight in self-defense or the defense of others."

Pill chewed on that thought for a few moments. Thieves in general, at least in this world, at this time, were largely unconcerned with the fate of most fellow creatures. This one had no problem killing from ambush if it meant that he got to accomplish his task and survive.

He had never felt the need to answer to some

'higher power' or, until recently, worry about any 'greater good' beyond his immediate circle of friends or battle mates, and few and far between were those that he committed to aiding outside of or beyond a single venture. Only family held that kind of tie for Pill Von Ferret. Even that was somewhat muddy water; a vampire for a father was inherently confusing... and his friends all fell into high risk mortality categories. After all, large-scale combat events usually guarantee casualties on all sides, and can the dead really be victorious?

Returning his focus to the being in front of him, Pill thought, 'And how do I know to believe you?'

The owl turned from a profile posture to facing the young elven thief. In the process it grew and changed and came closer. In a blink she was a shimmering, silvery, naked girl, with long, twinkling waves of curly hair to her waist. Her hands rested on his shoulders, cold as ice, with an iron grip. From out of her back, under the flowing argent tresses, wings spread and wrapped around him. As he stared into her violet eyes, the end of one wing terminated in the scaly head of a dragon, and it whispered into his ear, "I have no need or desire to deceive you. I will never lie to you. It would not be fair, as you cannot lie to me – not that you would."

She paused while he spun to face the dragon head speaking to him into his ear, gasping for breath that did not exist here. He turned back, seeing Sylvia's face and features saying to him, "I see your thoughts, smell your emotions, taste your words – our link is beyond magical, it's personal, chemical, biological, yet also metaphysical and logical – until now." At this she drew him closer and kissed him. It felt like the icy burn of leaving your feet in cold water too long and then letting the feeling come back slowly, painfully.

"Be careful," said the dragon head while the girl's mouth still occupied his, "the game of life is a deadly sport, and no one plays fair…"

***

They were all staring, fear on every face, even his undead father's.

"You saw her?" asked Corvin.

"Yes," was all Pill could muster in response.

Brine interrupted, "But, that's good! Right…?"

Corvin studied his son's almost-as-pale-as-his face and asked, "Well? Is it?"

Pill gulped and swallowed once, blinked twice, then said, "Partly. She's back anyway. And I'm confused…"

Chapter 28

Sibling String Pulling

The crowd was rowdy and raucous. The siblings had met each other over the past few days, never more than two together at a time. It took several meetings to work out their plan.

Getting the guard force of their target location to be enamored with Mynorca took no effort at all. She exuded both 'nice girl' and 'seductive woman' non-stop. When she sang, no one was immune, and she had been singing every night for several days.

The first day she had told the tavern owner that she would sing for free for one night, and if he did not want her to continue she would move on... but if he <u>did</u> want her to stay she would take a free room, free meals, and an accumulating ten percent of the bar profits every night until she left. The naïve man agreed. Each night she sang, and each following day word spread about her performance. The next night the crowd grew, but so did her cut of the profits. Tonight, it was up to fifty percent. The owner didn't care; he wanted her for himself. He should have cared – what he didn't know was that her half-orc half-brother had been watching him follow her when she went back to her room each night. He was waiting for anything inappropriate to happen, anything at all.

***

All Mynorca had done was tell the guards who came to watch her sing to come see her after the tavern closed in the common room of the inn. With a, "Let me change and be right down," to the innkeeper, she disappeared with a simultaneous (and effortless) hair flip and hip flounce, turning to head into the upstairs hallway to her room.

She opened and closed her door as she passed by it enroute to the back stairs where Yelsa waited with the door ajar. Normally very quiet when she wanted to be, Mynorca's movements made absolutely no sound at all. She made eye contact with Yelsa when they were outside. The latter smiled and deliberately slammed the inn door. As Mynorca scrunched her shoulders in a cringing grimace, Yelsa just grinned, waiting for her sister to recover as there was still no sound at all.

The half-gnome girl made a 'come-hither' gesture and walked toward the trees behind the inn. As they reached the well-worn path that in daylight was a pleasant riverside stroll the beautiful bard began to hear her own breathing again. They walked together for a few hundred paces in the dark before Yelsa finally said, "It affects an area. Pretty great, huh?"

In a ten percent stage whisper (something as a singer and performer Mynorca was quite adept at regulating) the taller sister said, "That was amazing! When did you learn that?!"

Sisterly praise always being welcome, Yelsa whispered back, "This last visit to the temple! The priest trainer did it to some obnoxious acolytes, but I was the only one who noticed… So, he taught it to me, as well as the way to pray for the extra power to make it work. Sometimes I feel like my mistress is communicating with me directly!" The little half gnome girl was almost glowing. The psychosis in her eyes was readily visible, but knowing it would never be directed at her, Mynorca was okay with it. One quick hug and they sped up to meet their brothers.

***

Chapter 29

Rrahmus and the King

King Kedrick studied his grandson as he entered the unfamiliar chamber. With just one glance at the King and the austere setting, he refocused on the door before letting it close. Turning, he said, "I would never have found that without detecting magic as you instructed! The crafting of it is amazing, the material is native, and the magic is beyond even me!"

"Astutely observed and concisely reported, as always..." said Kedrick. "Rrahmus, I also sense your surprise at never having been here before. You boys did have the run of this place, just not the parts you didn't know existed."

"Wait, there are <u>more</u> 'parts' I don't know about?!" blurted the Arch Mage rather like a flabbergasted grandchild.

"Let's focus on this one for now..." answered the King, sounding quite grandfatherly. He moved to the front of the central feature of the chamber, a large wooden altar. Low benches lined the walls, but Rrahmus raised a hand. "Wait Grandfather..."

The elder paused, watching his famous

descendant circumnambulate the room slowly, dragging the fingertips of this left hand along the walls. He paused at every gap in the benches but kept moving until he returned to the entrance. Facing the King, he said, "I know what this is. I had no idea there was one here. Why show me now?"

"Because we think we have an explanation for your 'Dark One's appearance." King Kedrick produced a large iron key that Rrahmus was sure was the second oldest thing he'd ever seen. It fit into, clicked solidly and turned a lock equally old, and the wooden platform sprung open, the back corners rolling toward each other, the whole thing hinging in the middle of the back wall. The stairs that had been on the left and right-side jutting forward from the front wall ended up sticking out to the sides at the back of both side walls. The relocation of the platform exposed a well just like the one in the dungeon at Fallon's.

Rrahmus asked, "Do you know where it goes?"

"So, you have used one before?" asked the King.

"There is an exact match in Rose Castle. It was matched to a spot in a wintry fjord far to the south. But I discovered that it was able to do more, and that it could be changed intentionally, like setting messenger routes. I know of at least one more, in a desert, far to the north I think."

"Yes," said Kedrick, "there <u>are</u> more. And they are very old – older than Metaerie – and, we believe, still magically linked to the old world. The possible explanation I spoke of is someone going there, then not being able to get back. Finding some version of the original separation spell, projecting here perhaps…"

"How long do you think?" asked Rrahmus. "How long for this person to go, be trapped, then find a way, or recruit help, to get back?"

"Well, it depends on who, and <u>what</u>, they were…" said the King, the implications creating more questions.

"Ah, longevity…" pondered Rrahmus. "I would have sworn that he was human, and therefore short-lived, but a First Man? Or an Original? Even a long-ago descendant of an Original could have lived much longer – potentially hundreds of years longer. That makes it even more plausible…"

"Well," said Kedrick, "you need to start at Icelle's anyway, and I'm sure more of your human friends will be there to start asking…"

"And I will. Grandfather, how many of these wells do <u>you</u> know of? And do you know how to alter their destinations? I've succeeded once, but now I don't want it to be able to reverse or revert…"

The King pondered for a moment, then after clearing his throat, said, "Our beginning here was a response to an anticipation of crisis. Not all men feared dragons, and not all men hunted pixies for sport, but in the old world it was the ones who defended themselves who were hunted down and exterminated. Those who fled, hid, and just disappeared were soon forgotten, left alone. Metaerie in the old world was mostly uninhabited – thought to be completely so, but that was incorrect. It is <u>our</u> history that ties it all together. Dragons could never fully blend into the human population without extra magic. Their innate shapeshifting to humanoid form could not remove their horns – the reason they always retained pointed ears. They could, of course, fix that, with the addition of a spell or potion, but most were not very adept at either practical or arcane magic. Understandably so, as their innate abilities, and of course just being a dragon, were formidable enough." He paused, remembering.

"My grandfather's grandfather said we were 'inevitable'. As promiscuous as both dragons and pixies are, and their only other options besides their own species and the wild animals were each other, it was bound to happen. A dragon in elf form and a pixie mimicking that form engaging in their favorite pastime, what could go wrong? Except that while dragons make eggs, pixies have babies. No one wrote it all down, but common belief among the historians is that it was during a celebration. A century after the separation from the old world the two races held their gatherings together to mark the first one hundred years of not being hunted. By the next year hundreds of huge babies were born to pixie mothers that could not fly, turn invisible, or shape-change. They all had pointy ears and looked like dragons in their bipedal form."

Another, longer, pause.

"Can you imagine it? The pixies thought there was something wrong with their whole race. An illness or a mutation. They were half right. Those hundreds of babies were our ancestors, and they only had eyes for each other; that was new in Metaerie! Much longer lived than humans, but not as long as dragons. Vision, agility, ability to hide quickly and well in any environment – very pixie-like traits. The extremely devoted family circles of pixies were devastated. A large portion of an entire generation of their all-too-few children turned out to be something 'new'. Fortunately, they did not abandon us." This time he paused so long

Rrahmus grew impatient and spoke uncharacteristically out of turn.

"Uh, sire?" Nothing. "Grandfather…"

"Hm? What? Oh! Sorry. Reminiscing a bit, I guess," said the King. "These lands had the ability to sustain us and were completely vacant of any Originals. The pixies and dragons had many meetings that next year. After much consternation, not a little recrimination, and just a smidgeon of admiration, a new land, fully inhabited with generations of both races, male and female, all colors, abilities and dispositions, was defined for our use. They raised our first, second and third generations. They made sure we could actually breed and reproduce successfully – that took half a century alone. As adults we had to learn how to create, maintain and optimally use our natural resources. It was the non-magical tasks that eventually proved to be the most difficult because our teachers were all magical creatures. We had some of their natural traits; the pointy ears of course, seeing in the dark, even an odd immunity to the charms and wiles of both of our forebears. But no innate magic and no practical skills. Neither farmer nor carpenter among them…"

"Nor practical magic users?" asked Rrahmus.

"Especially not that. There is one you've met who can fill that blank in for you some other time. Needless to say, accidental though it may have been, the addition of humans and witches to our population was of great benefit in the long run. Some are perhaps short-lived, but their industriousness knows few bounds and they can accomplish quite a lot in short time frames if they wish!"

The pair stood silent for a moment, each knowing the other was recalling momentous past events involving industrious human friends.

"I believe the symbols on the outside of the well are the links to other wells. Knowing as I do where a few others are, based on direction and distance, the number of symbols, and how many would have been necessary to link all of the old world, I think each well can only link to the wells around it, literally. My guess is that yours was changed accidentally in the past... Do you know for certain how you changed the destination location for the one at Fallon's?" Kedrick asked Rrahmus.

Rrahmus grimaced and said, chagrined, "Not really. Just that it definitely changed."

"So, if I'm right, and the wells further away are linked to some in the old world, perhaps our most recent unwelcome visitor is not a complete oddity, nor should it even be a surprise..." The King trailed off, considering.

Rrahmus, though centuries younger than his grandfather, was certainly far more familiar with the arcane. "If the method is truly a full-displacement transportation magick, then distance <u>might</u> be irrelevant. If the original caster tied the destination to a specific direction and distance, they could go nowhere. If it was linked to specific mechanics, objects or conditions then what you suggest is absolutely possible. I have to ask, has anything ever <u>arrived</u> here?"

"Not that I am aware of, but I believe that fear of that eventuality is why the cover was created long ago," said Kedrick.

Rrahmus continued his questioning, "Has anyone gone through it? Do you know where it went? If so, how?!"

"Yes, long ago. They arrived at a temple on an unfamiliar coastline, far to the south. We know because they found their way home. It was quite a scandal, long before your time."

Rrahmus waited for more information that was not forthcoming. "<u>They</u>?" he prompted.

"A senior royal guard was showing off for a girl. The girl worked in the kitchens. Her father and brother were grooms, the elder was a quite adept animal trainer. She would make them special luncheons or desserts, and they came to see her, but she was gone. Directed to the general area where we are now, they saw the guard holding her up over the edge of the well's side wall. They thought he was trying to drown her. They grabbed his legs and threw him up and in. With his armor on he sank quickly. The girl screamed then turned to see her family standing there. After yelling at them to tell them he was just holding her up because she wanted to look into the water and that she had asked him to, she dove in to save him. She did not come up, so they went in after her. No one knew what happened to them for over a year. They made their way home – well, most of them."

The King regarded the Arch Mage pointedly. His stare was returned. The younger spoke first.

"Royal guard? Palace cook? You're joking, right?"

"Not a bit," said the King.

"That sounds like a once-in-a-lifetime adventure, one to be shared with friends, family ... children?" Rrahmus' level of sarcasm was higher than normal.

"Not with young, curious, impetuous ones

perhaps?" countered Kedrick.

"Fair enough," Rrahmus acquiesced.

"Apparently I need to go see my parents."

The King nodded and closed the cover.

***

Chapter 30

Time for Some New Apprentices

"Tahmus," said the Elvish Arch Mage, "do you have any recommendations for new apprentices?"

"Not really... Not because they aren't likely to be quite good, but rather because I don't want to lose them from helping me...so, pretty selfish reasons!" his cousin the elven fighter laughed.

***

That was three days earlier. Since then Rrahmus had entertained a parade of variously accomplished young mages, and, not surprisingly, it was the members of his own family that, as a group, possessed the greatest magical aptitude and strength. Also not surprising was the fact that they had the least training, support and practiced application.

The last was unexpected. They had just consumed a lengthy and large supper, and most of the local crowd, including Tahmus and the rest of Rrahmus' family had departed.

The door was already ajar, but she knocked anyway. At least, those still at the table heard a knock...

Rrahmus looked up, and the usually (now)

unflappable Arch Mage raised one eyebrow. Only Graham saw it. He said to his brother, "We should see about the food – elves don't plan human-sized portions…"

Sean snorted, "No one plans Graham-sized portions! But I get your point." He elbowed Bronwyn with deliberate exaggeration as he stood up, causing the desired indignant eye contact. After seeing his wide-eyed but serious expression rather than the expected sarcastic smirk, she stood and followed the Yeomring boys out to the kitchens without a word.

After a subsequent exaggerated exhale by Rrahmus as he rested his chin on one hand and supported it by putting that elbow on the table in front of him, his two apprentices also rose to leave. The Arch Mage's eyes darted quickly right and left to meet theirs and he gave a slight nod. They left without any commentary either.

She entered slowly, hooded in a plain grey robe. Her shoes gave her away, though she knew it not. The soles were thick but made no sound, so double-layered for durability, but made of well-tanned soft leather. The uppers were dark brown, imbued with heavy oils to weather and waterproof them, and they had no buckles or laces. As they did not 'clunk' loosely or appear to make her walk oddly as those whose footwear pinch or squeeze do, they were custom fitted to her feet.

Wealth in general in the elven communities was largely irrelevant. Their social structure was oriented toward communal support and industrious labor using one's talents to help the collective in the best way possible. In times of peace and plenty it was wonderful. The elves well knew that it never lasted though. As Rrahmus pondered this, his visitor deftly flung her hood back, revealing a face well-known to him.

"Obviously your father knows nothing of this visit, as I am certain he would have mentioned it…" began the Arch Mage.

The responding grimace spoke volumes. The subsequent furtive look over her shoulder said even more.

Though her features were unlikely to inspire an epic poem, Rrahmus was relieved that neither his nephew nor his vampire brother-in-law were present. His youngest cousin looked so much like his dead sister it hurt. She was slim compared to the buxom human women he had been around for the last decade, nothing protruded from or distended her robe like the one worn by the recently departed Bronwyn. She had a small button of a nose, narrow but shapely lips, high cheekbones and forehead, which, along with somewhat tousled darkish blonde wavy hair all framed her piercing amber eyes.

At the moment those eyes were hungry, even desperate.

What she said was, "Take me with you!"

***

"Well?" Rrahmus verbally nudged his current apprentices. The question had been, "What do you think of our candidates?" The response had been some determined staring at furniture and architecture.

"Look," said Angus, "this is hard! They're not like us!" He wasn't whining so much as expressing frustration at his inability to judge those he did not know or understand. "Most of these kids are nobility! They are the next generation of elvish lords and ladies, destined to lead <u>us</u>! Tell me I'm wrong."

His cohort nodded thoughtfully, then said, "Yet, perhaps that's the point. To <u>lead</u> us they have to <u>be</u> us first. Who better than us to show them what their people need and want? And how to motivate and lead them? We <u>are</u> the 'them'..." He turned to Rrahmus and asked, "Did you set this up on purpose? Recruiting us from the docks, the ships, the melee square and the training yard?"

Though slightly taken aback at the premise of the question, the Arch Mage was also proud of its directness.

"Everything I do has at least two purposes, but many never come to fruition. Yes, I plan long term, but many positive outcomes are nothing more than happy accidents. What I <u>really</u> do is plan for most of the possible outcomes and then wargame in advance how to incorporate those eventualities into the winding of the path that I want. The ending is achievable via many different routes. Knowing them all and influencing them appropriately – there is the real work."

Fergus just sighed and said, "You still didn't answer the question. As usual."

"Because you knew the answer before you asked," retorted Rrahmus.

Angus laughed abruptly, saying, "Ha! 'Truth is always just on the other side of the mirror…' If I had a gold piece for every time I've heard you say…"

He was interrupted by having to catch the gold coin flicked unerringly at his head. It was followed by, "Do shut up. Now, apprentices, let me provide some screening criteria: you have to get along with them, they must possess the potential to be better than you, they must respect <u>us</u>, and, if I die tomorrow, you must

219

be confident that <u>you</u> can train them."

Fergus' eyes roamed from chair to chair around the room. He had deliberately had his interviews with each prospective new colleague seated in a different chair. One of his gifts was to see the past, or many pasts at once, and he did so now. After a few moments, he spoke.

"I'd say ten or twelve meet that minimum standard. The two mountain boys have the whole package for certain, the three fisherman's kids are quite social, skilled and teachable, I just don't know how to assess the rest."

"Right?!" said Angus. "Boss, your cousins are all scary good, but emphasis on *scary*... I don't know if I should slap them or bow to them..."

"To be fair, though, they are already trained in so many other useful and important things..." started Fergus.

"Okay, hold up," said Rrahmus. "Let's add some selection criteria then as well ... other abilities, levels of proficiency – perhaps we should include combat skills, languages, literacy, especially clear writing or even painting, previous travel, exposure to other races, climates, transportation methods..." he trailed off.

"Fine," said Angus, "but also age, or lack of it,

social status, or too <u>much</u> of it, public speaking, personal fears – based on recent apprentice events – and we need to know before we select people for tasks that are almost always under significant pressure that they can actually perform under pressure!"

"A public display would be best, but they may not want the world to know they are even attempting to do this, especially if they fail…" replied Fergus.

"Indeed," said Rrahmus. "You two have hit directly upon both edges of the recruiting sword. A public declaration exhibits intent and courage – except when it doesn't…" The apprentices both waited silently at this comment, each recognizing this was important. Rrahmus went on, "Those who have nothing to lose by it need no courage to try. Those who have much to lose, and perhaps the most ability, may never try, and we will never know they even had the urge. Add to that those who wrestle with doing what they are good at versus what they enjoy, or doing what is needed versus what is safe, and especially for the tween age crowd the ramifications are compounded even further. They are just coming into their adult skills, establishing their place in their social circles, and are often more concerned with approval than their next meal…" He paused again, remembering.

"In my case, Corvin was the adventurer. I learned practical magical combat spells to make myself useful to him and his friends. From the simplest flame or light source to moving objects from afar, my first spells were utilitarian, not arcane."

Angus asked, "Did you know that you were from a line of adepts?"

"No," said Rrahmus, "none of my family ever talked about it really. I found out accidentally, saving Fallon of all things. It was the emotion that set it off. He was – is – my best human friend."

Fergus asked, "Are all of your relations adepts?"

"I don't think so... the bloodlines wouldn't make sense...but who knows?"

"So," asked Angus, "What do we do? A contest? A public demonstration? A private task? A home-cooked meal...?"

They all laughed.

"Well, at least Graham would be happy..." said Fergus.

Rrahmus said, "None of the options mean the same thing to each candidate. We have to tailor the tasks to the weaknesses of the seekers. Everyone's personal quest for gainful and adequate employment of their talents starts somewhere. Perhaps facing their fears is exactly the starting point we need to see." As he said this, Rrahmus made his decision. "Solicit from each a written statement. It must include why they want to do this, why we should want them with us, and a list of their strengths, weaknesses and fears."

The other two exchanged a look, then Fergus said, "It feels nice, being included, even if we know deep down it was a charade…"

Rrahmus just smiled and left the room.

***

It was not until they had all read all of the candidates' letters that they sat down to discuss them a few days later.

"So," asked Rrahmus. "I have a few opinions, but honestly they could <u>all</u> be suitable."

Angus agreed, "Indeed they are all talented in their own way, and most would get along with us. It was enlightening to me to see how many were most afraid of failing others, whether by inadequate support or inexperienced leadership. They are all better people than I am. It really hit home to me to see how much of a self-centered troublemaker I am compared to them. A bit depressing really…"

"Well," said Rrahmus, "self-examination is healthy, but needless recrimination isn't helpful. I need ruthless more often than benevolent... we can't only have the best and brightest and nicest – to support our, or any, cause against evil, greed or corruption, the side of good must employ those who can fight the evil and win. Some will run from combat. Most won't go near enough to need to run from it. Some run toward it that probably should not, but most of those don't last too long, deadly trials are completely unforgiving when it comes to longevity. But those that are willing to fight, competent enough to plan, disciplined enough to train and practice, and with the temperament to lead charismatically, personally and from the front are invaluable. Those can accomplish any task, whether it be recruiting magical apprentices, fighting magical opponents and all types of monsters, or leading nations of magical practitioners. You two may yourselves yet be called on to do all of these." His current apprentices' mouths fell as open as their eyes widened at his words.

"Well," said Fergus after a long pause, "we can't take them all, can we?"

"No..." said Rrahmus. "But perhaps a division of labor is in order. Tasks, teaching, trials – I say we combine them, but separate us. Pick out who you think needs the most teaching, those that need technical training, and those who really just need practical experience. One group will go to Fallon's to finish preparing what we may need to find and perhaps finally eliminate Baru Dall. Another group will head to Yeomring Castle to begin the tracking. I believe my grandfather has something else he is not ready to tell me yet, so before we make our choices known I will press him as I believe he also knows more of what we need to proceed and the two may be related. I am not sure yet where I will personally end up focusing my attention, but at some point I feel I must address the lack of a Human Arch Mage. Think about it, give me your thoughts for the groups, we are wasting time."

***

Rrahmus' intuition about the King had been correct – he needed something, but it wasn't from his notorious grandson. As the Elvish Arch Mage stewed about how to tell his favorite cousin that his youngest daughter had decided to develop her magical talents while waiting to speak to the King, he paced the grand hallway outside the King's audience chamber.

***

As a youngster this hallway had only held angst and awe for the aspiring-against-his-parents-wishes mage. His natural talent found, he wanted to serve the needs of his people as to his abilities and best advantage. Unknown to any of his elders he had studied with a reclusive woodland mage who had helped him learn to track, stay hidden, fight with staff and dagger, make lights and fires and generally made himself useful to groups made up of his sister's suitors. Since she largely ignored them, they persistently went adventuring for whoever would pay them just to have tales to tell of their prowess and heroism to try to impress her. Unfortunately for most of them she only had eyes for the one that barely knew who she was.

Not yet twenty years old, Rrahmus had begged Corvin to let him go along. Young, cocky, even brash, Rrahmus had agreed to scout their route with Corvin (their actual scout), and the rest (who thought he was too eager) were more than willing to get rid of him for a while.

They were looking over a waterfall at an opposing cave in a rock face. He inhaled in preparation for asking a question, but before he could voice it, Corvin's hand sealed his mouth. The older elf whispered, "Not yet."

So, he waited. Nothing happened. For hours. And then when it did, he didn't know for a moment what it was... In his boredom he stopped looking, even took extra-long 'blinks', the last of which saw him blinking extra exaggeratedly, trying to stay awake, when he heard Corvin, off to his left, say, ""Where did they go?"

"Where did 'who' go?" asked the young mage.

"The spiders..."

Rrahmus' expression had been comical while Corvin's was serious, the latter's gaze scrutinizing the cliff wall to the front intensely.

The youngster asked, "What would they fear on a rock wall? Birds? A fire?"

"Actually," said Corvin, "a flock of birds could have that effect, but I don't see any. Fire, though it kills them and destroys their webs handily holds no natural fear for them, probably because they are quick and can get into their holes and crevices in time to avoid it, just as with birds. No, spiders fear cold..." As he trailed off, he was proven prophetic.

They could see the top of the cliff wall, a brown sheer face of fractured rock that dropped dozens of rods to a pool below. It was turning white.

Corvin continued, "The spiders can't escape cold by hiding. Birds and fires move on, but a biting cold can stay around, in some places for months. What could cause THAT?!"

***

Rrahmus had relived that day in his head many times since. The first had been in this very hallway, waiting to speak to his grandfather, just as he was doing now, and he involuntarily cried out in anguish when the door opened and Corvin's father (the King) and one guard looked out at him.

"Well," said King Kedrick, "you look like you've seen a ghost. Again."

"Grandfather," the Arch Mage began, "I think I am about to rock the family boat a bit."

"Come in boy, let's see what ails you," said the King. Alone this time, more experienced and confident, Rrahmus strode past the guard and straight to a divan where he knew the King would ask him to sit. The guard stepped outside and shut the door behind him.

"Well, grandson," began the King, "from your expression I would say your visit is tied to a fateful day in our past, but your demeanor tells me this goes beyond that."

Without preamble Rrahmus said, "Molly came to me to be trained. Tahmus doesn't know. She is by far the most accomplished of our candidates. I think he will object, strongly, to her choice and I need your advice about how to best address the situation."

The King's expression never changed. He was,

as always, direct, empathetic, and continually amused by all things social. If only Rrahmus' apprentices could see this – nothing ever seemed to surprise his grandfather. The King's smile remained unwaveringly genuine, if a bit fatalistic. "Well," he said, "we may as well get it all done at once!" Pulling a rope next to his chair rang a bell in the passageway outside. The guard there poked his head in with eyebrows raised, saying nothing.

King Kedrick simply said, "Send someone to bring Tahmus to me, now." Even as the door was closing, he addressed Rrahmus once more, "Now, while we wait, tell me just how talented my great-granddaughter really is..."

***

Chapter 31

Molly and Tahmus

King Kedrick stared at his grandsons with a fatalistic expression. "You two are killing me," he said.

"She is <u>not</u> a warrior!" Tahmus said, obviously furious.

"You are correct, cousin," Rrahmus responded calmly, "she is an adept and innate user of magic, one of the best I've ever seen..."

"That's not what I meant, and you know it!" The fear and anxiety for his offspring was readily apparent in the warrior's voice, and it almost cracked in frustration as he continued. "She is too young, too small, too inexperienced, too ..."

"Too 'daughtery'?" asked the Arch Mage slyly.

The King raised his hand and said, "Enough. We all know the fragility of life. We also know that the strongest steel has been tempered and tested, perhaps even re-forged and remade. What training has the young lady received?"

While Rrahmus studied a wall fresco, Tahmus gained an interest in the hilt of his sword. The silence was deafening.

The King sighed audibly, rolled his eyes and pinched the bridge of his nose with the thumb and middle finger of his left hand, spinning his staff with its base on the floor next to him with his right. Twiddling the man-sized length of heavy oak topped with an ornate mace made of enough steel to smash an ogre's head (and enough scuffs, dents and scratches to believe it had been used thusly in its past) made it obvious that the King was both very strong and an experienced (and impatient) warrior. He tried again.

"Explain yourselves. Now. Tahmus, you first."

"Sire… Grandfather… we thought to train her to utilize her talents for civic support, or healing, perhaps even historic record-keeping, when she was older and had found her true talents."

The King's deadpan expression made it clear that he was unmoved. Tahmus clapped his teeth shut.

"What you mean is that she is entirely untrained and almost of age, yes?" said King Kedrick.

Tahmus closed his eyes as he hung his head, mumbling, "Yes, Sire."

"That may not be entirely correct…" began Rrahmus.

"What do you mean?" asked the King.

"Yes, what <u>do</u> you mean?!" demanded Tahmus.

"Just that she is both a singularly accomplished adept <u>and</u> she has studied. Not with me, but with someone – or she could not be as accomplished as she seems to be." Rrahmus' declaration was met with confusion from his cousin and realization from his grandfather.

"That's impossible!" scoffed Tahmus.

"Perhaps not…" began the King. "You boys are well into your hundreds now, some of the most accomplished of our people, some would say at the top of your respective disciplines…"

"Grandfather," said Tahmus, "while I agree that my cousin and I are ambitious and accomplished, what does that have to do with Molly and magic use?!"

"Indeed…" murmured Rrahmus.

The two younger elves were dumbfounded by the King's expression. They had never seen him look as he did now. Over five centuries old and the undisputed leader of the most advanced humanoid race in their world, and he looked … sheepish. Almost embarrassed.

Passing his whole left hand over his face, the King said, "The reason is simple, though the explanation is complicated. Tahmus, you were raised by non-adepts, your beautiful wife is from a neighboring non-adept family, none of those expectations existed for you with

233

regard to your daughter. Our millennia old cultural oddities revolve around expectations and abilities. Part of why Rrahmus lives apart from us is our magical arrogance I'm sure. We elves are able to do things other races cannot, from seeing in darkness, viewing the hidden, and communicating with all creatures on an empathic level to enhancing our physical abilities for short periods – speed, agility, strength, stamina – to our longevity that allows us to study longer and more in depth, such as language, art, music – and magic." He paused. They waited.

"But just like the humans, some of us do not just <u>study</u> magic; some of us <u>are</u> magical. We elves are the original product of the ancestors of our world, you know this. We did not retain the inherent gift of flight, here in Metaerie our environs are under greater pressure than our old world. All new races are born with denser, solid bones. But the magic... the magic seemed to <u>pick</u>, to <u>choose</u> specific bloodlines to inhabit. No one is quite certain why.

Over time, our more mundane abilities, building, growing, leading and organizing, became more sought after for people in positions of power. Art, music, martial prowess and, yes, even magic, began to be viewed as specialties, rarities, areas of focus for free thinkers, individualistic types who might 'rock the boat' rather than maintain an 'even keel' in daily life." The sigh that followed was said, almost melancholy.

"Rrahmus," he continued, "your parents were both accomplished adepts; they still are, they were just from families who used their practical magic quietly in the course of their daily lives. My son courted your mother before either knew the other had similar abilities. When they returned from their displacement adventure, Tahmus, your father married my daughter after she helped him to deal with the loss of his mother who had died while they were missing. It was during the telling of the tales of their survival to get home that indications of natural magic became known, from both families. My family had hidden it for a long time. Their marriages, literally and figuratively, of abilities under my family name made people at the High Elven court very nervous! Worldwide, natural magic was viewed by elves as stemming from people (yes, even elves) that were unstable, of uncertain loyalties, even capricious. Their offspring, based on age, would likely be heirs to my succession. So, at the time, any oddity with regard to their children was likely to be seen as ominous. And it happened..."

"What, me?!" exclaimed Rrahmus. "I couldn't

have been seen as <u>too</u> bad, could I? Not at birth!"

"No," said the King, "but two of you could... twins are virtually unheard of in our race, but in this case it was to be as public as you could imagine. Politically our family was already viewed as potentially too volatile to be in charge – our propensity to risk life and limb to support our friends and neighbors, allies and associates, was not conservative enough. At the time we had no true existential threats. The dragons, our ancestors, largely ignored us. The pixies mostly hid amongst us. The First Men were our friends and their non-magical kin feared us, just as they do their own witches. Our central issue over the millennia was relations with the off-shoot hybrids of just dragons or just pixies – like the recent Troglodyte Troubles that you are all too well aware of now..."

Tahmus could not take his grandfather's rambling any longer. "Sire, did you say 'twins'?"

The following silence was complete. They could all hear each other breathing. The King broke it.

"Your parents were all best friends growing up. One set from a line of natural magical adepts who were accomplished artists, musicians and poets who worked as cooks and animal trainers, often sculpting meals and singing to their charges, the other set from a house of accepted non-magical but steady workers, well-off business and martial oriented civic leaders. The old King was dying, with no heirs, though even if he had, if they were unsuitable, the choices would still have been obvious... In order to keep everyone happy, he chose me. The stable, well-known, supposedly non-magical warrior who helped everyone in emergencies was to inherit the throne...and when he grew ill, I assumed the role, as far as anyone knew without either natural magic or a male heir. Then my son returned, to the amazement of all. And then both his and his sweetheart's natural magic became known in the telling of their tale.

The people gradually came to believe that they were deceived. Their choice to support my selection now somehow invalidated, despite no irregularity from me as a ruler, no negative interactions or grievances. No, despite impeccable results, somehow that early part of my reign was dogged by rumors of deception and scandal. And then it got worse."

The King seemed to collect himself with a few long, deep breaths, a little out of sorts, a condition his grandsons were not used to witnessing, and their mutual distressed expressions were noticeable enough for him to rouse himself to continue with a widening of his eyes.

"Both sets were brother and sister. Eventually they all wed, two sets of siblings, all related, all houses divided. And the weddings were held together, right here in the palace."

Now Rrahmus tried to refocus the King, "Grandfather, who are our parents?"

The King paused again, began again. "My daughter, and your other grandfather's daughter, both wedded each other's siblings, and both were from magical lines. It became known, and our councils came to terms with my heritage based on my success, finally, and were overwhelmingly in favor of not invalidating my coronation. What was NOT known was that he who had been my chief competitor was actually ambitious and vengeful, not common traits in our race, but not entirely absent either." Another pause. Tahmus rolled his eyes.

"In a few years after my coronation, the old King had died, and the voice behind my detractors was this competitor, saying that the old King's choice was that of a befuddled old man, that I had bewitched him somehow, things like that. The two couples, including my own son and daughter, had moved into this very castle with their children, your older siblings, with your grandmother and I, and I invited your other grandparents as well, your grandfather having taken another mate, but they declined in order to remain closer to her family." One more pause. Rrahmus sat down, intent only on listening now.

"The two young mothers became with child after moving into the castle, at what seemed exactly the same time just a few moon cycles after they arrived. At what was I am fairly certain exactly one year after their arrival, they were both due to give birth at any time. It was an odd night. There was no moon. It was so dark." The King met both of his grandsons' eyes. "We were attacked. It was treachery, from within, and many true loyalties were discovered that night... Magic crackled in the very air. In the midst of it all the two young mothers-to-be gave birth. That evil, arrogant betrayer found out, found them, and sent word for me to meet him there or he would kill them all." The King was crying.

"We knew for months that both girls were carrying twins. When I arrived both had given birth, but they, and their spouses, were all by their birthing beds on the floor, unconscious I know now, but then they looked dead to my eyes. Between them he stood, beside a table with four babies on it. As I moved toward him, with no preamble, he swung his sword down at the table, never taking his evil, predatory eyes off of me. Amid the screaming I only knew I could not allow him to be able to cast another blow, and with this very staff I caved in his head." The longest pause any of the three ever had to endure ensued.

"When the princesses awoke, they each held a healthy baby elfin boy, who they each raised in these very halls. You two. The truth of your lineage died with the blow of my scepter, but my instinct tells me now, as it has since that day, that you are in fact not cousins but twin brothers. Not even your mothers' have heard me say this thought aloud before. But, you see, it doesn't really matter which set of parents is or is not yours, for in truth the lineage is the same. You all come by your martial skills and courage AND your magical abilities naturally."

The former cousins stared intently at their King, waiting for him to continue. He did not.

The now brothers looked at each other. Then back at the King.

"But, Grandfather," said Tahmus, "there were four of us?"

"As far as I know this is the first time it has been spoken of since that night. I would like you two to honor that and keep it thus."

"Then why tell us <u>now</u>?!" exclaimed an even more exasperated Arch Mage.

"Right?!" echoed his brother.

"Because it is written in my royal journal, a magicked device that cannot lie. When I die it will pass on just as I do. You needed to know before that happens and be prepared for the associated next order of effects. And you should know where your blood lies in the world – for those of us with magical blood it will <u>always</u> matter! Never forget your family, you will either live or die alone if you do – and perhaps both..."

After some triple reflection, Rrahmus turned to Tahmus and said, "I will do everything I can to keep my <u>niece</u> safe. I promise."

Tahmus swallowed, cleared his throat and said, "I know. If I ever have one, so will I..." This came with a bit of a smile and twinkle in his eyes.

***

Chapter 32

Ogres at the Coast

A 'good' night's sleep, while difficult for everyone, was never a concern for most adventurers. Over time the constant vigilance, the ever-present unknown threat (all of which could kill you), and lack of regular meals or sleeping quarters almost always resulted in being disturbed by the slightest sound or movement out of place.

Pill sat leaning against a large rock, bundled under his one blanket and extra clothes, only his eyes visible. He could tell who his fellow insomniacs were around the encampment by their body positions, their tossing and turning, or the fact that a few were still up tending a few fires, talking in low tones. One such conversation was between Fallon and his father. Of course, Corvin could only be out at night anyway... 'Well,' he thought, 'I guess it can't be all bad, I got most of my rest cat-napping during the day anyway...'

They were still near the coast, with a plan to turn inland the next day, following the trade route path up the gradual inclines of the connecting valleys made by the river that came down from the Witches' Forest, a fairly direct route and hard to get lost. Not worried therefore about the route or preparing for any difficult travel, the thief was considering making a cape to fit over his cloak for eventual use in colder climates at higher altitudes. Or maybe buy one along the way; the highland peoples knew what was needed to survive their weather after all... Then he felt something wrong.

He looked, slowly, as far as he could, without moving his head, to his left and right, placing everything into a framed picture in his mind. Then he did it again and compared the two mental images. At least three boulders seemed closer in the second image. Watching closer now, he <u>saw</u> one of them move. Picking up a pebble, his hand came out from under his blanket and he flicked it unerringly at his father. The golden eyes immediately traced the path of the pebble in flight, and Corvin was already meeting his son's eyes before it struck him in the chest.

As Corvin had been talking and stopped, Fallon heard the pebble hit and drop. Before he could say anything, the vampire said, "We are about to be attacked. Raise the camp, now." He disappeared.

Fallon's voice was never hard to hear, especially when he wanted it to be heard. His first words, repeated three times, in a voice the goddess herself should be able to hear, were, "To arms!! Defend!!"

As the third exclamation died away, echoing off of the rocks, the sleepers were in various stages of awake, aware, and ... attacked.

The ambush came from two sides, south and east, or farther down the shore and directly from the water. They had set a watch, but the attackers had been quite creative. Knowing their own weaknesses, the ogres approaching had turned to their mages for an idea. While one cast a spell to create a shell of silence on a boulder, another lifted it magically and a group of them followed it, silent and unseen, with their bodies and their body heat masked behind the rocks. By the time Fallon raised the alarm, the watch was dead, and between two and three dozen ogres were running into their camp out of the dark, silently swinging their clubs, hammers, maces and flails at everyone in their path. The magical quiet made the screams of the wounded remain unheard until the attackers had moved on. They had no real beginning, just became audible suddenly, many in mid-shriek. The effect was horrible and distracting, and eerie did not begin to describe it.

Once the surprise was dealt with mentally, most of those being ambushed were no strangers to combat. Cloaks and blankets were flung aside, weapons retrieved, and with just a few coordinating shouts the night ignited in the chaos of melee.

The group that charged from the water began to meet resistance before they got to strike a blow. Pill reached for his bow only to simultaneously find it missing AND hear a bowstring twang next to him. His father was the best archer he had ever seen, and apparently his current status as a regenerated vampire (albeit a 'good' one) had not lessened his skill. Ogres began to have arrow fletchings sticking out of their eye sockets, throat hollows, exposed hands and wrists, making several drop their weapons. The first victim of such a shaft had been holding a wand and the arrowhead not only pierced the wielder's hand, it had broken the ornately carved stick in the process. The boulder being suspended by the ogre mage holding the now broken wand fell on the foot of one of the ogre warriors following immediately behind it. To those looking that could see in the blackness the effect was almost comical enough to stop fighting and have a good laugh. Almost.

Instead Pill just laughed quietly to himself while he began to dart back and forth through the ragged, undisciplined ogre raiding party slicing the heel tendons of every one of the almost giant figures, including the one whose pose was of an enormous howling child with a stubbed toe – and making absolutely no noise at all.

After disabling at least a dozen of the ambushers in such a manner the thief was finally rewarded with a crushing smash from a club that hit his skull a glancing blow on its way down and then his spine and shoulder blades at once. He fell, unconscious, his hard head saving him from a permanently paralyzing spinal injury.

Apparently one new thing about Corvin the Vampire (that even he did not know until he saw his son collapse without trying to break his fall) was his ability to produce an unholy screech that could be heard across the entire river valley, from ridgeline to ridgeline, creating several pauses in individual combat from both man and ogre. But not dwarf...

Brine had realized immediately what they faced, what his friend and mentor was doing, and that he needed to alter his situation to help. Picking those attackers that were mobility impaired and were not already vampire-archer pin cushions, the dwarf set about planting his battle axe into the base of their spines. He had dispatched half a dozen this way when he heard a massive crunching sound and looked toward it in time to see Fallon's sword exiting an ogre's rib cage. Having left his shield behind the big man's swing was from top right to low left, shoulder to hip, and Brine was certain it had penetrated deep enough to slice open the raider's heart. And then he heard the screech...

Corvin had used all of Pill's arrows. Using the bow had felt good, familiar, almost comforting. He set it down and moved to commandeer one of Fallon's short swords. He looked up in time to see his son fall, lifeless, under the blow of an enormous club, the head of the wielder sporting one eye with a feathered stick protruding out of it. His rage was immediate, and while he had to be told later about his sound effects, he flew, sword first, straight at the ogre's head. He hit the ogre's face so hard that the sword only stopped when the hilt crunched against the enormous skull, the impact so violent that it broke his own arm that held the sword. Corvin barely noticed.

Corvin fell to the ground next to Pill, scooped him up in his good arm and sprung straight upward out of the melee, circling to find the top of a rocky outcrop away from the fray. Even as he was setting his elven thief progeny down he could smell the blood flowing in Pill's body, feel the heat of life in him, saw no open wounds, and his relief sent his already focused blazing rage into an even narrower icy vengefulness. As he watched Pill's chest rise and fall with breath on his own, his son's hands reflexively went to a set of daggers on a pair of crossed leather belts around his ribs, feet moving to brace for an unseen foe, then relax.

Knowing everything was moving and functional led Corvin to believe Pill did not need a healer immediately, so he focused on his own arm. It was shattered above the wrist, and he felt the bones move, the muscles and sinew weave together like coastal seagrass finding their way around rocks. It almost felt invigorating.

Looking down at where he had come from, he spied Pill's fallen sword. One more glance back at his boy to see again that he was alive and would heal, he noticed a familiar dagger in his boot.

In a blink he was swooping down, scooping up Pill's sword and banking hard toward the rear of the ogre group, looping behind them. There were two of the mage types, covered in belts and pouches, standing together. The vampire came to a jarring halt behind them, the left-hand one getting its neck three-quarters severed by the sword in his left hand, and even as the bloody spray made his companion turn, the bone-handled dagger plunged upward under the rear-most point of its skull and well up into its brain. It froze, then when Corvin pulled the dagger out, it fell like a marionette whose operator just let go of all of the strings at once, all in a heap.

Looking ahead toward his companions, Corvin saw a flash of purple, gold, red, blue and orange swoop between him and his view of Fallon gutting an ogre warrior with an oversized spear held above its head, the spear falling from its grip as it died.

The few remaining undamaged ogres enroute to help their now audibly screaming comrades added their own cries of pain to the mix, and the night's darkness was ripped by flames lighting up nasty bits of torn bloody flesh flying everywhere, falling (in the vampire's eyes) to the ground in slow motion, blood dripping from it all. The ogres were now a handful of huge humanoid torches.

Before Corvin fully appreciated the attack for its beauty, speed and ferocity, it came back, doing the same to the rear sides of the same victims.

It was Plumley. He had not been boasting about his speed; he was twice as fast as the dragons in Corvin's experience. Corvin knew that most normal folk could not have kept up with it visually. It was truly impressive, and as suddenly as it had begun, the coastal half of the ambush was over, an utter failure.

To the south, however, the cries of pain, anguish and frustration were mostly human sounding... Fallon yelled, "We have to help Jankin!"

***

The King had been staring at his crown, holding it in his hands, flipping it like a child's toy. That's all it was, really, a toy for an over-sized child. He just wanted a wife, a house, some little 'Jankins', some horses and a dog or twelve... not a Queen, a palace, and thousands of subjects who only interacted with him when they had problems or wanted something from him.

At least when he was just 'Jankin' and people had come to him for help they had both wanted his help and paid him for it. Now it was just expected, uncompensated, and no matter what at least one of his subjects went away unhappy at the end of his arbitration of any conflict. He hated it. His cousins and advisors wanted him to raise a tax on everyone. When he asked what for they claimed it was to compensate him (and them) for their efforts; the travel and expenses involved with being the good stewards and arbitrators of the kingdom should be paid for they said.

He declined. By comparison to the average family they were all already richer than many could ever imagine. This endeared him somewhat to his people, but also made him begin to loathe his cousins. As he was descended from a second son, the deaths that had seen his coronation happen made the kin of the third son realize how close they now were to power, and they all accompanied him now, two advisors and two personal guards. He trusted the guards, brothers who had fought with him even before he became King, but the advisors, a brother and sister, twins in fact, were different; he always felt like he needed a bath after talking to them.

His mother, a rather mousy and quiet light witch, had always said that they did not share the same father as their brothers, that their mother was truly a dark witch and that the twins' father was a warlock from their same dark clan, not Jankin's uncle. Nothing was ever said publicly, and his parents (and theirs) were dead now, but he never forgot.

He regarded them now, sleeping nearby, the twins. He wondered if he was truly safe with them, then dismissed the thought. He couldn't help but think that as much as he disliked his current role it was better for the people that it was him in it and not one of those twins...

***

When Jankin heard Fallon's call to arms he was still wearing his padded armor under garment. He quickly threw his chainmail shirt over his head and grabbed his helmet, sword and shield.

Echoing Fallon's words as loud as he could, Jankin drew his sword along the inside of his shield while magically applying fire to the blade. The effect was a metal-on-metal scraping sound revealing a flaming blade. Everyone who had seen him do it in the past thought it was a magical sword and had no idea that the King was in fact a warlock himself...

Combined with his yelling, it drew the attention of the ogre raiders and his traveling companions alike. His human compatriots, including his retinue, personal guards and many of Fallon's trading crew approached as they could, in varying states of undress. One rather large former dock-worker, covered in tattoos but otherwise naked save for his boots and a large two-handed sword was accompanied by a similarly aged and tattooed woman who instead of boots wore sandals and carried an iron skillet and butcher's cleaver. In contrast, one of their traveling tailors wore an elaborately embroidered blue robe covered in gold suns and silver stars that matched his hair, but carried the largest set of iron shears that Jankin had ever seen. He could not have wished for better men (and women) at arms than Fallon's people, especially as many of his own people, armed and armored, were now cowering behind anything they could where Fallon's were running to fight.

***

In just seconds Jankin's royal intrigues and worries were made irrelevant, at least with regard to his current companions. The guard brothers were on watch and the first to die, without warning. As the ogres entered the clearing around a dry flood creek that was his campsite, the twins were smashed by clubs and maces next to the far bank as they hid under their blankets while Jankin was arming himself. He discovered that his squire was an adept with some training of his own, watching as the young man thrust his right arm forward, the fingers of his hand all straight out flat, pointing, and grabbed his right elbow with his left hand, yelling something the King didn't quite understand.

The effect was one he knew however! A bolt of raw lightning as if from a storm cloud shot toward the boulder suspended in front of them. It split into several pieces, and the lightning continued from each of them, each striking an ogre behind it, their flesh glowing

254

almost translucent enough that Jankin thought he could see their very bones. What hair they had caught fire, and Jankin chuckled in spite of himself – 'ogre candles'...

He glanced, horrified, at the bodies of his cousins, twin bloodstains running out from their blankets into the creek bed that were far too large to be survivable. Even as the two raiders struck again, Fallon's tattooed giant swung his sword like a scythe, taking two arms (complete with weapons) completely off at the elbows. As the two faced their maimer, one's eyes rolled back into its head in reaction to the clear gonging sound of an iron skillet being applied violently to the back of its head. The other dropped to his knees, his remaining arm hanging low and askew, mostly separated by a meat cleaver chop down through its shoulder and several ribs, leaving the cleaver stuck in the middle of its spine.

Their killer, the tattooed woman, ran out between them, escaping the blows of their fellows who were behind her. Armed now with only her skillet, she placed herself behind her man, poised to strike again. Ogres, being known for their aggression and fearlessness, were also apparently not stupid, Jankin noted – they clearly steered away from the naked tattooed pair...

As his squire mimicked the skillet and cleaver killer and moved behind his master, Jankin squared up and set his feet in time for a rush of three spear-wielding ogre warriors. The one on the left kept jerking toward his fellows, iron crossbow bolts emerging from his entire right side. The ogre to his right fared worse – apparently the tailor's partner had arrived and was handing him smaller pairs of scissors which he began throwing like hand axes, except flatly, like chopping a tree, to devastating effect at the ogre's legs, and one stumbled into the others and all three fell in a heap at Jankin's feet. The right hand one received a huge set of shears to the back of its exposed neck, the gnarled hands pressing down squeezed and clipped the spine with an audible snap, completing the surprisingly clean decapitation. The left hand stumbler received a narrow, curved blade in the hand of one of Jankin's northern climate sailors. Those hands, as dark as a mix of walnut and ebony, were weathered and scarred from years at sea. The face that accompanied the hands was hardly visible in the darkness, barely lit by Jankin's flaming sword blade, but as the scimitar plunged into the prone ogre's ear and poked partway out of the other, the bright white smiling teeth were easily seen. And then the scene dimmed briefly as the King plunged his sword into the back of the neck of the center of the now bloody and smelly trio... ogre bowels releasing was almost as offensive as their physical ambush.

And then the previously silenced cries of Jankin's watch and men-at-arms that had received the brunt of the attack could finally be heard.

After confirming with the handful of northern sailors to his left that they had more iron bolts, he shouted, "Cover me!" and charged.

His naked neighbors followed, slightly slower, while the tailors retrieved their scissors for repeat use.

Just then he reached the first ogre of the second rank, holding a severed arm and tearing off a bite of the forearm. The beastie saw him and hurled its snack at him. Though this was not the first time in Jankin's experience that this tactic had been used against him, it was the first time since he had become King.

He recognized the sleeve insignia on the disembodied shoulder as it hit his shield, the blood spattering on his face. He would have to tell that young man's family – parents, wife and children – that he had died defending their King, and that it was <u>his</u>, <u>King Jankin's</u>, fault and responsibility that he had died here.

His face in a snarl that made him almost

completely unrecognizable, he thrust his sword up. The ogre might have easily blocked the overly emotional attack, but at that moment a tremendous screech of anger and anguish split the night. The ogre lost focus. King Jankin did not. The sword point found the top of the ogre's skull from the inside.

And then the King's eyes went black. He heard a shout, a scream, and, "To the King!" and "King Jankin!"

By the time he could open his eyes he found himself lying prone on his left side, a naked tattooed screaming woman standing over him holding his shield and a familiar iron skillet. He did not get a response from his limbs right away, and there was a whitish ring around his vision. His defender seemed to glow in it, a berserk angel protecting him. She was quite the opposite of his gentle quiet mother. The words that assailed his ears were mostly a language other than his, but the few that were not would have made his mother blush even in the grandstand at a melee competition.

The shrieking harridan was amazingly fit, her calves and thighs solid, bulging muscle. He could have cracked walnuts against her posterior, clenched as it was to hold her position defending him. One breast had been sliced off in some previous battle, the scars used as central features of a tattoo of a shield with a family sigil he didn't recognize. On the arm under his shield (that only he could see at the moment) there were dozens of thin straight scars, markers or a count of something he was sure. The arm muscles were well-developed as well as she held his shield as easily as he did.

On her back were two scars the length of her shoulder blades, and as wide as an axe head at their centers. He saw her block a blow from a club fully one-third her size with his shield, saw her counter-strike with the skillet, heard an odd 'ting' and while wondering what had made it saw a giant tooth fall to the ground in the rocks in front of his face...

Apparently her mate was still fighting too as the severed ogre head that now landed and rolled to a stop facing him (recently losing a canine, the gap still bleeding) was kicked away by a booted foot under a huge tattooed leg.

Hearing no more immediate fighting, he said, "Here, help me up..."

His guardian angel stepped forward but did not lower his shield or her gaze.

Her mate lifted him with one hand by one shoulder as if he were a toddler.

Looking past the narrow spot between the

rocks where he had skewered the ogre that had thrown one of his men's arms at him, he saw a half dozen more ogres, including two mage types that appeared to be goading the other four to press forward. As he watched two blurry objects, one black, and one multi-colored and – on fire? – <u>flew</u> by the ogres.

The first, merely a shadow with some shiny spots, left the two mages with slit throats and guts, their necks becoming yawning red chasms spewing bloody rivers and their intestines looking like the rocks at the bottom of their crimson waterfalls. Before he could recoil at <u>that</u> the rest were slashed and engulfed in flame by what he quickly realized was their young dragon companion. They both made quick turns and return passes, resulting in two decapitated mages whose torsos fell forward as their heads fell off backward, their legs still standing solidly, and four screaming, flaming, flailing and running ogre-fires.

What seemed two lifetimes later to King Jankin was truly just a few minutes of deadly and unexpected chaos. As he walked toward the flaming not-quite-corpses thinking to put them out of their misery he stopped short when he stepped in something crunchy and looked down to discover his foot was in one of his cousins' chest cavity, likely carved out by an iron mace with sharpened and hardened ridges (that was laying nearby, still gripped in a severed hand). By the time he looked back up he had decided to let them burn to death. It did not take long.

**

Chapter 33

Jankin Reaches the Witches

The remainder of King Jankin's journey was more of a social jaunt, only dampened by the failure of Pill to regain consciousness. Along the way they passed the occasional farmstead, and while Jankin greeted everyone, Fallon assessed their trading potential and Icelle suggested stocking options... Stockades, stockpiles, livestock...

Their group, rather eclectic in its makeup, made most folks nervous. Originally large enough to be a small army, they were, though now reduced in number and carting some of the wounded, still well-armed and well-provisioned, therefore even more army-like. Their hosts frequently asked if they were expecting a battle. King Jankin always laughed, Icelle Yeomring would adopt a serious and thoughtful expression and nod slightly, and Fallon Rose would murmur under his breath, "Always...", none of which made anyone sleep any better.

After a few days they reached the outskirts of the Witches' Forest, the trees appearing dark and foreboding, allowing no one to even look inward very far between them. At least until Icelle dropped down off of his horse and strode up to one large old twin cedar trunk and placed his hands on it, saying his name as if in introduction. He turned and strode back to his companions and said, "We wait here. It won't be long."

Plumley had enough time to say, "What won't be long...?" before they were met by a welcoming committee of half a dozen trolls. One bounded toward Icelle like a jackrabbit with no front legs, moving in what was more like a series of insanely fast broad jumps rather than running, ending with the middle-aged looking human being scooped up, tossed, caught and spun around then set back down amid a howl of pure glee.

Icelle only smiled calmly and did not resist or evade at all. Fallon said, "So, you're an unofficial grandfather now?"

Before the fighter could respond, the troll said, "Papa, where Sean?!" while bouncing from one foot to the other.

Icelle said, in a very grandfatherly tone, "Not here little one, not yet." As the crestfallen troll wilted like a delicate flower in the midday sun, the bringer of ill tidings turned to his companions and said, "I believe we will be received well and not have to cook for ourselves this evening." They <u>all</u> smiled at that thought.

**

Chapter 34

When is a Witch not a Witch?

Queen Hazelmoon Toadscream welcomed King Jankin and his large entourage with mixed emotions. There were many of them, all seemingly bent on finding the source of their past troubles (specifically the violent persecution of witches), and for that she was truly grateful – she said as much as she sat down to a feast with them in her garden.

As far as the Queen knew none of the necessary parts to even start the task were present with them. She knew they needed a dragon, a pixie, a mage and a priest, all with special skills. That was disappointing. What she did not say was that her disappointment was greatest that the Elvish Arch Mage was not with them. Only slightly less of a disappointment to her, though felt much more intensely by her protector trolls, was the absence of her Captain of the Guard. They had asked everyone present, multiple times (each!) if they knew where Sean was. 'Where Sean?' had become a haunting echo throughout the grounds for hours. Though cunning, smart, and ferocious fighters, her trolls were definitely lost emotionally without their beloved leader, and their fixation was simultaneously adorable and exhausting.

"Ufu!" she called, and instantly the troll appeared at her left shoulder as if he had sprung up from the ground.

"Yes? Mistress Queen?" he said, head down at first, then looking to meet her eyes excitedly. His enthusiasm was constant and infectious.

"Please be sure to check the boundary tonight, that all of our guests are inside, and that no one is trespassing that would cause them, or us, any harm, please." As she spoke, she laid a hand on the troll's tree-limb-like arm.

Ufu, hopping from one foot to another, anxious to begin his task, knew his friend and leader would say not to just run off, but to make sure he understood and that he had said so.

"Mistress Queen wants guests safe, bad people out."

"Yes, Ufu, exactly!" Raising her slender arm from his she reached up to pat his cheek. It felt like the bark of an oak tree. He darkened a shade, from summer to an autumn complexion, then bolted away.

Hazelmoon turned to Icelle. "They miss Sean."

The master of her neighboring lands and keep

just said, "So do I."

To King Jankin she asked, "Are you confident in the loyalty of all who accompany you?"

"Absolutely not!" he laughed. "I've seen too much of treachery and selfish deceit since becoming King. I am quite certain that once this tracking effort begins in earnest it will lead me into King Chares' domain and I will have to deal with not only his successor but also those who came out on the losing side of his recent campaign of death and destruction. To think that some of my closest advisors and retinue are not sympathetic would be folly. I only trust those who fought beside me when they had nothing to gain by it from me personally, comrades in arms, and to only a slightly lesser extent, those in whom they in turn have a similar trust. No, leave no one untested my dear Queen. I'll not be the cause of harm in your beautiful domain..." he finished with a wry smile under a rueful expression.

Fallon had been largely silent since they had entered the woods under the witches' protection. The last time he had been with Queen Hazelmoon he had been asked to try to resurrect his long-dead wife, and though an attempt was not able to be made, just the thoughts of seeing her again had put him through several levels of personal hell. Hazelmoon had seen it all, knew his pain, and he was embarrassed that she had seen his vulnerability, but thankful for her support and understanding.

The Queen understood Fallon's hesitation and reticence, but she also wanted information.

"Master Rose," she said, waited for him to raise his head and meet her eyes. "I am sure your friend the Arch Mage has a plan?"

"He is relying on Aurelius and Slawhit to use their combined Originals' abilities to track Baru Dall as he remains certain that the mage was never fully 'here'...and he said that if I saw you I was to tell you how beautiful you are." This last was said somewhat tongue-in-cheek, but to his chagrin he realized as he regarded her that it was absolutely true.

King Jankin smiled, slightly raising one corner of his mouth, while Icelle, beside Fallon, turned and cast him a questioning glance.

Queen Hazelmoon Toadscream had a milky white pale complexion from rarely being outside in daylight. It turned several shades darker in short order. From sunrise pre-dawn pink all over to end-of-the-night fire embers orange, her blush was several seconds in the making. During that silence, her deep breaths made Fallon notice her figure as well as her face – still beautiful. He looked up again only to see her noticing his attention. Now she was as red as the darkest late-harvest apple. She straightened herself up and replied, "If you see him before I do tell him thank you. If you will excuse me…"

The Queen stood and walked away as lithely and fluidly as a large cat on a stalk. She was followed by three warlocks and six trolls and every eye in the place even as they all scrambled to stand in respect.

Icelle turned squarely toward Fallon. "Seriously?! Over a decade and the first time you show interest in a woman she's a possible love interest of your life-long best friend?! I mean, she's wonderful, but in the list of rules for being a good comrade, the one against this sort of thing is very near the top! You do know that, right?!" Icelle punctuated his lecture by folding his arms and staring, waiting. He had spoken softly, but Jankin had heard it all and mimicked Icelle, folding his arms and staring at Fallon as well.

Fallon sighed and rolled his eyes. Spreading his hands, palms up, in front of him, he said, exasperatedly, "I did <u>not</u> plan that! It was an accident, spontaneous, and only about ten seconds of my life! As far as I'm concerned, and hopefully you two as well, it <u>never happened</u>. We can just never speak of it again. Ever."

The other two exchanged a look. Jankin turned back to Fallon and said, "I won't, but I'll wager you do…"

Icelle said, "Speak of what…?" He returned to his meal, head down, mouth full.

Fallon put his elbows on the table and cradled his head in his hands.

***

Chapter 35

So That's the Red Desert

"I'm hungry."

The words hung in the air, still born, their last echo dying away in the rocks of the high mountain pass that they were carefully picking their way through.

The swarthy-faced elf in the lead dropped to a knee and held up an open right hand. Before he could turn his head, an enormous presence was at his side. Together Angus and Graham peered through the boulders on their left and right that screened the view from those behind – that just ahead and below them was the beginning of a vast desert of blowing, flowing red sands.

***

Rrahmus' test of the fountain in the lower level of his grandfather's castle had been a grand success. Armed with a linked item and a scroll spelled to bring him back to them, he left his family, apprentices and recruits against all argument. Finding himself popping up out of the water in a matching fountain in a rocky cave soaking wet and face-to-face with an enormous bear between himself and the exit, he instinctively emptied his hands, placed his thumbs together, all fingers spread like fern fronds. Raising first one set of fingers slightly then the other, as he watched the water drip from the bear's muzzle while it opened its mouth exposing fangs the size of his daggers, his hands ignited. The flame that burst forth from his fingertips came out in waves of color, each striking at the bear's exposed chest then angling progressively higher.

Starting out yellow, as it struck the initial wet fur it turned green. It then popped and snapped on the dried fur and turned blue, searing through to the skin. Both skin and flame turned red, and the unfortunate bear inhaled to roar just as the now yellow-again flames circled back and upward toward its face. Its lungs seared and no air forthcoming, the bear choked a little, failed to exhale past the now molten canal of its airway, and in seconds passed out from lack of air to its brain. Not long after, the bear died, still spasming and steaming, the smell of burnt oily skin and fur biting Rrahmus' nose; but he had already moved on.

Seeing no other threats, he climbed out of the fountain and exited the cave, stepping carefully around the smoking bear carcass. After looking around carefully, seeing no people, no animals, nothing but large crumbling formations of jagged rock, he realized how high up he was. The air was thin, and much colder than where he had come from. The valleys below were tiny dots of green, and the upper ridge lines only a few dozen barrels higher than the cave he had just exited.

If he had learned anything from the misfortunes of others in his younger days, it was his own brother-in-law's death that had driven him to find a way to achieve ready mobility in three dimensions. He jumped upward, his boots imbued with a levitation ability giving way to the flying capability of his robe.

In seconds he was above the ridgeline. To the south he could see a great body of water. North was a vast desert of reddish sand, swirling around occasional rock formations as far as he could see, which from this height was a significant distance. To the east and west were tall, thin ridges that looked like the rounded blades used by skinners and farriers to prepare hides, all aligned with the direction of the prevailing winds.

He returned to the cave. In the back he touched a tiny trowel to a bit of stone about waist high and a hole appeared. Placing a glowing gemstone in it, another pass with the trowel and the hole was gone. He did this two more times around the cave so that only open floor was between the three gems.

He started to remove a scroll from his pack,

then paused. Turning, he approached the bear. With both arms outstretched before him, palms upward, he brought his hands together, as if drinking from a stream. When he raised his hands the bear came up off the ground. Turning toward the exit, he walked out until the bear, half a rod to his front, was suspended over the edge of the canyon wall. Abruptly pulling his hands apart, the bear fell, bounced, fell some more, hit and rolled like a lumpy, off-balance barrel, then fell again. The Arch Mage did not wait to see it stop. He glanced around one last time, entered the cave, and read his scroll.

Reunited with his friends and family in a literal flash, they all watched as his clothes dripped and could smell burnt bear flesh and fur wafting from him while he explained their next move. He had to say it all twice.

***

Chapter 36

Retrieving the Old One

Angus did not turn to look at Graham, he just started talking. "Okay, you've been somewhere here before, right?"

"Right," said the battered-looking fighter with a lopsided sardonic smile that only the elf girl and her father saw.

"Does that help us?" came the follow up query.

"Maybe," Graham said, a little more seriously.

The smooth baritone with perfect enunciation from behind them seemed entirely out of place away from the elven palace they had just left. "With the sands before us, the ocean should be behind us, but if the fountain at Fallon's also points to somewhere in this desert, but not to <u>this</u> location, it seems an easy assumption that it is a <u>very</u> large feature."

Angus turned to face the speaker, painfully aware of how he sounded by comparison, a former wharf rat thief with a rattling gravel voice from sleeping outside on too many winter nights before being caught trying to slash and grab one of Rrahmus' pouches. "Sir Tahmus," he said, "you're right," and to Molly he said,

"Alright Novice, your turn."

The elf girl pulled a small bowl from her pack and filled it partway with some of the sandy dirt at her feet, then placed an iron leather needle in it. Putting a gold coin given to her by the Arch Mage (who in turn had said it was from the Old One's lair, a pebble from his craw that Rrahmus had flattened and stamped a dragon's head onto) in the center of the bowl, she grasped the needle and drew it around the bowl's edge three times, mumbled to herself, then dropped the needle back into the bowl.

Nothing happened at first. She sat the bowl down on the ground. Angus and Graham waited, Tahmus rolled his eyes. And then it jumped. The point of the needle struck and stuck to the edge of the coin, spun around it several times, lying flat on the dirt and rocks in the bowl. The coin shifted position repeatedly, spinning slightly until it eventually buried itself under the dirt, and the needle came to a stop, laying mostly on top of the dirt, but still touching the edge of the coin under it.

They all looked in the direction of the angle of the needle. All they could see was red sand into the distance.

"Huh," said Graham, "single point direction

doesn't give us a distance estimate though, and I for one am <u>not</u> going to walk off into the biggest desert I've ever seen without an idea of how far I may need to go and therefore have water enough for the journey... we got really lucky the last time..."

Angus said, "Then what do you propose?"

"Instead of following it in a straight line, we should mark this spot, below us, where we can see it from below. Mark that angle on the bowl, then pick an end of one of those rock formations directly to our front and head towards it. When we get there, she," he said, indicating Molly the Mage with a lean of his head, "does this bit again. The sharper the change of the angle, the closer we are."

Tahmus, the senior Commander of Elvish Knights, was impressed, and said so. "Using magic and logic together for locating the lost – truly amazing."

Angus nodded, climbed down over the edge, and with a snap of his fingers drew a flame along a flat rock wall, making an 'X' about as tall and broad as Graham. He then kept going downward toward the desert floor, followed by Graham, then Molly, then Tahmus.

***

They were almost halfway to the desert floor

when they heard a familiar female voice calling down to them, "Wait for me!"

Graham turned around, saw Bronwyn scrambling hurriedly down toward them, and wordlessly sat down where he could watch her while he did exactly as she asked.

Angus observed Graham 'observing' Bronwyn, snorted, and continued on. Molly flashed him a shy, embarrassed grin that almost traveled from one pointy ear to the other, and Tahmus only paused, looked at the two humans once each, shrugged and kept moving.

***

Chapter 37

Bronnie's First Mission

Rrahmus had decided to take as many new apprentices as he could to Fallon's after his grandfather agreed to let his formerly-cousin-now-niece be trained. Rrahmus' version of training the best was of course trial by fire, or experiential, and as he was sending his #1 apprentice, Angus, on a scouting mission and Angus was to be Molly's mentor, he saw no reason she should not go along. Tahmus had not agreed...

In the end, with Angus' other skills, the Elvish Arch Mage considered it overkill, but with Graham along, a veteran adventurer of amazing skill, he relented, saying Tahmus could go along too, but only as "hired muscle" and definitely "not in charge". To this Tahmus agreed. The Elvish Commander set his troops to preparing to deploy, readying arms, armor, transport and food, then left with them.

It was only after they were gone that Sean said, "That desert is a pretty inhospitable place...if anything goes wrong they'll need food, water and maybe a healer..." Even as he said it, Bronwyn jumped up, bouncing with excitement.

"Oh! Please, let me go! You said it's low risk, already an overly strong group for the task, I need experience too, pleeeeezzz!"

'Girls', thought the mage. 'Always using my own words against me.' Inwardly he chuckled. Outwardly, he said, "Well, you'd better hurry and catch up to them."

When she was gone he said, "Just like her mother. I just hope her father doesn't kill <u>me</u>..."

***

When she got to Graham's resting place, her hurry had her breathing heavily, a slight sheen of perspiration on her face and neck, hair slightly disheveled as a few of the gorgeous, shiny tresses were hanging askew in front of her face due to the downhill travel. Graham's smile grew just a little.

"Rrahmus...said...you...needed...a healer. He said...I would...be safe with you..." she said between heaving breaths, leaning over toward Graham, resting her hands on the front of her thighs.

It was only when she looked up that she realized he was shaking with silent laughter. Her petulantly fuming expression at his mirth only made him go from silent chuckling to laughing aloud. He stood up so fast it took her aback a little, but he just said,

"Safe? Interesting choice of words. Let's go find a dragon! You first m'lady…"

As she moved off after the rest of their little band, he reflected that he enjoyed 'watching her back' just as much as her front…and out of pure habit he continued to look behind them at their back trail for any followers or dangers, as well as Angus' 'X'.

The afternoon sun was waning by the time they reached the edge of the sand, and the air temperature had risen significantly during their steep drop in elevation. They could feel the heat coming up from the ground.

Graham said, "Without any known water source, we'll want to travel at night anyway to use less, and hopefully I can use the position of the stars and compare to what I saw last year to see if I can judge where we are in relation to where I was then. For now, we head to the left edge of that rock ridge sticking up straight out from this wall. Move slowly, conserve your energy, keep a cloth handy to cover your face if a dust storm kicks up." To emphasize this point he tied a shirt around his neck, knotting the sleeves together behind him so that it was snugly resting over his nose and mouth, then pulled it down under his chin and trudged off, now leading, saying, "Let's go, we're wasting daylight."

The priestess and two mages all had hoods on their robes that could be gathered at the neck to shield their faces, but Tahmus wore a helmet, and had removed it and his cloak in the heat. The best he could come up with was an extra pair of socks. Once tied in place he decided it had better be a life or death option to use them as a face cover as the odor wat not worth it otherwise. He needed some new socks.

***

The sun was gone and the moon was rising by the time they reached the rocks they had targeted. Neither the temperature nor the visibility had changed significantly as a result. The full moon rising was casting shadows and the sand was still hot to the touch. They found a fairly clear spot to eat, drink a little, and let Molly do what Graham now referred to as her 'bowl trick'. Bronwyn, not having seen it the first time, was quite excited to watch it.

Graham, watching the needle stop, said, "While we can no longer see Angus' 'X' on the rocky slope we left behind, I know we came very nearly on a perpendicular course from that stone feature to this one and they were very nearly parallel to each other. The new angle of the needle here is almost straight in line with the direction of this rock formation. We are closer than I expected or even thought possible. And based on the moon and a few star formations, such as Haukri's beak, I think the area I explored a year ago is about three to five days travel south and west of here. We traveled pretty much due north to get here from the fountain cave, and need to head due west to get to the Old One according to Molly's bowl... All that said, it took us a month to get home from there, including a week on a ship and traveling on horseback for most of it...and without an ancient senile red dragon in tow..."

Angus was depressed by the enormity of what was essentially an agonizingly involved escape plan. Tahmus was wondering if they had enough gold to outfit themselves if and when it became necessary and both Molly and Bronwyn, having never done any of the 'field' portion of their roles, found themselves just listening raptly like spectators to an interesting story about someone else. Graham continued, "Based on what I think from the angles of Molly's needle, we are probably three to five hours walk from wherever it is we are going. The desert gets cold fast, so while it is still warm let's get some rest. Sometime after midnight we will likely want to be walking to keep warm anyway. I'll take first watch."

***

While the others slept, Graham studied them. He knew now, that despite their skills, even Angus and Tahmus were looking to him to lead. It wasn't ill-founded. Angus knew ships, port towns, seedy taverns and sleight of hand. Tahmus knew how to lead large groups of fighters – swordsmen, archers and cavalry – even Graham had heard of his exploits against the giants in the south. But neither of them had been part of small group actions in an unknown and austere environment against unknown opponents with vague instructions and a brand-new team that had no experience together.

As a mercenary adventurer for hire, it happened to Graham all the time. He just wasn't used to being in charge. Technically he still wasn't, but Angus had plainly made no objection. 'So be it,' he thought, 'Boss Graham it is.' He woke Bronwyn for the next watch just for the excuse to watch her awaken and stretch and yawn before he went off to dreamland...

***

Before Tahmus could nudge Graham's toe with his boot, the human fighter had sat up and was pulling his boots on. The elf was too old of a campaigner to think he was so tired that his senses were altered, and said quietly, "Now how did you do that...?"

Looking up without lifting his head, Graham gave a little smile and answered, "Do what?" as he was already rolling his shoulders into his cloak.

Tahmus shrugged and walked away to share a biscuit and a piece of dried beef with his daughter. When they had all eaten Graham said, "For now we head consistently away from the moon. When it sets we should be close. I will look for a place before our target to huddle in, armor up if we know we are near, maybe have some hot food if we can stay unseen, like a cave. Just be alert, rotate who is in the rear, please, between you two, Tahmus and Angus. No offense ladies, you just don't have the necessary experience yet. If anything goes wrong, you get attacked by something, fall in a hole, a bird carries you away, whatever... YELL OUT. Seriously, too many times in my past people have not communicated a threat or problem when they had the chance and it just made everything worse. Keep checking the person in front of and behind you regularly and often, and if you lose sight of them, say something! And finally, remember that if you are in the rear and someone is behind you, say something because it isn't one of us!" They laughed at him. He rolled his eyes and walked off into the night.

***

The moon was almost down and out of sight when he saw the rock outcropping jutting up through the sand ahead and to his left. It looked small, and it was not long and narrow like all of the others he'd seen to this point. It looked almost completely round. Artificially round. Graham almost examined it too long. Bronwyn had caught up to him from behind as he slowed his pace even further than he had for the past four hours to make sure he didn't lose his little group, and she tapped his shoulder, saying, "What is that?"

He pulled up short to say, "I'm not sure, but it doesn't look natural..." and looked down before he stepped off forward again, only to realize there was nowhere to step that wasn't at the bottom of a canyon at least a dozen rods below. The sand was thick under his feet. As Bronwyn attempted to step around him for a closer look, he put his arm out to stop her and the sand gave way under his feet, sending one forward into space. Normally he would have stepped *into* a slip to avoid falling down, but now the opposite was true – forward meant a much longer fall!

As the overly large fighter fell backward, the arm meant to stop the much smaller priestess ended up throwing her to the ground, and to make sure she didn't pop up and go forward into the dark chasm before them, he held her there firmly. Once the 'Ooof!' of air leaving her lungs was reversed he had pulled his legs back and underneath him without releasing her, and the sand falling over the edge continued to reveal the undercut stone ledge the were on.

Finally, he looked down at her and said, "I'm sorry, there's…"

She cut him off with, "Look, I'll admit I find you somewhat ruggedly handsome, but this is a bit much for the, um, time, place and, well, company…"

Realizing which part of her anatomy he was pinning her to the ground by, it was the first time she saw him flustered. Even as the pre-dawn light showed his embarrassed eyes it also showed the quickly altered twinkle and gleam of his teeth in a mischievous smile and he finished his sentence, "no way we're moving yet…"

He bent down, now with both hands resting firmly enough on her chest to prevent escape (but not his whole body weight), leaned down close and stared into her eyes for a long few seconds…then kissed her…gently on the forehead. Gripping the straps of her rucksack he lifted her to her feet with him as he stood up.

Angus, currently next in their miniature skirmish line, had quickened his pace at what had sounded like a scuffle in the dim light, saw the drop off immediately, Graham regarding him questioningly, and Bronwyn once again flustered and out of breath. "Alright Graham?" he asked.

"Alright Angus – just stuck," was the response.

The others joined them. Molly was looking quizzically at Bronwyn, who ignored her. Tahmus said, "I think we're here – look!"

The light in the sky grew quickly in the flat terrain, and on the far wall of the chasm were several obvious entrances, tied together by stone staircases cut into the rockface. The far-sighted old elf said, "And it is guarded by ogres. With a larger opening below and left that looks like it was walled in – a definite candidate for a dragon's prison all right..."

Molly said, in a clear but quietly pure voice, "I will test again here, then again wherever we think we can gain access, just to be sure with a final, close-range triangulation." She did her 'bowl trick' and the needle pointed directly at the walled-in looking feature Tahmus had pointed out.

"Well," said Graham, "I'm convinced! Angus, can you get an ancient – meaning huge – dragon out of that? Who, as far as we know is not only blind, but perhaps injured and unable to fly?"

The elven mage thought, then said, "I'll bet he's not weak though, either way. The trick, as I recall from the Master, is to keep him from attacking <u>us</u>... I can make a hole in that wall that he can exploit. Keeping the ogres at bay is equally concerning though, as it will take time, and I have to be really close, like touching it close..."

"First things first," said Tahmus, "we have to move before they see us."

Graham realized they had descended from the slight ridge of the last dune they had crested, said, "Follow me," and headed off at a southeasterly angle quartering away from the canyon, between the leading edges of two sand dunes, like going between the bows of two ships. They were invisible to the ogres in seconds.

As they kept walking, paralleling the almost circular canyon, Graham observed, "This is basically a dry moat, with an approach only from above. I don't really like either of those things, though I bet a dragon would... I wonder if a dragon made this place..."

"Why would that matter?" asked Bronwyn.

"Because," said Angus excitedly, "they <u>never</u>

have only one way in and out!"

"Exactly," said Graham as he once again reminded himself to slow his pace for the benefit of his companions. "We need to find it, the other entrance. Perhaps it will be more easily accessed."

By the time the mid-morning sun was making Graham no longer want to put his armor on, Angus returned from his most recent trip to peer over a sand dune at the canyon wall now due north of them. Unlike the previous dozen trips, this time he was excited.

"You were right! There's an open landing ledge!" he practically shouted.

After he received a quartet of shushings, they all went to look. It was indeed a large cave opening – but this one had no stairs down to it. It also had no ogres visible above, though.

"Maybe they don't know about it?" suggested Tahmus.

"Or just don't think anyone can use it," answered Angus. "Which may be true – if it was still connected, he should be able to get out...right?"

"Okay," said Graham, "but that cave gets us a lot closer, and with no opposing force preventing us. The real question is can we get there? Ropes from above?"

"Only if we find a way to get on top of that feature, hopefully unopposed..." mused Tahmus.

**

They sat in a circle to eat while they considered, dropping backpacks and peeling off layers to endure the climbing heat. The three males sat facing the cliff and canyon, studying the cave opening. The females were facing toward the open sand, southward, with no mountains between them and the ocean anymore.

The conversation was desultory, as they each began to resign themselves to finding a way to defeat the ogres as all approaches involved getting on top of the lair.

Until Molly screamed. She was looking upward and southward, away from the canyon.

Tahmus leapt to his feet, drawing his sword and spinning around with almost the same speed as Graham – the latter was impressed, thinking that parental protectiveness was more powerful than he had previously imagined. When Graham saw what was flying at them, he was suddenly unsure if it would matter...

The dragon dropping down saw what he knew was a group of mercenary adventurers in front of his lair by both their appearance and odor – he smelled human and elf, saw robes and armor – and he went on the offensive. If not for the coastal deer in his mouth he would be flaming them by now. Instead he dropped quickly, rear claws extended – until he saw the elf's face.

Tahmus had resigned himself to a fiery bloody death. He knew that to kill a dragon with few casualties meant attacking early and with selfless violence to its core. He fully intended to be an elven torch before he plunged his sword far enough through the reptilian body to strike its spine to save his daughter.

And then the flying menace dropped its hind end, flared its wings, and almost hovered a few rods away.

All five of the humanoids had turned to face it by now and saw the deer drop from the jaws lined with fangs the size of short swords, blood flying. They all waited for the flames to come, Graham raising his entire pack with the shield fastened to the back of it in front of him, thinking to survive the blast himself and block Bronwyn from being incinerated behind him as well.

The dragon said, "Rrahmus?! When did you start wearing armor and using swords?!"

All six of the beings present were in varying stages of confusion. And then the eldest elf spoke, "I am

Tahmus, Rrahmus' cou – twin brother. You must be Audhan – he has told me much about you. I regret that I never met your grandfather before his untimely demise. In a sense we are here on a similar task – rescuing the Old One."

The ground shook enough to make entire nearby sand dunes change shape when the now adult gold dragon dropped unceremoniously to the ground.

Angus pushed his way between the two fighters, sprinting at the figure of shimmering gold but reflecting red from the sand. Even as the elf leapt the final few paces to grab the dragon in what appeared to be a miniature bear hug, the dragon was already chuckling, then rolling on the ground, mock-wrestling and howling with glee, yelling, "Aaanngusss!"

The next few minutes of social sorting ended up with Audhan feeling very lucky. He could have inadvertently killed one best friend and the brother, son, daughter and niece of three others. He was a quite inconsolable blubbering mess for a while. Finally, he did console himself – by wolfing down the deer that had prevented it all from happening. He said, "I have been trying to get him out, and I can't. The old lair he is in has been specifically spelled to keep dragons from damaging or penetrating it. The ogres know I'm here –

they told me if I kill one more of them, they'll stop feeding him. Now they just laugh when I fly over." He shed a few more tears at this, but these tears stemmed from anger and frustration rather than sadness.

"I'm not a dragon…" said Angus.

Audhan straightened up. "I thought of trying to get help, but I have been bringing him extra food. I don't know why he's here. I <u>felt</u> him. He must have been brought here unconscious, because by the time I recognized his presence he was walled in. I was off hunting, sunning, and sleeping, came back and literally crashed into the wall in the dark. When I righted myself before I hit the bottom of the canyon I flew to the other entrance, only to find the passage between blocked as well, and smashing at it only hurt me with no other effect at all. And then I felt him reach out – but he cannot sense me or any response at all."

Angus said, "It's magically shielded from the inside then. This could be much harder than we thought…"

Graham offered, "I'll bet they feed him through a gap. A dragon may not fit, but we aren't all dragons…"

"Ooohh!" Angus replied, "I'm getting an idea!"

***

Audhan was pretty sure there were a dozen

ogres left that he hadn't killed. He was even more sure that they smelled and tasted horrible, cooked or not. He had ferried their little group over to his cave on his back, one at a time. It got them out of the desert sun and was a far cooler place to consider their next move.

Angus went to the blockage of the old connecting passage. The new material filled a space easily four or five barrels high and just as wide. Turning to Audhan, he asked, "How deep is this? How far does it go?"

The dragon considered, then said, "Just shorter than me, from nose to tail." To let that measurement be easily established, he flopped down on his belly. Angus paced it off, went to the passage and started rustling through his pouches. Only Molly caught all of what he did, but with some material from one he reached for Molly and touched her shoulders, top of her head, sprinkled the rest on her feet, then placed her in front of the barrier. Her eyes widened in surprise, but she remained silent. Before Tahmus could voice an objection, Angus gently shoved Molly against the wall. The sprinkled bits lit up like faerie magic does in the evening trees in late summer, and an outline of stone the size of Molly began to disappear behind her. It lasted for several long moments. No one spoke.

Finally the lights stopped and Angus gently pulled Molly away from the wall, saying, "Stand here Molly. Don't move! I'm using you as an enhancer to increase my strength. We need to see if we can get through... Bronnie, can you see if the passage broke through? Graham, hand me a torch please?"

Angus took the proffered stick with one end wrapped in cloth, but instead of soaking it in oil, just grabbed the end and spoke strangely. When he removed his hand the torch lit up the area as if it were actually on fire. Handing it to Bronwyn, he said, "Quick in and out, just see if it's all the way open, okay?"

The young priestess nodded nervously, took the torch and ducked into the opening. She felt immediately uncomfortable in the tight space, but heard a reassuring voice from behind her, "If anything goes wrong, scream. I'll be right behind you, if I have to crawl through, sword first!" Graham's voice reminded her of being in a different 'restricted' environment that morning that she didn't mind so much... she kept going.

The light limited her view to just a few paces ahead in the small tunnel, but after a few dozen steps it continued outward, revealing loose stones and gravel. She should have just backed up. Straight backward and report the tunnel's successful access into the next chamber. But she thought it would be easier to exit briefly and turn around. When she did, off to her right she heard what sounded like an enormous dog sniffing to find a scent. She turned, and the torch revealed a red dragon over twice the size of Audhan. They both inhaled – Bronwyn to scream, the dragon to incinerate Bronwyn. His much larger lungs took longer to fill. She could see that he was emaciated, almost skin and bone, literally starving. Before he finished inhaling, she said, "Oh! You poor thing! Let me help you!"

The voice stopped him. Then, in that hesitation, a familiar smell. He straightened his spine, lowered his head toward her, letting her see one of his milky-white blind eyes.

"Thea?" he said in the lowest, rockiest rumble she had ever heard.

"No," she said, reaching out to gently touch his snout. "I'm Bronwyn, her daughter. I'm sorry to say my mother died many years ago."

"Did she…" he paused, tears appearing in his eyes, "did she ever speak of me?"

"I don't know. I was very young. I learned a little about dragons, a little about her friends. The only one I never met was called 'Marduk'."

The old dragon sighed, said, "Yes, that's me. She

was supposed to visit me. When she became well overdue, I went to look for her, in case she was hurt. But I could not find my way back. I was lost for a very long time. Now, I am just waiting to die…"

"No! Please! I need you to escape with me so you can tell me about her! It hurts my father too much to talk about, so I really know very little…" Now Bronwyn was crying too.

"Alright little one, for you I will try, but I am very weak," he said.

"Can you change to elf form?" she asked.

"Of course. In my youth we just called it man-form. Elves did not yet exist back then…" In just seconds an old, wrinkled, white-haired elf stood before her, his neck cowl falling to become a robe. He leaned against the wall to not fall over, two thin weak legs being harder to balance on than four large weak legs and a tail. She took his arm and led him to the tunnel.

"You will have to duck down. Just lean on my back," said Bronwyn as she led him out of his prison.

As they emerged, Angus said, "Well? Did it go through…?" Then the ancient elf stood up behind her, responding for her, the voice unchanged, "Why yes. It did indeed. Thank you!"

Audhan spoke first. "Old One! I heard your

pleas! I am here, and have been the whole time, for you!"

The old dragon-elf held out his free hand, and Audhan nuzzled it with his snout. "Ah!" said the elder, "A child of Platinus. Your truth and devotion honors you and your entire line. Always so good to all of us, no matter how you were treated. You are he the mage spoke of, the young one he accepted as his ward. But you have grown! His thoughts run through your head, a good connection you have." The Old One then started to fall over, his weakness overcoming him.

Audhan's transformation was rapid. His body retracted into a skinny, gangly but fit, and, right in front of Molly, naked elf. Her glimpse was brief but left a lasting impression. Even as her indignant father pointedly and exaggeratedly cleared his throat, Audhan's scales rearranged into golden plate armor that was part of him. Graham nodded appreciatively – that was new. He said, "Angus, will the passage be open forever now?"

The elf mage refocused, said, "No! It will close when Molly leaves, or in an hour or so even if she doesn't."

"We can fool the ogres I think," said Graham. "We need a creature that will fit through, then make it a dragon, and let the tunnel close…they'll keep feeding it and never know…"

Audhan turned to Angus, "Can you do that?"

"Actually," answered the mage, "yes. I can."

"Perfect," said the young dragon-elf, and he went to a back corner of the cave, returning with a sealed box. When he opened it, it squeaked. Reaching in, he handed Angus a mouse. "Will this do?" he asked.

"It might…" Angus took the mouse from Audhan, the torch from Bronwyn, and, placing the torch just outside the passage, squeezed down it and tried a spell he hadn't worked on in quite a while. He should have dropped the mouse sooner, but as it began to grow he soon had no choice. It mostly worked – it looked like a red dragon…but as he worked his way quickly back down his tunnel he heard the lowest-pitched squeak ever…he thought to himself, 'Hopefully it completely changes before the ogres notice.' To his companions he said, "Let's wait for dark and then get out of here." Then he noticed the blind old dragon-elf eating the rest of the mice out of the box.

***

Chapter 38

Baru Dall's Origin

Self-reflection and examination were not normal activities for the dark mage who sat surrounded by a motley collection of evil beings. As a young man he had never thought of himself as evil, or even 'bad' for that matter. Quiet, bookish, the youngest son of a house of well-known men of martial skills, he did not belong.

After all of his brothers save one were killed (in combat, accidents and at least one paid assassination), only he knew that the day his oldest brother was thrown by his horse on a bridge over an icy river and drowned it was actually due to a telekinetic attack by him, the 'baby' that would be Baron.

The two-legged wolves had come calling soon thereafter. Thinking to roll over the young, inexperienced heir with no tactical skill, they had arrived just days later, to 'pay their respects' and honor their fallen 'friend'. They brought a few too many men-at-arms to suit him. He let them view his predecessor's corpse in small groups, funneled into the small chapel a few at a time, then made them exit via an alternate route through the side of the chapel where the knights of old used to store their warhorses' armor, saddles and tack.

It fed out through the stables, where his mercenaries waited. They murdered ten groups of ten, a full hundred unarmed visitors before the first cry of alarm was heard...and ignored, put down to a distraught family mourner. A handful more groups met with slit throats and stabs to the rear of their necks and lungs before some of their cavalry's horse-holders questioned why none had come out yet if the space was so limited inside the chapel...

As his primary would-be opponent's senior advisor turned to echo the concern, the youngest of the Dall line plunged his own dagger into the priest's heart. As he bled out internally when the blade was twisted, he only had time to say, "Treachery!" and expire, falling in a sodden heap at the feet of his murderer.

It was his first combat killing. He had heard stories from some of his brothers and their comrades about their first time, how they were nauseous, or had a crisis of faith. Some even fell unconscious just from seeing the blood.

Baru grinned, turned to the advisor's valet, who was crying, seated next to his dead master, holding his head in his lap, the still open lifeless, vacant eyes looking at him in parallel to the younger, anguished ones. He slashed the valet's throat with violent glee. Then the bloodbath began in earnest. Later, when he sorted out who would support him, he found they were not farmers or sheepherders, tradesmen or loyal guards; the stable, normal, general population wanted nothing to do with him. When he distributed the belongings of the dead to his mercenaries, they agreed to continue to work with him as long as he helped them get more plunder. He wanted, no, *needed* to feel powerful, and he knew he couldn't get that feeling 'Lording' over peasants day in and day out.

He went into the chapel and found his mother still crying and praying for his dead brother. Behind the coffin stood an enormous symbol of the god she was praying to, and he knew at that moment that she was a good woman, a good mother, who loved him. The curse he uttered included a promise to anyone or anything unholy that would let him have power, not prowess or leadership, but raw ability to command others to do his will, control over matter and the elements, to bend the very earth to his whims.

His mother objected, telling him he was just misguided, sad and angry about the loss of his last brother, very supportive and motherly. Something inside his brain had cracked when he had started killing. It now broke completely. He felt strength grow inside him that he knew was not his own. It helped him to lift the standard in its entirety and plunge it completely through his mother's torso. The crunch of ribs, the 'thump' of the wood striking the bench behind her didn't keep him from hearing her last surprised breath escaping.

***

Looking back now, he knew that was the definitive moment of his birth, his emergence as the face of evil.

***

The black cloud that had coalesced around him with dozens of eyes spoke, saying, "Come to me. Find me. I will teach you..." It disappeared, leaving behind a book and a map. He left the chapel, locking the doors, left his family home that very day, never to return. He traveled with his mercenary company, following the map. He studied the book every day. They raided and pillaged every community they encountered along the way, getting more wealth, but losing members each time. Some were killed, others just disappeared into the night. Eventually the map led them away from settled lands, and only a few die-hard curious fellows stayed with him. They arrived at a mountain crag on a stormy coastline, and found an ancient gateway, blocked by a cave-in.

The remaining pair of brigands now had no use for him, so they drew their weapons to relieve him of his remaining valuables and kill him. He grasped the blades of their swords and screamed, head tilted back toward the sky. A bolt of lightning shot down, through his mouth and out of his hands, through their swords and finished by blasting them into the dross under the ancient arch. It killed them <u>and</u> opened a passage into the mountain. A voice rose from the very ground, saying, "That is just a tiny taste of what I will teach you! Come to me..."

***

Now, in this world, where magic was everywhere, and the few creatures that neither had it nor were touched by it still knew more about it than he did, it was beginning to seem as though his associations were more hindering than helpful. At home in his own world, the classically evil were largely geniuses, just few and far between. Here, like magic itself, evil was plentiful, but most of it was just <u>stupid</u>.

Gazing at the faces around him – the ogres'

arrogant leers, the bitter non-magical men's angry stares, and the curiously content countenances of the more efficiently evil of all in Metaerie, the dark priests, he realized he had misplaced his efforts.

The priests, whose followers were obtained by the promise of taking what they wanted from those who the priests told them did not deserve it – these deserved more of his focus and support.

Wealth from the workers was easy enough. Tell a worker that they are important and being mistreated and that you will help to fix it, true or not, and they will support paying a zealous tithe that is likely higher than the amount of tax they would have refused to pay at the point of death, if only because it was their choice where their contribution was sent (not necessarily what it was used for...). These priests had their human flocks convinced that their peers that had natural magic didn't just have an easier life, but that they *owed* a penance for it as their magically enhanced crops/buildings/fires/meals were taking energy away from the rest of the world's resources, and were the reason that these true believers fell on hard times. It was why their roofs collapsed, not because they were poorly built. It was why their crops failed, not because they were poorly tended. It was even why their food tasted bad, not because it was poorly prepared and cooked.

Fealty from the fighters was even easier. Just telling them that their efforts were needed and giving them a sword and a shield made them willing to take a pittance for pay and fight to the death, no matter the truth of the cause. They were quick to believe that their magical counterparts were only better at fighting because of the magic, not because they practiced, that their equipment had magical properties giving even more advantage. They were even more easily convinced therefore to not only attack them but to rob them, to obtain their magical weapons and armor.

These priests had even convinced their followers that those who had received lands from their Kings, given freely to the industrious and with no taxes levied against them, were receiving special favors, that it was the result of incestuous practices between magical creatures. They were persuaded with messages that resonated with those who saw themselves as exploited, persecuted and unlucky.

These became pockets of people who became bitter about everything around them. They ignored their neighbors who were rewarded because they worked hard, treated others well, saved and spent wisely. 'Those people' were just luckier, favored, even cheaters, to be reviled, beaten and killed.

These priests were his greatest allies. They were charismatic, motivational and experienced word-twisters, able to easily convince those of stunted intellect to view those with natural magic in a world literally created by the magical abilities of magical creatures as an abomination.

The irony of his goal here remained. He had been given limited magic in a non-magical world, then told his only way to get more was to steal it. The items used as the core strength of the spell to create this world were strong magicks, old in the old world before their use, and the source of all current magic in Metaerie. His teacher said that when magic died here it would grow in his world.

Only knowing of a few magical beings from his books, when he found a way to project part of his energy to Metaerie, he found himself in a dark temple full of tiny monsters at the edge of the world. They thought him a god, and he did nothing to deter them in their belief. Later, among non-magical humans, his abilities allowed the priests to perform 'miraculous events' (with his help) to sway more followers into zealous fervor rather than tacit support. What they did was therefore 'divine' rather than 'magic'. The priests had come to know better but had not cared. They were receiving more wealth and worshipers than ever before, and their egos could not have been more selfishly rewarded.

Comparing them now to his mother, he knew that these priests were neither loving nor charitable, neither humble nor penitent. No, they lived lavishly, gave only to achieve greater status, and served no one, not even him, not really. Yes, they were truly evil; he could only aspire to be more like them!

After trying to kill off dragons, but not finding any, then witches and faeries, he had not seen any increase in magic in his home world. Subsequent to his earlier defeat and several months of recovering, he had returned, stronger only in knowledge. He needed to destroy Metaerie in its entirety to capture its magic. That meant reversing its creation. His original assumption had been correct, that the creators had used a magical catalyst of some kind to enhance and bind the spell. To undo it he needed a massive magical negation. The major elements seemed simple enough: he had kidnapped one of the original magical creatures present at the creation. He was obtaining one of the original relics (again) to complete the spell reversal. And now he had decided that he would determine a method to use the item to kill the creature, negating the underpinning creation magic of both. Just as many of his revelations and discoveries these past few years had done, this one generated a personal interaction from his teacher, not a premonition or feeling, an out loud statement.

The voice came to him rarely now, but this was very clear, "You must strike the blow to receive the magic…" The arcane library he had found in the dark temple at the end of his journey in his home world had revealed several mentions of 'portal travel'. His troglodyte minions had confirmed such a thing existed, not knowing that he had seen one himself, in that very library. Now he knew; he had to physically come to Metaerie. The old books talked about a spear of great power – he had to find it. The oldest magic had to reside in the oldest dragon, one present at Metaerie's creation, and he had that dragon locked up already.

It was a simple plan then: get the spear and the dragon together at the portal, pop in, kill the dragon with the spear, pop back to his temple, absorb the magic of this entire world.

Simple. Evil. Flawless.

As he chuckled for no apparent reason, the

ogres regarded his black amorphous form curiously, the men shivered in fear, and the priests smiled wider.

***

Chapter 39

The Mage Isn't Home

Baru Dall had armed his brilliant troglodyte supporters with what he could – a decent plan, enhanced magic, and supporters. Their knowledge of Fallon's keep was a plus. He figured they really only needed to search Rrahmus' chambers. They just needed a way to get in. He spent precious personal energy getting the trog mage to transcribe a spell that would change his appearance and another to use on his priestly comrade and a few more. The rest of the plan was a bit diabolical, but simple enough.

The two had some quite evil accompaniment. They were non-magical humans, but ones with no compunctions about literally any form of murder or mayhem. Survivors of much of King Chares' campaign of terror against the witches, they were frightening even to the trogs.

The six of them arrived at Blaine's lower level one evening near the docks and took refuge in a fish cleaning chamber. Dramin combined some spells of change and permanence and by morning they all looked like elves.

They took passage to Rose Castle in one of Fallon's ships, sailing for a few days to get there. Their arrival had just a little fanfare, elves were common enough visitors, but groups of them were not. Their escort ushered them to Fallon's office to be received by his staff in his absence, but as he turned to leave once there, he was smashed on the head from behind with a hammer and hidden in a corner behind a bookshelf.

As he had hoped, the stories of Fallon's Faeries looked to be true – a glass jar with tiny wings in it sat on a map table. He said to the others, "Hide and be ready." He shook the glass jar.

The clear toned high-pitched sound was like a half-dozen tiny crystal goblets clinking together in a pleasant toast. The tiny wingless form that appeared said, "Can I help..." and then froze, held by Tarlek's magical grasp. Though she could not move, her anger was palpable.

Dramin said, "Stay hidden. Wait." They did, and were soon rewarded. Two more faeries, larger ones, popped in together, and were also immediately immobilized. As well as being larger, these had wings, which their captors spun coils of thin rope around and tied together and to the table, laying them down next to each other.

One of the evil men-looking-like-elves laid his sword on their bare necks. Dramin said to the little wingless one, "Your daughters I believe? I'll make this simple. We are not here to hurt anyone, just to retrieve an object that belongs to us. You get it for us, and get us out of the castle safely and your daughters live to tomorrow...sound good? I'm going to let you go now, but one word or action that I think is off in the slightest bit, and they die. Here we go..."

With that Tarlek released Lily. She was so angry her tiny body shook.

"Go into Rrahmus' chambers," said Dramin. "We know you can do it. Take this spelled scroll and read it. The magical items in that room will glow. The strongest and brightest will likely be the ones we are here to obtain. They are a simple old spear head and spear shaft. If there are others, bring them too..." She nodded, took the scroll and disappeared.

In seconds she reappeared with a spearhead in a glass bottle. Popping out again she returned just as quickly with a short wooden stick, carved with symbols. She simply said, "That's it."

Dramin passed a slightly bent wand over the items and they both shone with the deepest, brightest blue he had ever seen. "Now," he said to her, "remember our deal…"

Two of the men further bound and gagged the other two females, Djinja and Eyevee, and placed them in two separate backpacks. The mage re-emphasized, "Tell no one, or they die."

She led them out, popping in and out at corners and gates, sometimes causing a commotion to distract and then clear the path back to the docks. Once on a ship heading north, the trog-elf held the glass case with her wings in it up in front of her, saying, "I'll send it back with your daughters when we are safely away." Lily disappeared. Easy.

***

Chapter 40

Lady Kathryn

The day inside the castle walls began for her like any other. It was spring, and that meant evening fog, midnight rains, and by morning, blue sky and steam rising up as the sunlight struck the damp ground.

The smells that rose with it varied from barnyard to bakery. Throwing open both curtains and shutters she looked to the sun and breathed deeply.

Lady Kathryn had married well. Her family were mostly tradespeople. Her father was a wood carver, her mother a baker. They each came from mixed parents (magical and not) and neither seemed to have any innate magic, but both were quite adept at their chosen vocations. 'Kat' displayed no magic either, but if one asked those around her (and she heard the whispers often) they said everything she touched in the plant world grew better. Taller trees, more vibrant flowers, fuller shrubs, larger vegetables, and sweeter fruits – it seemed uncanny. She dismissed it all and believed it stemmed from just paying proper attention; how much water and when, keeping out competing weeds, protection from frost or too much sun. She knew it wasn't magic, just care and knowledge...

Her husband would occasionally tease her about her mother's bread and pies being <u>too</u> good and her father's works having uncanny resemblances to real figures...in response to which she always laughed and said, 'Practice makes better!'

On this morning the smell that reached her first was fresh bread. The first view, though the sun was in it, was marred by shadows in front of it...

High in the sky, but descending rapidly, were dozens of dragons, their myriad colors like the banners of an army taking the field, or so Kathryn supposed it would look. There were so many colors she did not know if she should sound an alarm or call together a welcoming committee – she had never heard of this many different types of dragons acting together as a group.

In the end she did both. With Icelle away, she knew how to take charge. In the central keep they had devised a simple system of signaling to the guard force as to where a threat was arriving. She went to her southern window and flung out a long, rolled-up red banner. It unfurled quickly, and as it did, she rang a distinctive hand bell outside the window three times.

She was pleased to see the battlement guards

on the outer south wall look up, thin their ranks there, and the rest begin springing to new positions on the north side of the outer perimeter walls.

The corn fields outside the wall were barely finished being planted and the workers were picking out weeds each morning to give the crop its best chance for water. They had reacted to the activity in the keep (the bell), but seeing the signal for threat on the side of the defensive structure that spanned from a rock face to the west to a river on the east indicating it was where they were was confusing. It was a few moments before any thought to look upward, and by then it was too late – the dragons were landing over the top of some them. The now-screaming field workers were even more confused as the threat was now between them and their safe haven...

Most of the workers froze or laid down in the corn rows, petrified. Thankfully, the current Captain of the Guard was fearless and had his men hold fast in place. When the first group landed, Lady Kathryn noted they did so on the wagon track, touching none of the planted fields, outside of the walls, and at the extreme range for any bowman.

What looked like a small tree wearing clothes frantically had the south gate raised and ran pell-mell to the dragons. All but three sat back on their haunches, resting. The lead two were completely unsurprised when the hurtling form dashed between them and jumped – tackling the large silver dragon behind them. Laughter ensued all around amid cries of "Auntie!" and "Ufu! Get. Off!" Eventually the elder dragon pinned the squirming troll to the ground, to the terrified workers' chagrin. After all, if a troll could be subdued so easily, what chance did they stand?!

But the cries went on far too long – and were punctuated by peals of laughter. She was tickling him.

A look back from the largest dragon, a golden male, and the tickling (and therefore laughter) stopped. Argenta released Ufu and when he stood up, she scooped him up by snaking down her long neck and flipping him backward over her head. Fortunately, trolls are quite durable, and he let out another squeal of delight when he found himself riding back to his gate on a dragon!

Argenta's solo parade masked the transformations going on behind her. When she arrived at the short drawbridge, she knelt on one front knee and leaned, allowing the joyous troll to hop down and shout up to the ramparts above, "These friends! Archers back to regular stations! Lieutenants come introduce!

Escort Lady!"

The parade of (now) elves was a cacophony of color. Their complexions and clothing all matched, most in robes or cloaks covering what looked like chain or ring mail, but a few had hauberks and bracers and greaves that were merely densely stacked layers of their own scales. Many of the guards' jaws dropped not at the beauty of the women, which was amazing, but at the flawless functionality of their armor.

There were weapons as well, one large old black dragon carried his sword across his back in his elf form at full size. The hilt was within his reach above his head over his left shoulder, the tip near his right ankle.

One of the larger gatemen, staring longingly at it as he passed, not noticing Argenta's brief nudity as she also transformed, said, "That's lovely, that is!" The silvery female (now) elf shimmered as she passed, saying, "Well. Less noticed than a sword." She snorted and said, "Humans..." and flounced after her sister with an exaggerated wiggle.

The guard, both single and <u>not</u> stupid, called after her, "Apologies Miss! The sword is fantastic, but still not as grand as you!"

Argenta looked back at him and smiled, remembering his face.

The guard turned back to close the gate, and Argenta turned away in time to meet Lady Kathryn welcoming her new guests.

The Lady of the Castle gave a quick curtsey, saying, "High Priest, Priestess, welcome to you and yours, as always."

Aurelius took her hand and his wife's at once and said a quick internal prayer of blessing, opening his eyes to see relief and peace in their eyes.

Ariene said, "Kat, don't worry about us. We are dealing with Auron's loss as best we can. We are all recently well fed, too, so fret not about being a surprised hostess of guests with extra-large appetites! We need to start preparing the site of the alien mage's departure to attempt to track him. Has Plumley arrived yet?"

Lady Kathryn's surprised look answered that question.

"Well," said Ariene, "if not I am sure he will arrive soon, perhaps with Rrahmus. We sent him to Fallon's some time ago to assist the Arch Mage with the proper spell research."

"Icelle and the boys also went to Fallon's just recently, I expect them back any day now," Kat replied. "For now, let's make arrangements for your group – we have improved the lower level, it has room for up to twelve full-size dragons to each have their own accommodation."

"Really!" said Argenta, pushing to the front, "we so rarely get to stretch out and sleep well away from home! That's great news!"

"Oh! Lady Argenta! Welcome to you too! Yes," Kathryn nodded, "Rrahmus and Fallon were insistent – they said it would likely prevent any repeat of the takeover at Rose Castle..."

Aurelius regarded her grimly. Silence reigned over all present until he spoke.

"Indeed, we were caught, unaware of a complete shift in behavior, motive and method – and altered intentions. Fortunately, it was fraught with internal ulterior motives on the part of many of the actors that were in our favor. Had it not, you would likely be hosting a different group than stands before you now." His face brightened and he continued, "Your family all acquitted themselves well in the aftermath, though. I heard you helped refine some defenses for the Witch Queen personally?"

Lady Kathryn demurred, lowering her head slightly, "We all do what we can..." she began.

"...according to our talents," finished Argenta,

her smile wide enough to reflect some sparkle onto the nearby walls in the morning sun. "The elves need to hear more humans echo those words..."

All of the dragons chuckled politely at that, but only Ariene spoke.

"Lead on, Lady of the Castle, thank you for your hospitality. I'm sorry to say that we intend to forward it with violence, if we can, against more of your kind who don't share your values."

As they followed Kathryn's guard into the second compound, Argenta hung back, as her hair would not allow her to move. Finally she turned around, knowing the cause. A desperate troll was holding it.

"Lady Argenta, please, where Sean?" She could have sworn some sap was welling up in the corner of the little tree-man's eyes.

***

Chapter 41

Pixie Resettlement

When she reached her chamber, she entered without any of her escort. Ubu pulled her back by her shoulder and stepped into the doorframe, sniffing.

Queen Hazelmoon heard the gravelly voice before being able to pick out the slight form sitting just inside her only windowsill. It said, "C'mere, lad! How are ya?!"

Ubu bounded in, plucking the slight form up under the armpits, studiously avoiding the wings, and spun a full circle and a half, setting the tiny winged man at the Queen's feet.

The pixie turned around and said, "H'lo, lass. Being Queen suits you," said Jobalm.

"Oh!" she said excitedly, "Are you stopping here on your way to Icelle's? How large of a group? Have you eaten? I can reopen the kitchen..."

"Mistress Toadscream, I am alone, at least for now. I left our gathering a little ahead of the rest. I intended to go home and see what I could do, but I realized I just don't want to. I thought, 'I'll go see if the witches can help me.' You see, my grandson doesn't have a home. Not a real one. And his best friend is an elf with no real home either. Their parents are all dead, though one can still walk and talk, at least in the dark..." They both chuckled at that.

"I see your dilemma. Would you like a new start? Inside the Forest perhaps?" asked Hazelmoon.

"And close to the Traders' main burrow too, I think. He needs to embrace both sides of his heritage," said the old pixie.

The Queen looked at Ubu and said, "The trolls all call him 'Tiny Cousin'. They think he has troll feet with dog claws," she smiled.

"They may be right! Who knows? Anyway, by the northwest corner of your Forest, along the river, there's some likely woods I think..." He looked up at her, cocking his head a little to one side.

She hesitated, knowing what he was asking. "By my old village you mean..."

Nodding, he said, "Slawhit and I agree with Aurelius that we need to stop hiding. We need to be open and involved, spread out more into the realms of men, especially the non-magical ones. That way we can help them, be more of a positive, supportive influence, show them that magic isn't 'bad' and that they aren't unlucky or persecuted or exploited. I hope it works; it sounds exhausting."

"There are a few here now that just arrived who I believe you know. You should see them before they sleep, they leave for Yeomring Castle tomorrow, and Icelle Yeomring is with them."

"I will," said Jobalm, "and you should stop leaving your windows open and unattended."

***

Jobalm left to go see his friends in Queen Hazelmoon's dining hall. The Queen went to check on Pill.

Corvin Von Hart, Sugarplum and Brine Drake had been taking turns staying with Pill Von Ferret every minute of every day. Brine was off getting some food, but only Plumley the Purple Dragon was in the room she had provided for him. It seemed to Hazelmoon that the nephew of the Elvish Arch Mage was too pale. She said as much. Corvin, it seemed had been outside the window in the night air on the roof. He heard her and came inside.

"I was worried about this," he said." I can't tell if he has internal injuries. We need an advanced healer…" He moved to the bedside and spoke in a commanding voice that he had learned came with his disease, "Pill! Wake up!"

He knew that he had broken through, but all that came of it was a feminine shout, that seemed to emit from Pill's eye, "You're Killing Him!"

Corvin looked to the Queen and said, "We can't wait."

Hazelmoon looked at Plumley, said, "Little Dragon, I need you to go to Icelle's. Find the priest healer Myron. Bring him back here. As fast as only you can."

The purple clad elf that jumped back out through the window Corvin had come in had a tail before he was all the way outside and all they heard was wings beating faster and faster as he sped away.

***

Chapter 42

What the Heck are Those

Eyes like alpine lakes at spring thaw.

Glistening around the edges with arctic white centers.

Teeth like the ribs of a large carcass in the desert.

The ends worn to sharp jagged points bent inward.

Layers of fur like saw grass over matted wool.

Rough and sharp, overly dense and horrid smelling.

Claws like freshly scraped late summer antlers.

Sharp ragged and bloody, bits of flesh still hanging.

Hunter turned to say something to his companions only to find them as wide-eyed as he was and one small hand over his mouth and a tiny female head shaking form side to side indicating he probably should not make a sound. He turned back to the view below. He did not have to wait long to understand the admonition to be silent. The creature he had observed had not moved, though its breath produced a continuous cloud of hot steam into the mountain air. When a similar cloud invaded his nostrils from directly below him, he recognized the fetid stench of rotten meat all to readily from his time in King Chares' army's field healing tents. The smell was so like that of his tent full of men and limbs that were formerly part of one body that it hit him like a wave of nausea, disgust and futility. It had not been there seconds ago, though he had remained perched above his overlooking ledge for several minutes. 'There must be a cave entrance underneath me,' he thought.

There was still snow up this high, a brief mountain pass crossing that his little friends told him was the shortest route to where he was heading. The wind was in their favor, coming up from the valley floor below them, running from the sun that was rising above the ridgeline across from them. It was not in favor of the large deer that ambled into view.

While the creature he had first seen remained motionless, the cloud of steam assaulting him from below split into two clouds and moved to his right and left, slowly, silently. In his peripheral vision to both sides two more of the nightmarish things appeared, but where the first had been about his own size, by Hunter's reckoning these were at least fully two heads taller than himself, maybe more.

The large buck, with antlers as long as Hunter's arms, kept coming closer. When it reached the level of the two creatures to its sides, the center one exhaled sharply, loudly, as if in challenge. The deer jerked its head upright and 'huffed' in return, looking for its competition. In that moment, the two side observers struck so fast that it was a blur and so hard that the noise was like a war hammer striking a leather-clad rib cage (which sound Hunter also knew well).

The creature to the right simultaneously smashed the base of the deer's spine with its left arm and severed the animal's left rear heel tendon with the claws of its right, a move intended to disable the prey from getting away. The creature to the left plunged both sets of its claws directly into the deer's hide, its right straight into the neck above the shoulder, its left up under the right front leg into the hollow, smashing bones and tendons and reaching for the heart.

Its attention now off of the threat to its front, the deer did not see the leaping form coming until the center creature arrived in front of its face, one enormous hand clamping onto each antler. The deer was then disemboweled and had its throat cut, unable to run, kick, bite or even just fall over to bleed out. Its eyes went wide, then glazed over, still staring at the nightmare baring its teeth in a devilish, and hungry, grin.

Switching hands to the opposite antlers, the center monster slung the deer over its back and turned around in one quick movement and strode straight toward Hunter and directly into the cave below his hiding spot, its two fellows following. Hunter noted that the carrier was female, the followers were male, and she was definitely in charge. He made a note of it for any future potential encounters, while hoping there would be none…

And then his diminutive companions were desperately pulling on him to leave. They moved swiftly, but not as fast as possible, taking care to make no sound beyond soft footfalls on rocks and bare ground. Finally, after at least a league (to his reckoning) out of their way, Hunter spoke.

"What in the whole of Metaerie were those … those things?!"

Without slowing down, all eyes glanced at Regor, who, noticing their attention, scowled. After some raised eyebrows from his female leader, the miniature harbinger of constant doom said, "Oh, all right…"

Apparently their side trip was over as they headed down into a ravine leading into the valley they had been paralleling to avoid the scary things they'd just left behind. As they descended Regor began to speak.

"Back when Metaerie was formed some creatures came along for the ride unexpectedly from the old world. What you just saw was a hybrid of an inarticulate distant human relative and an also largely inarticulate distant white dragon cousin. Both were savagely fierce, voracious killers and eaters, and completely indiscriminate in their choices of food supply. The combination is, as you saw, deadly. Fortunately for most of us they cannot abide warmth, and their natural white to gray coloring is perfect camouflage for snowy peaks and rocky caves so they just don't leave it. The lack of prey in these areas keeps their numbers low, and they don't seem to have many offspring, though they live in family groups. No one really knows what they call themselves, or even if they call themselves anything. They are known to us as the Sarkani Kulu.

Regor didn't notice Hunter's quizzical look boring into the back of his head. He was too busy shaking his head in chagrin at Chestnut and Barger bounding from rock to rock down the side of the creek they were following, quietly but with huge grins on their childish faces, enjoying themselves immensely. Based on a few glances from Barger, some of it was quite specifically at Regor's expense. A few hours later in the afternoon sun they finally descended into the river valley that the creek fed into below them. There were several creeks entering the river within less than half a league at this point, most rather noisily via channels through large boulders.

Needing to cross to the wagon track they could see on the other side, they headed toward a wide, rocky shallow area. "No reason for all of us to get wet!" said Hunter, scooping his three fellow travelers up. He plopped the boys on his shoulders and put Chestnut behind his head. She wanted to see, so she stood up, one foot on either side of his neck and holding locks of his hair in each fist, peering over the top of Hunter's head. Barger sat comfortably, while Regor hung on like he feared falling to his death (which he did).

Each commented on the view. From his right Hunter heard, "This is great! It's like having your own walking tree for a goat!" From above, "I can see so much farther from up here!" And from his left, "Slow down! I'm losing my grip! This was not a good idea! We're going to die!" Though the stifled laughter let Regor know his advice was being ignored, his doomspeak continued, unwavering...

The multi-layered chatter all around his head conspired with the chuckling of the shallow water running over the wide gravel bar where Hunter had chosen to ford the river and left them all equally surprised by the attack.

The impact came from their right and knocked the entire foursome sideways and upstream. As Barger was only resting on Hunter's right shoulder, he became separated from the rest and dropped lightly onto his feet in the shallow water that came up to his thighs. Turning to his left, the view was … confusing.

The large human had disappeared into the deeper pool he had been walking next to. Of Regor there was no sign, no doubt still clinging even more desperately to Hunter's shoulder underwater. Chestnut had flown from the man's shoulders as if catapulted when his tall frame pivoted downward after being struck and was lying, apparently unconscious, on a boulder in the middle of the river, blood pooling by her head.

The cause made Barger somewhat incredulous. It looked like the biggest badger he had ever seen was doing a handstand in the deep pool upstream. His tiny pot of rage boiled over in an instant. Hunter would have been amazed to see the counterattack; a tiny man shorter than his knees was running so fast that after a few steps he was literally running on the surface of the river. Leading with his sword (the blade the size of Hunter's finger) and screaming louder than a wounded wild pig, Barger saw the upside down badger's eyes narrow in surprise at its approaching threat, but too late to avoid the rush.

Unfortunately for the badger, its softest, most vulnerable underbelly was directly exposed to the little weapon and its wielder. Its tip angled upward and the enraged miniature swordsman launched it to just above the upside-down rodent's sternum, skewering its fur, stomach and one kidney prior to embedding in its spine. The impact jarred the tiny man's hands loose from the handle and the over-sized rodent into the deeper part of the pool beyond Hunter, who stood up immediately. Chestnut was still on the rock she had landed on, but was awake now. Barger grabbed ahold of Hunter's right boot top to right himself. Regor was still missing.

Before Hunter could ask Chestnut if she was okay or Barger what happened, the pool next to him roiled and bubbled with blood and a badger's head appeared, its mouth locked onto a tiny arm while a second, matching, arm and hand balled into a fist was pounding the creature in the eyes so fast that it was a blur. The effect was a successful release – Regor was flung at Hunter's knees and the badger loped back downstream to the gravel bar. As Hunter scooped up Regor and Barger he turned in time to see the large rodent jump over the downstream falls, a knife handle protruding from its belly, a trail of blood marking its path in the water.

A short while later as they sat in front of the rock face next to the wagon track drying their clothes and cleaning a few cuts on Regor's arm, the little group heard the approach of a large group of travelers.

***

Chapter 43

Pill is Still Broken

Brine had been being laughingly interrogated about his 'adventures with the froggy-folk' by Jobalm and eating when one of Hazelmoon's mages appeared to tell them of her discourse with what they assumed was the goddess. The mage (Brine could not tell any of them apart) was not an elaborative speaker, but when he relayed that a voice from Pill's eye said, 'You're killing him!', Brine bolted to go see his friend and mentor.

***

Now he stared at his teacher, looking like a blond-haired, pointy-eared rag doll that had endured multiple generations of little tomboy elf-girl daydream adventures – he was limp, barely breathing, rather rough and blurry around the edges. The last part may have been Brine's cloudy vision.

***

Jobalm had also disappeared when Brine did, except literally. Fallon had not noticed as he was sprinting after his dead friend's son the dwarf to find out what had changed with Pill, another dead friend's

341

son, who had seemed stable enough on their way here. He was about to enter behind Brine when a form coalesced in front of him. Stopping short to avoid smashing into Pill's father, the second dead friend, he said, "Corvin, can you see if he's okay?!"

The golden-eyed vampire did not turn around. "I am still young with regard to my 'extra' senses. He has warm, flowing blood, that I know. Mortalya summoned me, said he is bleeding inside somewhere, showed me how to find it – don't ask how..."

Brine heard the conversation, reflected that it was odd that the troll, Udu, did not react to the appearance of a vampire, and wailed, "He's alive! How do we fix him?!"

Corvin's hand on his shoulder, meant to be at least comforting if not actually reassuring, was so cold that Brine shivered. "I see a darker spot in his body, where the blood is pooling, cooler than the rest. The junction is between his spine and the back of his heart. The ogre's blow must have made his bones cut or tear something nearby. I can't fix it. Even if we cut him open and stopped that bleeding, the damage created would likely kill him anyway. We need a real healer. My only option would be to bite him, and I don't think he wants that..."

Fallon's eyebrows went up. "If we run out of other options, maybe there are worse things…"

As the ramifications of their words penetrated Brine's emotionally charged dwarven brain, he was prevented from responding due to two familiar forms tumbling into the room through the open window.

'Sugarplum' was a one dragon show of color, in stark contrast to Myron's dark brown robe and matching sandals. The tall, gangly priest tumbled off of Plumley's dragon back – disappeared as he changed to elf-form as he hit the floor, and Myron struck Brine squarely, avoiding hitting the wall behind the dwarf. Brine was not as lucky…

Many looks were exchanged in an instant, but no words were spoken.

Myron sprang to the bed, laying one hand on the elven thief's forehead, the other below his ribcage on the front of his torso. After a silent moment in the room, he said, "Oh, my."

Before anyone could question him, he said, "Corvin, stay back, what will help him might actually hurt you…"

Putting his hands up under Pill's armpits, Myron started making circles with his thumbs, then clenched both hands in his friend's loose skin of his upper back.

343

Pill's eyes and mouth opened in a gasp, he coughed once, then fell back, still unconscious.

Corvin said softly, "The bleeding is stopped, I believe."

Myron put the back of his hand on the younger, living, elf's forehead and said, "It's not enough. There's too much blood loose in his body. I don't know how to remove it, and it will harden and slowly destroy some of his organs. We need a different type of healing for that…"

The roar outside was deafening. Everyone reached for weapons except Udu and Plumley. And Pill.

"Sugarplum! Bring him to me!" came a lower register pitched but distinctly female voice.

The purply elf said, "That's Sylvia. We had better do as she says…"

Fallon, Myron, Corvin and Brine each lifted a corner of the pallet bed Pill laid on and carried it to the nearest exit. The large silver dragon that awaited them said, "Tie the whole thing to my back! I am taking him to my parents!"

Once they had secured him to her, she launched without a word.

Plumley had followed them and said to Myron, "I'm sorry, I have no lift left for now. I cannot return you right away, I'm spent."

The rough-looking cleric saw the despondence in his summoner's demeanor. Just as Queen Hazelmoon arrived, he said, "We all have our limitations. I don't like mine either."

***

Chapter 44

Hunter's NEW New Friends

The group that appeared was not what Hunter expected at all. First and foremost, they were moving too fast. Secondly, their feet were not touching the ground... The buzzing in his head that he had put down to a possible head injury was in fact a dozen pairs of wings moving as quickly as those of hummingbirds. Though only one was much bigger than his current companions, they all drew up short, stopping at the sight of the wet and bedraggled caravan of one (and some riders on his shoulders).

"Oh, great!" said Regor in his nasally, whiny voice, full of sarcasm. "Pixies. They'll get us killed. Or at least blamed for their mischief. Or..."

"Regor! Stop!" said Chestnut. Uncharacteristically, he did actually stop.

"Well," said the leader, dropping to land a few (human) paces to Hunter's front, "would you look at that? I didn't know any of you renegades were still alive! How wonderful."

Before the rest could even absorb both the implication and the insult, little Chestnut was on the ground in a flash with a finger in the pixie's surprised face, saying, firmly but not shouting, "You know <u>what</u> we are, and your shame is not a regret for <u>us</u>. But you have no idea <u>who</u> we are, so … BE NICE OR BE GONE!"

The Patchy and Splotchy males moved not a muscle, waiting. The pixies behind the speaker were also silent, landing like feathers, even the hum of their wings was gone before he responded.

Hunter tensed, feeling protective of the tiny girl, even if her actual protectors did not seem to. The pixie looked like one of the dodgy, half-starved cats that had hung around his healing tent after a battle, glowing eyes in the torch or fire light reflecting raw hunger. This one was <u>not</u> a tamed beast…

"Alright little one. I respect your honesty. Now hear mine: I don't regret your existence. By the goddess, I don't regret <u>anything</u>. But I'm not nice to anyone – ever – so I'll do as you say and be on my way."

And true to his word, he started flying off along his original route, following the river, without another glance at any of them.

Chestnut was left pointing at nothing, her face puzzled, until the other pixies approached. The one in front, a pudgy redhead with an enormous smile and flashing blue eyes above a white robe and brown leather sandals and matching belt, said laughingly, "Ignore him – he's just cross all the time. Are you okay? Why are you all wet?"

Even Chestnut had to laugh at the bubbly winged ambassador of amiability. After his dour companion he was quite pleasant!

"We are taking this poor lost human home. We found him in our mountains. He was separated from his host after a battle and spent the winter wandering."

The pixie, who looked like a candle partially melted in the sun and bowed out in the middle, spoke from under the flaming wick of his hair, saying, "What's your name young man? Where are you from?"

"It's Hunter," said Hunter, "and I grew up just east of the Witches' Forest."

Another voice from further back in the pack of pixies spoke, "But you don't believe that is where you are from, do you?"

The pixies parted and a larger form walked toward them. Regor's eyes were immediately drawn to the feet. Under a grayish, nondescript robe, rather than tiny shoes or boots, the speaker wore…fur. And claws. They looked like … dog paws.

It spoke again, "Do you believe it?"

The young man wilted like tall grass too near a

fire. "No. I was raised by a horrible family that treated me awfully and I did not look, sound or act like any of them."

"Ah!" said the too-tall pixie with dog feet. "Now there is the truth. Well, we draw near to an important gathering of powerful users of magic and seekers of truth – if you come with us, I can see if they will help you too. That is, if your escorts are willing?"

Chestnut walked up to the pawed-pixie and grasped his hand. "Oh!" she said, "You're something new! I'm Chestnut." Her smile was child-like and infectious.

"And I am FLAW. Delighted to meet you," he said. To Hunter he said, "You'll have to wear my robe and carry me on your back to keep up." As he said it, he removed the robe, revealing a kaleidoscope of clothing colors – Hunter's eyes could barely 'keep up'…

"What?" was all he said.

"The robe," said Flaw, "it lets you fly!"

"Ah! Ok," Hunter replied to the scramble of color, taking the proffered robe and donning it.

While he was experimenting with how the robe worked, the redhead said to Chestnut and her friends, "We can carry you folks too, if you like? Or you can go home if you want?"

The largest of the three finally spoke, "Chestnut," he said, "we go where you go." Regor nodded in vehement agreement.

***

The trip was exciting, exhilarating, and unexpectedly exhausting. The multitude of ways Hunter had to position, hold, tense and exert his body to control his flight, especially with Flaw on his back, required far greater effort than he had anticipated. He was <u>tired</u>!

Thus it was that when they crested a stony-cliff ridge overlooking a large fortress of nested square walls being aerially patrolled by several dragons he dove headfirst to the ground, accidentally avoiding smashing his head on the rocks by putting his hands down to break his fall which actually directed the robe to right itself, slowing, and letting him drop gently to the ground, feet first.

Flaw was nowhere to be seen...

Hunter was joined by the two lead pixies, Walhe and Ohrb. The former looked at Hunter and said out of the corner of his mouth, "Y'alright?"

Hunter, nodding hesitantly, heard Ohrb say, "He's fine, just spooked, that was a pretty abrupt landing..."

The young healer turned to Ohrb to say it wasn't the landing that had spooked him, when he saw the redhead leaning over a quivering, coalescing form – Flaw had been invisible!

The rest of the pixies kept flying, landing on a rooftop of the central tower below them. Hunter could see them talking to what looked like a tall, pale-haired woman.

And then he bolted to hide behind a large rock outcropping, having seen the woman turn into an enormous, familiar-looking silver dragon. Not that he could have escaped if he had tried, but she arrived next to him in mere seconds.

Her voice was both metallic <u>and</u> melodic to his ears. She said, "I take it you've seen dragons before," in a matter-of-fact observation. "So – what did someone like me do to someone like you...?"

***

As he regained consciousness, Hunter startled violently. Looking around the unfamiliar room he was greeted by familiar faces, save one. That one was a female elf with pale hair and bright blue eyes who smiled kindly when they met his. He shrank from her in fear, but with nowhere to go, and hearing her say, "What's wrong? Are you ill?" calmed himself.

Hunter said to her, "You're a dragon!"

Her look of concern softened back to kindness as she said, "Yes, I am. But how did you know?"

"I thought you were going to roast me alive earlier!" he said.

"Interesting. This is the first time I've ever laid eyes on you!" came her surprised response.

Just then another female elf of similar appearance, but a bit older than the first, walked into the room. The younger one asked, "Aunt Argie, did you try to cook this boy?"

The other answered, "Why no, sweetheart, at least, not yet…"

The room spun a little until Hunter realized that she was teasing, baiting him. He had closed his eyes, and opening them now he saw them both looking down at him with a third, much smaller, female face between them. That one said, "Get up, silly, no one's going to eat you! I'm the smallest thing around here, and if anyone is at risk of being a snack, it's me!"

All three females laughed at that. He sighed.

The older elf-dragon said, "From your reaction, I take it you had a negative experience with a dragon…"

"Negative?! How about terrifying?! We were attacked in the middle of the night, hundreds killed, dying like dry logs in a bonfire, except running and screaming and pleading for help!"

The younger elf-dragon said, "And you were their healer…" The silence that followed was deafening.

He finally said, "I didn't even like them… I disagreed with what they were doing, they had no real value or respect for life, and … if I failed? Their demented priests just raised up the dead as zombies or skeletons the next day anyway. I would see men who died holding my hand crying, or screaming during an amputation after a battle, going to fight again by the following sunrise, their limbs moving, but their eyes lifeless. It was awful. One of the worst things was when the leaders made us go forward each morning to watch the initial attack. They took great delight in seeing the zombies raised from their victims leading the vanguard into their former families, friends and neighbors. They toasted each other at night, boasting of the cries of anguish they had created. They celebrated the anguish of people who had not wronged them in <u>any way</u>." As he recalled his own anger and anguish, he relived it, getting angry all over again, sitting up a little, then remembering who he was talking to, he quieted down and laid back.

He continued with, "To be fair, it is what they

were doing when they died. They were toasting, boasting … and then roasting. Like pigs put too close to the flames catching fire, I could smell the searing flesh, hear the fat sizzle and pop, see the hair sparkle like greased kindling… and hear the screams. I still hear the screams…"

Unused to hearing directly from a survivor of their aerial attacks of flying and flaming, Argenta and Sylvia exchanged anguished looks of their own.

"Young man," said Argenta, "I am so sorry to cause you distress. You seem very caring and sincere and I applaud that. I can't help but think you did not belong with those people… it saddens me to wonder how many men just like you we may have killed, not knowing that they were not bad people, but perhaps just swept up in the group by one affiliation or another." He could see her crying, and when one of the tears fell to the floor it tinkled like a piece of silver jewelry on the stones.

The sound grew louder, making him turn his head, seeing Sylvia's cheeks covered in tears. She said, "I was there, at that raid that night. We had been attacked that afternoon and tracked down the camps. It never occurred to me that there might be some among you that did not hate me, that some in your number might not want me dead. I am so sorry..."

Hunter the Healer couldn't stand it. Though he knew they were dragons, capable of crushing, shredding, torching or even eating him in an instant on a logical level, what he saw, and felt, on an emotional level was two good and caring females, crying over <u>his</u> feelings.

He reached out and grasped one hand of each of them. Taking one long calming breath in and out, he let his calm flow into them, his peace of both mind and body moving throughout theirs, finding little wounds, rough edges, of body and brain, smoothing and soothing them in just a few moments.

Chestnut jumped on him and hugged him around his neck, and he could tell from the warm wet feeling under his beard that she was crying too. And then none of them were.

He let go of the elf-dragons' hands, lifted little Chestnut up in front of him to look her in the eyes and told her, "It's okay little friend, I left the bad men behind. I knew I didn't belong anyway, and they were horrible people, and I couldn't bear to see any of the dead ones marching off to fight again after that."

Sylvia's shock wore off first. "Did you just <u>heal</u> us? Or charm us...? Or ... I don't know what?"

Argenta answered, "You're a witch-healer, a natural. Did you train as well? You must have, I think, to hide it, or your former companions would have killed you themselves. Did the rest of your family share in this dilemma?"

He set the tiny Chestnut down, noting her confused expression. "In fact, I did not resemble the rest of my family in any way, appearance or actions. If I had to guess, I was at best a foundling, at worst perhaps kidnapped. I'll probably never know now, as I'm fairly certain that they're all dead, at the hands of you lot. To be clear, I don't blame you, and I will try to move on from my ill thoughts about it… And, yes, I can naturally 'heal' people – some animals too."

Sylvia asked, "Are there many more like you? Natural healers? I am a priestess myself, like my mother, but we must commune with our deity in prayer daily to do what we do, and our abilities are finite…"

Hunter waited for her to finally trail off, not interrupting, before he answered her question. "I have no idea if there are others. There definitely were not any more like me with King Chares' army, that's for sure."

Sylvia said, "When you feel up to it, I have a very good friend who may need someone just like you

357

to save his life... Just know that he also was part of that night raid a year ago. I need him alive, so if you say 'no', I will understand, but I won't let any further harm come to him... For now, we'll let you rest."

Sylvia and Argent left. Chestnut laid down between his left arm and his side, head on his shoulder.

Hunter's thoughts were a jumble, but soon he was asleep.

***

Chapter 45

Plumley gets started

It was officially the strangest group that the youngest present had ever seen.

Brine Drake was superfluous to this occasion, or so he thought anyway. Dragons, pixies, First Men, a King, a Queen, Lords and Ladies, witches, warlocks, and trolls, oh my. Plus one dwarf and a ... whatever Flaw was.

Standing in what seemed to him to be a random spot in a cornfield (though he knew better), they were all staring at probably the shyest creature he knew. Poor Plumley's purple scales rippled with reflected gold off of his wings from the sun when he moved, dazzling the onlookers just enough to keep his eyes hidden. The slightly-built dragon circled the whole group at least three times then began to spiral inward.

A flicker of flame got all of their attention. It sprang into being, not exactly in the center of where the purple dragon looped, and Plumley adjusted his perimeter accordingly. The flame was strangely omnidirectional, had several points or tips, pointing in all directions, in three dimensions, like an actual ball made of flame. Unlike most magical balls of fire, it was nowhere in the color spectrum between yellow and red or any shade of orange in between. This ball was a deep, dark, ocean-at-night blue. As Plumley worked his circuitous way closer it got brighter.

Brine, as usual, was dying to ask why, but his normal information source for such things was still unconscious.

***

Chapter 46

He's Still in There

It was the longest 'conversation' he had ever had with the goddess, of that he was certain. They had each laughed back and forth at what the other had to say. She was pleasant, her voice melodic and almost musical. It felt like they were flirting in a tavern, the words gone by flying out of his head as soon as they were spoken. There was an underlying wrongness in the ease of their patter, but he could not focus long enough for it to matter. He lost all track of time, until he heard his name. It sounded like his father, but that was impossible.

"Pill! Wake up!" He stopped engaging with the voice in his head briefly, then continued. But then it seemed his conversation was interrupted. His father was telling the goddess that his boy needed to come home. She agreed, but he declined – he was enjoying himself. Then it was just the two of them for a long time. She never really came into focus now. Instead she seemed to cycle through different versions of every winged creature he had ever seen.

He felt eventually as if he had imbibed a bit too

much of something, though he didn't remember having anything to drink. His vision was darker, too, and had a pinkish tinge to it. She ignored him for a bit again, yelling at another girl, but then she was back, and he felt much better, his vision was much clearer.

And then he jumped – the voice that made him start was another woman yet, louder than all of the others combined, as if her voice were magically enhanced. It sounded sort of familiar, but not really. The goddess ignored it, so he did too.

A while later the goddess spoke with yet another female. He wondered if she had any male friends other than him? Unlike the others, this one talked <u>to</u> him. Unlike before, though, this was quite one-sided – he could not respond.

'Hold still little elf, this might hurt a bit...' He screamed. He felt like his entire body was on fire, only on the inside! Every blood vessel felt like someone had boiled the blood in a cauldron and put it into his body all at once. And then a hand was squeezing his heart, and another his brain. He was definitely immobilized, and not by choice, he just didn't know why, or by whom.

When he calmed down, he realized that his pains were all gone, but so was the goddess.

Chapter 47

Plumley's Results

The ball of blue flame continued to get brighter as the purple dragon circled closer. Then he launched into flight, following the same circle he had walked and then ran, now tighter, smaller, faster, and then... nothing. He disappeared, but the blue ball of flame did not. It got brighter, then seemed to freeze, as did everyone watching.

Ariene spoke first. "Sugarplum?" she called softly.

It was Queen Hazelmoon, slowly turning in a circle of her own, who noticed the line of broken corn rows, the small earthen berms underline outside his initial circle, leaving a straight line through several of them, leading away from the blue ball of flame. She ran to where it ended, and was joined immediately by several pixies. A chubby redhead said, "Plumley? You okay?"

The small purple dragon came into the Witch Queen's vision again, shaking his head like a wet dog, only slower. "My first step is done," he said. "It won't fade now until I use it."

Aurelius, in elf form, said, "Well done

Sugarplum. Now we need some magical help and preparation to continue."

To Icelle and Kathryn he said, "We need to keep your people away from this until we can use it. We will guard it, but not in dragon form, in case we are observed. Will you please spread the word that it is dragon magic gone wrong and that it could kill them if they get too close? That should help."

Fallon interjected, "When the purple one there recovers, we need him to go find Rrahm. I'm not sure anyone else is up for this."

The old gold dragon turned sad eyes toward the fighter not one-tenth his age and said, "Truly you remind me of our centuries of failures young friend. We came here to avoid the outcome of our behavior and proceeded to just duplicate it. I had high hopes for Auron to cut his teeth fighting, then learn magic from the best. We dragons have not had an Arch Mage of our own in an age, and we have been far too removed from our descendants." Meeting Slawhit's and Jobalm's eyes in turn, and then his mate's, he said, softly to Ariene, "We must start to be examples of not just power and might, but of goodness and right. As I recall, young Master Fallon here was told not too long ago that symbols have to be seen – well, so do examples."

To Fallon he said, "I hope he is already enroute – with as many pixies and dragons as we have spread about we could have either half a dozen new wars or species by next year. Or both!"

Chapter 48

Heck of a Wakeup Call

The large room was bare stone except for the wooden table and a few buckets, open to the chill night air. Normally used for hanging meat underground, the windows were up high, the curtains open. The starlight was obscured by the torches burning brightly all around just under and in between each window.

All Hunter knew about the elf before him was that a whole lot of powerful beings from many different races wanted him to live.

When he had described to the rough-looking human priest named Myron how he had attempted something similar before, the man had looked horrified. When he was asked why he had tried it, he had honestly answered, "Because they were all going to die and be raised as undead eventually anyway, it literally couldn't hurt to try."

Then the arrival of another mage and his family made the task much easier.

"The trick," he told them, "is to use enough heat without burning him to death." That had drawn more horrified expressions from many of the highly influential people. And several dragons. It was that thought that set him on his path.

**

A huge male gold dragon held an iron needle that was at least a rod long pointed downward at Pill's torso. Myeer, wearing a large pointy hat very similar to Rrahmus', had his hands above the elven thief's head and stomach. Corvin held a round, spiral-bladed dagger under Pill's back, where Myeer held him, suspended in the air, not above but rather beside the table. Tara, a cute-as-a-button woodland witch, now Myeer's wife, stood at Pill's head, her hands on his lower ribs on both sides of his sternum.

Several more humans, dragons and pixies surrounded them, looking on with great interest.

Hunter grasped the bottom of the long needle and plunged it into Pill's body cavity, seeing in his mind the thickest section of coagulating blood and letting the tip of the needle rest in the middle of it. He removed his hands, nodding to the dragon.

Aurick had been chosen from those present among the dragons as the youngest, largest male, with the greatest capacity for extended, controlled flame. Gripping the needle with his impervious-to-fire claws, he inhaled deeply, then blew gently. A narrow, focused, blue flame began to strike the end of the needle. The iron began to grow hot, eventually glowing a cherry red along its entire length.

Tara began to chant, quietly, and Pill's skin started to turn white radiating outward from her hands.

Hunter had his hands down on Pill's body too now, the outside edges of his palms downward. They became the dividing line between the blazing heat and the freezing cold on the unconscious elf's skin. Hunter looked at Corvin, saying, "It will happen quickly now, be ready!"

The vampire could see the loose blood inside his son start to brighten, to liquefy, getting thin and flowing freely. While Hunter controlled the conflicting heat and cold from damaging Pill outwardly, Corvin stabbed his boy in the back, carefully avoiding damaging anything inside, only poking through skin and cavity wall. His success was instantly visible as blood began to gush out of the wound around the spirals of the dagger blade, much more than should have come from just the wound itself. The bucket below steamed a little in the spring night air from the almost boiling blood striking the cold of the bucket, and all present could smell and taste the iron in the air.

Corvin waited until he saw the dark spots in his

son's body lighten, and tissue around the almost molten needle starting to burn before he said, "Enough! Take it out!"

Aurick pulled upward quickly, reached far out away from the rest of the group, and laid the metal down, still glowing, on the stone floor, a few small sizzles from it contacting the dampness on the stone breaking the silence.

Tara also lifted her hands away, her palms looking like they held snowballs.

Hunter told Corvin calmly, "Remove the dagger, sir, and back up a bit, I don't want to harm you."

Corvin pulled downward on the dagger, dropping it into the bucket, it's tip also seeming to glow red, and backed up, able to see both wounds, front and back, close and knit cleanly, then the internal holes close up as well. Pill looked healthy to him.

Hunter removed his hands and walked around the elf, asking Myeer to "Please put him on the table." Then he laid his hands upon the thief's head briefly. Looking up at them all, he said, "I've done what I can, but his mind is closed to me – what is his full name?"

Corvin said it softly, "Pill Von Ferret."

Aurelius approached, touched Pill's chest and then head and called out, "Lorknowis, please show me how to heal this boy!" A blue glimmer flashed over Pill's whole body. The dragon High Priest said, "He is healthy, but will not awaken. It is as if he is resisting me…"

Corvin said, "He is bound. To the goddess. But not as a worshipper, rather like a high priest would be, and death was cheated…" The vampire reached down and picked up the bucket of Pill's superheated blood, tipped it up and drank deeply from it. In that moment those who could see his eyes saw them swirl, a myriad of red, blue and gold, several times, settling back to gold, but then his very skin seemed to light the room even brighter.

Moving to Pill's side he told Hunter, "Put your hands back on his head. Reach out to him. Call his name."

The young healer did as he was told, and Corvin placed his hands on top of Hunter's. "Mortalya!" he shouted, then to Hunter, "Together," he said, and they called out in unison, "Pill Von Ferret!"

"Now," said Corvin, "Make him say his own name." When the young man began to object, the vampire-elf-father said in a hoarse shout of desperation, "Do it!"

Hunter focused on Pill's thoughts, found him in a conversational mood, and asked, 'Can you tell me your name?'

The thief thought his name, knowing the young healer could understand.

'No,' Hunter tried again, 'Out loud. I am outside of your consciousness.'

The elven thief's mouth opened and said, "I am called Pill Von Ferret." And then he screamed. It was unnerving, loud, long, and primal, the scream of existential fear, knowing certain death is approaching.

Pill sat up on the table, and said, "Oh no. Not again."

***

He was screaming. No, that's not quite right. He was shouting above a horrible cacophony of sounds, mostly the floor shaking, flames crackling and rock breaking...and as his surroundings came into focus in the blackness he pictured a scene that he knew must be a nightmare of his own creation about Auron's death.

The shades of flame he could see must be when his friend had roasted some of the young wyverns. He could see the dragon's corpse blown open in front of him. Pill found himself turning around, seeing a larger dragon-like creature that the thief assumed was the wyvern Krystal and Sean had told him about. And then it ended. He knew it was a dream, but he still wanted to save his friend. He tried to shout, "No! – and then his vision went blank, awash from light that he knew was Auron's gaseous bile igniting, the flames that had incinerated the wyvern but had not saved his friend.

***

He sat up, still yelling, one arm thrust out in warning, palm up … being observed worriedly by several friends and family members and lying in a strange bed.

***

Chapter 49

The Growth of Elvish Nobility

'Division of labor for tasks requiring several different skill sets requires the leader to understand all of the parts in order to properly position and allocate assets to optimal advantage.'

Rrahmus could still hear the echoes of his father's voice lecturing about leadership in the training yard behind the castle. As a boy the Elvish Arch Mage had been quick, agile, and adept with his hands and mind, usually bent on stealing an extra helping of dessert after dinner that he could have just asked for...

The elf's mind had always been difficult for others to identify with, especially his own family. His parents (at least those who he had for his whole life up to now assumed were his parents!) had made sure he could survive – build a shelter, make a weapon, hunt, make fire, forage, even cook, but also to fight.

He wanted to 'slap around' with the other boys, but his father had had other ideas. 'First,' he had said, 'you have to learn to get hit, fall down, and get back up.' Rrahmus' quizzical expression was famous, combining widening his mouth, raising one corner of it and dropping the opposite eyebrow – it oozed obvious sarcasm completely silently.

'Can't I just avoid getting hit at all?' he had asked.

'You can try, of course,' said his father, 'but everyone gets hit eventually, and it's better if the first few at least are in a controlled environment...'

His father had been right of course, but what rambunctious, rebellious adolescent wants to believe that...

So, he learned in spite of himself. He learned where to strike for maximum effect, how to fall and minimize his own risk of damage, to use his and his opponent's weight and momentum to advantage.

When he got hurt his sister was there to patch him up. When he got too cocky his cousins were there to knock him down. It was after a knockdown and a patch-up that he was relegated to the armory while he healed. He followed the smith and his assistant around, helping where he could. Over the next few days he learned two very important things about himself: One, he thought magic was fascinating, and Two, he was a natural at it.

The blacksmith needed to move from task to task, and would tell his assistant (that Rrahmus now knew was a rather accomplished mage) what he needed in advance, like, 'Heat that blade for bending,' or 'Freeze that mold,' and 'Mix that clay,' or 'Stir that oil.' But unlike other assistants around the castle, he didn't actually move much... Instead he had several wands in a bucket, symbols to identify them carved into the ends he held them by that could be seen when they were tips down in the bucket.

The mage would select the appropriate wands for the task then move them to the task, usually with a toss and a point of a finger at the proper target. One type in particular was Rrahmus' favorite – it was a simple two-tined large wooden fork and the mage had several of them. It was used to shoe warhorses, many of which were notoriously contrary. It clamped their foot to be worked on in either up or down mode. Up to receive a shoe or their hoof trimmed and down to keep the horse from leaving in the middle of the process...

Rrahmus had always been quick to observe, to analyze, to mimic, and by the middle of his third day of fetching for the mage he just tried a wand himself – it was for blowing sawdust off of the worktables after the smith worked handle materials for his axes and hammers. It was a bit too successful...

He had selected the correct wand. He held it

377

right, said the right words, but was unaware that the strength of the winds was controlled by the speed and force of the wielder's exhaled breath... He was rather excited to be doing something new (and that he knew he shouldn't be) and when it didn't work right away, his rapid exhale of frustration launched a handful of axe handles off of the work table and out into the yard, tripping a few of those training there.

They assumed, of course, that he had thrown them, and, with his reputation as a bit of a prankster, they rushed to pummel him.

Normally he would have gleefully obliged, but with one arm in a sling, he made a new plan...

Tahmus was the fastest, and he pulled up short, one foot staked to the ground. His sparring partner's left boot caught fire, and their arbitrator was running away with a stick that was normally used to whack dust from hanging rugs repeatedly smacking his bottom as he ran.

Tahmus and the smith were laughing too hard to do anything else. The mage just squinted his eyes at Rrahmus and recalled his wands, telling Rrahmus to 'Take a bucket and quench that lad's boot.'

***

Later, his father and both grandfathers sat with

him out on an upper veranda in the dying light. They had four chairs, a small table, a bucket of chestnuts, a bucket of cold water, four cups and four hammers. They didn't say anything to him, and he dared not speak, knowing better, or so he thought. They all dipped their cups to get some water and began using their hammers to shell and eat some chestnuts. Rrahmus just kept his eyes down.

After a while he grew impatient and looked up... and stared in shock, mouth wide open, watching the hammers smashing down on nuts with no hands holding them! The nuts were jumping out of the bucket on their own as well!

The older elves did not acknowledge his flummoxed expression – no smiles or laughter – just continued to quite nonchalantly open their mouths and catch pieces of chestnut without moving and chew them up. After a few more minutes his grandfathers both stood up, one ruffled his hair and the other patted his back, and they left.

His father said, 'You'll have the chance to spend part of your time in the library with the mages if you like. It's up to you. We've never seen one so young do so much with no training so quickly after just being exposed to practical magic. I will absolutely support you doing it. My father will not, at least publicly, so be prepared for that, and keep this little meeting to yourself. That will be a lifelong test, to not give away other people's secrets. Not all of our people support daily use of magic as normal behavior; in fact, many see it as dangerous. They are mostly those who do not have any aptitude for it, but just because you don't see someone use magic, don't assume they don't know how or are incapable. Do not underestimate anyone. Ever.' He had placed his hand on Rrahmus' shoulder and ended with 'Gift or curse, using it is up to you!' Then he too left the balcony.

Rrahmus watched his father leave, clothed in layers of undergarment, padded leather, overhung by curtains of ring mail on his chest, back, upper arms and legs and fitted with custom greaves and boots designed to make his distinctive twisting limp seem less than it was.

The boy that he was then had stayed out all night watching the summer sky on that veranda contemplating his future. He had finally fallen asleep deeply enough to not wake when his mother and father collected him and carried him to bed just before dawn.

The Elvish Arch Mage now stood on that same veranda, recalling pulling his father out here not long after that day to show him an update on the hammers and chestnuts. He had a bench standing on end with a bucket before it on the ground and another beside it. He made a nut fly up in front of the bench, and a knife laying on the table beside him shoot forward and pierce it, sticking in the bench while the pieces dropped into the bucket. All his father said was, "Well done, son. Use it wisely."

Today he used the veranda to send his apprentices into the world.

"Fergus," he said, "start them off with simple, practical daily tasks at Fallon's. Let them make themselves useful and become part of the family. Then pair them up with our folks on the trade routes – no more than a few trips to each location! They need world and people experience. New geography, sociology, and the magic to go with them. Got it?"

His apprentice said, "I've got it. And you're going to Icelle's?"

"Yes, eventually. I don't have a clear target there for a portal spell – I'll fix that this trip. I've figured out the rest of the steps to track the mystery mage, just not the actual methods yet, I'll have to do that with what I have at the time. I also need to share the possibility of finding the Old One with the dragons.

They, and the pixies, should be converging at Yeomring Castle any time now. You're in charge – don't let them bully you!" Rrahmus smiled at this. Fergus did not, just rolled his eyes and sighed heavily.

After the apprentices going home to start their training were gone, he turned to face his father who had arrived that day. "When this is settled, I'll come back so we can spend more time together. I'm sorry for staying away so long…"

His father smiled sadly, hugged his son, stepped back and said, "Dramatic lives all have sad endings eventually, son. Regrets make the dutiful rue their choices, no matter how noble. If you come back, and if I'm still alive when you do, we can sit here and eat chestnuts for days. Regardless, just know that I'm proud of the elf you've become. Be safe if you can, and if you cannot, be deadly."

Once again, his father turned away. Rrahmus was sure he was already planning how to tell his mother that their son had to leave again. He was also sure after seeing her that she had not come to see him off on purpose as she hated goodbyes.

He turned away. He threw a large handful of sand into the air, letting it cascade down then freeze like a curtain in front of him. With a flame from his finger drawing an outline of a doorway with one hand, the other began sweeping across the sand, each time revealing a different scene beyond it. Finally finding the one he wanted, he stepped though it into the parklike clearing just behind the Witch Queen's castle.

Instantly Sean stepped through behind him, and the troll that had been about to accost the Arch Mage let out one of the strangest sounds he'd ever heard. It was part squeal, part shout and part … purr like a cat? Whatever it was it was followed by a bellow of, "SEAN HOME!!!" and a flattened pair of new arrivals, Rrahmus being knocked into a tackle/hug on the ground in the garden, his hat and staff flying in different directions.

***

Chapter 50

To Icelle's

It was a strange band that set off for Yeomring's castle that evening. Despite Queen Hazelmoon's assurances that the bulk of the journey was within her demesnes, and therefore protection, Rrahmus was uneasy... He believed her, but traveling in pitch black on a magical route only visible by his human mage counterparts, even if they were natural warlocks and he could see somewhat was a bit of a role reversal, and making the trek with Sean (who could NOT see), a half-dozen trolls and a cranky old pixie still left him little to be comforted by...until he found he could see their magic route literally laid out on the ground before him. He said nothing, but felt relieved nonetheless.

He was quite certain that his beautiful hostess was keeping something from him, and considering that she had already told him that his nephew might be dead, it must be a significantly more dangerous or painful item, and that was a bit unnerving.

His other distraction was observing Sean and his trolls. They were like little brothers to the young fighter, who was himself a little brother, and Rrahmus overheard him explaining his concern for Graham to them, "So, the Arch Mage there, he sent him to go find the oldest red dragon in the world through a magical portal to a faraway desert where he may be being held by the worst foe we have ever seen...that's got to be safe, right?!"

The trolls were well acquainted with the threat of dragon's fire, and each one patted his shoulder to show their concern for their 'uncle'.

Their eventual arrival was unexpected, but not unanticipated, and Jobalm made sure that advance notice was given to keep them from a violent reception, returning with a few other pixies. Their last league was uneventful until they reached the south gate and when it opened more trolls assaulted Rrahmus' young human traveling companion.

Witches, mages, pixies and dragons alike all laughed at the joyful reunion.

Fallon, Icelle, Pill's father the vampire, and King Jankin stood by a young man, and Fallon corralled Rrahmus at the first opportunity to say, "Rrahmus, Elvish Arch Mage, this is Hunter. He was a healer in Chares' army, and you may want to query his history a bit when you have time – after you talk about how he saved Pill!"

386

Chapter 51

Let Me Sum Up

"Let me recapitulate for you all what I think I know," said Rrahmus to the gathered assembly. "The Dark One, Baru Dall, is once again trying to do <u>something</u> here in our world. His interest in originals, both races and items, leads me to think that he has some source that tells him that he needs them to do whatever that 'thing' is. So far he has been largely unsuccessful at anything except attacking unsuspecting villages and slaughtering their inhabitants. At this point the 'why' is becoming irrelevant. We have to stop his murderous forays into our world. We need to identify, locate and kill Baru Dall and <u>all</u> of his followers and associates."

The Arch Mage paused, letting his words sink in. "And, we need to make sure that he cannot return." His tone changed, and he said, "Actually, honestly, he has also been quite successful at recruiting support. He got most of an entire non-magical kingdom of humans to slaughter not just their own race, but frequently their own neighbors. He recruited some troglodytes as well, and now … ogres!"

After another pause he continued, somewhat chagrined, "To be fair, who among us has not visited violence on others based on their differences? What we call 'evil' behavior from an ogre, they may call part of their culture. What we call 'fair play', they may just call, well, stupid. More than once in my own life I know that I have unleashed what was absolutely over the top unnecessary mayhem because I felt I was out of other options. This may be one of those occasions, but for our entire world, not just any one person, group, village or even kingdom. To use a cliché, we may need to burn down a forest just to light a torch..." As he concluded he was staring straight into Queen Hazelmoon's eyes.

In the past this type of declaration before such a large and varied group would likely have ended in an outburst of raucous discussion, opinions being vehemently exchanged, and the occasional class, racial or ability insult tossed in. Not today.

His assembled audience sat facing northward outside of the northern gate of the Yeomring's outer defenses, eyes frequently glancing at the corn rows behind him. The planters had placed stone markers at the head of each row with the names of fallen soldiers on them in parallel on either side of the gate approach road. On the back of each marker was a number, the number of attacker's bodies that were buried in that row from the recent siege.

        Many assembled this morning had been present for the event and could recall the scene – the fires, mangled bodies, piles of armor and charred horse remains, the smells of burned flesh, fear imbued sweat and the dying flatulence of every type of creature present all mingled with dragon gas, and the roar of the collective shouts of command, screams of hundreds of wounded or dying, and thousands of underlying grunts from individual close combat actions; all were punctuated by just a few overpowering, unforgettable noises. The bellow of Baraghi the Giant's death throes, recognized by the plaque just behind where the current assembly now sat, the clanging of the stone gargoyles striking armored knights – these were new to their experience because of their emotionally conflicting nature; giants dying had never before been a bad thing, and knights being smashed to a fatal pulp was not supposed to be a good thing, yet they had to resign themselves to those realities while in the midst of life and death decisions, the deaths of comrades, at the hands of their neighbors who were being led by a powerful and seemingly insanely evil user of magic who claimed to want to destroy magic itself. They remained silent, just as torn and confused now as they had been then.

And now at the head of the valley where the mountain path entered to become the northern gate approach road through the corn fields was a new marker. A grand sculpture of pure gold shone brightly in the sun, large enough to see clearly even though it was half a league away. It was a large male gold dragon.

Only Aurelius responded, "I will not speak for Slawhit," he began with a glance at the ancient pixie seated next to him, "or for the men, elves, dwarves … or trolls," this last said while patting Ufu's head. "I don't want to confuse my anguish at the loss of my son with the best interests of our peoples and our world." He paused, his keen predatory eyes regarding the new statue for a moment. "We came here," he said, louder, for the group and the men-at-arms on the wall behind them to hear, "to preserve our very existence. Since then, for millennia we have flourished. In that time we have seen, by design or accident, newcomers arrive and new races arise, and despite the conflict of individuals, the squabbles inherent in all interactions of sentient beings, we have continued to thrive. To be sure, our motivations are personal and selfish – family success, power, greed – but all of these have survival at their roots. Common goals for common good will never replace the deep-seated animal instinct for survival, but groups can temporarily overpower it if the they can be convinced to work together to defeat a common threat."

Pausing, the High Priest and leader of dragons (in elf form) stood and moved beside Rrahmus, placing a hand on the elf's shoulder as he turned to face his family, friends, and partners. He said, even louder yet, "We here do not need convincing. We need to ensure that we have a common understanding of the threat, the risks, and what we can, and intend to, do about it. I will commit my dragon brethren to stopping this adversary from gaining entry to or maintaining a foothold in our world. In <u>my</u> world..."

Rrahmus waited a moment out of respect (and to let the shouts of support from the walls die down), then said, "I know how to find him. What I don't know for a certainty is how to stop him, but I have an idea."

Slawhit seemed to launch straight upward and then flit over and come to rest again sitting on Aurelius' shoulder. He said nothing and the expectant quiet became such that they could hear the bees buzzing in the fields. Finally, he said, "We will help with communications. I have sent my kin to known travel points in all directions. They each know how to find their nearest counterparts, can travel at speeds faster than anything you can imagine, can be invisible at will, and are ready to send messages at any moment to anyone, anywhere. And should they encounter problems, they are <u>not</u> alone... We pixies will see this thing <u>done</u>. Long before the first dragon was killed in the Old World, we were hunted for sport. I am the only one left who was there except my friend, the oldest red dragon. I remember. I also recall learning to fight back before we decided to leave – it was largely unsuccessful. Our magic is so much more potent here! It is a <u>part</u> of us, a part of our world...killing us won't recharge the Old World with magic. But destroying Metaerie entirely? Putting it back where it came from, perhaps undoing the spell that made our world? <u>That</u> just might do it. This is, I believe, another fight for our very survival. Unlike the last time, though, we cannot run away. We. Must. Fight."

There were no cheers this time. Slawhit's words were cold and grim, direct and dire. They broke into smaller groups to set abilities to tasks.

***

The groups below were divided largely along racial lines, coordinating the who, what, when, where and how, and hopefully with whom. As Sugarplum looked down from his perch on the roof of the Yeomring inner keep he could see them all clearly. But as they broke apart a new group formed. He looked closer and determined that they were all female...

***

"Lady Yeomring, thank you for your hospitality," said Queen Hazelmoon.

"Indeed!" said Ariene and Argenta together. They laughed, and Ariene continued alone, "The quarters below are so spacious and accommodating to us in our natural forms, I don't think I've ever slept so well away from home in my entire life!"

Their hostess smiled shyly and said, "And you are welcome to use them any time!" To Hazelmoon she said, "My Queen, I was your guest for quite some time recently as well, it is the least I can do!" Turning and crouching a little, she said to her new arrivals, "And how are you faring, Miss Chestnut?"

The tiny (in stature only, not personality) woman answered sprightly, "Oh! Quite well Mistress! The dwarf ladies made me a snug little bed on one of their shields so I wouldn't accidentally get stepped on..."

Dendra Drake, Wonder's widow, laughed at

that, which was good to see, though her clothes and armor were still all black and unpolished. "We did have a bit of a stir in the dead of night when an owl came to see her – we thought it was trying to eat her! Turns out it's her flying mount, come to find her…"

Krystal McNab said, "I think, and I'll wager Tara agrees with me, that we also feel safe here because of what we survived here. Because the worst threats we ever saw in our lives were overcome right here. Thank you for having us and please let us know if there is anything at all that we can do to help you with this friendly invasion of your home!"

Tara and Jitters walked inside the gate all the way to the inner wall where there was a table lined at the outer edges with apples and biscuits that the males around them had been helping themselves to and walking away. Motioning the other women to join them, they moved to either end of the table, reached into the 'empty space' against the wall and began to hand out cups of tea and pastries, laughing as they did so…

Even Lady Yeomring laughed in spite of herself, saying, "Ah! Illusion versus expectation! Well done, ladies, well done."

***

Chapter 52

The Long Blue Line

The path was clear. The pixies could follow it like a beacon – or a long blue snake. Able to fly dozens of leagues each hour, if they tired, they made one of their number detour for reinforcements, then handed the task off so they could go rest. The Arch Mage, unsure how long his spell or Sugarplum's route marker would last once they were activated, had told them that speed was imperative.

The route was indeed circuitous, and it looped a few times as well. Many of the locations it passed through were now just burned out ruins of villages, towns, farms, and bridges. The pixies were mapping the route at Rrahmus' direction. His spell had made Plumley's path visible to all pixie eyes, one of his ideas that had come to fruition, the grisly method evident to all who saw Slawhit now wearing a patch over the socket where his left eye had been. Hunter had once again partnered with Corvin to accomplish the task with little other damage to the ancient flyer. The idea had come to Rrahmus after hearing how the two had healed Pill.

When approached by the Arch Mage, all Slawhit said was, "Are you certain it will work?" At Rrahmus' negative response he said, "Well, if it's only one eye you need, go ahead. Maybe it will take away half of the visual memories of the evil I've seen... and done..."

Casting the spell also required a donation from Sugarplum himself – a bit of his wing, one entire claw, and one of his eyes as well. The tribrid did not hesitate either.

The alchemical portion was simple, it combined their vision and the blue flame's method of creation. The application was also simple, but a bit nauseating. Plumley drank the potion Rrahmus had made, then regurgitated it into Slawhit's eye socket, still looking like molten rock. Rrahmus placed Sugarplum's eye in with it, and Hunter melded it to the ancient pixie's body.

The rest of the spell was a shared vision potion made with Slawhit's eye, which he drank.

"Now," said Rrahmus, "all that remains is for Plumley to step into the blue flame to start the path. We don't know how long it will last...but you, Slawhit, can transfer your vision – <u>his</u> vision – to any of your people, by spitting in their eyes. And if it works, they also can transfer it the same way. I know it sounds disgusting, but it has to be that way. I think."

Jobalm stepped up, saying, "I'll be the first test." His tone made it clear he would not be told 'no'.

Plumley stepped into the blue flame, his purple coloring making the growing inferno seem much redder, but then a blue beam shot out of it, up and over the mountain before them and disappearing. He said, "I can see it. Can you?"

Rrahmus replied sadly, "No, I saw a flash and then it was gone from my sight."

Slawhit, however, said, "I can still see it!" Without a word he turned to Jobalm, who nodded and forced his eyelids open wider. The elder pixie spit in them. Jobalm turned, blinking the alien fluid out of his vision, and said, "Well I'll be a three-eyed squirrel – I can see it too!"

**

Aurelius was horrified by the arcane process that Rrahmus had used, but fully understood the necessity. He was appalled at how it defiled two amazing beings, but he rejoiced at their voluntary participation.

He told the Elvish Arch Mage, "The mind that could conceive of the combination of arcane events required to make this work absolutely makes me cringe. However, their example of voluntary sacrifice to do this is an inspiration to us all. I cannot think of one better. Perhaps the greater the sacrifice the more horror is attached to it?" He paused, but as no response seemed forthcoming, only a single slightly raised eyebrow from Rrahmus, he continued, "I only have one remaining question – what do you think will be the long term effects on the pixies?"

After a moment's thought, Rrahmus finally spoke, "Can <u>you</u> see the path Plumley made?"

Turning from their bench on top of the inner courtyard wall on the north side of Yeomring Keep, the dragon-in-elf-form High Priest said, "Why, yes, I can still see it right now."

"So only Sugarplum can <u>create</u> the sign, but you can all see it?" asked the mage.

"Something like that, yes," was the response.

"Well, as I did everything I could to make sure this worked and therefore made sure not to skimp on materials or do anything that would cut it prematurely short or diminish it unnecessarily, it is entirely possible that the effects could be permanent...why?"

Aurelius hesitated, then said, "Dragon sight is not just for 'seeing' – it is part of our overall magical abilities, rooted in our makeup, passed down through our lineage...and while some things are common to our entire race, others are specific to color, type and family. Sugarplum is a tribrid – an amalgamation of several branches of the 'dragon tree' if you will – and it remains to be seen, I guess, what he will, if anything, pass on via this event... Fire breathing pixies would definitely be new..."

"As would baby pixies with purple skin I suppose..." mused the mage, "but it is already done, so I guess I'll just have to be ready for the blame!"

***

Chapter 53
Return of the Map

The searchers did not take long to return a detailed map to the instigators – it only took a few days, and Jobalm himself handed it to Slawhit personally.

The elder pixie no longer wore the patch over his new eye, it had healed quite quickly. It did not move as it should as it was too large for its new socket, so he frequently just moved his entire head to use both eyes. He also could not keep it closed, so it watered a lot from dryness. Aurelius and Rrahmus agreed to attempt some modifications once his healing had settled down. For the moment, the three unrolled and studied the map.

After a moment Aurelius spoke first. "Well. He has certainly traveled more of our world than I would have expected..."

"I see several forays to the late King Chares' castle..." said Rrahmus.

"How can there be points and routes that don't touch each other?!" demanded Slawhit.

They were silent a moment, then all said together, "Separate visits!"

"We need more eyes on this..." said Rrahmus.

"And copies made I think," said Slawhit.

***

A flurry of activity began. It included the gathering of blank scrolls, pens and ink, and the most traveled of those assembled. It was semi-organized chaos. First, a copy was made to be copied, and then The Counter arrived and made it actual Chaos. Along to document this historical undertaking on the part of the entire dragon race, he soon had four more copies being made, leaving one of his magical stylus' remaining to document the documenting. It was an even faster flurry than before, faster than anyone else could come close to matching, his magical pens literally flying over the pages.

Scant minutes later there were maps on tables in every room large enough for eight to ten sets of eyes to stand around them. The results were varied but immediate, and some were quite unexpected.

King Jankin easily noted the path of wanton destruction through his domain that had led to the battle at this very spot. He also noticed a few locations that the dark mage had visited that had NOT been destroyed... those might warrant a visit, soon, to verify their intentions and allegiances...

Sean pointed out a location far to the north,

saying, "This has to be well into the Red Desert. We encountered the edge of it about ... here, I think," indicating a spot just inland of a great expanse of water that had tiny pixie writing on it saying, 'open' and 'salt water'.

Rrahmus replied, "Your brother, and mine for that matter, are already there. Nearby anyway, as you know, looking for the Old One. So that makes sense."

It was Krystal who asked, "Is this the last point or the first? I'm confused."

Jobalm, completely worn out, trudged over to her on foot and stepped up onto a human-sized chair to see what she was looking at. She pointed and said, "I...I think I know where this is ... a narrow point in a great river, well upstream from the ocean, northeast of here, and just near it is written, 'kobold lair'..."

***

Chapter 54

A Ship?

Tahmus stared at Angus like a rabbit with five ears. "You want to do <u>what</u>?!" he demanded.

"Get on a ship. We have to get home. I don't know where the fountain here is targeted to go back to, and I don't think I can fit these big lugs magically into the location I know is safe. So, unless you have a better idea, <u>we</u> need a ship."

Graham asked Tahmus, "What's wrong elf-lord? I am pretty sure I can get us to the port in a few days or less. There were plenty of ships the last I saw it."

"How do you plan to pay for passage?!" said Tahmus.

"Me? Not a problem, I always have some spare coin on me. Actually, for my lifestyle, all coin left at the end of each day is 'spare coin' come to think of it. But I figure we'll see if one of Fallon's ships is around as a first choice. Angus can get us on any of those quite easily I'm sure. If not, we'll just have to empty some of Audhan's pockets I guess..." This last he said exaggeratedly slyly with an elbow to the younger dragon-in-elf-form's ribs, who jerked in surprise at the unexpected strength of the blow.

Audhan snorted, rolled his eyes, and said, "Is nothing private anymore?"

"Not in a party this size my friend! Plus, my brother spent some time with Auron, and I figure you guys have LOTS in common..." the large human winked melodramatically.

"Ah! That explains it," said Audhan. To Tahmus he said, "Not to worry, Sir Elf, we can book passage easily enough."

Tahmus looked at all of them grinning at him, the two girls actually giggling a bit at his frustration, and walked away in the direction they had been traveling, assuming that Graham had already been leading them toward the ocean.

***

Chapter 55

One Eye Open

This waking up to people staring at him had to stop. It was completely unnerving for someone whose life had depended on not being seen or spotted. Off to his right, his father's fangy smile and bright golden eyes didn't help either, nor did the frozen hand holding his own, but he smiled and squeezed it back anyway, and then a warmer one was placed on top of both of theirs and he looked up to see Rrahmus' face, his expression concerned.

He said to them, quietly, "I feel awful … am I dying or healing…?"

"Healing!" said a female voice off to his left. 'Ah, Sylvia,' he thought, 'I missed you.' What he said was, "Well, that's good!" and allowed his smile to grow larger.

Another female voice, even farther to his left (or so he thought?) spoke *inside* his head, and he started at that, not because it was a female voice in his head – he was used to that by now – but it was a *different* one! The words were worse. 'It's not to be little elf. She's spoken for, sadly.' He looked beyond

Sylvia and found her mother's sister, Argenta. His smile lessened, but he said and thought ... nothing. He had gotten used to this sort of dialogue by now.

Sylvia grabbed his left hand and Corvin released his right, as if jolted. "Oh!" she gasped, "I'm so sorry! Are you okay?!"

The vampire smiled, thinly but with an expression of great understanding, and said, "It is merely ... unsettling, not painful my dear." Patting his son's head he said, "It's almost daybreak, I should go anyway. Good to see you awake boy." And then he was gone, disappeared like a midnight wind gust. Now *everyone* was unsettled...

***

The spot Krystal had pointed out was known to many present, but it was Pill who said, "Isn't that where you McNab's are all from?"

She did not reply but nodded quickly before she left the room crying.

Into the following silence he said, "What?! What did I say?!" to all of the reproving eyes around him.

It was Fallon who pulled him aside. "Did Reaver never tell you the story? About Render?"

As he shook his head the elf realized that was a

mistake – his head still hurt constantly. Fallon noticed his grimace and waited for him to refocus before he continued, quietly.

"Render did what we all said we wanted to do: He made enough wealth to build his own place, married a nice girl, settled down and started a family. I heard Reaver was with them for a while, but maybe not – it was after our 'incident' so I lost track … "

The old fighter looked away and blinked rapidly a few times, cleared his throat and sighed. "Anyway," he continued, "they were good and generous people and they attracted others. Tradesmen who came by, fighters who wanted to train with the melee master – you know how similar it sounds to my own tale… Except that while his little keep grew into a village, with a training yard, smiths, shops and cooks, he had no real continuing income, and his nest egg began to shrink…so when he was approached about leading one last party of adventurers, apparently Sephara agreed to let him go. No one knew she was with child, but she was. The story, as related to me by one who went with him, was that they set out to remove a rather nefarious character who was acting as a ruler over a huge community of kobolds. In fact, I think he is here. You should have him tell you the story."

***

It turned out they could map out every trail on the map as separate trips and based on many inputs about which locations were visited multiple times, all roads seemed to lead to the same point of origin. The kobold lair on the most recent trip was the center of it all.

When Pill and Fallon went looking for the fighter who had been with Render on his last mission each shared with those they asked briefly why, and they drew a lot of interest in hearing the story along with them. Fallon finally found him in the blacksmith's area, drawn to it by a particularly odd series of different colored lights coming from it. It was not Icelle's smith at the forge however, but a very dark-skinned elf, whose bright white teeth gave off a kaleidoscopic reflection and flash from the flames when he smiled at the old fighter's entrance.

"Fallon!" he cried. "How many old fighters does it take to repair a sword?!" he joked.

"None!" cried Fallon. "They just steal another to keep fighting and leave that to the smiths!"

"As they should!" cried four voices together before bursting out laughing.

"So, what brings you to the forge in the dark?"

asked the elf.

Fallon, turning toward the two onlookers, focused in on the one <u>not</u> wearing an apron, pointed, and said, "Him."

The target stopped laughing, sat up straight and said, " 'Ere now, boss, what've <u>I</u> done?! I'm just gettin' me sword straightened!" When the laughter died down, he continued, "No, seriously! I bent it on one o' them ogres, I did!"

The current leader of the Rose trading concerns smiled to calm his flustered friend, "Georgie, I just need you to look at a map and regale us with a story from your distant past – and if you need a sword in the meantime you can use one of mine!"

They all laughed again. Fallon's weapons were notoriously heavy.

Just then the elvish smith, said, "Ah! It's ready!" and pulled the heated blade from the fire and quenched it in a barrel of water.

Though Fallon had seen him do it before, when he brought the blade out of the water barrel the old fighter squinted his eyes and (mostly) looked away. He found himself cringing (as was his host) when the guest smith ran both sides of the steaming hot blade along his tongue.

After rinsing it and wiping it down and running it across the adjacent stone wheel a few times on each edge, he pronounced it fit for duty and handed it to its owner.

"All right, George, back to lopping off parts for you!" said the elf.

The fighter took the sword admiringly. He appeared to be of an age with Fallon, his chainmail-over-black-leather armor showing plenty of damage and wear and white salt stains from his own sweat. His dark hair and graying beard were both handspan length and shaggy, but his boots, belts and weapons were clean, oiled, and shiny. He said, "What do I owe, Ebon?"

"A good meal and a story sounds good…" said the smith mischievously.

George glanced at them all in turn and said, "Well, where's this map, then?"

**

The sun had been gone for hours and the cooking fires had burned to embers when they all gathered to hear George speak. He looked nervous and kept touching the pommel of his newly-repaired sword as if he thought he was going to have to fight his way clear of the gathering crowd.

Before he could bolt, Fallon approached with

412

two tankards of ale and handed George one. They crashed them together and drained them in a second. Both burped loudly and everyone laughed – making George remember that they were there, and that they were all expecting him to speak! It made him want another ale or six...and then he saw Ebon. He called to his friend.

"Here we have one who should really set the stage so to speak, so you understand why we went on this mess of a mission. Tell 'em, Ebon!" he said animatedly.

The dark elf hesitated. He looked this way and that, then finding the face he wanted, raised his eyebrows, and shrugged in askance. Aurelius nodded slightly.

"Well, first of all," he began in his booming blacksmith voice, "all is never as it seems..."

Stepping back from Fallon and George, he stepped behind a hay wagon and removed his sword belt, hammer, sandals and tunic that went to his knees and began to grow... Ebon was a black-scaled dragon, and he was <u>huge</u>.

Fallon's expression did not change, but George's became one of indignant consternation. " 'Ere! Ho'd on! <u>Years</u> of 'round ear' jokes and 'seeing in the dark' pranks, and you're not even an <u>elf</u>?! If you weren't a dragon I'd pop you in the nose, I would!" George railed at his friend.

The response began with a rumble of laughter. "I etch steel blades just out of the forge with my tongue – that didn't give me away at all...?!" was the incredulous response.

"I ... I don't know what all elves can do!!!" said the flustered George.

More laughter ended in a gentle rejoinder, "Fair enough I suppose. Well, let me tell the story and then see if you think a dragon should tell it or an elf..."

He began by sitting quite primly for a black dragon that most knew as a rather roguish fighter and blacksmith, wrapping his tail around all of his feet. His voice was a pleasant baritone now, a change from his usual rough, raspy rumble used among his fighter friends.

"A dozen millennia ago, when our world was still 'settling' itself and the older creatures were finding their way and stabilizing territories, some of our younger males just wanted to be alone for the most part. The first few hundred years are usually the worst, especially without a mate. One such young black like myself was not very keen on hanging around waiting

414

and he eventually found himself far to the east along a rugged coastline of tall cliffs riddled with caves. No one saw him for several gatherings – for those who may not know, we do still get together every ten years."

One of the castle guards spoke into the pause, "Hundreds of years without a mate? No wonder dragons get cranky…"

When the uproar died down Ebon himself was still chuckling, "Yes," he said, "I see your point… As it turns out this particular dragon did not wait that long – our Counter back then went searching after he missed his third or fourth gathering. What he found was a new race. Apparently above the cliffs where this one settled was a vast rolling prairie inhabited by dogs and deer and rabbits. He ate the deer, the dogs ate the rabbits, and at some point the Counter's guess was that he got a bit too friendly with some of the dogs, but in a smaller dragon form rather than elf form… that doesn't make it any less weird, but it explains the result – a darkly colored wingless lizard with horns and the face of a dog that lays eggs… you know them today, over twelve thousand years later, as kobolds, but originally he called them 'cobbled dragon dogs'. It was shortened over time to 'cobbleds' and eventually the translation and spelling was miscommunicated so much between dragons and humans that for most of <u>you</u> they became 'kobolds'."

A few side conversations started as he finished, but one voice rose over them. It was Aurelius', and he said, "We were like children then, untethered from fears and competition, our abilities and actions magnified in previously unknown ways. We have since adopted specific racial and cultural rules – well, guidelines really – that keep us more within some boundaries of behavior, especially with each other. We fail periodically..." He glanced at Sugarplum, "but most times we find later there was a reason for it to happen..." he concluded, glancing at Slawhit and Flaw. The ancient pixie nodded thoughtfully.

"Uh...okay," said Ebon, "Well, as one of those children's children's children, let me introduce my friend George..." and he stepped back behind the wagon and disappeared.

George, left alone and empty-handed as Fallon walked away with the large, now-empty, cups of liquid courage, found himself once again the center of attention and his rapidly reddening face and neck made it obvious that he was <u>not</u> okay with it.

"Ah. Yes. About 20 years ago Render McNab came to see me. 'E brought a bottle, and while much of that evening is fuzzy, we were off a few days later."

Chapter 56

Render's Last Adventure

It wasn't a great group. That was the first thought he communicated to the few he knew and trusted. Their skills were lacking, they were mostly unproven, and he was fairly certain a few were outright brigands.

Render reflected back to a few days earlier when he had been approached.

"You could probably handle this all by yourself," his guest began. "They're already terrified of you – if we just start the rumor of you riding out against them, they might simply flee! And if it worked, I'd still pay you the same…"

"So, what's the rub?" asked Render quietly. "Why do you need them gone so badly that you're willing to pay but not to fight?"

He'd struck a nerve. His guest went from nonchalant and chuckling to red-faced and angry. Though his voice remained quiet and calm it transformed from effusive to clipped. "I control a thousand leagues of farmland and graze for sheep. There are caves underneath it all. When the kobolds move in, they start a new village for about every 4-5 dozen of them, and they breed like dogs. They started at the cliffs and worked inward. Every village wants their own entrance and exit to access the surface! They make holes all over the place! And they steal my crops <u>and</u> my sheep! Not once in a while... Every. Single. Day. And when they cook, they build huge fires underground – it heats up the underlying rocks to the point that it kills my crops and the grass that the sheep graze on. They are rapidly turning my beautiful, profitable, lordship into a barren wasteland. If there is to be any hope of agreement, moderation, or compromise, it cannot be me who swings the sword. Kobolds are vindictive vendetta fighters... I need an outsider."

"And, as you said, they already fear me..."

"They still tell stories about you to their young to keep them afraid of humans. How your mighty sword arm cleaved two or three of their warriors heads off at a time, that you fought for hours, and at the end, your sword broken, you were using some of their own dead warriors as clubs. I'm sure the feats have grown 'greater' over the years, but the fear is real enough, and after all that's what really matters..."

***

George was relieved to see Fallon approaching

with another ale, storytelling was thirsty work…

He went on, "So Render says we're to pick out some of the bigger villages and take out the leadership, put the young ones in a state more inclined to negotiate… I says, 'How many of them are there?' He says, 'No idea, but, hey, they're just kobolds…' Well, let me tell you, there were definitely too many, even with Render along, especially when you get betrayed!"

***

They rode until they began to see herds of sheep, a few weeks travel to the east. Then they looked for signs of poaching. It didn't take long to find. The buzzing of hundreds of flies could be heard a dozen rods away and smelled at half that. Upon viewing the carcasses, Render was visibly angry. "Small wonder that Lord Sanswood is upset by this. They killed a dozen sheep at once, only took choice cuts of meat, and left the carcasses to rot in the sun and kill the grass. Three times the meat that they did take was left behind. What they need is an arrangement where they tend the sheep for a share of the meat, then both would value the other and not behave so… Such as hiring the likes of us to attack them without warning." To the scouts he said, "Follow the tracks. Find the entrance…"

***

The scouts were all back in under an hour but one. The lead scout was one quarter elvish. His ears were rounded on top, but he could see in the dark. His name was Leoli, and his report was succinct. "There are two warrens ahead, on either side of a rolling grassy hill. Both have lookouts waiting. They pop up like prairie dogs every few minutes like they are expecting something…"

Render asked, "Is that normal?"

"No," said the scout, "they usually barricade and guard from the inside where they can see and hear better…"

"So, either something is wrong, or they know we're coming."

"I left one man to watch, but I suggest further investigation – bypass these, circle around, see if the behavior is consistent."

All were quiet except George, who asked, "Bypass north or south?"

"South I think, away from the cliffs and the larger populations," replied Leoli.

"Do it," said Render, "we will follow, low, slow and out of sight. If it seems to be a trap, we ride for home and don't look back. Got it?" Nods all around. If the fearless one was acting cautious, better for the lesser to listen…

***

"So," said George, "we did as Leoli suggested, we crept around to the south, 'round at least a half dozen more hills, each one hiding a couple more kobold dens, all with guards peeking out. Then I saw Render's face go white like a ghost and his knuckles cracked he gripped his sword so tightly. That grip would've broken my neck, believe me! He pulled us all back and left me with the horses while the rest crept up to peer over a hilltop. Leoli came back to get me, said it was the home of the man who hired us, and he was out in the yard in front of his own gate, talkin' to a bunch o' kobolds! Looked like leader types, too, with fancy headpieces and groups of followers." George paused, his face grim in memory. "They all came runnin' back to the horses, talkin' about how this was the perfect opportunity to take out some leaders and rescue the boss all at once, and Render said…"

***

"FOLLOW ME! One sweep through, one sweep back, and off for home! Do not dismount, do not slow down, kill as many as you can, I'll get our benefactor!"

At least they were experienced enough that there was no shouting, no attacking war cries, just the thunder of dozens of running hooves across the uneven prairie.

They swept through the scattering mobs of kobolds. By their differently colored garments they looked to belong to at least a half dozen different clan groups.

The larger men on horseback had to reach quite far down to strike the single barrel height horny dog-faced little lizards. The great swords the attackers carried on horseback were up to the task. They were long, and heavy enough that they didn't even need to be swung to split open a kobold skull.

On the first pass through fully two-thirds of the kobolds died. They were sliced, smashed, stomped, and skewered, and their screams were shrill and surprised.

When Render pulled up short to turn around about a dozen rods past the open yard of the keep they'd ridden past, the rest of his cavalry line did so too.

A few had small arrows stuck here and there, but none seemed too serious. One horse had a small spear stuck in its barding but didn't appear to be bleeding. "All right!" he said, "Well done! Now we go again – I'll retrieve our employer, you kill the rest, but don't stop 'til we're clear and back to where George had the horses!" And with a double-heel shot to his horse's ribs, he led them again.

***

"And we did just like he said," recounted George. "Render swept down, his horse runnin' over one kobold while he swept another two of their heads off with one swipe of that enormous sword that he carried. He had gotten far enough ahead that when he drew near the lord he slowed, grabbed him up and dropped him on his horse in front of him, yellin', 'Hang on, we'll save you!' And then somethin' went terribly wrong."

This pause was exceptionally long, even for George. He cleared his throat twice before continuing.

"Render fell off his horse. We were all stunned. He landed square on his back, with a sword hilt sticking out of the side of his armor at an odd angle. It made no sense at all – until his lordship that hired us yelled, 'Shoot!' and arrows started to fall like rain into our midst. We were droppin' like flies in a fire. I saw that 'lord', still moving away from us, riding backward on Render's charger, moving slowly as no one held his reins. He looked ... gleeful.

Well, I snapped. Archers be damned, I charged after that betraying scum. He saw me coming, the look on his face changin' when he realized that his treachery was discovered and I was about to make him pay for it. He fumbled at Render's longsword still in its saddle scabbard, but he didn't know how to loosen it, and when I saw he was about to jump from the horse, I didn't wait to strike – I drew and threw my broadsword from just a few paces away, just as he jumped. But he didn't jump to the ground! He jumped <u>at</u> me! No fear in that one. Skewered clear through by my sword, he hit me like a wall, knocked me to the ground. He landed astride me, his knees on my elbows, and began to pound my head with his fists until I realized I could reach my sword hilt, the one already <u>in</u> him. I wrenched at it as hard as I could with both hands. Once up, once down, spun a quarter turn, then once left and once right. I'll never know which one did it, but one of those slices must have severed his spine, 'cause he lost his leverage when his legs went limp, so he grabbed my throat. No quit in him either!

Thanks to the gods, he had neither Render's strength nor mine as I peeled his fingers back, one from each hand, hearing them break as I broke his grasp. I rolled over and my sword point that was coming out of his back stuck him to the ground like a tent stake. I mirrored that with my long boot dagger through his neck, the blood oozing out slowly as he didn't have much left I think. He pulled his lips back in a grisly grin and he died that way, never speakin'."

The only sounds heard in the vicinity now were the splashes of the rushing rivers both under and adjacent to the castle.

"I used to say," George said quietly, "that I'd rather collect my weapons than my wits, there are more of them... That's what I did that day. I took my dagger and my broadsword out of that scum-suckin' dead traitor and turned 'round to go get my friend. But when I looked he still wasn't movin'. And he had company – only one of our number was heading my way. The rest had fallen, either from wounds or because their horses went down. And then they were overrun. Men and kobolds alike came pouring out of the gate of that keep. It was only then that I finally realized the depth of the deception, that betrayal had been the plan from the beginning.

Leoli caught Render's horse and brought it to me and we <u>raced</u> away from there. We went due west, nowhere near our original trail by those kobold warrens. We got away with our lives ... and some pouches I liberated from the dead 'lord' before we ran." He drew his sword and said, "Krystal McNab? I know you're here somewhere, can you come up here

425

please?"

When the surprised young female fighter did as she was asked and came forward her eyes were red and her cheeks wet after listening to how her father had died.

Turning the sword that Ebon had just repaired so that he was holding it with both hands flat in front of him, he said, "This was your father's. It was still on his horse when we rode away that day, and I have carried it ever since. It is yours now if you want it. I tried to give it to your mother twenty years ago. She said, 'Render always said, "You own what you use, whether bought or won, what's left when you die can go to your son." Well, he has no son, and you won it, so it's yours to use.' I have used it ever since, but I think it needs to be returned to its family. Here you go!" he said, handing her the weapon, hilt first. He continued, "She <u>did</u> take the money I gave her that I'd liberated from the dead lord, as we could tell right enough when we finally got back that <u>you</u> were on the way... and by the looks of you she did her job quite well." He bowed his head.

"I ... I want you to keep it," she began in the most unsteady voice any present had ever heard her use, "but at the same time I <u>really</u> want it, just to have something of my dad's..."

She drew her own sword, put Render's into her simple leather hanger, and gave <u>her</u> sword to George, then hugged him, saying, "Thank you so much. For the sword, yes, but more for the story."

***

Chapter 57

The Pieces are Present

Baru Dall was tired, but happy. It was an odd combination for him. He usually described his approach to goal accomplishments as 'layered' and 'gradual', a slow and steady method of managing his own expectations that prevented a lot of disappointments. This day brought him unadulterated evil glee.

**

He knew based on their previous behavior that Dramin and Tarlek could not be trusted, so he made it a point that they did not know where his base of operations was to be. He took a team of his best, most dedicated guards, and met the trogs at a port several days travel away, a location where he had instructed them to go.

They were already there, waiting in a port brothel being run by an unscrupulous agent of his when he arrived. When they saw him, each produced a small box from their robes, and with no preamble opened them on the table they occupied in a back corner of the common room. Dramin passed a wand over them, and each glowed so brightly blue that they lit up the entire room.

Slamming the lids shut, his lips parted, revealing shiny white teeth in a death's head grin.

"Now this," he said with elation, "makes up for your previous bungling." His eyes narrowed. "Your payment is waiting outside – money, spells, potions, weapons and poisons – everything you need to get your king back on his throne. A throne that will serve me or I will kill him myself. Understood?"

Both troglodytes nodded, still not speaking.

"Good. Go. Do not fail or do not come back…"

They left.

He looked at his priest. "Get the dragon. By the time he arrives at the river fort I'll be back, and stronger than ever. Keep these safe – like the life of everyone you've ever known depended on it." And he disappeared.

***

He sat in his cavernous library (in an actual cavern) holding the oldest, smallest, and hardest to read book in it. He was looking over the top of it at an equally ancient broken fountain. Cracked near its base, the water had been gone before he ever saw it, but he knew now what it did from the troglodytes. And if the portal spell he'd found went near the fountain's mate, to another, deeper well, it could not be coincidence.

The magic was simple enough, but didn't allow his transit to be complete. He had form and ability when he was in Metaerie, but not solidity. He knew now after many such trips that his body stayed behind. His power was so much greater there even in an incomplete form that he knew he would be unstoppable if he could complete his physical transfer.

The portal spell, in his estimation, had been created to replace the ability to go to the vicinity of his newly finished river fort after it broke in the distant past. He needed to sleep, eat, and repair this fountain...

***

Chapter 58

To the Sea

"Alright," said Angus, "we have passage booked on a ship. It is heading to Fallon's eventually, just a few stops in the wrong direction first, but not back to here, so we won't be discovered that way…"

Looking pointedly at Audhan and Tahmus, he said, "Our story is that you are taking your grandfather home for a family wedding. His escort and human bodyguards are accompanying us. Audhan, you have to be with him at all times. Neither of you can leave your elven forms for any reason for the next few weeks, I'm sorry. I have convinced them that the Old One here is a wealthy eccentric who has gone blind, and to let us board the cargo plank in the dark. And if any of them ask you for anything at all, tell them to speak to me! They've already been well paid…"

Tahmus, the military leader, bristled initially at being told what to do. Turning his head while clenching his teeth he saw Graham, sitting on the ground, leaning back against a tree, quietly sharpening the shortsword that he used as a dagger and camp knife. Saying nothing, his face reflected his inquisitive listening but relaxed and accepting attitude. It struck Tahmus that perhaps he had been in charge for so much of his life that he couldn't stand <u>not</u> being in command. When had he lost the fatalistic acceptance of the good foot soldier? He smiled, turned back to Angus and asked, "What about our names? Most elves we might encounter will know mine, but not my face. You, Angus, on the other hand, may be well known to many sailors, and a false name might raise unnecessary suspicion...?"

Graham spoke before Angus could consider and respond, "I have a similar issue, as does Bronnie – many would put my name and size together as a Yeomring, but not without both usually – lots of folks are used to seeing big stupid fighters. Bronwyn's name and beauty together, at least in the coastal trading areas, will immediately peg her as Fallon's daughter. The lot of us together? All sailors talk too much in their cups, and we'll get enough of their attention as it is in the taverns."

Bronwyn's face was flushing a deep red despite Graham's matter-of-fact tone, and when Audhan said to the Old One, "The poor human girl is as red as you Grandfather," even the oldest inhabitant of Metaerie chuckled.

"Sir Tahmus," he said, "you'll be my stoic son,

Thom. Audhan and Molly, you're my grandchildren, cousins Audie and Mollie. Graham, your size befits a stoic background too, and I dub thee Sir Grim of Frostland, Giant Slayer, my bodyguard, and traveling with us is your younger sister Bonnie, who is preparing to be a priestess. Angus my friend, you have to just be you, on loan from my longtime family friend the Elvish Arch Mage. Who, in point of fact, robbed me once in his youth, but I hold no ill will about it. How's that?"

Angus, sporting a huge smile, said, "It sounds perfect sir." They were all smiling now.

***

Chapter 59

Pill is Up and Around

It had been a long night of planning, sorting and socializing, most of it productive and positive. Only when Pill, ever the quick healer, went to find and thank his saviors, did a wrinkle that rankled occur.

He had found his father in a lower level guard room, teaching Icelle's archers how to set up and use an indoor training range for winter and bad weather activities, and to incorporate blade work, hand-to-hand targets and movement into their training regimen.

He stood there watching for a while, unnoticed, listening, hearing familiar phrases from his childhood. "If time is not an issue, let go when it 'feels right'. If time is an issue, make it feel right!" Corvin had set up three firing lanes with three shooting positions each, staggered along the shooting lanes at different distances from the furthest targets. Each lane incorporated a moveable wall on the right, another on the left, and a constructed window to shoot through, all of which could be moved to change the environment. It also allowed the archers to get used to having comrades on their right and left, in front and to the rear. And then he heard it, "And above all else..." said his father with a pause for emphasis that Pill interrupted in a booming voice that echoed off of the subterranean stones, "Aim small, miss small!"

As some of the archers jumped in surprise, Corvin was already smiling before he turned around. The gold eyes were still eerie, but the look was warm (though the skin was not), friendly, even loving, that the vampire gave to his son.

"Too right son!" beamed the pale elf with oversized fangs. "Would you care to comment for the class?"

Pill thought a moment, regarding the setup, then said, "Bags of sand and stick dummies at first. Throwing sand at the windows will teach the shooter to stay back in the room, unseen from left, right and below. Stick men around the corners of the walls to engage with your blades will aid in weapon transition speed." As he spoke Corvin began moving some of the dummies into the described positions. Pill continued, "And then you escalate, throwing rocks or sticks instead of sand, and having a live sparring partner attempt to attack you instead of just striking at a stick figure. You get the idea. And at the edges add some hard targets for thrown weapons, like daggers, hand-axes, darts or even stones."

"Shall we demonstrate for them?" asked the vampire slyly.

"I'm still a little weak," said the thief, "but I'll give it a shot … or three …" Seeing one archer holding a bow that looked like his father's, he said, "D'you mind if I use that for a minute?" The bow was almost as tall as he was, made from the bones of some large species of deer. The arrows were fletched with white goose feathers, scores of them sitting point down in half barrels by the wall near the entrance. He took a handful, stepped to the first point on the left and said, "Remember this: always deal with the greatest threat to <u>you</u> first if you can, because if you get killed or incapacitated you don't get to fight anymore. Save yourself to save others with your future actions."

With that he shot the furthest left hand target in the face, drew his shortsword, spun around the corner of the wall and struck the neck of the dummy Corvin had put there so hard it severed and the sword blade stuck fast into the wooden wall. Leaving the sword stuck there, he turned back and rushed to the next point in the center lane, a window, and knelt, shooting the closest center target in the sternum, then dove out of the window into a front shoulder roll without letting bow or arrows strike the ground. He crawled to the right-hand lane's furthest wall type firing point and turned back toward the group watching, drew back and fired an arrow into the <u>back</u> of the head of the same target! He then rolled up onto one knee, switching to a left-hand grip, leaned around the wall and shot the far center target in the ear, swung the bow around the wall, hooking the dummy there by the arm and, pulling it towards him, stabbed an arrow in his off hand into its neck. Letting go of both bow and arrow, the experienced thief drew a dagger from his boot as he stood up and threw it into the dead center of the face of the furthest right-hand target.

The whole series of engagements had taken less than half a minute. The archers watching were, to a man, staring with their mouths open in awe. Corvin was just leaning against a wall, smiling.

Pill said to the group, "I don't recommend that you start with that, but as you train, prepare for battle as you would for dinner in a tavern common room – everyone gets to choose their own table, seat, and companions. They can be to your left, right and rear just as easily as your front, and if any of them are like my father there," he chuckled, "even above you..." Corvin's smile got bigger.

"And remember, just as you watch a play before you on a stage, or engage targets on a range like this, real life is happening in every direction, all the time, even you may be otherwise occupied, with eating, sleeping, training or mating. Plan your lives and make sure you always have a weapon close to hand and know where the rest are, their capabilities and how to use them. The enemy always gets a vote as to what they'll do next…"

As he began retrieving the blades, arrows and bow, his father addressed the group again. "Now that you've seen what is possible for an experienced practitioner, let's start with a quick assessment of where your skills are now." Pill handed Corvin the bow and arrows, and the latter turned and, in a blur, sent three quick shots squarely into the heads of all three furthest targets.

"I taught Pill his archery skills. The sword work is all from Fallon Rose and Render McNab. The blade throwing is all his own doing… and he is usually much stronger and faster than he is today, he was after all unconscious and dying for several days quite recently… Let's begin."

Pill put one arm around his father's shoulder and said, "And for your parts in keeping me among the living, thanks Papa." With a quick squeeze he took his leave, continuing around the lower level of the keep.

Around a corner in a long corridor that previously had just been rough cut stone, he passed over a grating above rushing river water, then found many torch-style lamps, each opposite a new opening, large chambers cut into the rock, each with an entry passage that turned, leaving the inner area some privacy from the hallway, but with no actual doors. From one he heard the familiar voices of some of his favorite dragons.

"Hello...?" he said from the hall, projecting a bit to let them know he was there rather than walk in on dragons unannounced...

"Pill my boy!" came a response that shook the walls a little. "I'd know that sneak-thief voice anywhere! Come in, come in!"

"Lord Aurelius, sir," said the elf as he turned into the chamber, with a slight bow.

Seated around a man-sized table in some stone chairs with cups all in elven hands were Aurelius, Ariene, Argenta, Sylvia, an elf he didn't recognize, and a human that looked familiar, but he could not place.

"Ladies and gentlemen," said the Dragon High Priest, "the rescued stray of the hour, Master Thief, Pill

Von Ferret!" Though he chuckled, the old dragon continued, "Kidding aside young elf, it gratifies me to see you looking so lively, as even I could not heal you."

"That is part of why I have interrupted you, before this crazy world comes unhinged and I lose my place, I need to find and thank those who saved me. I just left my father and I was told there was a dragon involved as well as a human witch healer. I figured you lot would know where I should start…"

"Look no further my friend, they are both here. On the end there is Hunter the Healer – ironic name, no? – and he is, or was, an unwitting warlock. In fact, we're pretty sure that you and Auron killed his whole family in your flying raid over a year ago, where he was a healer in King Chares' army before the battle here."

Pill stepped over to the human, who stood up too quickly and spilled his drink. Setting it down like it was burning him, he offered his right hand, which Pill shook vigorously, saying, "Thank you so much. I was trapped in my own mind, and it can be pretty dark in there. I don't know what to say about your family. I … hope you can forgive me?"

"You are most welcome," was the reply. "It is who I am, and it's always gratifying to succeed in reviving someone that so many care about. I am

443

discovering that those I knew as my family as a young man were likely impostors, and had they known about my magical talents would have likely killed me themselves, so no forgiveness is necessary, but thank you."

Looking to the unknown elf, who now also stood, the movement flashing several reflections from the gold accessories in and on his clothing, Pill said, "You must be the dragon – a relative of the High Priest himself perhaps?" He heard Aurelius snort behind him. The 'elf' in front of him said, "I am – distant cousins – and my role was minor, just heating an iron rod, anyone could have done it…"

"Perhaps," said Pill, "but you actually did it, and deserve my thanks and lifelong gratitude for it." They also shook hands. Sylvia stood up and said, "We are all just so pleased that you're alright. Pill, this is my betrothed, Aurick." Her eyes met his and they were sad but hopeful. His were disappointed but resigned. What he said, to both of them, was, "Congratulations."

As the whole group made small talk, Pill and Sylvia's eyes did not change, but also didn't meet again. He gave the excuse to find others to thank and left.

*＊＊

The early morning hours saw everyone doing

something new. The decision was made to send a significant force to the location where the dark mage seemed to have entered their world on multiple occasions. The timing was opportune as a large contingent of dwarven infantry had just arrived, committed to their cause. Gathered to train months ago they were answering the recent call for aid.

Aurelius said to a gathering of all of the leaders, "I am uncertain when I shall pass this way again, and before we depart, I wish to bless this entire assemblage, both en masse and individually. I will be at the northern gate all day today."

***

As the night watch began to be relieved, they were told to go see the High Priest before they went to eat and sleep. The first few who arrived were greeted by Ariene, side-by-side with her mate, both in dragon form now. Before her was a barrel of water, which she dipped one long claw into and drew a line down the left cheek of each man in turn with the back of her claw, the smooth, dull side. Each face flashed with a silvery shimmer that was then gone immediately, then they turned to Aurelius.

The old gold dragon was surrounded by bags of gold nuggets of seemingly uniform size. Another, younger gold dragon was placing them into a series of small, flat-bottomed iron bowls all about the size of a large coin. As each man approached Aurelius breathed a jet of flame at one of the bowls. The bottoms held a design worked into the iron of the bowl. As the molten gold settled flat and began to cool, Ebon in his dark elven form struck each with a hammer, driving a special marking die into the top, and Sylvia and Argenta took turns picking up the iron bowls and slamming them onto the top of a tilted cask with water on half of it. The newly minted coins would clatter out and they would slide them into the water to fully cool. Aurelius would then speak a few words and give the coin to the person waiting. They kept going, a blessing and a charm for everyone, one every few seconds, from dawn to dusk.

***

In the common room/eating area for the castle guards the night watch were lingering over their food. Most had fought in the siege here the year before, and when they had arrived, they'd found some of its heroes breaking their fast after the long night.

Fallon had been asking Sean, "So you plan to head back to the Forest with the Witch Queen?"

"If that is what she wants," the young fighter replied.

Pill said, "Every troll I see tells me how delighted they are that you've returned and asks if you're staying... you've got a bunch of rather durable dervish fighting puppies!" They all chuckled a bit.

Sean said, smiling, "They are my children, no doubt about it. I asked Graham if he thought we could train them well enough to send them to other places. He couldn't stop laughing." This last was said rather ruefully. "The ones here are devoted to my mother, just as the ones I had left behind are to Queen Hazelmoon. But they ALL love me. Perhaps when he gets back here he'll take on some here as a test case to see if he can take them on a mission of some kind with him..."

Brine Drake said, "I'm going to visit my kin camping outside the walls, see if I know any of them. Have we set a departure yet?"

King Jankin said, "Two days hence I think. Coordination is set, supplies will be gathered today, arranged and distributed tomorrow."

Icelle asked, "Do you plan to solicit volunteers along the way?"

Fallon said, "Well, we do have Flaw with us, it definitely opens up more options for recruiting..."

"Has anyone asked Hunter?" Pill inquired. "Having a natural healer along couldn't hurt, especially if we stay true to form and do our level best to almost die on a regular basis...speaking for myself of course..."

Rrahmus said, "I did, and he has a personal vendetta against Baru Dall – he's in."

Yar Drake, with a bit more white in his dark red beard than the last time they saw him a few years before, said, "We've 100 fighters, 25 shield maidens and a dozen priests. Leif put me in charge, and I have two subordinate commanders. We've supplies for a few weeks to a month, depending on available forage..."

Icelle said, "I'm not in charge of anything but my own little world right here, everything I can see from the tower above us..." He paused. "However, if I had some assurances that the previous attack here would not be repeated, I could perhaps commit some support to this lunacy..." He looked at Pill and said, "You must be feeling better – I heard about your little 'demonstration' to my archers!"

Fallon, laughing, said, "As did we all I think – you and your father teaching archers, Lady Yeomring will have the best defense ever!"

Rrahmus said, "We already have potential aerial reconnaissance assets virtually everywhere. The pixies have not pulled back, and Aurelius tells me the dragons are still looking for several of their number, including the Old One and Audhan. I'll wager we can investigate for any possible approaching forces in a day with their help."

"All right," said Icelle, "If there are no issues over the horizon, I'll match the dwarves force with sword, horse and archers, but I'll be staying here."

"Fair enough," said Jankin and Fallon together, then laughing.

***

The lady of the castle imparted a smile or a kind word to everyone she encountered. Her morning had started with her husband telling her that the greatest danger in their world in a dragon's age was likely located, a force was being dispatched to try to deal with it, and, most importantly, he was staying home with her. She was positively glowing.

As she entered the bakery she picked out in her mind sweetbreads for all four of her family members, then remembered that Graham wasn't here. When she returned to their dining chamber balcony on the second level of their keep tower, she found Icelle, Sean ... and Krystal McNab.

She said, "Well, good morning young lady! Lucky for you I brought enough to feed Graham, but he's not here!" She set the fresh baked goods in the middle of the table and said, "There, let me get some cold water." She retrieved a bucket from a hook under the eave that had been there overnight and some cups from a sideboard table. She filled them and sat opposite her husband while Sean and Krystal sat next to each other on one side of the table. Her smile dimmed briefly as she glanced at the empty chair opposite Sean's, but came back right away. Graham was the most amiable, practical, and durable man she knew. He was also the biggest, strongest and one of the quickest, and that left her feeling assured that he would likely survive anything he faced and come home safely. Her smile got bigger. Icelle laughed around his mouthful of bread and shook his head at her, knowing her thoughts as if she'd said them aloud.

Turning to Sean, she asked, "When do you plan to head to Queen Hazelmoon's castle?"

Sean said, "Mother, the Queen has decided to help in the mission to rid our world of this evil. She is personally involved as her family was killed, as you know. She is your friend, and she will not ask me to go. I know father is staying here, so you'll be safe. To add to that I will leave one third of her warlocks and my trolls at both her castle and yours, taking one third with me to protect her. And though she didn't know, I invited

Krystal here this morning to ask her to stay with you as well..."

Lady Kathryn's face had grown paler and clenched her jaw progressively tighter as he spoke. When he was done, she inhaled to respond, and in that moment, Krystal backhanded him in the chest.

"Are you kidding me?!" she said to Sean angrily. "We have traveled and fought together for months at a time and you think I'm the one who is staying behind?! You stay behind! I've been waiting here for months for your return, and I think your mother is absolutely wonderful, but if you think this is okay to even ask, you don't know me at all!"

Icelle sat further back in his chair, smiling enough to show some teeth now.

Kathryn sighed. "My son, always the protector. You want to save us all. But you try to do it by putting yourself in danger, and don't see that those who care about you don't want to lose you either! Ugh. Adult children." She pointed the sweetbread in her hand at him. "If you care for this young lady then you tell her that. AFTER that, her choices are her own, and she will choose to incorporate your feelings into her decisions or she won't, but in neither case will it be up to you! If I had any control over your father, he'd still be a woodcutter living with me in a shack high up in the mountains. 'Gold and Glory' comes at many prices, some social and some lethal. Now, you go protect <u>our</u> Queen as you promised. <u>And</u> tell me how I'm going to feed six trolls! Good grief." She huffed, folded her arms dramatically, noticed the bread still in her hand and took a bite. Chewing furiously, studiously ignoring the wide-eyed Sean and Krystal, she looked up at her husband and said through the breadcrumbs, "And if <u>you</u> think you're staying here while my baby marches off to get killed, think again! Hmph!"

***

Chapter 60

Dragons on a ship

Boarding the ship had been uneventful. The elves and Audhan could see in the dark and the Old One was blind and had to be led anyway. Graham it seemed not only could move like a cat but see like one as well and he 'guided' Bronwyn all the way to the screened off area of two hammocks that had been arranged for her and Molly.

It was in the pre-dawn darkness that things got interesting. Some rather bumbling steps up the stairs to the main gang plank stopped short as it was stowed aboard for the night. The noise woke all but the oldest of them, and the ensuing conversation was anything but quiet.

" 'Ere! What're you about?!" cried the deck watch.

"We need to speak with your captain, it's rather urgent," was the terse response.

"How 'urgent'? He's sleepin', and I ain't wakin' 'im for somethin' I'll get a beatin' over… Whaddya want?"

"We need you to transport a large bit of cargo

that will be here in a few days. The price will be worth his while!"

"We already got good payin' cargo, and we're leavin' at daylight. Why us, and how many days is 'a few'?"

"Honestly, somewhere between three and seven days, I'm not certain and definitely don't want to mislead you, but yours is the only ship we've seen that is large enough. Please, let us speak with him now? At least let us come aboard..."

"Oh, no! I'll not be the one who allowed boarders on my watch! If it's more space ya need, hire two smaller ships, and shove off."

The voice was exasperated. "Look, this isn't a bunch of bales or barrels! It has to go in one hold!"

"Oh, really?! And what, pray tell, izzat huge?"

There was a pause, a deep sigh of resignation, then, "It's a dragon."

"Are you out of your wobbly-legged mind?! A DRAGON! No. Not. A. Chance. No one is dumb enough to let a fire-breather onto a floating pile of kindling! Now – GET LOST!."

"We will literally give you its treasure hoard."

Now the pause was reversed.

"Tell ya what – I'll tell the cap'n about yer offer

454

– tomorrow, when he's awake. We probably have to swing back this way at some point anyway to get on with our run into the Center Sea and we can talk again then. In a half moon cycle or so. Okay?"

The voice could have chilled hot soup still in the cauldron over a fire. "Make sure you do. And know that we need to go the opposite direction. We need to cross this water to the south and head east – which I was told is the direction you are heading now. What if I paid you for your current cargo and let you sell it to two other captains so that I don't have to be delayed a month?" The last bit was clever and a little cunning, but ultimately desperate.

"Like I said, I'll ask. Now shove off," said the deck watch, definitely sounding less certain that before.

"Ask him now and I'll pay you a personal bonus…" was the sly retort.

"And will that 'bonus' include growing me a new tongue?"

The only answer was the sound of booted feet thumping down the wooden stairs and walking away.

***

Graham, Angus, Audhan and Tahmus whispered together.

"if they're moving the mouse, shouldn't we care

where to?"

Angus said, "My job is to get him to Rrahmus at Fallon's."

"But Rrahmus isn't going to Fallon's," argued Graham. "At least not yet...and we are already on this ride to get out of sight – if our rescue is discovered, shouldn't we avoid being where people are likely to look? What if we get off at the end of the ship's route and wait for it to come back? Then we just see where they take him and report it."

Audhan said, "Or some of us just stay behind..."

They agreed to decide when they got there.

***

At daybreak the ship sailed. Soon after it did, the night watchman told the captain about the dragon shipment offer. The group watched and waited. When he approached them a few days out to sea to ask if they were okay with a delay ashore at his current destination so that he could relay back and forth one time with another cargo and then take them straight to Fallon's instead a slow trading route, they agreed, though outwardly reluctant. Later when alone they celebrated as the excuse they had needed was now not even their own!

***

Chapter 61

Army on the Move

King Jankin looked in front of him, down the ridge line that he had just crested. Across the long verdant river valley to the northeast he could see dragons circling and landing on the opposite ridge. He knew these mountains held great herds of sheep and goats, herds that only got larger in the direction they were heading.

Below him, Icelle's cavalry were walking with their horses, their armor stowed, a rather rag-tag looking vanguard. Behind them followed his infantry, most of their gear in a few wagons, along with the archers' bows and baskets of arrows that were currently passing him.

The leaders of all of these groups sat with him now. Fallon was looking behind them at the dwarves coming up the hill, their faces dour – until a conversation sparked and their faces lit up with smiles and laughter, a somewhat insightful view into how dwarves interact with each other as opposed to non-dwarves. Even though many of the Shield Maidens were actually married and heading off to fight with their husbands, they did not march with them. It likely served a broader function than just camaraderie and unit spirit though, as Fallon noted more than once when a round shield of a 'maiden' flew into the ranks of the dwarven infantry, usually striking a culprit of an off-color remark, likely about his own wife or one of her close friends. Each was followed by much merriment throughout the column as the commentary was told and retold while the shield was picked up and passed back to its owner without any commentary at all, lest the final messenger be attacked unnecessarily (and at closer range, with deadlier weapons).

Fallon had no idea yet what they would face, but he liked his odds already. He saw Yar Drake at the head of his troops and thought of the dwarf leader's brother, Wonder, and then of Reaver McNab. Turning back he saw the motley collection of friends and supporters that they had gathered along their trail and smiled. Pill and Flaw were trudging alongside a wagon being driven by Brine Drake. In it were Hunter the Healer and his tiny friends. He was currently examining a dwarven foot that had blisters the size of a sword pommel. As Hunter took care of them, little Chestnut talked the poor dwarf's ear off. The victim/patient stared at her, wide-eyed and silent, occasionally glancing around in a silent plea for help.

When Hunter was finished, the blisters were gone. With his boot replaced the dwarf shouted, "Thanks!" to Hunter as he dove out of the wagon without waiting for it to stop, tucked, rolled into a low stance and ran to his place in his column amid laughter from his fellows (some of whom had already encountered the little 'Healer's Helper' as they now called her) and a little, high-pitched voice calling after him to not wear his boots so loosely.

Their food wagons, hung with water barrels on the sides, each had one of Queen Hazelmoon's guardian warlocks riding along with the drivers. Every now and then there would be a flash or puff of smoke of various colors emerging that he would react to with a start and then pointedly ignore. Rrahmus and the Queen, riding together, had both noticed his actions and now looked to him immediately when it happened, frequently laughing together at his discomfort. His pangs of jealousy didn't help.

***

Chapter 62

Dragons OFF the Ship

The voyage was largely unremarkable with one exception. Angus, working with Molly on some spells to pass the time, almost caught the ship on fire. And they were worried about dragons! Bronwyn however doused the blaze easily, and necessarily as the flames were under her hammock! Before any crew arrived to investigate their yelling, Graham covered up the miniature flood and noise with a mop and a bucket and some rather bawdy songs sung loudly and a bit off-key, swabbing away at the deck in the girls berthing area.

When they finally arrived in port, the captain asked Thom if they wished to disembark first, or wait until nightfall. Having already decided that they were unlikely to be recognized, they exited readily. Audhan was familiar with the area and had a cousin whose lair was nearby where they could stay while they waited, out of the local public scrutiny (and he and the Old One could stretch out and sleep at full size).

They bought some supplies and headed inland. Once away from the view of random observers, Audhan changed form, put the Old One on his back and flew off.

The rest kept along their original path as the road generally headed in the right direction and would make his return flight shorter. In under one turn of an hourglass he was back. He said, "We're all set. My cousin is not home, but it won't be a problem. I will give you all charms of his that will let you in and out, and hopefully keep him from eating you..."

Graham just rolled his eyes and began putting on his armor while the rest had expressions ranging from incredulity to horror. He said, "I'll head back to the tavern at the edge of town to see what's going on around here. Meet me back here about an hour after dark. I'll light a fire or a torch to mark my position."

Audhan nodded and took Molly and Bronwyn to the lair.

Left with Angus and Tahmus, Graham said, "That dragon is a great kid. Rrahmus loves him. But he may need advice. Please make sure that he gets it?"

The two elves both looked quizzically at the broad back of the enormous human as he strode away with a ground-eating stride. He looked odd wearing his armor instead of carrying it on his back for a change. The handle of his enormous sword stuck up above his right shoulder, looking like an oar pulling against the air, driving him forward. His helmet swung from his left hand like a dangling anchor.

Tahmus said, "I wish I had a thousand of those..."

Angus replied, "To do what? We haven't been seriously threatened by the giants in decades."

"It's an age-old commander's dream I guess – an army of soldiers that can both fight and think, that are both logical and loving? It sounds amazing." He chuckled. "It never works out that way though."

***

Chapter 63

To the Fort

Farsight was living up to his name. He and his brother were watching the trail from the town to the riverside fort. He saw his sisters go by following the river's edge. Not long afterward a fight spilled out into the street. They were too far away to hear, but he was fairly certain that somehow his sisters had the men of the town fighting each other! They kept waiting, hiding in ambush, waiting for returners to keep them from getting to the fort and interrupting their plan. And then he heard a soft, broken female cry of pain and fear behind him and he smiled in the darkness.

***

The woman came running out of the darkness into the rings of torchlight looking back over her shoulder, oblivious to the slanted beams on the shore side of the road leading from the town to the fort. Designed to let the drawbridge rest at the appropriate angle without putting tension on the boards or the lift chains, it was <u>not</u> designed to be stepped on by half of a boot while running. The cry that followed the rolling of her ankle was both cause for alarm and yet strangely alluring to the two guards atop the walk above the raised bridge. When they looked closer, both immediately recognized the mass of curly red hair sobbing on the ground below them.

One yelled down to her, against all of his instructions, "Are you alright Miss?"

"Of course she's not alright!" said the other, "She's twisted that ankle for certain. But there's naught we can do about it, so leave it be."

If the first guard could have seen Mynorca's face as she stared at her hand rubbing her booted right ankle, he would have agreed and that would have ended it. But before she turned her beautiful face towards them, her satisfied, cunning smile was replaced by a wounded, pleading look. When she spoke the accompanying plaintive words, "Help me! They're after me! Oh, I'll never escape them now..." and sobbed into her arms folded over her knees, he was sunk.

What he said was, "Release the lock, I'm opening the bridge. Now!"

The older guard's tone brooked no argument, and as he set his poleaxe down to lean it against the inner stone and mortar wall he thumped the butt of it down for emphasis before stepping into the bars at the end of the iron-banded log that served to spool the chains up and down to open and close the drawbridge.

The younger (and wiser) guard said, "Fine." He pulled the iron handle that took the bars out of both chains at once. Thus unpinned they could spool freely, and soon were. As they did, the younger guard looked over the edge of the parapet and said, "Miss! You need to get to the other side of that shelf beam or the bridge will crush you! Hurry now!" He had seen the songstress perform a few times and even in the dim light quite enjoyed watching her wriggle to comply. He would carry her himself if needed he thought.

When the bridge was down, he said, "Okay, now clamber over on and as we raise it, just slide down to the bottom!" This time he was rewarded by a view as she pulled herself onto the bridge on her hands and knees, smiling up at him, her blouse being perfectly affected by gravity. Then she rolled onto her hip and spun to a seated position and began to scoot downward as they raised the bridge.

"Besides," he said conspiratorially to his elder who was busy raising the drawbridge by himself, "she'll just be trapped between the bridge and the portcullis anyway. And now she owes us a favor..." His smile almost matched Mynorca's. He knew she had noticed him during her performances in the tavern. He was a bit of a dandy who wore loose-fitting shirts and tight trousers, his boots shined, and his hair, beard and sword always glistened from a coating of the same light oil.

As he mused about his other options with their newly acquired beautiful captive, when the words, "Lock the pins," came, he did so reflexively, not looking up. Too late his peripheral vision caught the butt of the poleaxe as it smashed into his temple.

***

Mynorca was the only one who heard the stifled maniacal chuckle from behind her under her cloak. "Sh!" she said quietly.

"But they are so dumb!" came the whispered response.

"Of course – they're men. Now shush!"

Soon enough footsteps came down the inner stairwell to their left. Completely made of stone and walled off from Mynorca's view, the stair opened into the back of a reception area that they faced. On the other side of an iron cross-hatched portcullis with openings so small she couldn't put her hand through, there was a half-wall, perfect for spearmen to defend from. On each side of the room behind that wall were racks of bodkin-style spears with long, narrow hardened iron points designed to penetrate mail, armor and shields that she knew could skewer her where she stood from behind the safety of that wall.

The helmeted head that peered at her briefly around the edge of the stone wall disappeared again quickly, and she heard, "You're safe now, Miss. No one can hurt you. I just can't let you in, at least not yet, it's against the rules."

She let go a small sob, "Alright. I mean, thank you for protecting me. Those men were so horrible! They tried to attack me, but then they fought over me and I ran! But now my ankle hurts terribly, and I don't think I can sit down in here, but, if those are your master's rules I don't want you to get into trouble on my account…"

She could hear the quick clanks of metal on stone in the stairwell as his helmet gently knocked against the wall as he argued with himself internally. She almost had him.

"I'm so sorry Miss. I just don't have the authority. I've done what I could to make you safe, now we'll just have to wait for my comrades to return and get you the help you need."

She gasped, "Oh, no! Then I am surely doomed, as they were some of those who attacked me! I just

469

need one strong protector! One who will come away with me and help me leave this evil place!" The sobbing, increasing throughout, was inconsolable now. A small pointed, gnomish boot to the back of her calf at 'surely doomed' had helped with the tears.

This time the helmet appeared on the other side of the large square of mortared stone that encased the stairs to the top of the gate. "MY men attacked you?!" he said.

"Some of them..." she sobbed. "A few tried to protect me, too, that was how the fight started."

It rang true, not only because it <u>was</u> true, but because he had knocked out his own watch partner for his rapacious thoughts just moments ago. And tied him up, for he didn't want a blade in his back. That was going to be hard enough to explain...

"The only way I can protect you is to let you in, but no one can know I did it, or that you are here at all... It may sound really odd, but I think I can do it... You'll just have to hide. Unfortunately the only place to do that would be in one of the cells..." he finished lamely.

"What?!" she exclaimed, "You want me as a prisoner?!"

"No-no-no!" he said quickly, "It's just that no one would look for you there! I can sneak you food, and then in a few days when things calm down, even if they go looking for you, we just slip away in a different direction."

She was silent a moment, then said softly, "You're pretty smart, and you've not attacked me. I'll trust you."

The iron portcullis was counter-weighted on a single chain system that was operated from the side. He went there now and opened it just enough for her to duck under it and come inside, then lowered it back down right away.

"We have to hurry," he said, "I have to be back on the gate walk before anyone finds out I'm away from my post."

"And your partner above?" she asked.

"He is no longer a concern..." he said darkly, and started to turn to leave.

Mynorca froze, waited for him to turn back, and took in an impressive heaving breath that made him freeze as well. She removed his helmet and kissed him, softly at first, then hungrily, pressing her whole body against him. And then she stopped, replaced his helmet, and stepped back. "Don't run, please," she said coyly, "my ankle still really hurts!"

He started to turn away again, did a quick

double take, then moved slowly but directly toward a door in the back left corner of the room. They were then outside, in a courtyard, where the middle was open with no roof, but the walkways along the building walls were covered with drainage roofs and spouts to fill freshwater barrels for siege preparations. It was indeed a well-planned fortress. Almost to the river, in the center of one wall, was a strange semi-circular half door, and a matching-shaped iron trap door in the floor in front of it.

Opening both, the guard revealed an angled passage downward with steps cut into the native stone. He said, "Down here. You go first."

She did, and soon she saw five doors sent into a native stone wall that had to be below the waterline of the river, but she saw no moisture anywhere. He pointed to her left when she looked back for guidance. When she opened it he said, "It's full of long term provisions, essentially our root cellar, but no one goes in here, and we don't have any actual prisoners, so the rest are full of goods too, but those we use more often. Don't worry, you'll find blankets to keep warm too. I may not be able to do anything sooner, but I <u>will</u> bring you food in the morning."

She hesitated, then nodded and squeezed his

hand, appreciating his slow crimson blush.

The sound of the bolt closing on the locked door bothered her not at all.

***

Though a bit tall for a gnome girl, and <u>way</u> over the line mentally into the psychotic side of evil behavior, Yelsa did not behave randomly. She was fiercely loyal to her siblings; they were her only true connection to the rest of the world. She <u>belonged</u> with them. Not even the priests who taught her knew what she wanted from life, only that life itself held little value for her.

When she slipped out from under Mynorca's cloak as she kissed the fort guard, Yelsa looked back from cover in time to see her sister look back for her as well as she was being led away. The beautiful redheaded human girl's expression was a very sisterly, very twinkly, squinty smile of secret unconditional love. Faith that she would not abandon her as their father had done to all of them. Yelsa knew that she was trusted, valued, and ... loved.

She considered killing the man the second his back was turned, but knew that as long as he waited for his companions to return she could search the place unhindered. Now she just needed the thief skills and strength to make sure she could look everywhere she wanted...so off she went to open the riverside gate on the upriver wall.

***

"So, how many do we plan to kill?" asked Hailee.

"One at a time dear brother, one at a time..." said the half-elf.

"Fine. How many total?" was the exasperated response.

"Our collective inquiries and observations tell us there have been thirteen distinct personages in the fort by the river. Ten soldiers, one builder, one priest and the 'master'. No one has seen the 'master' in a season, the priest, builder and four soldiers just left on a journey, and two always remain inside. That should be it," said Farsight.

"Be WHAT?!" said the half-orc, frustrated as usual by story problems involving math.

"Four. We should, at most, have to deal with four. Okay?"

"Yes. Thank you. Just a handful then, and not behind fortress walls. No worries," said Hailee.

"No," said Farsight, forgetting his audience for a moment, "a handful would be ... urk!"

The enormous paw, made up of a thumb and three oaken bow thickness fingers that grasped his throat reminded him, quietly, "Four," with a whisper in his ear, "but I only see two … ssshhh…"

The two men that stumbled toward them were quite obviously injured, and the trailing one, though not limping like his companion, was dragging his sword tip in the dirt, looking frequently behind him. Their conversation soon became intelligible.

"…so many at once. And our own comrade against us! Can't believe he stabbed Carl in the back like that…no warning, nothing!"

"Yes," said the other, "and as he is a better swordsman than you or I, you should have done the same. At least then we wouldn't both be wounded…"

"Oh please! You fell over a bench getting out of his way while he took a swing at my head! You deserved an injured leg."

"You stabbed me!"

"Not on purpose! When you fell, he tripped over your flailing legs and when I ran him through the sword point accidentally found your leg. I said I was sorry! At least we're alive…"

The two were drawing even with their ambushers when all four heard a very loud clang of metal on metal, one, two, three times, then a loud scraping noise of metal on stone, a pause, then a combined crunching splash.

Even as the injured coward turned back to ask his rescuer/injurer what he thought it was and what to do, all he saw was his companion's look of surprise as his head came away from his shoulders, a great axe blade appearing where the front of his neck had just been.

Following the structure of the axe to its handle, then hands holding it and arms and body they belonged to, he saw the enormous half-orc grinning at him.

His puzzled expression froze in place – forever – as Farsight reached around his neck from behind with both hands and used the daggers they held to pull the man toward him as violently and quickly as he could. It didn't quite decapitate him, but near enough that when the half-elven thief pulled his blades clear and the body began to topple forward the head stayed upright all the way to the ground, then whip-cracked face down into the road with a crunch of finality.

The brothers looked quickly toward the town, and seeing nothing coming their way, dragged their respective victims off of the path by their heels (Hailee had to go back for the severed head of his victim), then using a broken leafy branch swept away (or swept dirt over) as much of the blood as they could see – or at least Farsight could see, before it cooled.

Then they waited all over again, but rather than more guards or searchers, they were only approached by their crazy sister. Her tap on their shoulders sent them both into instant violent reactions that were completely useless against a half-gnomish girl who was sitting down, back to a tree, giggling with uncontrollable maniacal laughter.

After regarding her briefly, and with a glance at each other, both posed to counter-attack man-sized opponents, they each rolled their eyes and shrugged, sank down beside her, and laughed with her.

When they subsided, Farsight finally asked, "What was the clanking and crashing behind us?"

"Not me! The guard that kissed Mynorca killed his partner and threw him off of the fort wall into the stones of the moat."

Hailee said, "The guard … killed his own man … because Mynorca kissed him?"

Her little smile was mischievous and playful as she said, "Close enough!"

"So, now what?" asked the thief.

"Well," she said, "Mynorca is locked up, he is

the only one left and can't leave the gate watch, the side door is open, and Grunnach is waiting for us there!"

They both gave up, stood up, and waited for her to lead the way, which she did, happily.

***

Chapter 64

Inside the River Fort

Yelsa led the way out to the river and down the riverbank to the right-hand edge of the cut where quite recently the drawbridge had been lowered for her lovely sister. She nimbly stepped out into the water and trudged steadily across to the island, the water never even getting to her ankles or into her heavy boots, and got nowhere near the bottom of her charcoal gray robe or the black cape she wore over it.

Farsight crossed right behind her, making almost no noise at all. Hailee had to step gingerly from stone to stone, not because he could not see them, nor because he didn't know where they were – he had placed them himself – but because he could not help but splash, since his boots were the size of gnomish shields.

Once across they made their way to the riverside boat loading and unloading side service entrance on the upriver side of the fort. At the outer gate under the stairs they were greeted by another grinning sibling. The half-dwarf let them in and locked the gate behind them. "Well," he said, "we're all in!"

They looped around and up into the right-hand spiraling stair and through an upper, matching gate into the parapet walk that went completely around the top of the outer wall. There were dome shaped covers over stone vents here and there indicating fireplaces below, and drain holes for the rain to run off, both outside where they exited through sculpted stone figures to force the brunt of the water's eroding force away from the walls, and inside into collection barrels for drinking and cooking in case of a siege.

Yelsa gave the layout. "There are stairwells in all four corners. The one we just passed to get to the gate is the main keep with the master's quarters. The guard house barracks is in the other front corner. Those two are three levels high. By the river on this side where we are is the storehouse, and in its cellar, Mynorca is in the far left chamber, long term stores. The riverside corner farthest from us is the chapel, the kitchen and dining rooms are below us. The only guard left is at the gate. Other than him, we're alone!"

Farsight said, "We need to make sure he stays there, search the keep, the chapel and the storage. Yelsa, you know right where Mynorca is, so take Grunnach and let her out then head through the storage first and meet us in the chapel. Hailee, let's take care of the guard and check the keep."

***

The half-elf thief stood at the point in the upper portion of the stairs up to the top of the gate overlook where only the top of his head and eyes were above the level of the upper floor. His target was pacing too much and too quickly and erratically to be normal. The guard kept peering over the wall, looking down at the moat below. Farsight was sure he was looking at his partner that he had murdered and then thrown onto the rocks below. The thief had hoped for a pattern of behavior to exploit but was rapidly losing hope. This man was dealing with a guilty conscience.

And then his opportunity arose. The guard lost his internal argument and headed for the stairwell, his gait finally purposeful and decisive, his gaze down and left, looking at the point below him where he would have to turn with the stairs. He never saw the shadowy form in the shadowy side of the stairwell away from the torches above, nor did he see the arm that shot out to lift his back foot as he stomped downward. The trip spun him so quickly and unexpectedly that he did not get his hands out to break his fall, and when his forehead struck several stairs down, his neck snapped. Farsight heard the last air escape his dead lungs and thought that if they did this right, the internal killings would look accidental.

He retrieved Hailee and they went to the keep, leaving the guard where he lay.

***

The first door they came to looked imposing – it was large, thick, heavy, and ornately carved, but with no obvious handles or locks or even a clue as to which way it swung to open.

"Great," grumbled the half-orc, "Magic…"

"Not necessarily!" said his brother, who knelt down and put one ear close to the door. After a moment he shook his head.

Hailee pushed hard, right in the center of the door, with one enormous hand. There was no sound of hinges or scraping and the door flew straight backward a few paces and stopped. The siblings exchanged a silent quizzical glance in the light of Hailee's torch held in his other hand. Both shrugged and entered the room, each stepping in on opposite sides of the door.

The room was large, open, with a cobblestone floor and large mortared stone walls with high open windows at the top. There was a large round table with a dozen chairs around it in the center of the room. Around the walls were several cupboards, revealing nothing but cups, plates, utensils, and bottles of various spirits. When Hailee tried to open one his brother slapped his giant hand and took it from him, saying, "That could be poison, or a potion, or even really rotten ale. Knock it off. There are three more doors in here – pick one!"

The pouty half-orc face made the half-elf want to laugh, but he kept a straight face. Barely. After a moment, his huge little brother moved, pointing, explaining his logic out loud, "That probably goes to the kitchens Yelsa told us about," he said of the door to their left. "This," he said pointing to the door straight ahead on the far side of the table before them, "lines up with the stairs from above. But that one…" he said turning to his right, "That one goes back toward the front wall of the fort by the moat… So, let's verify the first two, then focus on <u>that</u> one."

"You're smarter than you look," said his little big brother.

With a huff/grunt and shake of his large greenish, somewhat porcine head, Hailee backhanded Farsight in the stomach, the latter losing all air with which to speak (likely the intended effect) and trudged to the left hand door.

Farsight, bent double from the brotherly

483

remonstration, spent a long moment regaining his wind, then, duck-walking a little, joined Hailee, knelt, and listened at the door. This one had a large ring right in the center. Looking back at the door they had entered he saw a similar ring, and, looking up, saw a similar rail system above him. He placed his ear to the door and heard – nothing.

Rising and moving to the side, Farsight nodded to Hailee. The larger brother reared back to strike the door as he had done before, and before the horrified smaller brother could stop him, Hailee's arm shot forward – and stopped just short of the door, gently grasped the ring, and pulled the door open, slowly and quietly, revealing the kitchens beyond as he had suggested.

"And you," chuckled the half-orc around his tusks, "are dumber than you look…"

One adrenaline releasing sigh later and Farsight pushed the door closed. "I suppose I deserved that."

"Yes, you did."

"Fine. These are inner barricade only doors – see the matching rings on either side of the door built into the walls? And the heavy iron bar meant to slide through all three? They only lock from the inside. Our uninformed host is not here, that seems certain now."

They quickly repeated their process at the center door, revealing the stairs they expected, without the sibling foolishness. Moving on, at the right hand door however, there was no ring.

The half-elven thief knelt down as before, and, looking to the side, leaned forward to press his ear to the door – and fell headlong to the ground. In his flailing to recover, he could see that Hailee had pranked him again and was almost doubled over laughing, holding the door open where he had pushed it while his brother wasn't looking.

Farsight, still on the ground, kicked his brother in the shin. It did not remotely injure his target, but it did make him feel a little better.

Once again moving to opposite sides of the door, this time the brothers senses were assaulted in the light of Hailee's torch.

Every wall was covered in painted murals of battle scenes. In each the victims were all humans, with most not wearing armor or possessing any decent weaponry. Their attackers were dragons and mages with grotesque faces and horns.

The light barely reached the far wall, but in the corner to the left was a huge and ornately carved canopy bed, the work similar to that on the outer door, but with the same grotesque faces as on the walls. Next to it was a rack of very old weapons, rusty, dusty, and uncared for, then a set of shelves lined with dozens of books and bone and wood scroll cases, then more shelves lined with jars and bottles and small casks. Farsight was sure some of the contents were moving...

And then he saw the chest. It was dark wood, banded in yellow metal – brass or gold – either way it was shiny and drew the thief's sole focus and attention. He began to move toward it, almost involuntarily. After a few steps he noticed that he wasn't going forward anymore. Frustrated, he looked down for obstacles, only to notice that his feet were not touching the floor and that he was being lifted by the sides of his leather armor. "C'mon! Leggo!" he said quietly.

"No," was the quiet but firm answer. "Not until you snap out of it. I know how you get!"

The dangling feet kicked a little in futility, followed by a sigh and shoulders slumped in defeat.

"Fine. I'll be good," said the thief.

When his brother set him down, Farsight paused a few seconds, studying the scene. He recounted his observations for his brother. "The weapons are neglected, the scrolls and potions dusty and untended, and this chest looks almost as new as a freshly made item, but is obviously very old..."

The response was a low grumble, "I <u>told</u> you this place was magicked. This is a bad idea. This place belongs to a wizard, not some old rich merchant..."

"Touch it," said the thief.

"What?!"

"Just touch it, you're more durable. If there's a magic protection, you'll likely survive where I would not."

"No."

"Yes!"

"No!"

"Fine. I'll do it..."

As the half-elf began to reach out his hand toward the chest with a slightly tremorous bounce, it was slapped down, the reverse of earlier with the bottle.

"NO!! I'll do it!" said Hailee. And he did.

And nothing happened. They were both shocked that he had not been shocked.

Farsight began to examine the locks. There were two. What he saw was not good. Small holes above each were likely the openings for two classic poisoned-needle traps, designed to kill or incapacitate those who opened the chest incorrectly. The problem was that each hole could also be the point to insert an extra tool – another 'key' of sorts – to keep a trap from being sprung. As he debated, Hailee said, "I could just smash it open with my axe..."

"And if the trap is poisonous gas? Or acid? No. Not at least without Yelsa here to heal me if I need her. No, let's go to the chapel."

***

When they reached the small place of worship in the opposite corner of the compound, they entered to find their siblings staring at a remarkable spectacle. There were a half dozen wooden pews, benches with high backs and slightly tilted up seats.

Mynorca turned to greet them with her usual sincerely warm smile that she reserved just for her family. She said, "Come, sit down a moment and see if you have any thoughts about this."

Hailee could only sit in the front row as he would not fit between the rows. Farsight sat next to him.

They had all seen altars, pulpits, dais', and stages – this was different. It was a pool with stairs leading up to its edge like a fountain, but the only artwork was a golden-hued sculpture behind and above it. It depicted an armored knight on a warhorse with a lance stabbing a dragon from above. Behind the knight on his horse was a robed mage, hands extended, shooting bolts of lightning at a pixie on the dragon's back, one bolt striking the rider's wings and the other his head.

Farsight, still staring at the spectacle before him, said back over his shoulder, "Sorry, Sis, your guard friend fell down the stairs and broke his neck. I'm pretty sure he was going to retrieve his comrade that he killed for you and then threw off of the fort wall into the moat headfirst..." When no response was forthcoming, he continued, "Also, we went through the master's chambers and all we found was that he's likely a wizard and has a trapped chest in his room."

Yelsa said, "What the guard told Mynorca about putting her somewhere safe, that she wouldn't be found with the long term stores? That was a lie. The other four rooms down there are filled with bags of rubies from floor to ceiling." For emphasis she dropped one over the thief's shoulder and onto his lap. He let the initial quiver of greed that passed through him subside, then said, "If this is being kept in unsecured rooms and with only a few guards in the whole place, what is in that chest?!"

"Before we go find out," said Mynorca, "Here

are a few bags of rubies each for all of us to have in case we have to run or split up." It was reminiscent of a mother telling a bunch of children to bundle up against the cold before going out to play.

***

Chapter 65

Lily is a Sneak

Lily first made sure that her daughters were safe for the moment. Then she went back to the ship she had just left, knowing it was in port and unlikely to have moved. She could not risk staying gone long enough for it to be out of position and lose them as much as she wanted to report the two traitorous troglodytes' theft to Fallon's security chief.

Getting Djinja and Eyevee out of their clutches had been easy enough. Popping in and out while invisible defeated their captor's ability to notice her. Letting them out and transporting their portal items home was done at their next port in minutes. But though she stayed to try to retrieve the stolen items as well, the trogs had relocated them into a magically sealed chest. So, she stayed with the ship.

At the next port she went back to Fallon's again. This time her colleagues at Fallon's told her that the mages were still all gone and they had no method to contact them. The frustrated little wingless fairy took her wings in their glass summoning case and moved them into Rrahmus' chamber on a high shelf so no one would inadvertently call her away while on a moving ship and not be able to get back to it. She returned and started gathering information.

The trogs were actually quite arrogant <u>and</u> dumb. They didn't check on their hostages for weeks – again. Lily was sure that they didn't really care if they died, but they certainly did not let them go as they'd told her they would either! If they had intended to, they would have discovered their absence much sooner. As it was, when finally <u>did</u> notice, they still had no idea that they'd escaped. The cabin ogre they questioned said that perhaps he'd accidentally put them into the washing with their other crockery. They just laughed.

At the third port stop, they switched ships. When they boarded the new one, she waited. This one was crewed by ogres, not men. That couldn't be good. They didn't come ashore at all, just let the two troglodytes come aboard with their baggage, retrieved the gang plank, and cast off again. Lily, invisible, blinked herself to the unoccupied high rear deck of the new ship as it eased away from the wharf in time to see a third troglodyte greet the priest and mage, who deferred to him, bowing. No, not good at all.

By the next port she had gleaned who the lead trog was, why the ogres were helping, and who was behind it all. Now she just needed to figure out who to tell and how without losing track of them.

***

Chapter 66

Had to Try

Farsight said, "Let's make this good, okay? We steal as many rubies as we can and still make the rooms look full. We just pull bags from the back closer to the door. A boat serves us best I think... Yelsa, will you take Hailee and get a boat and meet us at the side gate riverbank pier?" Getting a nod, he said, "Okay. Let's move some gems!"

In an hour they had ten bags of rubies each loaded into a boat Hailee had acquired not far upriver. As they got together to discuss leaving, Farsight said, "I want what's in that chest..."

Yelsa said, "You can't just take it with us, it gives away the robbery too easily."

Mynorca said, "Fine. We go check it out, together. Hailee, stay with the boat. If anyone comes, drown them, and let the river take them. If there's too many, just shove off in the boat – we'll find you downriver, okay?"

Hailee nodded, smiling.

In another quarter of an hour they were back, Farsight carrying a bag over his shoulder with a

495

bandaged hand and looking a little orcishly green...

"What hap-..." began Hailee.

"Don't want to talk about it," said the half-elf.

"Let's go."

***

Chapter 67

Keep the Old One Safe

"So, what did you learn?" asked Tahmus.

"That we missed an odd meeting between some troglodytes and some other 'folk like me' several days ago," replied Graham as he continued to remove his armor. As he pulled the chainmail shirt over his head it gripped his undershirt and padding, pulling them up too. He dropped the mail with his eyes covered and it clanged and scraped metal on metal as it struck his already removed breastplate where it lay on the ground. Still blinded by his clothing, he pulled off the padded leather, leaving only a light weight spun shirt up around his face and neck, revealing his torso.

All eyes had already been on him anyway, but now the scrutiny was increased, especially by Bronwyn and Molly, noting the large, rippling muscles – and the scars on most of them. Long slashes, short stab wound marks, even sets of claws had cut him more than once. When he brought the shirt down, he carried on his report. "When I asked about it, the innkeeper said that the two had waited for a few days for some men to arrive by land. They wore robes and he was certain that the ship that brought them was crewed by ogres. That on its face was odd enough as the two are age old enemies. When I said as much, he agreed, as was their staying at the inn and not on the ship – 'Sailors just don't normally waste coin like that,' he said."

Angus, cooking what smelled like mutton over a crackling fire, looked up and said dramatically from across the large mountain cave, "No we do not!" with a broad grin.

"Anyway," continued Graham, "he said it was even stranger when they left as the 'trogs' left on the ship they came in, while the creep they met, a human in dark mage's robes, and some of his men went back the way they came – the way we left to come here, by the way – but more of them got onto yet another ship. A small ship heading to where <u>we</u> just came from…"

Audhan spoke first. "You think they are the ones that came to get the Old One."

"I do. But there must be more to the story. He was guarded by ogres, but these didn't go get him… Why not?"

Angus walked over and handed the large fighter a leg of sheep, freshly roasted. While Graham took the morsel and devoured it in seconds, Angus said, "What if those trogs are helping to conceal his prison? We know the ogres man it. I'd love to know where those 'men' went..."

"Well," said Graham, "we have a few weeks of waiting for that ship to return to find out I think."

Audhan said, "Whatever their plan was with him, getting him out of their prison and just hiding here foils it, no?"

Tahmus agreed. "Right. <u>We</u> can do some investigating, but I say the girls and the dragons stay <u>here</u>."

The various responses he received all at once were of many pitches and volumes, but they were unanimous in their disagreement. When they died down to a dull roar, he bellowed back (at the ceiling far above), "Fine! Do what you want! Who needs logic or safety anyway?!"

He noted the bemused smiles on the faces of the Old One and Graham and shook his head before sitting by the fire and carving himself some mutton. The old fighter would not want it said that he had died hungry.

***

Chapter 68

An Empty Fort

"So, now what?" asked Bronwyn. Her comment appeared to bounce off of the enormous back in front of and largely above her. Graham did not respond.

Instead, the tawny gold-colored wolf at his side turned to look at her and said, "Sshh." Audhan had tracked the scent of the men from the port tavern to this place, but when they found two freshly beheaded bodies in the dark, they paused to investigate.

"It was an ambush," said the dragon-in-wolf-form. "These two came from the town, but they were also in the tavern. Two more left with them, but have not been back this way. The ones that went by us to the closer port, at least four, must be those trying to book passage for the Old One. They have not returned either." He paused, then circled near where the drawbridge to the riverside fort in front of him lay. Walking back into the trees, he continued, "Two others, not any of the guards, were here. One of them was at the ambush site with the two ambushers. None of which explains the dead body in the moat or the lack of guards, either at the gate or on the walls. This whole place is creepy. I'm going to fly up and have a look around..."

***

Audhan landed back on the same bank he had taken off from, on the upriver side of the fort, deciding to proactively answer the several pairs of questioning eyes at once.

"The dead guardian in the moat was also on the wall above. His comrade is also dead, fell down some inner stairs. Neither seems to have combat wounds. The two that entered through the drawbridge were met by the ambushers and one other at a side gate, and again inside in an odd chapel with a large round pool in it."

Turning to Graham he said, "And they have rooms full of bags of Grandfather's rubies."

"Greed doesn't have to accompany a lust for power, but neither does it have to be independent of it," said Tahmus.

"But they're gone...?" asked Angus.

"Yes," answered Audhan, "but quite recently. The mage was here. This is his place."

"Why here?" asked Bronwyn.

"Likely the fountain," said Tahmus.

"Where did they go?" asked Graham.

"The tracks all converge here at the river...I say

they took a boat," said Audhan.

"Well," mused Angus, "The Old One is safe with Molly for now, let's follow them!"

They all agreed with that, just not how... Graham said, "We need to go now. Those bodies in the trees are fresh and will draw attention come daylight... I know," he said, looking at Tahmus, "we should wait and buy a boat... I know, stealing is wrong... But getting killed by an angry mob for something we didn't do is <u>way</u> worse than some short-term guilt that we can come back and correct..."

The elf stewed on that for a few seconds, then said, "Fine. Just don't make ME do it."

In a quarter turn they were floating downriver in a newly acquired small fishing boat with a removable mast and sail and sides lined with reed baskets. As they sped along the current with the aid of Audhan's tail, the only comment was from the dragon. "The smell of fish is making me hungry."

***

Hailee stared at his brother's bandaged hand as they floated down the river in the darkness. Farsight stared at Yelsa. Yelsa stared at Mynorca. Her softly curling red hair looked alternating black and silver in the moonlight as she swayed her head, humming an old slow tune that none of them recognized.

***

The river was lazy and slow, flat, and dark, with the moonlight making it easy to make out the banks lined with trees. With the extra power supplied by Audhan's tail, the result they wanted was easily achieved – in under an hour Tahmus sighted the boat ahead of them when it was still several dozen rods away and he quietly let the rest know.

Angus whispered, "A handful maybe, including one large something… I have a plan…"

It looked to Graham like he had a piece of shiny black glass, and after saying a few odd phrases about 'deceptive darkness' and 'bending like long grass before the wind', set it down in the boat. In a few seconds Graham could no longer see him. Or Audhan. Or the boat! "So, what's the rest of this 'plan'?" he whispered.

"Get close and listen, take them unawares, maybe on the water, maybe on shore?" said Angus.

As if by request, they were soon close enough to hear a rather musical voice say, "There, at the next bend, there's a soft sandy cove – steer for that."

The lead boat did exactly as the woman's voice directed, and it eased into a shallow backwater.

As it drew near the shore, the occupants began

to hop out to drag it up to beach the bow – and were stuck fast when the water all around them froze into a sheet of ice several inches thick. As they spun their heads and struggled, trying to be quiet, but also checking on their siblings to figure out what was happening to them, figures swarmed them out of the darkness.

Hailee felt his sword and axe yanked from his back and heard, "I'll just hold these big fella, you rest easy for a minute..." Realizing that the voice was speaking from very near his ear and that his weapons had been drawn out easily and <u>upward</u> from his own tall back, he knew his unknown assailant was both large and, more importantly, <u>not</u> trying to kill him. He let his hands swing out wide from his sides, empty and in full view from both front and rear, and said, "As you say..." and as he said it he saw several elves and a human girl do the same to the rest of his family. There was only one brief moment where he thought violence might break out.

Tahmus had Mynorca's wrists held behind her back, Angus held one clenched hand toward each Grunnach and Farsight, who were completely immobilized. Bronwyn and Yelsa were face to face, and though no words were being spoken the contest of wills was obvious. Yelsa's eyes, normally possessing a rather crazed look, had an extra edge of hatred, but they were not looking at Bronwyn; she was focused on Tahmus, her sister's captor.

Just as she appeared to be losing control and started to raise her hands, a soft voice came from a reptilian head that appeared in front of her eyes, saying, "You love her very much, don't you?"

The little half-gnome priestess' eyes went as wide as they had ever in her entire life to that point. She stammered, "D-d-d-dragon!"

"Yes, but I don't plan to eat you... At least, not yet..." smiled Audhan, several of his extra-large teeth sparkling in the darkness. She dropped her hands, and to almost everyone's surprise, smiled back...

"You're ... beautiful!" she replied.

"Uh... thank you..." said Audhan, somewhat taken aback.

Mynorca's laughter fell on all of their ears like tiny raindrops made of quietly tinkling silver bells. All of the elves looked at her curiously. Bronwyn turned and glared at her, but Graham laughed out loud, saying, "Sorry miss, I assume you're naturally 'charming' and not trying to influence us in any underhanded way, but, either way, this particular group is <u>not</u> the right audience!" He continued laughing at the expressions all around him. Only the tusked greenish fighter whose weapons he was holding said under his breath, "You called that one!"

It was Angus who finally put them all at ease. "Listen, we don't want to kill or rob you. Honestly, we may find a way to even compensate you if you help us, because it seems clear to me that you aren't residents of the fort you just came from. Raiders, perhaps even thieves — no offense intended! — but not regular occupants. Interested?"

It was the slightly-too-large gnomish female that turned to him and said, "We took some of what we found, but we didn't find what we were looking for. And then we stayed too long, so we left."

"So," Tahmus began, "can we make this a bit more friendly and keep anyone from losing some frozen toes?"

Hailee spoke over his shoulder to Graham, saying, "Don't worry, I'm good with this, but I'll make sure my brothers are too..." As he finished talking, he pulled one leg and then the other from the magical ice with almost no effort, clomped over to Farsight and Grunnach and stood in front of them. "I know you can hear me. The mage here is going to release you," he got a nod from Angus, "and when he does, you'll not do anything hostile or stupid, got it?"

Grunnach made no sound, but rolled his eyes a little. Farsight's mumble was both angry and non-cooperative. Hailee looked at Angus and said, "It's okay, I got this." Reaching back toward Graham, he said, "Axe please?"

Graham obliged, and without shifting his feet the half-orc swung his axe through the ice on either side of Farsight's feet, the cracks making two sides of a triangle. Moving behind the now (muffled) yelling half-elf, Hailee waited. Angus spread the fingers of one hand in an exaggerated fashion, and Farsight began to squirm – right into the enormous arms of his brother – that pulled him backward in a bear hug that broke the last side of the triangle of ice that continued to trap his legs. Hailee lifted him up onto one shoulder and trudged to shore, setting the wriggling, cursing figure down on a log, one hand grasping both of his brother's while the other covered his mouth.

"You shouldn't talk like that in front of the girls," he said quietly.

The much smaller face went from anger to shame to acceptance before an exasperated, nose-breathing only sigh indicated that the struggling was over.

Angus released the half-dwarf as well, still watching the half-orc and half-elf in amusement. "So," he said, somewhat conspiratorially, "What <u>were</u> you looking for?"

Grunnach inhaled to answer, but before he could Yelsa said, "A magical gold hoard. Quite a large one actually... we followed it twice, and we know it went to the fort, but it's not there."

Now all of her four siblings were shaking their heads at her. Graham, who had moved over to the log and sat down next to Farsight, handed Hailee his sword and said, "Is that ... 'normal', for her?"

The half-elf stuck out an empty right hand in introduction, and said, "Actually, no. I'm Farsight, this is Hailee. <u>That</u> is Yelsa, our normally quiet sister."

In moments introductions were accomplished. Grunnach recognized Angus, and Hailee (as Graham only said his first name) said, "Heir to Yeomring Castle..." causing all of the siblings, including Mynorca, to look at him again, which in turn caused Bronwyn to glare at her again and Graham to laugh again. He walked out on the ice and brought their boat to shore, dragging it by the bowline across the ice, and tied it off to a tree.

Hailee mirrored his actions with the siblings stolen boat while Angus sat down between Audhan (now in elf form) and Yelsa and asked about the gold.

"What made you think the gold was in the fort?"

When the story was done, he only had a few more questions. He asked Farsight, "If you failed to get into the chest, how do you know the gold wasn't in it?"

The thief replied, "It was far too small. Bags of unprotected rubies that fill entire rooms? No. Whatever is in that chest is much more valuable, at least to the mage that lives there..."

"So you just decided that you'd done well enough and it was time to go?" This was said to the group.

The grumble of, "Yes, finally..." from a low tusky voice made the inquisitor laugh and the thief wince. The high-pitched perky voice that said, "Mynorca told Farsight that he was only allowed one healing per trap attempt, so I cured his poisoned finger and bandaged his hand and we left." The thief's grimace grew more pronounced.

"Okay," said Angus, "then what happened to the gold? Spent? Melted down? Smuggled out? If so, why? To where? Bags of rubies...may I see one please?"

The little half-gnome girl produced one from her robe pocket and handed it to the mage without question. He looked at it briefly, handed it to Audhan and said, "Same as the ones you found?"

Audhan's expression was serious as he handed it back to Yelsa. "Yes. It fits, with as long as he was imprisoned."

The older elf moved to where he could see them all. "Are you certain that there was nowhere the gold could still be hidden in that fort?" Five heads shook from side to side in the negative, revealing to him a true sibling resemblance. "Did they ever leave with a heavy cart?" Farsight repeated the motion. "How about a boat?" Several shrugs. "I'm out of options." Tahmus shrugged in resignation.

Angus said, "Audhan? There may be another possibility..."

The dragon-in-elf-form looked at him, confused. Angus spelled it out for him. "What if the mage has someone who likes gold and can fly ... in his service?"

The expression that took over Audhan's face was grim. His eyes flashed gold in anger at the thought. Yelsa's heart melted. Audhan sputtered, "Roary would never aid a disgusting person like that mage!"

"At least," said Angus, "not willingly...how long has it

been since you've seen him...a decade or more?"

***

.

Chapter 69

The Approach

"We should reach the western edge of the coastal plains by tomorrow evening," Rrahmus said to the group at his fire. Their suppers consumed in the fading light, they watched as he and Myeer made colored flames chase each other about like wisps, changing shapes and colors. A tiny red mouse fled a cat outlined by blue lightning, and when the mouse became an orange wheel rolling into an as yet unburned log, the cat became a green arrow that shot through it.

"And then what?" asked Fallon. "We have diminished in number significantly…"

"True enough," said Aurelius, "but we cannot blame the King for responding to his own immediate existential threat, which we, by attracting his subjects and followers to our cause, actually made worse by leaving a larger power differential in our wake. The more of his experienced and capable fighters that chose to aid us, the more vulnerable he became. And it seems that King Chares' successors did not fail to realize it. I just hope that our calls for others to aid him are in time to be of service to him."

Queen Hazelmoon said, "As long as the pixies are sure that my Forest and Yeomring Castle remain clear of their intended destructive path, we, of course, remain committed."

Icelle just smiled and nodded. Sean rolled his eyes, and Krystal promptly smacked him with a backhand to his bicep which only prompted an even more exaggerated eyeroll with accompanying arm raise, which made almost everyone smile.

Only Flaw seemed out of sorts. Pill asked him why.

"It's true. The hate-filled men march again, this time against their human rivals only. They are no longer led directly by the evil, other worldly mage, but don't their actions stem from his influence? Where they had perceived mistreatment and disadvantage before, now they have actual losses, deaths by the score, lost loved ones. No matter how misguided or even evil they may be, they can now cry out those names as they attack, call upon them for strength in battle, recall their twisted, torn, bruised, burnt and bloody bodies as they exterminate all in their path. How can it end? Won't it just get worse?!"

The response was a bit gravelly. The dwarf behind Yar Drake, one of his commanders, named

Draluca spoke up. At least half of his hair was white, falling in stripes into his beard under his ears and at the corners of his mouth. "It only ends when both sides agree that it's over little friend. That could be one of three ways: 1. They compromise and just stop fighting. 2. One side surrenders. Or, 3. One side completely annihilates the other. That there is the truth of all contention, every argument, physical, logical, or emotional. Two out of three choices are absolute and leave half of those concerned either dead or ruined. The practical answer is to never really 'end' it. If one side is sufficiently beaten down enough to stop fighting, whether verbally or physically, even if just temporarily, then both can enjoy a reprieve, a respite if you will, and at least for a time avoid the melancholy that accompanies total destruction of an opponent or the despair of totally submitting to an enemy.

Folk never really let their emotions go away, they just hide them, some better than others." He paused, stood up and stretched, his back cracking audibly several times. "Though if you do encounter an unemotional sort, never try to reason with them. The being with no fears will never make a deal, never truly accept defeat, only death. Talking to them is a waste of time." With that he turned from the fire and with a bow to his leader, left them.

Flaw looked at Yar, whose face was troubled, and said, "I still don't understand. Can't there be a way where people don't have to die to decide their differences?"

Yar said, "My grandfather thought so. You see, dwarves exist today because we were not abandoned to annihilation." Looking at the faces around the fire behind Flaw, he found both Jobalm and Slawhit. He asked, looking at the latter, "Grandfather, do you mind?" The older pixie said, "You tell it as you please Master Drake. It is only my past. It is _your_ history."

"Very well," said Yar. "You see, Flaw, though what you see of us today seems established, with well-known archetypical attributes, like size, strength, abilities and features, knowing _why_ we are how we are is easily done if you know our origin." As he spoke, he drew the attention of more of their companions.

"The short answer is that we are just another branch of elves. Created in the same way. It seems in this case that the initial differences, height and personality and facial hair, became self-fulfilling and self-replicating, and stemmed from the lineage and coloring of the dragon involved. Back then we were still just smaller, darker, furrier elves.

It was the second year after the joint dragon/pixie centennial celebration. The first year had resulted in hundreds of elf babies born to pixie mothers. Unlike pixies, who give live birth in a year, dragons take two years to produce an egg. Those eggs wait until certain conditions are met before they hatch. Those same celebratory couplings that left many pixie females pregnant with what were to become elves in a year, also created another anomaly – at the two-year mark female dragons began to give live birth. Maybe it was due to being inside a creature that normally produces eggs that are harder and denser than rock and immune to fire, but these babies were smaller, denser, and the size of dragon eggs."

Realizing that his audience had both grown larger and quieter, Yar spoke up, and in a slightly less grave tone, said, "Pretty soon dragon lairs around the world had hungry babies running around underfoot, trying to bite or smash literally everything in sight. Food wasn't really a problem...we'll eat anything!" Laughter spread out from the fire into the darkness.

"But how did you live? Grow up? Become who you are now?" asked poor Flaw almost desperately.

"Well," said Yar, "many of our relations already knew of the pixie babies. The effort was well underway to raise them together, and so the first thought was to do the same. But the pixies had their babies outside, in the trees, and their offspring kept that link – the elves still love their treehouses! We were born in caves, underground, in dragon lairs. In fact, it is where our underlying desire for mineral metals and gemstones comes from. My father studied it. He argued that our ancestors even determine what we like – children of red dragons like red stones like rubies or garnets, greens like emeralds, blues like sapphires and white want diamonds, and so on. I have yet to have seen him be wrong!

So, just as they separated their 'elf' children to an area to live in, grow and develop, so were my kin sent off by your forebears to a large complex of caverns near the sea. I think now that initially they sought to contain and observe us, as they did not understand our motivations – even as children we all want to dig and mine and find things underground; it is in our very nature.

For the dragons, we carved out lairs for our ancestors, grand halls, entire underground cities. But dragons largely live lonely lives. Solitude and grand beauty fills their hearts, and the byproducts of their existence fill their treasure hoards." Here he paused, then said, softer, "We can't create gems and precious metals, but we do know where to find them in nature! All the stories about dragon hoards and how fiercely they protect it? Nonsense. They just give it away and make more! In fact they tend to desire the ones they <u>can't</u> make themselves. Dwarves on the other hand will give away food, shelter, clothing, even fight alongside you to the death, but DON'T ask them for their shiny baubles...!"

The laughter took a while to die down this time.

"Flaw," said Rrahmus patiently, "our history is rife with what we would now consider mistakes of judgment perhaps. Our current reality is the sum of those actions and how they have evolved. We can look back now and judge those actions and agonize over them if we wish, but it won't change them. Only by discussing them openly can we avoid similar future pitfalls. The dwarves back then were called the 'dark elves', and it wasn't long before they were threatened with annihilation by the offspring of what we now know to have been the 'Phase Gods' of the old world – the giants. Thankfully they only bonded with the basic elements and their children need their own type of environment to survive for very long and the young dwarf civilization still had some adult dragon and pixie supervision that recognized the threat and relocated them quickly from their first home, their 'Dwelling at Arves', the cave-riddled point at the ocean end of our southern mountain range. The caves were occupied after a fashion – by dirt, stone, fiery lava, icy pools, and misty tunnels. One day giants of all types began to come out of them. The dark elves were only in their second generation. What made the giants want to kill them? I have no idea. But a benevolent guardian can surely never hurt when it comes to survival. The two had no 'disagreement' to settle, no argument between them, other than the giants were hungry and the dwarves were the first thing they found to eat."

Flaw kicked hist feet out and dropped to his behind on the ground abruptly, shoulders slumped in emotional defeat. "I don't want to hurt anyone," he said.

Pill leaned over to his little friend, put a hand reassuringly on his back, saying, "Evil is all about perspective my friend. We see a hungry being, whether an ogre or a bear, an orc or a dragon, and assign malevolence to it if it wants to eat us, but not a sheep. The sheep might find it evil if we want to kill, cook, and eat it, too, no? It is a constant battle between needs and values as seen through each individual's eyes...like me keeping you from being a hobgoblin snack…" The thief smiled and the little furry explosion of color smiled back at him.

"Okay, I sort of understand."

***

The morning sun rose behind them, finding Hunter making food for his little partners. Barger was saddling his goat, telling Regor that they were going to catch him a needed mount today from the sheep herd he'd seen across the valley the night before.

"I'll just ride in the wagon and try not to fall out and get run over," Regor said in a defeated monotone.

"Nonsense!" said Chestnut, "you're going to need a mount to ride in combat!"

"Great," said Regor. "What about you?!"

"Don't worry, my winged friends will help me, day or night. I would call an owl for you, but it's daytime…"

"Oh no!" he said. "I won't get on one of those things! They fly so fast and high and …"

"Yes! Yes, I know. Exactly why you need a sheep!" Chestnut said brightly.

Barger and Hunter laughed together – not even Regor could change Chestnut's mind or dampen her spirits.

As they rode away together on Barger's goat, Regor's protests fading into inaudibility, Myron approached.

He said to Hunter, "Have you considered taking your natural abilities and healing training to the next level? I could sponsor you to a well-respected trainer..."

Hunter blushed, replying, "I'm not sure I'm a good enough person to do that kind of thing..."

"Oh! You think all healing priests are 'good'? Well, while it is both idealistic, and flattering, the truth is a bit more mundane. Our 'deities', as near as I can tell, are just as capricious and squabbly as we are, with very different ideas about how to behave, just like us. The difference is, they can't <u>die</u>. They all have followers, I think, because while they cannot die, they also cannot physically manifest among us. I suspect it is akin to the spell that created our world, perhaps even a different version of how this Baru Dall is coming here but not completely. They need us to have any influence here, and since we don't live that long in immortal terms, they always need new acolytes, making the recruiting process never ending... Anyway, no hurry, think about it. You've got skills, why not put them to their best use?" With that, Myron left him, head swirling.

Chestnut said, "Why are you worried about

being 'good'? You're the nicest person I know!"

***

Chapter 70

Songs Are Hard

"It occurs to me," said Icelle, "that we are short one key skill set in this bunch of ours..."

"What's that?" asked Aurelius. In his elven form, they, and Fallon, Rrahmus and Yar were looking down at a small hamlet that seemed abandoned but matched their map of where Baru Dall had made his way <u>from</u> multiple times.

"We have no bard. If we all die, who will tell the story?" asked the aging fighter.

"No one, even if we had a bard; if we had a bard and we <u>all</u> die, it's irrelevant..." said the dragon. "The bard would be dead too..."

Fallon chimed in with, "You dragons have a scribe – a magical one even. He's already keeping a record of all you do, right? Since we are with <u>you</u> (or vice-versa?), won't our actions therefore also be recorded?"

"A little," said the High Priest. "I see your point, though, Icelle – our history of these events could die out with us. Chaos, our 'counter', isn't really a chronicler. He does track a fairly well-ordered set of data about our lives, but it is from the stories we tell him. He normally tracks, at a minimum, births, matings, meets and deaths, perhaps some location data. So, if we die here, that is all that will likely be known is the approximate location and time, from whoever comes to find out, not the why or with whom or the specific circumstances."

"Do we really want people to sing about our demise?" asked Rrahmus. "Let's find this crazy interloper and kill him and put an end to this."

As the sun faded to a final bright orange beam above the horizon, Fallon began to sing. They all looked at him, eyes wide, but no one spoke. The soft ballad about why he fought was slow and melancholy. When he finished, they got up and filed away back to their camps to wait for morning.

***

"I hate to ask, but could you slow down a little?" The voice sounded both nauseous and apologetic. Its owner was sporting a distinctly greenish tinge on the parts of his face that were visible among surrounding brown patches of pieces of clothing. Riding on the back of a rather slowly ambling sheep about one milk bucket high off of the ground, Regor was holding on to its neck wool for dear life.

Ahead of him, Barger, on his goat, turned

around and said, "What did you say? Hurry up, they're leaving us behind!"

The voice mumbled back, somewhat desperately as it's mount sped up, "Wasn't … talking … to you!"

Barger shouted back over his shoulder, "We'll rig you up a saddle later – hang on!"

***

The column they were trying to catch erupted into a cheer for the little Patchy as they came into view riding down a softly sloping grassy hill into the river valley currently occupied by dwarves and dragons, men and horses. Word had spread quickly about his mission, from Chestnut of course, and many bets were lost by the skeptical that day.

Barely faster than the dwarven infantry, but faster nonetheless, they soon caught up to Hunter's wagon, resulting in a squeal of happiness from Chestnut. "You did it!" she exclaimed, clapping her hands excitedly. She turned to Hunter, punched him in the shoulder with a tiny fist, saying, "See?! I <u>told</u> you he could do it!"

Hunter shot her a mystified look, and started to speak, saying, "Huh?! <u>I</u> said he …"

527

"We'll talk about it later!" Chestnut interrupted, "For now let's just congratulate Regor for accomplishing such a huge task!" Hunter clapped his mouth shut and looked out over the backs of the ox team in front of him, still befuddled.

***

Rrahmus was eating a midday snack of a dried biscuit and some smoked fish with Fallon, debating whether they should just occupy the target area in force or send in a well-armed and experienced reconnaissance patrol when they arrived. Now that King Jankin was off on his own mission, they all deferred to Aurelius. Though he was the Regent of Dragons, he was also the High Priest of Lorknowis and would always prefer a peaceful outcome (though all knew he would fight, and personally, if needed).

The Arch Mage was convinced that this was his issue to plan, so he considered. It came down to skill sets and abilities, as Icelle had mentioned. Did they need shock troops? Sean, with his trolls and Queen Hazelmoon's warlocks were a deadly combination. Myron was an amazingly talented combat healer who could fight, and he said the same of Hunter. Pill and his apprentice Brine Drake had been working on many of the scouting tasks expected of thieves in this environment, with the help of the gruff little Splotchy, Barger. The entire pixie contingent's flying and invisibility coupled with their somewhat ruthless morals made them a force to be reckoned with all by themselves, and their numbers were growing by the day.

Finally, he spoke to his lunch partner. "The pixies from the east are saying we may have a problem."

"What?" asked Fallon.

"Kobolds. More than they've ever seen. Just a few here and there, but at every single entrance to every warren, cave and hole between here and the ocean to the east. And not just in the early morning and early evening, but all day, every day. They say, where's there's a few you can see, there's at least a few dozen if not a few hundred that you cannot..."

The old fighter looked at his friend curiously. "You don't think this goes all the way back to Render, do you?"

Rrahmus thought for a moment. "I don't know what to think any more," he said. "All I can think now is that we need more information, as usual."

Fallon got up and said, "I think the dwarves are better suited to handle that kind of threat vice heavy cavalry, but I'll make Yar and Icelle aware."

"Just remember, this mage doesn't think like us. He may yet surprise us again with both his motivations and targets…"

***

Yar Drake leaned on his axe, sweat running down his temples into his beard and falling out from it onto his breast plate. His expression was simultaneously fatalistic and exasperated. "Kobolds?" he said, a bit dismissively. "No problem. We hate 'em anyway. I'd feel better if you kept a squad or two with you regardless, though…how long do we have?"

"Sometime tomorrow I'd guess," said Fallon. "We are heading into the village this afternoon. Can you cover to the rear and right flank?"

"Of course," said the dwarf, shouldering his axe to leave.

As he left, Icelle asked Fallon, "So, cavalry in the open on the left, infantry between them and your party?"

"Yes, please."

***

Chapter 71

The Ghost Town

Their approach, had anyone been there to see it, would still have been undetected. Reunited with Pill were two pixies he knew well. After one complete circuit of the village, flying while invisible, they returned to the small copse of trees that Pill and Brine and Barger all lay watching from.

They heard a greeting before they saw anything more than a flicker of shadow on the ground. "Aiee, Pill, what are we supposed to find here anyway?" The speaker, a copper-haired and pudgy pixie who was barely tall enough for his wings to not drag the ground sounded frustrated.

"What <u>did</u> you find?" asked the thief.

"Nothin'," said a second, flat voice, accompanied by the appearance of another, taller, thinner, and grimmer pixie. Walhe said, "A few bodies. Older ones, picked clean, are human. The most recent are kobolds. A few weeks at most. Nothing worth eating, that's for sure ... eh, Ohrb?"

"Walhe, that's disgusting, even for you," said the redhead. To Pill he said, "Someone ate one."

"Hm," said Pill. "No fires, no people – any animals?"

"Just crows and flies," said Walhe, still smiling at Ohrb's comment.

"All right. We go in. Walhe with me, Ohrb with Brine. Barger, go tell Sean to start a circle around both sides with his trolls. Every door, every attic, every cellar. If anything moves, scream bloody murder and come <u>out</u>. No one goes in after anything alone, got it?"

Receiving nods all around he stood up and off they all went.

***

Nothing happened.

Over an hour of slowly investigating every house, shop, root cellar and attic, barn and shed, netted them exactly zero contacts or information. Pill finally went into the center of the village, near the well, which was dry, and told Walhe to let the leaders know that they may as well come in and use the village as shelter while they took their investigation up a notch – likely a magical one.

***

"Well Uncle? Now what?" Pill asked Rrahmus.

"Now we wait," said the Elvish Arch Mage. "We know he's been here more than anywhere else. It <u>has</u> to be his entry point. I would love to know how long it was between his visits and how long he stayed each time, but I don't. So, this is our best option."

***

Chapter 72

Waiting to Return

Baru Dall was eating a midday snack of a dried biscuit and some smoked fish as he considered his final triumphant return to Metaerie. His progression had been the best he could do each time he had visited.

He had thought co-opting an entire race was good, but it didn't really gain him any true power. His research of the catacombs full of scrolls and spell books in his home world had gleaned a few things, like what Metaerie was and how and why it had come to be. The records were written by some who had witnessed parts of the process.

One day he had stumbled across the actual spell. Unfortunately, it was tied to a magical geography defined by the spell casters and tied to the members of the group that had cast it. In his experience, if magic was tied to a circle (or any other shape) of power, violating the circle meant destroying or nullifying the spell. He had been confident that finding and destroying an item used in the spell casting would accomplish the same thing. To date he had found several, destroyed them all while in Metaerie, and accomplished nothing.

He was forced to alter his thinking. Metaerie was not just <u>created</u> by magic, it literally *was* magical. Every spell he cast there, even in only partial manifestation of himself, was highly more effective than at home. When he felt rested enough, he tried one every time he returned to his body. Every time before it had resulted in disappointment, and this time was no exception. The power was there, not here. His goal up to now had been to bring that magic back, and as the greatest practitioner (perhaps only?) he would become the most powerful person in his entire world.

The passing of the years had changed his mind. To undo the spell required a <u>reversal</u>. Like changing the weather (which he now knew how to do), it would take a few key components going backward to get the flow started. He was <u>very</u> close. He found and imprisoned a being who had been part of the original spell. He now had an item used to actually <u>create</u> the spell, not bind it or repeat it. He just needed to fix his fountain into the portal that he now knew it could be, get his full being into Metaerie, bring back those originals (being and an item) and destroy them <u>here</u>. That should start the flow reversal sending the magic back to his world. And if not, he would still have a reliable way back and forth between the worlds, with vastly greater power available to himself until he figured it out!

His smile was self-satisfied and smug.

***

Chapter 73

New Partners

Audhan had taken a few handfuls of the rubies and was in the trees doing something with his hands and some very dark flame that he was breathing out. Yelsa stood with him, fascinated.

Tahmus said, "Look, we might not under any other circumstances be friends or even civil acquaintances, but we are truly worried about a risk that just may genuinely be a threat to our entire collective existence. If you can just view the whole world as your extended family for just a little while...?"

Grunnach, who had been talked over, cut-off and/or ignored for almost their entire encounter thus far, said (in a louder-than-needed and forceful voice), "We. Will. Help. What do you need us to do?"

Angus couldn't help himself. "Fascinating family," he said.

From the trees behind him, in a high-pitched and almost maniacal voice, Yelsa said, "Aren't we just the cutest? Well, at least I am..."

The laughter was infectious all around, and even caused a brief flash of extra-bright flame from the same trees whence came the voice.

Tahmus, once he could control himself, said, "Who can identify any of the gold you were chasing? We need to verify if where we are hiding our friend is actually safe. And who knows what the fort's occupants look like? We need to decide whether to co-opt, observe, capture or kill them…"

Graham said, "I think we need three groups. One to follow them from the port, one to check Roary's lair, and one to wait at the fort."

Just then Audhan and Yelsa rejoined them. He held ten of the Old One's rubies, now wrapped in gold wire and hung as pendants from braided gold wire necklaces, which he handed to everyone present. "I can only do so much," he said, "but these will protect and identify us all, to each other, and to the Old One. If I did it right, you should all be immune to both mine and his fire breath as well…but I am a bit hesitant to test it! Rrahmus is a great teacher, but I am rather inexperienced…"

Graham looped his around his neck and stuck out a bare arm. Hailee, not to be outdone, did so too.

"Um," Audhan began, "I worked with Rrahmus a bit, but it's been awhile, and this is kind of tricky using dragon-made items as well, so … are you <u>sure</u>?" Neither moved, nor even blinked.

"Okay..." he said, and changed into dragon form, briefly revealing a rather gangly and youthful pale body under his tunic. Once he was fully covered in golden scales, he inhaled and breathed out, softly at first, quiet enough to hear the crackle and clank of the stones in his dragon's craw igniting his flammable stomach gases, and a yellowish flame washing over the two exposed arms...and still neither moved.

Graham's eyebrows went up, but Hailee broke down and spoke first, "Wow! It's like water parting around a rock in a stream! I mean, I _feel_ that it's hot, but it doesn't hurt!" Graham nodded in agreement and said, "Well done, kid," to Audhan. "So?" he continued, looking at Tahmus, "What's the risk versus priority?"

Mynorca spoke up first, "I am a risk with the fort guards, no matter where. They have all seen me and will undoubtedly recognize me – they all came to hear me sing."

"I have to go to Roary's lair, that's a given," said Audhan. "And I don't think we need strength at the fort, just observation, but independent actors who can survive the most environments should cover the port I think."

"All right," said Angus, "let's break this down. If

they have a dragon with them, how likely is our mouse ruse to last?"

Audhan said, "Seconds to minutes."

"And then what? The guards come running back to tell the boss? Near as we can tell he's not around, so what else?" As Angus pondered out loud, Graham interjected, "We need to check on the Old One and Molly. Now. I'm not a wizard, but I'll bet a dragon could have flown from that prison to Roary's lair by now..."

Tahmus said, "Angus? Do you mind?"

The senior Elvish Arch Mage's apprentice looked at his mentor's twin brother and said, "No sir – tactics and strategy are your specialty, not mine!"

"All right then," said the experienced elf fighter, "Audhan, can you carry three?"

"If you mean yourself and these two," indicating the two largest non-dragons present who were still comparing their not-burnt arms, "then no."

Angus said, "Perhaps I can help with that... I'm not as adept as the Arch Mage yet, but I can do this one!"

"Then we'll do two groups. We check the lair first. If it's all okay, no worries. If not, we move the Old One and go to the port. Everyone else will head back to the river fort and watch for the return of the mage and/or his men but stay out of sight. We just need a healer... Yelsa, want to see a dragon's lair?"

The little half-gnome girl's eyes shone with delight and she nodded and clapped emphatically.

"Good. Angus – watch for us on the river or the road. If you don't see us in a week, get out of there."

***

Chapter 74

Baru Dall's First Visit

The premise had seemed simple enough. Magic was all about influence. The book he read it in was the smallest and oldest book in his library/cave. It described categories of it. Influencing 'things', inanimate physical objects, was easy – reliable, predictable and repeatable. Animals were more difficult; they had desires and dislikes and fears to overcome. Brief, unstable control could be attempted, but longer-term relationships took multiple steps. People were even more complex, but easier to influence when they were focused on their more basic natures, like food and frolic. The worst, it said, were magical creatures. It listed them: Dragoons and Peexs and Wytchs.

So much more information was now available to him! When he had first arrived in Metaerie he had appeared in the middle of what seemed to be a tribal council of a group of creatures with doglike faces and lizard tails. He found himself atop a pile of thousands of gold nuggets the size of his thumb. They had what looked to him like another man trussed up and bound to a rotating log with each end on two rocks like a spit to cook a pig and were even then stacking wood underneath him. The man was chuckling softly and shaking his head. He would never forget that scene.

What the man said to him when he noticed his presence was quite memorable as well. "You're going to ruin everything!" The words did not seem to match the man's mouth, but he heard them clearly inside his head.

"What do you mean?!" he answered, realizing that the small half-dog/half-reptilian things had now noticed him as well and were approaching. Using the spell to come here had been an agonizing decision, not knowing what he would encounter upon his arrival. He had several spells rehearsed and ready. He was unprepared for the effectiveness of that magic in this world. The result of his preparing an 'understanding' spell was obvious – the soon-to-be-roasted man could communicate with him and vice-versa. Beyond that, he could 'feel' what the man wanted...he was hungry and planned to eat the dog-lizards. That made no sense, but he detected no fear in the man at all.

His choice was forced, as the little beings had come to a decision, and apparently he was to be added to the menu. He turned toward the rotisserie victim even as he felt the fear from the others. Very odd. Hands outstretched, waist high, palms up, he met his target's eyes and said, "Help me to rule this land and I will feed you!"

Turning back to the advancing creatures, he reached in to take out an ancient hand bell from a pocket in his robe, only to realize that it was not there. For that matter, neither was his robe! He had linked the spells he needed to several objects, and standing here naked without the robe, its pockets and the items that he had stored therein, he was right back to a complete disadvantage despite his proactive attempt to avoid just this situation. He immediately realized his error, but still had a plan. To those approaching he yelled, "Serve me or die!"

They paused, then continued their approach. He raised an arm toward the roof and from his index finger directed a massive bolt of wild electrical energy. The effect was far greater than he had intended, the effect much more powerful than what he had achieved at home. Fortunately he had practiced this set of moves and was not distracted enough to forget. He raised his other palm up, facing him, drawing it up from his chin to the top of his head, achieving instant invisibility. Yelling, "I will return!" he focused on an empty bit of floor behind the little dog-lizards who now rushed at the spot they had last seen him and he 'jumped', magically, to the empty space. And then he waited and watched.

After much head scratching and pointing, they lit the fire under the spit. The chuckling from the man on the spit turned to outright laughter.

His bewilderment complete, he did not see the crowd surge from behind him, pushing him over and trampling him, quickly knocking him unconscious.

He awoke back in his own world, where almost no time had passed. He would prepare better next time.

**

Chapter 75

Baru Dall Arrives – Twice

He had been lucky to survive the first time he used the relocation spell. Knowing he had not been able to take objects made him examine the spell. From the one written history that he'd found describing the event he realized that he was in possession of a copy of the spell for someone who was inside the outer ring of its influence – they went *with* the objects, even the water, rocks and dirt, not needing anything else but themselves, linked together, to move. And this spell was older than theirs, so if they could modify it, so could he. So he did, a few weeks later.

This time the man-on-a-spit was gone, but there were far more little dog-lizards, and no gold nuggets. His robe made the trip this time, and as he reached into its pockets, he neglected to defend himself from the dozen small swords to his sides and rear that stabbed and slashed him to death in mere seconds. Even as he passed out watching himself fall into a pool of his own blood in Metaerie, he awoke, unchanged as far as he could tell, home once again.

He was a little weakened, but not too much,

and he decided to go right back. Casting a small, bubble-like protective sphere around himself first, he went back, his understanding spell also recast.

His appearance caused immediate consternation and a half dozen of the little things charged him, only to bounce backward this time.

"I warned you!" he said, "Serve me or die!"

This time he rang his bell right away, having arrived with it already in his hand.

There must have been a handful of different tribal groups of a dozen or more each within a few paces of him, and they all froze in place, listening. He said, "It is in your best interests to serve me, as I will always take care of you, even more so when I rule this world."

The apologies were overwhelming. It seemed that when he left the first time the trussed-up man had not burned to death, but in fact seemed impervious to fire. When they had tried to skewer him, he had pulled them into the fire with him, a fate that had befallen at least a handful of them before they gave up and backed up to archery distance and then he disappeared.

They said they should have listened to him before and they absolutely would this time! When he assured them that he would care for them like children as long as they remained loyal, they began to calm down. "It may be a long journey, but if you commit to aiding me, I will lead you to greatness!" he said.

He had not believed himself then. Despite the awe and adoration on their little dog faces and the rapid switching of their lizard tails, he had known then that he was manipulating them, using them to his own nefarious ends with no actual regard for their well-being or even survival. Now, over a decade (of their time) later, something had changed. To support his façade of leading them he had been forced along the way to actually take care of them. He felt what he could only assume was something akin to fatherly pride. What had been a loose-knit group of squabbling packs were now a nation of organized clans living in mutually supporting harmony. Well, almost. No large group ever got along perfectly... But he saw the correlation; the more he invested of his effort into them, the more he *actually* cared about them.

Ever the pragmatist, he knew they had outgrown their environs. Their caverns and tunnels had spread out over hundreds of leagues, largely uncontested after the death of Render McNab, previously their worst nemesis, through the treachery of one of his first recruits.

During his most recent visit he had told them it was time to spread out, go on an offensive 'swarm' to take over new territory that they needed to survive and grow, and that doing so would help him become even more powerful.

Their dog traits were likely the reason for their fierce loyalty, and they were excited about 'getting in the fight' as he had kept them out of it before, saying they "weren't ready". His real reason was he thought they would just get massacred, be a problem fighting alongside men, and maybe, just maybe, a part of him would feel bad if they died... Now he didn't need them, but they could cause mayhem and distraction to keep any potential opponents busy and away from him and his true focus.

He was about to repair his portal fountain. His detection methods let him know for certain that the ancient magic was still there and working, it just didn't have the correct catalyst. He understood it now. His fountain had pieces missing at its base and could not hold water. The stone foundation was not magical at all, only the sculpted, shaped stone above was. It was a simple portal, like a door laying down flat, but needed water to complete its effect. He had found the right spell to shape stone now and knew he could do it as he had at his river fort.

Baru Dall knew that with as powerful as he was in Metaerie without his entire physical body that if he could get there completely he would be the most powerful being that that world had ever seen. He was so close it was maddening, but he willed himself to be patient.

While his kobold minions overran the domains of men, his new partners the ogres would be his army and personal guard with an expected troglodyte navy soon to follow. He began to gloat, then ate, drank, and slept, resting in preparation for fixing his fountain portal. If he couldn't destroy Metaerie's magic - - - he fully intended to <u>rule</u> it!

***

Chapter 76

Dark Tidings

More pixies arrived from the plains approach out of the east, talking to Slawhit and Jobalm. It was dark, and Corvin, sitting with Pill and Brine, noticed them first. "Dark tidings in the dark?" he mused.

The two older pixies went to Rrahmus and Fallon first. They then looped to a few tents and wagons, gathering up Queen Hazelmoon Toadscream, who was wearing an ankle length black fur robe with dark purple trim, Sean Yeomring and Ufu who were covered in grass and leaves from where they had been wrestling, Yar Drake still in his armor, and Icelle Yeomring in a beige woolen nightshirt, some hastily pulled on breeches, boots and a sword. The dragons were nowhere to be found.

"Odd," said Jobalm, "one usually can't misplace a dragon..."

"No," agreed Slawhit, "but this cannot wait. The kobolds are moving fast, and are excited, purposeful, even chanting as they move to the surface. They do not appear to be focusing here, but in a widespread wave, moving west toward every human settlement south of us."

Fallon asked, "So is it an invasion? They are just sweeping across the land?"

"The most notable aspect of this is <u>what</u> they are chanting…" said Jobalm.

Slawhit paused, looked around at them all, and said, " 'Baru Dall'. Over and over and over. All of them."

Yar said, "But if they're moving south and west of us, they'll go right through the non-magical human settlements that were his biggest supporters…"

Rrahmus asked, "Do they appear to be driven by some other external leadership?"

The pixies both shook their heads 'no', then Jobalm said, "Truly Master Drake it would seem he has set them against his own allies."

Icelle said, "We have to get word to Jankin."

Slawhit said, "We'll take care of that."

The Queen said, "It's too late for me to try to return if they are upon us, but should we attack them preemptively or hope they pass us by?"

Jobalm said, "It almost seems as if the one place they are specifically avoiding is right here, and all points north of here, which is a good sign that this may be where we find Baru Dall himself."

"Then I'm staying," she said.

Corvin said, in a voice that seemed to spring out of pure darkness below two glowing gold eyes, "I can help to ensure early warning of any approach during the night hours."

Pill was still slightly uncomfortable with his undead father's new speech patterns, but it was better than not having him around at all.

"However," Corvin continued, "please don't shoot or cast anything at movement in the dark without positively identifying that your intended target is indeed an enemy? I will have less trouble soliciting help, and you all will be less likely to be bitten in your sleep…"

There were a few awkward chuckles, but the point was made.

The sound of wind rushing at them made them all look up and around to find the source. In seconds it was obvious. A sizable winged creature dove from the sky, plummeting out of the thin clouds and straight down into the village well, a flash of red coming from it as it passed through the low angled moonbeams under the clouds. The splash was enormous.

"Was that a …" began Fallon. "…dragon?!" finished Rrahmus.

Pill exclaimed, "Where'd the water come from?! That well was dry a few hours ago!"

Corvin said, "I'll be right back," and disappeared.

And then reappeared before the others had even begun the discussion of whether they should go check it out.

"The well is full of water, but I don't recommend drinking from it...I am fairly certain it is part of a magical portal somehow – it tastes...old. And there's nothing in it – I looked."

Collectively taken aback, the information was too much to fathom.

And then a half dozen more dragons arrived, and though they approached much more slowly, their circling descent and landing caused many to hide in fear, behind rocks, trees, and shields. They exuded irritation, anger, and disgust, which just made it worse. It was only when Aurelius called out to Rrahmus that some hesitantly looked out from their hiding places to see the Elvish Arch Mage approaching the huge, angry gold dragon, and were comforted to see him moving calmly and confidently to his friend's side.

"We must move quickly," said the dragon. It was then that the riders began to be seen getting down from their places on the dragons' backs. The one on Aurelius looked like Rrahmus but wore armor and embraced the Arch Mage quickly.

"Were you following another dragon?" asked Rrahmus.

"Yes, but not to catch him, at least not yet, why?"

"Well, one just flew straight down into the village well behind you a moment ago..."

Turning just his head around quickly on its reptilian neck, Aurelius shouted, "Argenta! Mind the well entrance! Just in case he can come back out that way!"

The female silver dragon jumped to a great height, flapped her massive wings a few times to get headed in the right direction, then glided to a landing on a rooftop adjacent to the well.

As the dragons all approached their leader, Rrahmus broke into a run toward one, shouting, "Audhan!!!" and another hug followed. His passenger was a little beat up – her whole face was soot-covered, her once long, beautiful hair hung in splotches with bare spots in between and what remained was singed and as fire-damaged as her clothing.

"Oh my! Molly! Are you okay?!" asked her uncle, his anger, deep down most of the time, feeling like a small flame exploring a ball of tinder.

"I'm fine. My robe and hair are ruined, and I may get a few scars, but my new friend Yelsa here saved me from the worst of it by healing me right away," she said, indicating a rather-large-for-a-gnome girl hiding behind her.

The Arch Mage hugged Molly gently, then scooped up the little priestess healer and squeezed her tightly, saying, "Thank you ever so much!" then set the squirming female back down quickly. "I'm sorry!" he said, "I didn't mean to startle you!"

"You're most welcome Mr. Arch Mage, sir. Your brother did the exact same thing." Yelsa answered shyly.

The reunion that most missed was when a large figure slid off of Ariene's back and sauntered toward the group around Aurelius. In seconds, another large form came hurtling at his back out of the darkness, flying, feet off of the ground, for a mid-air tackle. Ariene watched in amazement as Graham's tall, lanky form dropped flat to the ground while spinning so that he was facing upward and grabbed the flying shadow out of the air amid a strangely low-pitched squeal of laughter and the words, "Not Sean!" followed by open troll hands alternately smacking both of Graham's shoulders in glee.

Sean walked up as a muffled, laughing voice said, "Alright, alright, Ubu, let me up!"

The troll stood, let Graham stand, then stepped aside as Sean tackled his brother back to the ground. Another couple of trolls arrived, but they stepped aside as another Yeomring male landed on his two sons – it was too much for the trolls, so they piled on too.

The scuffle had grown loud enough to draw some attention finally and was spotlighted in Fallon's lantern. The six participants froze like deer – then slowly stood up, brushing leaves, dirt, and twigs from their clothes/bark, all smiling a bit sheepishly.

At that moment Argenta's passenger stepped into the light and said around his tusks, "Fascinating family..."

Graham laughed at the joke, but unexpectedly the trolls bristled and growled. Graham quickly faced them and put one hand up in front of them, saying, "Whoa there, fellas! This one is on <u>our</u> side! We just fought together in fact. This is Hailee, and Yelsa there is his sister!" The trolls were not the only ones confused now, and explanations went on all around them for several minutes. Most of the collective stories had been shared when Hailee decided to address the group.

"So, we land outside this huge cave with two

men near what looks like a blank wall at the rear. They're just standing around with spears and torches. No bed rolls, no fire, no food, in the middle of nowhere on a mountain side...nothing curious or suspicious about <u>that</u>, right?!" he said sarcastically.

"Audhan here is all they can see, 'cause Angus shrunk us, but we aren't weighing him down 'cause he also 'levitated' us. I think that means 'float'? I don't know. Anyway, dragon boy here says, in his booming scary voice, "Where is the Old One?!" and these two don't say a word, they just throw their spears at him... Next thing I know, they're on fire and running past us to the opening on the mountain side. They didn't even slow down at the edge. Must have been a few hundred barrels worth of fall, screamin' and burnin' the whole way down until they stopped, sudden-like, one right after the other." He paused to look at Graham, who nodded, so he continued.

"But then we hear more screamin'. From <u>inside</u> the mountain! 'Cept it's a girl... Tahmus here went nuts. That's his little girl right there – " he said indicating Molly, "and she sounded mad, scared, and hurtin' all at once. Now, he's got some kind of charm that should open the door, but the stone doors are barred from the inside somehow. Me and Graham are standin' there wantin' ta help, but we're smaller than Yelsa at the moment and, like I said, floatin'. <u>She's</u> the one who says, 'You're small, not weak!' So, we ran over and bashed the door, together, and 'bang!' it goes slammin' open, there's some yellin', and then we see this red dragon standin' over these tied up elves." Molly closed her eyes as he continued.

"He looks up, but doesn't see us right away, 'cause, like I said, we're tiny, and we're inside, where we pushed the doors to. And right behind us comes this tiny, crazy elf, tiny sword held high, tiny, high-pitched voice screamin' an angry war cry, and I am not surprised that the dragon hesitated. It was just the right combination of comical and curious. The dragon stepped back to turn around, maybe in shock, maybe in defense, maybe just out of morbid curiosity, who knows, but Tahmus kept on a beeline towards Molly, to protect his little girl. Whatever that dragon was thinkin', he grabbed up the other elf, which I know now was the Old One in elf form, and he turned in time to see Tahmus shielding Molly as best he could with his little body. He got a blast of flame for his trouble, and when the dragon saw that he wasn't burnt, it turned and jumped/flew out of the door, bowling poor Audhan here over like an alley game pin." One more pause to regard Audhan with a little sympathy.

"The poor kid was spent. Flew all four of us all the way there, then spent his last bit of flame to get us inside. If we were full size maybe Graham and I could have tried to grab him, but when you're half the size of a badger, trying to grab a full-size dragon, well, it just didn't happen."

Aurelius himself said to Hailee, "Young fellow, that was very well said." To the group he said, "We had gone hunting for a late supper – we find that it seems to terrorize fewer of our friends if we hunt after dark and away from your gatherings. We saw a flash of light, up high on a nearby mountain. It was so bright and sudden and then gone, it could only be dragon fire. It must have been Audhan. By the time we got there, Roary and the Old One were gone. It begs several questions, but I think Roary is somehow being used. Controlled by this Baru Dall. He is Audhan's cousin, a few times removed, and his haunts are few. We know where this entrance of his has an exit, and it is already under watch. And now we need to retrieve the Old One."

"With great respect sir," said a small voice, "If you have need for someone to get into a small space, I will volunteer." It was Barger, and his companions' comments of, "Oh dear," and "What?! No!" were both easily heard and ignored.

Aurelius said simply, "If we do, you'll be the first consulted." The miniature male bowed politely, then shushed his friends. The dragon turned and called to his other companions, "Sugarplum, Ebon, Karmien, come here to me please." A familiar, small purplish dragon and two large black and red dragons approached.

"Plumley," he began, "can you still see the other worldly mage's magical trail?"

"Yes, I can," was the quick reply.

"And if he returns, will you see that too?"

"I ... uh ... believe so, yes." Said the young tribrid hesitantly.

"Then I want you two to fly from here to the kobold cave entrance every hour. And if you see any sign of him, or Roary, you tell the others first to give them warning."

The trio bowed formally to their Regent and flew off immediately.

Pill waited a moment, then said, "Aurelius, sir? What others?"

"We have several dragons of all types waiting along this cave complex from end to end. It was an original lair, back before our world was made. It is known to all of us, and has a dark history. It is where the first dragon was killed by men." Aurelius' face was grim, even for a dragon.

Pill said nothing, just nodded and looked at his boots, the voice in his head distracting him. It was Argenta. Again. 'Poor elf boy...'

'How do you do that from so far away?!' he wanted to know.

'I was focusing on my brother-in-law and you wandered in,' she responded.

'How does <u>that</u> work?'

'Geography and relationship,' she replied. 'If I know <u>you</u>, and I know <u>where</u> you are, I know <u>where</u> to find your thoughts. I can't just hear everyone in one place, but Aurelius <u>thought</u> about you, thought that you were really asking him where Sylvia was, and he likes you, so he didn't want to tell you that she is with her mate at the other end of the caves.'

'Mate?!' his mind screamed as his body wandered away to sit by a tree all by himself. That was new. With Mortalya he couldn't move...

And as he sat down, a nesting bird on a branch above him looked down and said in his head, 'Oh, can't you?'

Two female voices laughing in his head at the same time was almost too much. Scrunching his eyes tight shut and placing his palms to his temples, pressing hard, he saw some sparkles of lack of blood flow briefly, then took a deep breath and thought, 'You're going to say that I never tried. Fine.'

He stood up, walked to find his uncle, hugged him, stepped back and said, "I'm going to find the Old One. I may need help. I'm not waiting for the crazy mage to come back, I'm going into the caves now."

Rrahmus thought about it, then said, "I agree, you should. I believe he has found a way to get here completely. Yelsa described a fountain that can only be an old-world portal, and he's built a fort around it. Krystal confirmed earlier that these buildings below us are her old village – Render's village. And it's tied to a prehistory dragon lair? Too much coincidence. I'm going to the fort I think. We need to get ahead of Baru Dall's next steps, and we need to share the necessary skills for each task."

Fallon approached with the Yeomrings and the half-siblings in tow. He said, "Apparently there's a fort with a fountain and a chest that Baru Dall left behind at the river just a bit further past the cave entrance the dragons are watching, on the edge of a river."

Several smiles and headshakes made him turn in time to see Yelsa's head nodding emphatically all the while smiling comically. He did an exaggerated double take, then continued.

"I think the dwarves can keep the kobolds off of us, but Graham says the mage got something from two froglodytes, and <u>they</u> got on a ship crewed by ogres. The Old One's prison was <u>also</u> guarded by ogres…"

Rrahmus pondered, "You think there was more to the ogre invasion…"

"I do now," said the old fighter.

"We're not prepared for that, at least not here. Plus, why would it be an ogre force here? To what purpose?" said the Arch Mage, exasperated.

"Why unleash the entire kobold population against those who were his allies?" asked Graham sarcastically. "Let's face it, this guy is <u>nuts</u>."

"Well, I am definitely going to this fort. Whatever he has there, or plans to do there, has to be my focus. Goddess forbid that it is also the point of an ogre invasion… Good grief." Rrahmus swiped at the sweat now accumulating on his brow in the warm night air.

"Icelle is still the best bet on that flank, even against ogres. His cavalrymen are <u>good</u>," said Fallon.

Graham said, "You'll have a healer, a thief and a couple of fighters waiting for you; Hailee and Yelsa's other three siblings are already there, with Bronwyn and Angus, watching for whoever shows up."

Sean said, "I'll ask the Queen, but I'm fairly certain she will agree with us working in the open – trees, rivers and forts sound better to most warlocks and trolls than caves."

"Fine," said Graham, "then I'll go with Pill. As usual, we'll need fighters and sneaks, healers and freaks. I mean mages! Ha." His old adventurers party mantra was not lost on most present – just Yelsa.

"I thought I was a freak," she said sadly. "Why only mages?"

Everyone else chuckled. Her biggest/youngest brother reached down and picked her up to hug her. "You're just perfect," he said. "Will you help Graham and his friends in the caves? I don't want to leave you alone, but I should probably go to the fort if there's going to be ogres, no?"

Seeing Yelsa's horrified face at the thought of her brother not being with her, Graham said, "No, I think Sean's trolls will be fine, especially with Queen Hazelmoon's warlocks. Besides, only the smallest dragons can go, and Audhan will be perfect for the caves..." Yelsa's expression changed to instant joy. "I'll go with Audhan and Hailee!" she said gleefully. "I mean, and you, too, Graham..." she said a bit more shyly.

***

By midnight it was settled. As the moon began to rise, everyone was in motion. Myron and Myeer would stay with the dwarves. Barger, Brine and Audhan would go with Graham, Hailee and Yelsa, led by Rrahmus, Pill and Argenta. Rrahmus told Sean to find those watching the fort, and stay in contact with his father and Angus, but if Baru Dall used these caves as his way in to Metaerie, this group needed an accomplished mage, 'freak' or not. Hunter and Chestnut were enlisted to help at the fort too, her owls could help her transmit messages in the dark. Oddly, Regor was nowhere to be found.

The rest of the dragons and pixies were all determined to be free to insert themselves as they saw fit as the events unfolded. Flaw said, "You need me at the fort to help determine if any captives, captors or combatants are being truthful. I want to go with Pill, but dragons and mages in tight spaces make furry people, well, *nervous*..." His friend the thief laughed, put an arm around his little shoulders and said, "I'll miss you too."

As they broke up, Queen Hazelmoon, with Sean and two trolls in tow, approached Graham and Hailee. She addressed the latter. "Young man, though you may not know it, you are quite the naturally charismatic speaker. Even the trolls stopped growling after a moment or two, and with the history between trolls and orcs, that's a bit surprising. The gnome girl is your ... sister?"

"Half-sister, Mistress," he said. "As far as we know there are five of us, all with different mothers, all of different races. They all said our father was simply irresistible, that when he was with them they believed he would be with them forever – and then he was gone – but we were on the way!"

"Did he sing to them?" she asked.

"Yes! In fact our full human sister, Mynorca, is an amazing singer and musician! And she could talk a bear out of hibernating!" he said brightly.

"Well, I'm no clairvoyant, but I'll say this – you all have a place to live in the Witches' Forest if you want to..." she said regally.

***

The moon was quite full, and when it was in full view, there was a loud squalling. It was coming from a scuffle heard in the trees between Fallon's fire and Hunter's wagon. Thinking they were being infiltrated by kobolds and that this was the beginning of a surprise attack, Pill, Brine, Fallon and the Yeomrings sprang into action. Arriving in various states of armor being put on for what was to come, they found what appeared to be a rabid squirrel attacking Regor's sheep. Crimson wool was everywhere. The sheep's throat was torn out, its underbelly ripped open from ribcage to tail, and its attacker was rending off and eating pieces of its hindquarters from the inside where there was no wool or skin.

It seemed to gradually become aware of dozens of eyes watching, and its chomping slowed down, a piece of long leg muscle hanging out of its mouth, swinging back and forth, dripping an arc of blood as it turned its head to regard them.

"Well!" said Brine who was closest to it, "that's not normal!" Smiling, he looked around to see who appreciated his joke – and failed to see the squirrel's eyes narrow and gather itself to spring at him. As it flew toward him another projectile hit it in flight, but failed to significantly change its course. It clawed the poor dwarf on both sides of his neck and bit him through the adolescent beard on his chin.

It clung there, convulsing, blood pumping around the elvish blade of Pill's dagger, tearing at Brine's skin as it died. And then it let go of him and fell to the ground. The bleeding slowed, and as it did, they looked on, horrified, as the little body writhed and shook until a pale white and very dead Regor lay before them. And then Pill understood. The patchy little browny was a were-beast. And it bit Brine...

"Don't move!" he said to the dwarf, "Let's get you a healer..." And in his mind he thought, 'Before I have to kill you...'

***

Chapter 77

Meanwhile Back at the Fort

"Angus!" Farsight whispered. "Do you have a spell or something that can tell us if someone has been here?"

"No," came the terse response.

"Then what's the plan?" asked the thief.

"I have the ability to do some abnormal things without spells," said the mage, and he began to rise up in the air, moving toward the top corner of the fort in front of them.

While they watched he 'floated' around the upper perimeter and passed out of sight, then returned to view eventually on the opposite side, then did it again, lower, looking in every window and vent or opening he could find.

When he returned, Grunnach said, "Do all elves fly?"

"No," Angus replied, "the Arch Mage made special boots for me. They basically let me walk on the air, in any direction I choose if I focus a little."

Farsight said, "Oh, I <u>need</u> some of those!"

Bronwyn asked, "Any sign of anyone?"

"No," he said, "and the two bodies we left are still there, though a bit worse for the wear, especially the one in the moat, the fish have been at him quite a bit already."

"Fish have to eat too," Mynorca said smiling.

"True," said the mage. "We should pick a few vantage points to watch the road and the gates I think. From here we can see both fort entrances and most of the way to the town road. Where else?"

Farsight said, "To the right of the junction with the town road is the route along the river to the nearest seaport. There is a hill on this side of it that has a view of the town, the road crossing, and most of the way to the port."

"Alright, you know where it is, you and Grunnach can both see in the darkness pretty well, so you go. We three will stay here. Remember, <u>don't engage</u>. Watch, observe, report. We can't help if we're dead..."

***

Chapter 78

Old World Diseases

"I saw him die," Pill told his uncle.

"You mean you had a vision of his future death?" asked Rrahmus.

"Fine. Sure. No matter what set of semantics you choose to describe it, I killed Brine." Pill's frustration only increased when actually saying his name did not create either a vision or a visit from the goddess, as he was certain that it meant that nothing had changed.

"I want this thing off of my face! I'm sick of not calling people by name without risking having to watch them die, I've gotten way too used to talking to a fickle goddess, and not knowing what will happen makes me always hope to win. I think I'm going slowly mad!" The thief threw his dagger into a tree for emphasis.

"Seeing too much truth is often a burden," said his uncle. "Have you asked her to release you, or how it can be done?"

"No," Pill said dejectedly, "but if she did know it doesn't mean she'd tell me."

"Okay. We still need to know if it's even

possible I guess. And how to heal Brine. Myron is with him now, and Hunter too."

***

Brine looked fine. He had no visible wounds or scars. Myron pulled Pill aside and said, "You saw it. Did the creature bite or scratch him?"

"Creature? You mean poor little Regor, who happened to look like a ghoulish squirrel and was eating his sheep mount after gutting it, as if it were normal? The fearful little browny that I skewered with a dagger just a bit ago? Yes, he both scratched and bit Brine. Why?" Pill's frustration was obvious.

"Hey, I also thought Regor was a wonderful little guy, but he was infected," said the priest.

"With what?!" demanded Pill.

"One of the three oldest diseases, all from the old world, all brought by humans. The first, natural magic, we embraced as our creators all had it, and it is familial. But we also brought along several lairs of infected humans too, hidden ones, accidentally. That is how we ended up with vampirism, such as what afflicts your father. Neither fully dead nor wholly alive, daylight burns him and moonlight heals him, he still answers to the Mistress of Death – and if the tidbits I've heard are true, so do you…" Myron hesitated.

"Is <u>she</u> responsible for this?!" exclaimed the elf.

"No," said Myron calmly, but he led Pill further away from Brine's ears.

"This is the rarest of the old diseases. It affects only certain people, and differently by race. Those afflicted, outside, under a full moon, turn into a murderous version of a furry, carnivorous animal, usually one similarly sized. At least, that's what I was taught. And they usually just kill something easily available, generally smaller than they are, eat it, and wake up the next day naked with a stomachache. The first time they change they attack the biggest thing they find to gorge themselves. I think that is what just happened here. Passing it on is actually rather rare, and I don't believe anyone really knows how it's done, just that bites and scratches are a risk."

"Is Brine dangerous right now?!" Pill cried.

Myron once again walked further away and spoke even softer, "No one is really sure. Possibly. We do know that in the animal form it is, absolutely. In his humanoid form? I just don't know, sorry."

"Can I take him with me? In the caves I mean?" Pill said in a much calmer voice.

"It might be the only safe place for him if the moonlight is the true trigger of the condition... But I believe that it takes a moon cycle for it to dominate him, and I don't know if he has to die, like a vampire, or if it is immediate."

"Is there a cure?" The elf's eyes were pleading.

"There is a way, yes. Maybe more than one. He may or may not survive it no matter what we might try." The ragged healer was at least consistent in holding out no real hope at all.

Pill turned and charged in to see Brine through the back of Hunter's wagon.

"How d'ya feel?" he asked the dwarf.

"I feel … fine?" was the answer.

"Has anyone talked to you about possible dangers?" he said, looking around at Fallon, his uncle, and Brine's uncle, all standing back watching as Hunter and Queen Hazelmoon examined the young dwarf. His 'healing' had left no sign of the squirrel/browny's attack, and he did not look feverish.

The young dwarf looked to his mentor for a straight answer and said as much.

Pill said, "It's a disease. No one knows for sure how it works or what to do, and all of the possible cures can kill you."

"Master Thief," said Aurelius from behind Pill, "your protégé here requires divine intervention. I know you practitioners of the clandestine arts are not usually enamored with that type of influence or interference, but I also know that you have an unusually close relationship with such a presence. If you do pursue it, my only knowledge to share is that such an act is a once in a lifetime request for each petitioner...so choose wisely."

Pill looked from Aurelius to Brine, and said, "Let's go save the world."

***

Chapter 79

Frog vs Trog

'Finally!' Lily thought. 'A familiar ship!' The little fairy was in repose atop the highest sail on the tallest mast, feeling a bit like a princess in her tower, dozing, waiting to be rescued, when the lookouts below her woke her while changing the watch in the wooden basket they sat in.

She saw a ship in the distance ahead of them. She knew those sails. And they were approaching. Then she realized that both ships, and several others, were closing in on the same port. One had large green frogs depicted, which she was sure had to be King Runebane's work. She wondered if Hak the gnome was aboard; she was always amused watching him eat – he took bites as big as she was.

But the others in the port area were mostly smaller, rowing style attack ships, though she neither saw nor heard any evidence of fighting. The first sailing ship she saw in port with its pale-yellow wood from the northwest deserts had to belong to Captain Rabat. She could make out the dark-skinned crew scurrying about. The farthest out was Roland's ship. Fallon's brother-in-law, his sails sparkled at the edges as the lines were hung with polished coins, just like his clothes.

She knew what she had to do.

***

Blaine looked out of his oceanside upper window at the mass of ships arriving into his already full port and knew that he was about to have a problem. "Ogres and troglodytes and men," he sighed out loud.

"What's that?" The muffled question came from under his recently departed blankets. One bare foot attached to a shapely female leg stuck out into the cool morning air he had let in when he opened his shutters to see why it was so noisy.

"I have to go," he said as he pulled on his breeches and boots. By the time he had on a shirt and a sword belt, the foot had disappeared again.

***

When he arrived at the docks, Blaine found an odd assortment of people arguing about the moorage space. Looking at the racial makeup of the vocalists and the ships in the harbor, he began to get very nervous.

Putting on a brave smile, he waded in... and was accosted by an ogre who wanted his friends to be allowed to tie up first, a man who wanted his ship allowed out before that happened, and a quiet gnome with a huge sword who looked at him fixedly but said nothing, just jerked his head to one side and walked away in the same direction. He said to the rest, "Just a moment, I'll be right with you!" and followed him.

Hak turned behind some full barrels and spun to meet Blaine. "Ya can't let the ogres tie up. They're here ta start a war, and they're workin' for the mage that kidnapped your girl Tara."

"What?! How am I supposed to stop them?! Look at them! They're ogres!" Blaine protested.

"Listen ta me. King Runebane is on one o' those ships. The ogres are tryin' ta put the old king back in charge. I am fairly certain, on good authority, that he's here too...I will show you which ship. To appease the ogres, tell 'em you'll let one o' theirs tie up first, but make it that one. We need ta manage this, and I'm positive those ogres will not behave well in your little town..."

Minutes later the ship captain who wanted out was assisted through the maze, and the ogre crew with the troglodyte passengers came into the vacancy. Unfortunately, the divide and conquer plan must have been recognized as the rest of the ogre ships filed in behind it and began tying their crafts together, bow to stern, and using the ships like a floating road.

Hak had a new plan. He boarded the trading vessel next to the stern of the lead ogre ship, was social with the crew, a mix of gnomes and dwarves, and, borrowing a few oil flasks, some bits of line and a lighted stick from their kitchen for his pipe, when the second ship tied off, fulfilling his fears, it was time to flush his quarry.

Tucking short ropes under the ones tied around the oil jars covers, he lighted them with his smoldering stick, blowing on it to blaze it up several times. The crash of breaking pottery on the rear deck of the first ship below him went unnoticed, but the one that splashed all over the forward deck of the second ship also set a few of the ogres standing there ablaze, and it turned out that ogres, loud when they are <u>not</u> on fire, are even louder when they are. These were soldiers, not crew, laden with armor, shields, gear and weapons, and when they jumped into the water, they didn't come back up. Hak decided that should give him enough time to deal with the occupants of the first ship without worrying about interference from any of the follow-ons. He ambled back down to the dock to wait.

Ogres, like troglodytes of old, don't feel the need to cook their food and therefore had no real need of fire on their water vessels. Hak was counting on that to also mean that they would be ill-prepared to deal with a fire aboard ship. He was soon proven right.

However, unlike ogres, the three troglodytes that emerged from below decks were very strong swimmers. As the ogres tried to get their gangplank settled onto the pier, a sudden blow from a huge gnomish sword sent it spinning out of their hands and down into the water out of reach. He could see beyond the howling ogres, into the eyes of the trogs. They were debating whether to attack him or to abandon their escorts and swim to safety.

Already the ships behind them were reversing course, untying, and rowing away from the flames — directly toward three much larger and better-armed ships that Hak knew well. His patience was rewarded.

The three banished trogs were excellent swimmers — but not in robes and armor. Doffing them all quickly, they dove into the ocean. Hak said, "Alright fairy girls, your turn," and swung his sword in time to deflect a spear thrown by a desperate ogre crewman.

Djinja and Eyevee had joined them in their froglodyte quest to find out what the ogres were up to as they knew their mother was likely to be found at the same time. That reunion had happened an hour ago, and they took flight now, tracking the troglodytes from far above.

Though King Runebane had been anxious to lead this effort, Hak had suggested that since this was a largely naval oriented conflict in the making, he should allow his senior ship captain to have first crack at it (and ensure the King's safety).

Roglok stepped up next to Hak now, knowing their King was still aboard another ship out in the harbor. "Is the old king with them?"

"Yes," said the gnome.

"And the traitor scum?" asked the froglodyte.

"Yes, both."

"Then I may need help. Their magics are twisted, but not weak..." he looked sidelong at the gnome.

Hak picked up the ogre's spear at his feet like a toy, looked out to sea at several ogre ships sinking from enormous holes created by broad-headed arrows three times his size attached to ropes as thick as his wrists. He said, "Roland and Rabat will be done soon. Let's end this before they make port." Looking up he found the flying fairies and followed their trajectory toward the shore away from the cliffs. "See? They are heading to the swampy area beyond the beach. You up for a swim?"

Roglok's response was a thin, cruel smile, followed by him diving into the water to follow their prey with almost no sound. Hak began running to the landward side of the docks, an enormous sword in one hand and the ogre's spear in the other.

Blaine, ever the businessman, had seen it all. From the dwindling ogre population, he knew he would no longer have to worry about their appeasement. He turned to his nearly-adult ward, Bam, and said, "Go help the gnome. I'll try to keep everything from burning."

The large teenage human, promoted from raising supplies up the cliffs to loading and unloading ships (frequently with a barrel or two on his shoulders), picked up his long-handled maul, a sledgehammer with a stout bladed edge on one side of its head to open or break apart barrels and casks, and easily caught up to Hak. His help was quite welcome.

***

The boy and the gnome waited quietly in the tall beach grass. The brief, ragged, one-sided conversation let Bam know who they were up against.

"No warning," Hak said. "They'll kill us just for seeing them." The human was okay with that. He had seen the aftermath that Baru Dall's army had left behind in the villages of his friends between Blaine's and Yeomring Castle.

Hak nudged him, pointing upward. Eyevee was waving at them while Djinja flew rapid circles around her, making a target bull's eye effect. Straight ahead. And then they emerged from the water, but only two of them. Neither Hak nor Bam hesitated. As the troglodytes made the transition from swimming to wading and stood up, Hak let fly with the ogre spear and Bam threw his hammer over the top of his head with both hands.

Tarlek Soul-Collector never saw the spear, never heard anything over the roll of the knee-high waves breaking around him. The spear went through his ribs until the wider, fur-lined and bone-rimmed throwing handle hit his chest. At that point the force of the impact knocked him from his feet. As they came up another incoming wave flung his flippers upward and forward and his body weight falling onto his back drove the spear deep into the soft sand. The water began to turn darker, and a nasty, oily, foul-smelling slick appeared around the wounded trog even as bubbles began to appear around his mouth.

Dramin Fire-Bringer saw the spear. Flinging up one hand he attempted to shield himself, then spun toward Tarlek's attacker and cast out invisible arrows from the claws of his other hand. The maul coming at him was too dense and heavy for his defensive ward to handle. It slowed but got through. The blade missed, having spun too much, but the top of the hammer's head struck him squarely in the sternum. As he both heard and felt the crunching of his rib bones, the spin of the maul continued and the handle struck his face, from chin to forehead, all at once. Unconscious, he dropped straight into the surf, bobbing like flotsam in the waves.

Hak, knocked back by the mage's attack, never saw the third troglodyte, the old king, who had come ashore down the beach and circled back around behind them in the tall grass-filled swampy backwater behind them. He slashed Hak's throat open from behind, the strength of it leaving the gnome fighter's head pulled back by its own weight, a yawning red ring around the holes of his air and stomach tubes, spouting blood like a fountain that sprayed onto Bam's right arm.

The boy spun, hearing the huge trog let out a half laugh/half yell of triumph as he saw Hak's sword fall from his lifeless left hand. He picked it up awkwardly, but in time to fend off a swing of the huge old troglodyte's dagger.

And then Bam's opponent froze, and the bulbous eyes got even wider. He spun from the top down like a well-used rope falling from memory back into its coiled shape, revealing what looked like tiny wings. As Bam blinked his eyes to adjust his impression he realized that they were actually the handles of two long, slender bone daggers with feathers tied onto them. Their wielder, Roglok, now stood looking down at his old king. He said, "It ends here, your former Highness. No more will we be betrayers and monsters."

All he got in response was a quizzical look above lips gurgling out black blood due to punctured lungs. The old king tried to draw a breath, achieving only to fill what was left of the open-air space in his lungs with blood. The great swimmer was drowning on dry land.

Roglok told Bam, "Toss me that sword, son." Bam did it without hesitation. Roglok said, "For King Runebane, and all true Froglodytes everywhere. It ends here." With a final physical punctuation, the froglodyte sea captain decapitated his old king.

Asking Bam, "Can you carry our friend the gnome there to a healer? It seems too late, but with magic I just never know anymore…" He waded into the surf with Hak's sword and took off Dramin's head as well. As he looked to do the same to Tarlek, he realized that the priest was awake, watching him, stuck to the sand. Roglok said, "You should have chosen better friends," and swung the sword one more time.

They walked back to Blaine's, Bam carrying Hak, Roglok carrying Hak's sword and three heads.

***

Runebane stared at Hak's lifeless body. Small in stature perhaps, but his larger-than-life protector and true and loyal friend, closer to him than any froglodyte had ever been. And he would have to tell Ms. Toss.

The King of the Froglodytes turned to his priests, who immediately looked to the state of their flippered feet. No chance then. He had them wrap him up in seal hides and stow him below decks on his ship to take home. He would have a place of permanent honor among the Froglodyte people. But that would have to wait.

***

Chapter 80

Into the Waterfall

Rrahmus, Pill, Brine and Barger had ridden on Argenta's back, Graham on Ariene and Hailee on Aurelius, and Yelsa rode gleefully on Audhan, all arriving together in the bowl below an old waterfall that hid a cave entrance. The water had now found another way around, but still filled the pool created by the original falls. The trees above now had roots that hung down like a curtain. The pool was surrounded by dragons of all colors and sizes.

Greetings were brief and quiet. Only Rrahmus saw the awkwardness between Sylvia and Pill. A patrol order was easy enough, only the human and the half-orc couldn't see in the caves without light. Pill looked at Brine and said, "I'll go first. If anything too big shows up, get the big boys up front and get them involved." He turned and entered alone, not looking back. Brine followed. Rrahmus waited, handing torches with leather covers on top to Barger and Yelsa. "When it all goes black, or when we need our large friends here to fight for us, take the covers off of these, okay?"

Barger was confused, but Yelsa was fascinated.

She reached up to uncover her torch, but Rrahmus held up a hand, "Oh, no! Wait! Please…? You don't know it yet, but this light can be blinding!" He chuckled a little. "When I was younger, they didn't always work, but now? Some are just <u>too</u> bright! Let's not find out right here…"

They could all tell that Yelsa still <u>really</u> wanted to open it anyway. Audhan said, "That will be <u>fun</u> to do later, somewhere deep in the caves where there's no light at all!" The half-gnome girl's eyes lit up, and she and Barger followed Rrahmus inside.

Graham and Audhan exchanged a glance as the young dragon followed them in. He and Hailee waited. Graham had a torch of his own, which he lit, then they followed. Argenta called after them, "I'll be trailing behind – I have to change, I'm too big in this form."

***

Normally in complete darkness Pill was able to pick his way along easily, most things being clear to him a good 20 to 30 paces ahead. Caves like this where there were normally fires and lots of movement of warm-blooded creatures tended to be even darker with soot and humidity. This cave had been empty for some time. It was dry, cold, and the walls picked clean of any edible debris by the crawly things that hid in the corners, cracks and crevices. And where the soot was no longer, the moisture, in rivulets, likely after rains, from the old riverbed above, made deposits that invited lichens and mosses that gave off many colors of iridescent color – and light. Pill could see for as far as there were no rocks to block his view.

It occurred to him that perhaps this was where the river above had first diverted to after wearing through the ceiling above him. Here and there were pools of still water, with sand and pebbles at the edges.

Occasionally he heard Brine behind him, but other than that, nothing.

After what seemed a league underground, he found himself looking out over a bowl with dwellings up high on one side. He waited for his companions before continuing. When they caught up, Hailee said softly, "This is where we found the kobolds massacred."

Pill asked, "How were they killed? Were they burned? Bitten and eaten?"

"No, slashed and stabbed, with spears and swords, pretty sure by the guards from the river fort," said the half-orc.

"So they killed these kobolds, male, female, adults, children...all of them. Presumably ordered to by Baru Dall, the patron of all kobolds. Why would he do that? What is here that they can't see or know?" Pill mused.

"And now," said Argenta in elf form, "those very kobolds are attacking everything in their path south of us, seemingly deliberately avoiding this region. They have to know of this colony. So perhaps he has given them some excuse to not come here? Or even used this as the motivation to get them to go on a rampage?"

Seeing no threat, they continued down to the silent village.

Graham stopped at a small barricade, noting that there were no bodies about. "This is wrong. Kobolds guard their families like packs of dogs. There was no confrontation here at the guard post? Even if they were completely surprised there should be some sign." He pointed, "Most seem to be gathered near the center, the adults anyway – gathered for what? A meeting? Or a greeting with someone they knew? This is treachery…"

Audhan said, "We have to find Roary and the Old One."

They moved on.

***

Chapter 81

Here's Baru

Baru Dall looked into the pool before him. His lopsided smile looked slightly more crooked than normal. The first step was complete. His fountain was restored and holding water nicely. And though crystal clear with the bottom fully visible in the torchlight of his cavernous living chamber, the rabbit, frog and fish that he had dropped into it were nowhere to be seen, transported immediately once fully submerged. To *where*, of course remained to be seen... He just needed to have one more successful 'partial' trip to verify... He checked his belongings one last time and cast his spell.

***

He arrived as he always did, but this time he planned to go immediately to the fort on the river to check for the arrival of his animal test subjects. Later he would come back, retrieve the spear, gather up his hostage and return. It would not take long. He had made some modifications to his spells of relocation, and had several prepared – from here to his fort chambers, from there to the ogre prison in the desert (hopefully unnecessary), from the prison or the fort to home (which was really just canceling his current spell). If the critter transfers worked, he would be back for the spear right away; it was too valuable to risk trying to get it back through the fountain before he tested the full functionality of them in both directions. The glass jar he held he smashed to the ground, and when the smoke cleared he stood in his bedchamber at the river fort. He checked on the spear and its shaft – still in the chest.

Walking out into the chamber between the gate/bridge and the courtyard, he skirted the stairs and headed toward his chapel. Striding to the fountain, lighting torches magically from a distance as he went, he took in a deep breath through his nose while clenching his teeth with excitement. There on the fountain's lip sat a frog, and there was a bunny in the water, frantically trying not to drown. He wondered how young it was, for most rabbits were strong swimmers in his experience.

He picked it up and threw it back down again, hard, into the water, and it was gone. Turning, he grabbed the frog and repeated the action. He looked for the fish and found nothing. 'Good enough,' he thought, and canceled his projection spell.

**

Chapter 82

Information Overload

In pixie terms a flurry of activity all driven by furious effort toward one goal was described as 'flurrious'. That was the word they used when they needed to impress on their fellow pixies as to the importance of something, and it was being said often in the conversations taking place as Aurelius and Ariene landed back at their camp near the well in Render's old village.

Slawhit and Jobalm and Flaw were surrounded by pixies of all shapes, sizes, colors and styles. And they were all talking over each other, like children at play, except they were grave, fearful, and seemingly anxious for input. They soon got it.

"Shaddap!!" Slawhit's booming directive echoed in the nearby empty buildings.

"The ogres are coming!" said a voice.

"The kobolds have attacked!" said another.

"The troglodytes stole ancient relics from the Arch Mage!" "You mean 'froglodytes'," "Which Arch Mage?" "The old trog king came back to challenge Runebane!"

This time it was Jobalm's turn, "One at a time, for the Goddess' sake! Let's go with ... alphabetically this time..."

In the few moments it took to sort <u>that</u> out, Fallon, Sean, Queen Hazelmoon and Yar Drake arrived in time to hear all of the reports.

Aurelius summed it up at the end. "Okay. The ogres are sailing this way, we are not sure exactly to where, but over half are already dead. Relics have been stolen from Rrahmus by the old troglodyte king's advisors and given to Baru Dall. They tried to help their old king return to power, but those three are all dead, along with the gnome bodyguard to Runebane. Fallon's brother-in-law Roland and several other Rose trading ships are chasing the ogres. That may be problematic if their mothers decide to get involved – not everything 'divine' is actually 'good'... the Hags fall into that category, certainly...

So, as I see it, the coming combat will be land, sea, and magic. Yar, I recommend you start a flanking offensive against the kobolds. Someone will have to explain it all to the human kings. Icelle's cavaliers can do the same to the north and west; if any ogres are already on land, with the help of Sean and his trolls and the good Queen Hazelmoon and her warlocks, they should be able to contain that fort."

With a glance at his wife, Aurelius concluded, "We dragons will start with the threat at sea, where the ogres are trapped on their ships and at greatest risk from our deadliest weapon – fire."

Slawhit told Jobalm, "We'll send messengers to everyone. We can continue to be the communication service, we're perfect for it. Jobalm, we have to alert the Arch Mage. Maybe he will know why his relics were stolen…"

Aurelius stood to his full dragon height, head held high, and spoke forcefully, "Listen! All of you! Remember that <u>this is war</u>! We are not waiting to be attacked! This fight goes back at least a decade! None of this is what any of us had planned to be doing on this night! But we are here, now, so let's do it well and hope we can all regale each other about it another day; a day when we finally get to live our plans and realize our dreams! Remember that you do this not only with, but <u>for</u> each other! Seize the initiative! Do not hesitate! And <u>fight</u>!"

The spontaneous roar of motivated enthusiasm took Aurelius back a bit. Though he had fought before, many times, he was a priest and healer by training and inclination. He was a leader to his race, to his fellow believers, but not to legions of warriors – others were much better suited to that task. At this moment all he could think of was his dead son, and that he did not want any more of his 'children' to suffer Auron's fate if he could help it. He suddenly understood what his warrior friends had told him for centuries, that even though the fight might start over land, or love, or power or treasure, once it starts you fight for the comrades next to you, and until the fight is over, that is all that matters. He could see it in their eyes, these men, dwarves, pixies, dragons, even trolls – they would fight for <u>him</u>. He felt both pride <u>and</u> humility.

And then he heard Sugarplum yelling, getting rapidly closer, "He is here! He is here! The mage, Baru Dall, he is <u>here</u>!"

"You all know what to do!" bellowed Aurelius. He told one of Plumley's companions, "Karmien, go with the dwarves. Gather your kin. Stop the kobolds!" He turned, roaring so that only dragons understood, some flames escaping as he did so, "Follow me!" and took off to the north, toward the cave entrance, the river fort, and the sea.

***

Queen Hazelmoon Toadscream looked at her little group of loyal subjects and friends. To Icelle

Yeomring she said, "I have no experience to help you. But I can send with you your son, his trolls, and my warlocks…"

"My Lady," Sean interrupted, "You cannot be wholly undefended!"

"I won't," she said. "One," she said to her chief warlock, "will you and three trolls accompany me to this fort on the river? And," she continued, turning, "Krystal? I sincerely need both a competent fighter to guard me personally when I use my magic – and another woman to talk to in between times who understands what's going on never hurts…will you stay with me?"

Sean was torn, Krystal could see that, and she wanted to be with him, but she also saw the practicality and utility of doing what the Queen asked. She saw him nodding slightly.

"Your Majesty, of course I will," she said. To Sean, she said, "If you die, I'll kill you!"

Icelle turned to his commanders and said quietly, "We leave now. Split up, search every road and path between here and the ocean. You each have two pixies assigned to send messages. If you find ogres, send for help, do not get engaged! Break contact if you have to, they will not be difficult to relocate. Let's go." To

Sean he said, "Screen my right flank, okay? Make sure you and the warlocks have horses that can keep up with the trolls." In a softer tone he said, "And don't die," and grinned, saying, "She sounds like your mother..."

Sean replied, "You don't die! I'm not explaining it to mother!"

***

Ebon stared at Flaw, who just said, "Please?!" Jobalm had flown to warn King Jankin, and Slawhit to warn Rrahmus, but the little furry pixie could stand neither the thought of being left behind nor of not being there for his friend Pill. They soon caught up to Slawhit, and Ebon left them with Aurick before winging away toward the ocean, with a few more dragons in tow.

***

Chapter 83

Watching is Boring

The boat had not been there a moment ago, he was sure of it. Angus shook his head and blinked hard, wetting his eyes and forcing his mind to focus on the current view before him. Yes, it was a boat. Even as he nudged the sleeping Farsight with his boot, he saw both men and ogres exiting onto the upriver platform next to the side gate of the fort he was watching.

The half-elf's eyes opened with full awareness, took in Angus' posture, slowly moved to follow his gaze.

To keep from being overcome by boredom or tunnel vision, and to keep communicating and checking in on each other they had decided to move one person between their locations every few hours. Tapping his brother the half-dwarf, Farsight counted a half dozen ogres and as many men enter the fort. As far as he could tell no one stayed on the boat.

Grunnach said, "Should we get the girls?"

***

As they rotated locations it was bound to happen eventually that Mynorca and Bronwyn would be left alone together. The latter stewed after Grunnach left for about an hour before she <u>had</u> to say something.

"I really barely know Graham," she said.

Mynorca turned from her observer duties, looked the younger girl straight in the eyes, smiling, and said, "You are adorable. Don't worry, he <u>loves</u> you. And I just like strong men to chase after me, which I can guarantee <u>he</u> won't do. He's not my type, you have nothing to worry about from me." She looked back down the road they were watching.

"He … he 'loves' me?" asked the young healer.

Without looking again, the beautiful performer said, "Friend, he looks at you like the best born day present ever, the best meal ever and his favorite sword all at once. Trust me, you want to keep that one."

She stiffened and said, "There are heavily armed and armored men, some mounted, some not, sneaking through the tress. Stay down, stay quiet." As they watched, a few of the men and riders periodically peered out into the road, and then dozens crossed all at once, a skirmish line as far as she could see. A few even crossed the road behind them! Mynorca was sure they would be missed and able to rejoin the others by the fort unnoticed. Until the cute little healer girl went running out into the road, yelling excitedly…

Mynorca got ready to run, gathered her things,

then looked up and saw one of the riders jump off of his horse and immediately he was being hugged by the crazy girl who was holding him so tightly that when she jumped up and down in her excitement only her lower body seemed to bounce in place. And now she was pointing to their hiding place. Terrific.

The songstress stood up and waved – her chances with fighting men were much better up close anyway...

* * *

Chapter 84

Fire on the Water

The pixies were faster and spotted the rose emblazoned sails in the dark as they flew over dozens of the smaller, oar-driven ogre craft. There were only a few on the deck in the dark hours of middle night. Their sails were full, and the larger ships were gaining on their quarry.

Landing on the railing behind the helmsman, Walhe said, "Is Captain Roland on this ship?"

The poor fellow spun, drawing a cutlass and completely releasing the wheel with both hands, and saw...nothing. He felt the ship start to turn under his feet, so he spun back to grab the helm and correct it, dropping his cutlass, knowing he would need both hands at this speed, and as it clattered to the deck, he looked down at it first, then up to the horizon – and into the eyes of the speaker, who had now made himself visible and was sitting cross-legged on the forward railing of the helm area.

"You should really be more careful," said the mouth under the eyes.

"Alright," said the helmsman, calming himself,

"The captain here is Captain Rabat. Captain Roland's ship is behind us a little way."

The pixie fell to the deck, face first, his wings stopping him short of smashing into the polished wood. He deftly picked up the helmsman's cutlass and flipped it toward him, gently. It took all of the self-control he had for the helmsman to not dodge or flinch and let the wheel out of his control again. The tip of his blade went smoothly into its scabbard and fell until the hilt struck home.

With an exaggerated exhale, he told Walhe, "You are quite disturbing." The pixie just smiled. He replied, "You should see me with those that I don't care for..."

"I'll wager on the truth of <u>that</u>..."

"Can you get your Captain Rabat up here without making a racket or sounding an alarm?" asked the pixie.

"He already has!" said a voice through the railing, only a few inches of an arrow showing.

"Oh! Good then!" said Walhe, "You need to know that I am your marker to keep the dragons from roasting you. Wait, I know that voice – you're the captain of Fallon's from the northern desert! I asked you about your scars – controlled scorpion stings you said – sounded awful…"

The arrow disappeared. "Walhe! … Did you say 'dragons'?"

As if on command, a long sleek silver dragon and large muscular black dragon dropped onto Rabat's deck. The first said, "We need to have a meeting I think. Of those ahead of you Captain, are any of them friends?"

"Lady Ariene," said Walhe with a small bit of pomp, "meet Captain Rabat."

"You have lovely dark brown skin," she said. "Not black like Ebon here, but we don't really have any brown dragons. Are the scar designs similar to tattoos in nature? Is your coloring from the sun or are you born with it?"

"I am now as I was at my birth, my Lady," he said with a slight bow. "Among my crew there are both – some who get as dark as I am from the sun, others who are lighter but from my same family line."

"That could come in quite handy in a night fight like this – hard to see you in the gloom I'd imagine for those who cannot discern heat. But, quickly now, I have some fire to manage…" She smiled.

"There is only one ship ahead that I prefer not to be burned if possible," he said. "It is mine, you see, stolen from me, manned by betrayers... for the ogre ships I care nothing, but that one I would like to get back, if it can be arranged?"

Ariene looked to the smallest form present and said, "Walhe, I believe that is more your specialty. Ebon can help. He is quite strong, good at both acquiring and using weapons, and also very hard to see in the dark." With that, she flapped a few times to rise off of the deck without pushing against it to jump and thereby risk breaking it, then flew upward, where those below could now see dozens of dragons circling lazily above them. A few moments of silence below later and they watched as the dragons sped off to the east.

Minutes later, as flashes of light began to dot the night sky on the horizon, Walhe said, "Well, gentlemen, that's my cue to go get you your ship," and he winked out of existence.

Ebon said, "He'll need some help. I may be back to get some loyal crew from you to take over to it to sail it when we're done – there may not be any left..." and he left in the manner that Ariene had.

A few moments passed. "Cap'n?" said the helmsman. "There were some big dragons and a tiny little flying man here just now, right?"

"Yes. They were <u>not</u> your imagination," said

Rabat. "Now, set your course toward those flames..."

**

Chapter 85

Original Lair

The tunnel ended in a chamber that dipped down and was filled with still water. The ceiling rose as well but was still visible above. With no reason to be in a hurry to die, Pill waited with Brine and Barger, then when Rrahmus and Yelsa peered into the chamber he said, softly, "It must come back up, yes? But after how far?"

Rrahmus asked, "Brine? If the water is still?"

The youthful dwarf, and experienced miner, thought, then said, "The sides are carved, not rough, this is intentional. It could have been hewn around an obstacle, or angled to join another existing passage. Either way, without knowing how far, or if it is a dead end, or maybe just blocked, I can't say, nor can I see in the dark underwater. Sorry sir."

Hailee and Graham slowly followed Audhan to the edge of the water, unable to see at all, their torches having burned out long ago. Graham said, "I smell pond water."

The silvery female elf behind him began to glow. He and Hailee stepped apart, letting the light grow and illuminate the round chamber. "This is familiar," Argenta said. "This is an old dragon lair trick. We need to go. Forward or backward, but we can't stay here."

Rrahmus decided for them. "Back for now, let's plan a bit?" he said and moved in that direction, only to narrowly avoid being bowled over by a three-headed monster the like of which he had never seen, the heads stacked vertically.

Yelsa screamed and swung at the top head that seemed to veer off on its own toward her to push it away – with the hand that held her torch. The force of the swing shot the leather cover off of it at Slawhit's face. The light blinded them all, and Aurick in elf form stopped so suddenly that Flaw, who had been on his back, shot forward and into space...into Brine... They both tumbled and then fell down into the water. The splash was the only sound as the flash of light had stopped them all in their tracks. The two that had submerged did not come back up.

Argenta, moving back to get out of the round chamber, called to all of them, "Get out of there! Follow me! This is a trap!"

Pill, still standing at the edge of the water, made eye contact with both her and his uncle, then turned and dove into the pool.

Hailee grabbed little Yelsa and Graham lifted Audhan with one hand and each swung them back into the entry passage as they went themselves.

Slawhit and Aurick, instinctive flyers, went up, the latter jumping as he changed into his dragon form, to get away from the water.

Audhan, pressed up against Graham, saw the ruby necklace he had enchanted glowing in front of him. He lifted it over Graham's neck, turned back toward the chamber opening, stepped in slightly and tossed it upward toward the two flyers, saying, "Take this! Wear it!"

Yelsa saw what he did and took hers off and did the same. Both were caught by a quizzical Slawhit, though with a bit of difficulty as his independent eyes were still getting accustomed to his new perception of depth and space. And then the opening into the chamber shimmered – Audhan and Yelsa pulled back into the tunnel, and it solidified, looking like a blank stone wall. Hailee thumped it with a hammer punch using the heel of his fist – it was stone.

They all heard the sound of rushing water coming toward them and backed away, but nothing came through the new barrier. They heard it rise, the sound like a bucket filling under a waterfall, getting quieter, then there were a few muffled shouts, then … nothing.

Rrahmus approached the wall, put his hand on it, and it glowed bright blue. "Ancient magic," he said. "Much stronger than my own. Pre-historic I'll wager, old world, like the fountains. I wonder if the pool works like they do…"

Argenta cried, "What do we <u>do</u>?" the words rising in a crescendo to finish nearly roaring.

"I have one option perhaps," Rrahmus said quietly. They all moved back as he put his arms out wide, one holding a dagger that seemed to just appear in his hand, the other holding a small hard stone used for sharpening blades. As a group they tried to slow their ragged, adrenaline-filled breathing. The Elvish Arch Mage continued, "I am not as good at this as some of our priestly friends, but here goes." He spun, eyes closed, arms out, in a circle, three times. The blade of his dagger glowed, then lit up, the steel shining brighter than even Yelsa's magical torch.

Rrahmus opened his eyes, put both hands on the dagger, and spun three times more, raising it for one circle, lowering it for another.

"Well?!" asked Argenta.

"If I could sense the dagger that I know Pill carries, my own blade would have turned red at some point. It did not," he said. "That means he is too far away. They are gone."

Graham and Hailee both nodded and turned to leave, Hailee gently taking the torch from Yelsa's little hand.

Rrahmus, rarely at a loss, was devastated, as were the dragons.

Yelsa asked, "Where's Barger?"

***

Chapter 86

The Frying Pan

Pill was relieved to find Flaw and Brine alive and undamaged, sitting on the edge of the strange pool he found himself in. As he swam to the edge, they asked what they should do now. When he stepped up and out of the water he said, "Find a way out, or a way back?"

As they pondered their predicament the water roiled a bit and they turned, taking defensive postures, only to see Aurick and Slawhit appear, the latter absolutely disgusted.

Slawhit said, "Well, at least I know where we are and how to get out. Move toward that wall above you, young thieves." To Flaw he said, "Grandson, pick up that poor browny next to you before he falls back in and drowns."

They had not even noticed poor little Barger until that moment. He completely blended in with his surroundings. Flaw picked him up easily and moved to follow Pill and Brine up the slight slope. Aurick, his dragon form so recently adopted was so shiny and golden that it became a light source for all of them. As he approached the wall, two sections of stone swung out and away from them. They immediately pushed into the new space, which initially continued upward, the slope rising vertically another barrel or so in height. In front of them at the top was a quivering, wavering hole in the air.

"Go-go-go!" said Slawhit, "This may be our only way out! Whoever was here just left! If it's that dragon with the Old One, we could catch up to him! If it's the mage, well, we could all die... But no one lives forever, and he might be alone!"

They all stood aghast when Flaw turned and stepped into the undulating hole in the air and disappeared.

Pill ran after Flaw (and therefore Barger as well as Flaw still had him in his arms). Brine ran after Pill. Slawhit zoomed ahead of Aurick and out of sight. The dragon dove forward, changing to elf form to fit in the available space, his tail pulling into his body just in time to miss being closed on by the shrinking opening.

***

As the hole disappeared a figure appeared behind it. Roary hadn't known that Baru Dall had been here until he heard the glass breaking from his spell to leave. Now he realized that he couldn't see the opening it had created from the side opposite! It had been here the entire time! The mage had not seen them in the darkness. He would just have to make a fire and hope that Baru Dall came back soon and could see them the next time. He had said several times that this was where he always came to first.

***

Aurick barrel-rolled into a room lined with old scrolls and potion jars and … his friends, staring at a chest. It didn't belong here, the chest. The walls and floor of the room were hand-cut, decent work by an above average stone mason, the bed and shelves knocked together by an average-at-best carpenter, but the chest was functional artwork. It had gold locks, corners and buckles, even the trim where the lid met the trunk was meticulously fitted gold.

Pill, seeing their last companion arrive and the air tunnel behind him close, said, "I have to open this, but following can't wait. Brine, can you lead?"

The dwarf said, "Of course, but where? I looked out this door, there's three more…"

Barger was awake, and though he was rubbing a knot forming on his head, said, "I can track by smell. Are we following someone?"

"Perfect!" said Slawhit. "Smell that pillow over there on the bed, I'm sure it has the owner's scent…"

He followed up with, "Brine, right behind, Aurick next, then me. Flaw, you stay with Pill! Let's go!"

As they left, Pill said, "Any intuition about his box old friend?"

"My father's nose smells blood and poison," said the flightless pixie "there (sniff, sniff) on the left-hand lock."

"Needle trap, got it, thanks," replied Pill, taking care to keep a knife blade above his pick as he turned the tumblers. "Just in case there's a second trap, go stand by the door please," he said.

He also stood to the side when he opened the chest, and when nothing happened, he looked inside. It was filled with an assortment of gold, jewels, an elaborate set of rings, a necklace, an orb, a scepter and a crown, all set in specific places cut into beautifully polished mahogany designed to hold each piece. In each back corner were two bags that obviously were not part of the original contents. Opening them hesitantly he knew immediately where he had seen them – in his Uncle Rrahmus' chambers at Fallon's, while he tried to figure what they did. Whatever Baru Dall wanted with them couldn't be good. He took them.

The box he knew had to be the crown jewels that Yrag had made for King Jankin, stolen by one of

Fallon's betrayers and given to Baru Dall, who obviously intended to <u>wear</u> that crown someday soon...

Pill took a special pouch out of his backpack and pulled it down over the box. Flaw's eyes bugged out a little, as he could tell that the top of the box was wider than the mouth of the pouch by at least four times. And then the whole box was in the pouch and gone. Before he could ask, Pill said, "I'll explain later. Let's catch up with the others. Can we follow your nose?"

Nodding, Flaw left the room, shaking his head soon after. Walking to the left-hand door, he pulled and it opened, revealing the inner area of an entrance behind a portcullis and drawbridge. Flaw walked right past it, glanced briefly to his right at a dead body in a stairwell above him, then continued around the stairs, down a corridor to the right, then to a large double door, where he hesitated.

Pill did not. He pushed the doors open, one with each hand, hard, drawing weapons while they were still swinging and stepping inside ... a chapel.

Near the front he saw his comrades again, staring at a fountain. They spared him a glance, then looked back. Pill and Flaw approached quickly. "What is it?" Flaw asked.

Slawhit said, "An altar. A fountain. A portal. A

pool. Maybe all four. We heard a splash, then came in quick, only to see the dark mage disappear, standing where we are now. So, the splash wasn't him, but neither is there anything in the water…"

Pill said thoughtfully, "My father used to say, 'Just because an arrow has a tip on both ends, it doesn't mean it can shoot backward'…"

Brine's eyes crossed at the observation. He said, "What?!"

Pill explained, "I think it means that if you go forward, even though you may turn right back around, you don't really go back; the place you left is no longer the same. If this is a portal, and we go through it, is the portal at the other end pointed back to here?"

The dwarf sat down in the nearest pew. "Let me know what to do next. Puzzles are not my thing, and I'm tired."

Barger said, "Look! A fish!"

Indeed, a small fish had broken the surface, swam a short way toward them, then, frightened by the browny's exclamation, went back under – and disappeared. They all leaned forward to see better. The pool was clean and clear, and the fish was gone.

"Well," said Aurick, "some portal somewhere is pointed here anyway."

And then the fish broke the surface again, farther away, but when Flaw said, "Another fish!" it dove and was gone. "Okay," said Pill, "but was that the same fish? Or a different fish? If it's the same one, we have a reversible portal with a reasonable chance we can risk using it and seeing what is at the other end. If not..."

Aurick said, "Well, my father taught me to fish like a dragon..." He changed to his dragon form and hovered his head over the middle of the pool. He did not have to wait long. A fish appeared and he put his snout and mouth over it and scooped his lower jaw under the fish and slurped both it and the water around it into this mouth. Snaking his long neck over to the floor, he spit it out, held it down with his nose and deftly poked out the fish's right eye with the end of a claw. Picking it up with his tongue he turned and spit it out and down into the water.

Flaw looked slightly ill, staring at the removed fisheye on the floor. Aurick saw it and said, "Don't worry little friend, if he comes back, I'm eating him anyway. I'm hungry!" The toothy smile did not comfort the little half-pixie...though he felt a strange desire to roll around in the fish scent on the ground, he had no desire to eat it.

The frog that popped up right next to them was a surprise, but it jumped backward and into the water and disappeared. In its place was a one-eyed fish that Aurick scooped up again, spit out again, and flipped it over to compare its eyes. He said, "Well, Flaw?"

The pixie nodded, said, "It's her. She recognizes me." The dragon's double take went unnoticed. Even Slawhit narrowed his eyes.

He said, "Flaw, can you <u>talk</u> to the fish?"

The wingless descendant said to his eldest ancestor, "No. I just <u>feel</u> what she's thinking I guess."

They all heard the bellow of anger from the other side of the fort.

Pill said, "I think he's back already, and found his chest is missing. My uncle the Arch Mage and Aurelius himself didn't succeed in killing him the last time we know he was here. What chance do we have?"

Slawhit said, "So, we go in the fountain that <u>he</u> didn't use, knowing we can get back here? Wait there until we think maybe he's gone again?"

"Resisted Aurelius <u>and</u> Rrahmus? Let's go," said Aurick. The fountain was too small for the width of his dragon body to get through, so he changed to his elf form and hopped in. It only came up to his chest. He ducked under the water and was gone. They all followed, quickly, quietly, with no splashing.

***

A single coin fluttered down to the bottom of the pool.

***

Chapter 87

Minions vs Bad Help

It was not possible. He did not believe it. He couldn't. Finding Roary in the old lair was surprising. Finding out that the Old One had been rescued, hidden, accidentally found and re-kidnapped? That was amazing. But that he somehow missed by mere minutes a group of at least an elf, a dwarf, a pixie and a dragon and that they had used his own magic tunnel to escape to his own chamber and somehow stolen his chest with the spear he needed to kill the ancient dragon was just too much.

Baru Dall's assessments of his various minions led him to the conclusion that only he and his extremely powerful, but luckily hypnotically suggestable, dragon friend (who he ultimately planned to kill anyway) were competent. The kobolds couldn't keep their mouths shut. The ogres were just as big and dumb as their reputation. Even his fellow men (the ones willing to believe ill of their magical neighbors even when presented actual evidence to the contrary) were simultaneously woefully lacking in intelligence and convinced of their own brilliance.

The only solution was to finally just get it done; destroy Metaerie and everything in it and absorb its magic.

He led the dragons to his fountain in the chapel. "Alright," he told Roary, "just jump in, and take the ancient bag of dragon bones with you. I'll meet you in a moment, I'm just going to do a quick search of the premises for my chest."

Roary, a red dragon in the prime of his adulthood, in his elf form was quite the physical specimen. He always made the mage uncomfortable, with his strength, physical good looks, mental prowess, loyalty and confidence. He was literally all of the things Baru Dall was not. He lifted his ancestor, bound and gagged, in his arms, walked up the stairs on the front of the fountain, and jumped in, falling to a sitting position where they were both under the water.

***

When he stood up and tossed the Old One out onto the ground over the lip of the fountain, he felt the dagger, thrown into his back, sink up to the hilt under his left shoulder blade. The momentum of both actions drove him forward, so he plunged out of the water over the edge of the surrounding stone, his right hand slapping against the outer masonry, sending him into a practiced roll.

Unfortunately his maneuver drove the dagger in deeper when he rolled over on the handle. Fortunately he was already changing into his dragon form and the tip of the blade missed piercing his heart by the thickness of a rose petal.

Continuing his roll over onto his claws and knees, his growth was soon enough to be seen by his attacker behind the fountain, who well knew what a dragon looked like. Pill turned and ran into the opening in the wall behind him that Roary could not fit through and around a quick corner where Brine and Barger were waiting.

The burst of flame that jetted past them down the hall was searing hot. All of their faces became reddened and sweaty in an instant. The growl was clear, "I'll deal with you in a moment."

The thumping steps retreated, but a second roar erupted. They heard, "What?!" The sound ran out only as it faded into the distance.

"I think that was Roary, and he brought the Old One," said Pill. "I also think that our friends have given Roary bigger problems. Now let's see if we can mess with the mage."

The room they'd just left, a large underground

torchlit chamber was adorned on one side with paintings, all of them painstakingly detailed scenes of death, with clear depictions of events from the recent past in Metaerie. There were dragons flying over camps of men, incinerating them, kobolds being ridden down and beheaded by armored men on horseback, gargoyles plummeting into the breastplates of mounted knights – all events that Baru Dall would know of, and all from the perspective of a story related from the view of himself or one of his minions.

They entered a room/cavern, of rough-hewn doorways, naturally formed walls, but hung with rough-weaved wool tapestries with alternating lines of different colors in both directions. They contained reds, greens and blues mostly. A few had undyed black or white wool as well. The room smelled musty, old, and was lined with shelves filled with jars and pots and map and scroll cases, and books; many, many books.

Pill didn't hesitate. Even Brine gasped quietly, "What're ya doin'?!" He replied, "Search the other passages, quick now."

He took a torch from the wall and touched it to the bottom of every wool hanging. He had spied an oil lamp and poured it out over the biggest bookshelf and lit it from the bottom. He pulled the jar-covered shelf on the left down into the flames, and the scroll-covered one on the right down on top of that. Turning, he looked at Brine, who stood in an adjacent room, staring upward.

"Well? Any other way out?" he asked.

Barger, who had been following Brine to each entrance, was backing up, saying, "Um, Mister Pill, sir? I don't think he can hear you... Remember Regor?"

The dwarf stood in the middle of an open-air staircase, looking up at a very full, very close, very large moon. And he was getting ... furry.

Pill said to Barger, "I won't do it."

"Do what?!" said the little splotchy.

"I won't kill him!" said the elf, desperately.

Brine turned toward them, rolling his badger head from side to side, cracking his neck like a fighter after a practice bout in the training yard, smiling and exposing gleaming white fangs, flexing long dark claws.

Barger ran, yelling back, "Tell him that!"

Pill, shaking his head as Brine charged him, kicked the half-dwarf/half-badger in the chest, knocking it backward into the stone steps, then ran after Barger.

***

Chapter 88

Flight to Fight

Argenta and Audhan burst forth from the waterfall cave entrance first. Only Rowena was still there. "We have to get to the river fort, fast! They passed us by! And we'll have passengers," Argenta said hurriedly. The older, larger dragon asked no questions, but let Graham and Hailee scramble up onto her back. Rrahmus went with Argenta and Yelsa with her adored Audhan, who led the way.

Straight to the fort they flew, as both lead carrier and passenger had been there before. Audhan landed in the inner courtyard, changed to his elf form quickly and led them to the chapel.

They ran to the fountain. Little Yelsa couldn't see over the edge, so she went up the stairs and sat on the top one. "What's that?" she asked, pointing to a small coin near the edge but on the bottom. She immediately started to dive in to get it, but Audhan plucked her out of the air, set her down on the floor. "Whoa little lady," he said, "we don't know where this goes. I'll get it."

He changed back to his dragon form and easily

plunged just his head in and retrieved the metal piece with his tongue and teeth. He turned to face Rrahmus, sticking out his tongue, waving his arms to show his claws, not easily used near his tongue.

The Elvish Arch Mage deftly plucked the item from Audhan's tongue. "I can't quite make it out, it's like it keeps shifting," he said, bringing it close to his eye for better scrutiny, "It's almost like the one…" the medallion flew into the Arch Mage's eye, "…Pill had that let him connect…"

He felt like he was suddenly weightless, standing in a raging inferno, surrounded by reds, oranges and yellows. Some of the flames seemed to gather, form feathers and wings, and then a whole, large bird with huge, sharp talons and an enormous beak, the largest bird of prey he'd ever seen.

'Why am I here?' The thought was in <u>his</u> head, but from a familiar female voice. 'Mortalya?' he thought. 'Why are you in <u>my</u> head?!'

The bird spun a slow circle, then looked at Rrahmus again. 'This definitely changes our relationship. Being my liaison to the world is a job for an experienced priest, usually a follower, often a flyer. A thief was a surprise, but this? The power you hold, both arcane and social? This may create some concern… Oh well, no one likes me anyway, they all fear me, now they'll just have more reason to …"

***

"Rrahmus! Arch Mage!" Argenta was shaking him. "What do we do?!" He shook his head to clear it, looked in the water in front of him and saw a dead body floating in it.

***

Chapter 89
The Fire

When Roary went after Pill, Aurick had stepped out from behind an ancient column, one of two between the old pool he had exited and a large opening at the other end of the huge chamber. He picked up the Old One, and ran toward where Slawhit was waving for him to follow. As he ran, he could see that every nook and crevice had jars and papers and roots and leaves and bones of all types stuffed into them. Between these and the paintings, he knew that this was Baru Dall's research chamber for his dark magic.

As he ducked around a corner, he realized it was just a bend in the enormous chamber. Slawhit and Flaw stood near an ancient altar. He joined them as they hid behind it just in time to hear a roar of frustration.

Flaw cut the Old One's bonds as Slawhit removed his gag.

"Old friend," said the pixie, "I'm afraid we are back in the old world – our world. I can feel myself aging just thinking about it." Turning to Flaw he said, "Here young one," and put the necklaces Audhan and Yelsa had given him around Flaw's neck. Looking back to the only other living thing that was as old as he was, he said, "We have to overwhelm this old-world mage whenever we encounter him. And apparently he has enthralled a dragon of his own?"

The old dragon-in-elf-form said, "It's Roary. My direct line. Enthralled is literally correct. I don't know what magic was used, but it is complete. I have only the hope that the mage's death will free him. Until then, stay behind me if he attacks." He paused in thought. "Ah, Slawhit. The land of Platinus. Do you not wonder what changes are around us? Do you know where we are?"

"The magic lair. Where we began the spell. You are leaning against the altar," said the pixie nostalgically.

***

Barger and Pill burst out back near the fountain in time to see Baru Dall reappear. They did not slow down they just ran past him.

The mage looked at them as if they were dolts. He opened and closed both hands, and they stopped, frozen in place, held by enormous magical invisible hands.

"Let go!" Barger yelled. "He's coming!"

Baru Dall laughed. "You fear someone m than me? Interesting." Turning to Pill he said, "Are you so frightening, elf?"

Roary, who had stopped at the noises behind him, came back and was listening intently.

"Only to some," Pill said, his tone making Barger stop struggling. And talking.

The mage approached Pill, opened the thief's backpack, and, seeing the bags with Rrahmus' stolen relics in them, said, "Master thief, are we? I could use someone like you..."

"Master Magician," said Roary, "the Old One is here, but he has been taken, likely by the companions of these two. They ambushed me."

"Ah. I need to face him anyway. These two aren't going anywhere. Now, let's see what I have here..." Opening the two thick cloth bags he took out a spear head and a piece of wooden handle. He and Roary began walking away from the immobilized elf and browny to where they assumed the Old One had gone. As Baru contemplated bringing the two ancient magicks together, Roary screamed. This was no roar of rage or bellow in combat – it was the primal scream of pain, surprise and mortal fear.

Brine the Were-Badger had come upon the

...iest moving being he could see, Roary,

...is training and muscle memory instincts

...ı Pill combined with the bloodlust and need

to feed of the lycanthrope. As one set of his over large

claws severed Roary's right heel tendon, the other

slashed open the dragon's body cavity from underneath

as he walked, making an opening from hips to sternum,

his organs literally dropping out onto the chamber floor.

Not slowing down, Brine spun as he passed Roary's

neck, and with all of his infernal strength, sliced through

scales, muscle and cartilage, ending the dragon's

scream abruptly.

And then the bloodlust fully took over. As

Roary's body crashed to the floor, the Brine-badger

buried its snout into the dragon's neck, rending, tearing,

chewing – and never noticing the spear plunging toward

his own neck. As he collapsed onto Roary's neck, his

legs twitching as the spear was wrenched back out of

his spinal column, a tear ran down Pill's face. Baru Dall

gave a slight, pleased smile and turned to go get the

'Old One', his new weapon tested successfully. He just

needed to kill the only dragon left alive that was part of

the original spell casting that had created Metaerie. The

spear, whole and functional, looked old and dull now,

but it had glowed bright red when it had found blood in

the crazed badger's spine, and entered as if razor sharp, like a hot knife through warm butter. Its magic was old and bloodthirsty.

Baru Dall didn't see the necklace's appear around Pill and Barger's necks behind him, nor did he realize that they had gained their instant freedom from his spell. But he did see the spear start to glow, despite seeing no threats in front of him. He turned around in time to see Pill and Barger dumping Brine's now dead dwarf body into the fountain. The anger surging through him made the spear turn bright crimson in his left hand as he curled his right, letting a small ball of flame begin to grow in it.

As the flame grew while the mage prepared to hurl the ball forward toward them, Pill dropped his backpack, removing a triply-folded leather flat case. Looking up and seeing Baru Dall's pose, he tossed his backpack into the fountain behind him to save it from the ball of fire he knew was coming. And then it hit — explosive sound, searing heat and total lack of air to breathe. But when it ended, oddly, he felt no pain. Looking from his hands to Barger's face, which was currently looking amazed at his survival, his gaze was drawn down to the ruby pendant the browny was wearing, glowing bright red. 'Ah!' he thought.

'Protection from fire?' Maybe it was, maybe not, but either way they were alive, and he was not about to waste that fact.

The case at his feet held a dozen more of *his* type of combat supply – daggers, knives and hand-axes. Two of the knives were flying at the laughing mage before he could see through the smoke of own creation. As he reached down for two more blades the smoke was clearing and he saw a flaming, charred body behind Barger. It was Flaw. His innocent, guileless eyes were wide open and unmoving, his catastrophe of clothing colors all singed and covered with soot. He was smiling.

Devastated, confused, enraged and perhaps just a bit invincible, Pill Von Ferret went with axes next. His throws were angry but true. The first stuck, but the mage had turned away, so it was in the ribs of his back. He could see the blade of one of his knives sticking out of the back of the mage's neck above it. It must have gone through his mouth but missed the spine. The second axe spun too much but still struck solidly. Then he saw why the mage had disengaged – the spear had fallen from his hand and was laying on the ground, Pill's other knife stuck in its handle.

And then he saw Barger, scooping it up and running around Roary's body even as Baru Dall bent down for it. Pill grabbed up his case and also moved to the far side of the dead dragon's body to meet the scurrying browny, to protect him.

Two dragons and a pixie rounded the bend in the wall of the huge chamber, and the huge, ancient, blind red dragon said, "Save yourselves, this one is mine."

Aurick dashed toward Pill just as the thief told little Barger, "Keep the spear, jump into the fountain!" and turned to throw more blades at the dark mage.

Barger ran, leapt up onto the edge of the fountain and jumped, giving a slight cry of dismay before he splashed in and disappeared.

Pill was in mid-throw when he saw the spear appear in the mage's hand, his other shooting massive bolts of lightning at the Old One, the jolts making the ancient dragon rear up in pain, then come down breathing flame everywhere.

Slawhit had seen Flaw's body just before and flew to his side. A burst of angry ancestor adrenaline allowed him to lift the lifeless body of his millennia younger grandson over the top of the fountain and let him go. He turned toward Baru Dall and used the mage's own body as a barrier, protecting the pixie from the Old One's flames.

Pill's third knife arrived just after the bolts of lightning had departed, and the fourth he let go instinctively even after the dragon's flames began washing over him.

He heard Slawhit say, "Here! Right here!" but also heard Aurick cry out in pain. Turning to look at the latter, the elven thief saw that the gold dragon was ablaze along his whole right side. Sylvia's mate. Who had saved his life... Was not immune to dragon fire in this world? The elf ran to the gold dragon and placed his magical ruby necklace around Aurick's neck. The blaze on his right wing stopped, just in time for another wave of flame to wash across the entire chamber.

Without words as there was no air to draw enough breath to speak, Pill pointed at the fountain. Aurick understood, and with a flap and a leap, dove in, changing to his elf form as everything Pill could see turned to flames. His attempt to spin made him scream in pain, the skin cracking on his back it was already so charred and crispy. He could only think that his father's jacket must be ruined.

The about face worked, though, and he saw another sight to remember. Slawhit's wings were burned off. He was sitting on Baru Dall's shoulders, holding him by a pair of blade handles, one in each ear.

One was his, one was Pill's. The mage still held the ancient spear.

The Old One had walked closer with every breath, and Slawhit yelled one more time, "Here, Marduk! Right here!" After his deepest breath ever, the old red dragon's final exhale was absolutely flambulous. The air was orange with flame, the spear head and handle were too, and soon even the walls and roof were molten hot. As the scrolls and potion jars began to explode and incinerate, the roof collapsed on them all, burying them under thousands of cubic rods of liquid rock. The water of the fountain steamed away quickly and soon after the fountain walls melted too. As the rocks settled, it was not long until the nearby seawater began to seep in. Encased in melted stone below, from above it just looked like a portion of the ocean cliffs had subsided under the waves.

FIN

Chapter 90

Loose Ends

Icelle's combined infantry and cavalry had pushed to the sea, encountering no resistance. By the midday tide some charred flotsam began to arrive. It was soon followed by Ebon the blacksmith in dragon form. He swooped up and down the water's edge, waving his wings to the soldiers until he sighted Icelle and landed. He confirmed that no ogres would land anywhere near here on this day.

***

Sean and a trio of his trolls and Two the Warlock were told of the finding of two women in the woods. When they arrived, skirting the town to the west, Bronwyn hugged him, and Mynorca said, "Hm. Shorter, but definitely Graham's brother." His quizzical look made her laugh just as Queen Hazelmoon, Krystal, more trolls, warlocks and the Rockripper siblings arrived. Krystal looked like she was going to punch Mynorca until Sean pulled her aside. "Charms don't work on me," he said. "Well, none but yours..." with a smirk and a twinkle in his eye. To Mynorca he said, "Speaking of Graham, let's talk to the rest of your bunch."

***

Sean found his brother in the river fort's kitchen. He was eating while half a dozen strange men were cooking and being directed by Angus and an animated too-tall-for-a-dwarf fighter with the top half of his armor removed in the heat. Hailee was making a necklace out of what looked like a dozen ogre ears. All he said was, "It figures," and sat down to join them.

***

Final Chapter

EPILOGUE

"Quite a day," Icelle said to no one in particular, looking down at the harbor below.

The 'no one in particular' in question was pacing along the parapet walk around the outside of his upper keep. Where before only one bench marked "REAVER" had sat, there was now one more. Newer, but of the same design, the word "PILL" was worked into it in gold coins, outlined in thumbnail sized polished rubies. The mage who sat there, touching his nephew's name, no longer had the mischievous twinkle behind his eyes. He said to Icelle, "Do you think I was wrong to kill Brine?"

The old fighter turned and his stare bored holes into Rrahmus' eyes. "No. The disease is uncontrollable. That wasn't Brine. He is still a hero, and not just to his own people. Leif told me that they received a matching stone bench to this one... I assume designed by Audhan and Ebon, with stonework by a fairly competent stonemason..."

"Or a mage with access to an obsessive gnome with a magical rock hammer...?" asked Fallon as he paced past them both again.

A new, exuberant face appeared, bounding up the final steps to join his friends. Fallon accosted him, "Tell me again why this is a good idea?!"

Jankin the Fearless' happiness was not diminished by Fallon's dour expression one little bit. "Why, because it is the will of the people! Just as your daughter and Icelle's oldest boy working with Hailee and his siblings on the orcish frontier is a better idea than sending in untrained green dragons and wild boars, having a competent and compassionate ruler is much better than sending a ruthless expert killer to facilitate peace and harmony!"

Rrahmus, touching the large medallion pendant on his chest, said to Fallon, "You may have killed, and been expert at it, but you were never ruthless. You have enduring faith in the causes of the just, eternal hope for the fairness of actions between people of good heart, and will stand as a bastion of charity for those who need your help; you truly are perfect for this."

Jankin said, "When the pixies reached us with the news of the coming kobold invasion I was trying to arbitrate who would be Chares' successor; and failing miserably I might add, no matter how fair I was being. They were just as horrible as my own cousins. My pleas to work together to fight the kobolds were ignored. I knew Yar was coming, and then they were upon us. Rather than let them hit us over and over again and surround us, I took all who would follow and punched through them, swung around away from the dwarves, took a breather, then did it again. Over and over, at least a dozen times. The last time I charged when no one else was ready, by myself. Then the dragons arrived, and that ended it. The pixies followed them as best they could, and of all things, an entire group of Traders that were there went after them, chased the kobolds down into the tiniest holes they could find. Not many survived." He paused. "I didn't care. I was covered in soot, sweat and blood, some of it my own..." He unconsciously touched a rather livid scar over his right eye. "The more moderate, less greedy, of Chares' old followers realized that we had saved them, despite their inaction. Magic wielders, dwarves, Traders, dragons and pixies, all risked their lives and saved them. One of the potential successors was advised by a priest who had the audacity to suggest no change to their previous position, that in fact it was actually the perfect time to exploit my now even greater weakness. He said it right in front of one of the dragons, who roasted him on the spot, dragged him into a corner of the square we were in and ate him in full view of those assembled." They all envisioned his description, and all shook their heads, amazed.

"I had no idea what to do. I bellowed at them to get their house in order, and that I would be back for either a hand or a sword, and I stormed out. As I said before, I am <u>awful</u> at this!"

Further discussion became moot as they heard several sets of massive wings flapping nearer. A large gold, silver, red and black dragon each landed on a corner of the parapet.

Rrahmus handed his best, oldest friend a pouch and said, "This is for you. Tell Jankin to open it before the ceremony." He squeezed Fallon's shoulder, then mounted the silver dragon.

"Where to?" Argenta asked quietly.

"Anywhere but here," Rrahmus replied. "Let's go find my father."

***

The other three powerful dragons, black, red and gold, landed in the fields just above the docks, now nicely terraced for growing fruit. Icelle Yeomring dismounted from Ebon, Jankin the Fearless from Karmien, and Fallon Rose from the last, Aurick, the dragons positioning themselves behind the men, all facing up the long hill.

Three more dragons swooped down to land like rearing horses, silver, green and white. Queen Hazelmoon Toadscream leapt off of Sylvia to stand next to Fallon. His daughter, the lovely Bronwyn, sprang off of Verity, the green dragon helping her and Graham in their liaison to the orc homeland, and Krystal, his non-blood-but-niece-anyway, vaulted nimbly off of Bianca, the white dragon found captive in the old lair near the McNab's old village.

Two massive peeled logs lay before them all, ready to be ship's masts. Sean and Graham Yeomring each approached the logs, drew their swords and chopped them into the wood like axes, leaving them stuck there, colored cloth in black, blue and green hanging from the hilts.

They were followed by dozens of village elders and family leaders from all over, magical and not, planting their swords in commitment of their support. Several ship captains, including Roland, Rabat and Roglok, followed suit.

Yar and Leif Drake each planted an enormous battle axe in each of the logs, one from each hand.

King Kedrick, his grandson, and now Elven Chieftain, Tahmus, Arch Magus Angus, and his apprentice Molly came next. Molly gave bouquets of flowers to the men, the petals matching the colors of their dragon companions. Tahmus gave strong but slender daggers, with handles similarly colored to match their dragons, to the women. The King of the Elves bowed slightly, turned and threw two daggers, one from each hand, into the ends of the logs right in front of Fallon and Hazelmoon, the handles made of bone with intricately carved skulls on each of them. He said softly, though it was heard by each of the several thousand present, "For my great-grandson."

One more dragon arrived, the largest, oldest, living gold. Aurelius also had a passenger. The Froglodyte King slid down one foreleg, carefully holding an enormous sword. He stood in front of Fallon, presented it with a half-bow and said, "He would not have missed this." There was a brief obnoxious cheer from the gnomish contingent present, which both Fallon and Runebane acknowledge with a pair of slight bows.

Aurelius took out two lengths of golden wire. Facing the waiting throngs, he tied one to both elvish daggers, uniting the logs. The other he turned back and tied to Fallon and Hazelmoon's wrists, saying, "Your union makes us complete. Perhaps the strangest family ever, but family nonetheless. Be blessed," he said, touching his medallion of a dragon reading a book to each of their foreheads, then he moved around behind and in between them.

The silver dragon that swooped in low over the crowd landed where Aurelius had been. Ufu somersaulted over Ariene's head and landed at the Queen's feet. Ariene said, "Your Majesty, your new Captain of the Guard at the Witches' Castle."

Ufu put his arms around both Hazelmoon and Fallon, squeezed gently, then moved behind them and in front of Aurelius.

Jankin stepped forward, dumping out a pouch as he did so, and a large chest appeared. It was not locked and opened readily to his hand. "Fallon Rose, old friend, new husband, you are now indeed the Consort of the Queen of the Witches. Indeed, she is my Queen as well!" He set the upper edge of the lid of the beautiful box aflame with his finger as proof of his lineage.

As the crowd murmured, he removed the objects inside. He handed Fallon the orb. It flashed in the sun, shiny onyx and gold, saying, "To remind you to weigh the costs of your decisions, this is filled with the ashes of both friends and enemies alike." Next, he proffered the scepter, a mace the size of Fallon's own not small arm. "To bring the obstinate in line for the good of the kingdom!" Quieter he said, "Please kneel my friends."

As they did so, he raised his voice and said, "And to remind us all that I was a horrible king and that the people chose YOU!!!" He placed the crown on Fallon's head, pulled the doubly royal newlyweds to their feet amid cheers the like of which had never been heard in Metaerie since the moment of its creation.

Behind them from the decks of the ships in the harbor, thousands of pixies took flight, the buzzing heard by all as if in the midst of a swarm of bees.

All who had known them soon recognized the patterns they were making as two faces could be seen looking down on them all, the faces of Slawhit and Flaw.

The End of the End